Scotch & Water

by

Garvey Duggan

# Long Dash Books

Printed by:

**InstaBook Maker** ™

*All rights reserved*

No part of this book may be reproduced or transmitted in any form or by any means, electronic or mechanical, including photocopying, recording, or by any information storage and retrieval system, without permission in writing from the author.

InstaBooks are distributed and printed through:

**Long Dash Publishing**

**89 Walnut Street**

**Montclair NJ 07042**

For more information:

*www.longdash.com*

©2006

This book is dedicated to my mother, Rosemary.
Thank you for passing on your gift of gab.

And in loving memory of my father, Thomas,
a man of few words.

Special thanks to Steve and Donna for all your help.

Cheers!

# Prologue

Dino DeLuca never should have gone deep-sea fishing. He should have stayed on the beach with his bitchy wife, his snotty children and his pain in the ass mother-in-law. But no, Dino wasn't content whiling away the hours on the pristine beaches of Tyle Island, a picturesque haven that sits fourteen miles off the coast of Massachusetts. In Dino's own words the small Island was "friggin boring him to death." Alas, if Dino had just settled for "friggin bored to death" he might not have ended up "friggin dead."

# Chapter 1

Dino DeLuca was a big, dumb, goon from Atlantic City, New Jersey who was sent to Tyle Island three days prior to his fated fishing trip by his "employer" from back home. His assignment was to "oversee" the construction of Tyle Island's first gaming casino. "Oversee whut?" was Dino's initial reaction upon learning of his latest task. He was a goddamn hit man after all. He could oversee three bullets to the brain and the odd dismemberment, but what the hell did Dino DeLuca know about building a casino? Of course Dino didn't verbalize this question of authority; one in his line of work didn't question authority. Rather, he packed up his family, drove north, took up temporary residence in a rented cottage and impatiently waited for work crews to arrive so that he could "oversee" the clearing of trees on a piece of land that had once been Tyle Island's largest nature refuge.

I should probably take this opportunity to mention that the people of Tyle Island whole-heartedly opposed construction of a casino.

As I stated earlier, the tranquility of pre-season Tyle Island was too much for Dino DeLuca's small mind to bear. So, after another goddamn day of sitting on the beach with a cold wind whipping sand into places sand shouldn't go, Dino decided that he needed a little action. Possibilities for action on Tyle Island as compared to Atlantic City were limited, but Dino was determined to find some quote-unquote fun. So, he dumped his bitchy wife, snotty children and pain in the ass mother-in-law back at the rented cottage, drove his big black Towncar down to the docks and growled at a few of the locals until he chanced upon Milo Donoghue, a fisherman who was known to finance his ever-increasing bar tab by taking on an occasional private charter. The following morning, a

Friday in early May, Dino met Milo at the Old Harbor dock. The two men boarded Milo's boat, The Mary Rose, and headed off for a fun filled day of recreational fishing.

Five hours later, a lobsterman returning from a morning of baiting traps plucked Milo from the ocean. Milo, an old salt who had fished Tyle Island for fifty plus years, was shivering and waterlogged but none the worse for wear. After a nip or two of whiskey to warm his chilled bones, he told Police Chief Tatum and a group of curious locals the details of his misadventure at sea.

The blues were running and Milo, knowing the waters as he did, hit the school dead center; four pounders were practically jumping into the boat. Both men were having a grand old time when off their bow pulled a thirty foot Boston Whaler carrying a handful of women who, according to Milo, 'weren't wearing enough clothing to cover what the good Lord had given them. Their titties be spillin' out everywhere,' he added in an embarrassed whisper to the chief. Needless to say Dino's interest in blue fishing took a back seat to the boatful of scantily clad woman. But when the vessel of ill repute moved in for a closer look, Dino was surprised to be greeted not by the big-haired, make-up laden women who had first caught his eye, but by two over-sized men wielding equally over-sized guns.

"What the hell did you do Milo?" Chief Tatum asked.

"What anyone in their right fecking mind would do. I dove me ass in the water and swum like hell."

The Islanders all nodded, yep, that's what they would have done too.

"Do ye mind calling the Coast Guard for me Chief?" Milo asked as he reached for his trusty fifth of Jim Beam, "The Mary Rose is adrift out there, and dead body or no, I'd like to be gettin' her back safe and sound."

# Chapter 2

At last count the year round population of Tyle Island was 512, although two residents were pregnant, one with twins, so sooner or later the number would rise to 515. Shaped like a comma, the Island is seven miles long at its' longest and 3.4 miles wide at its widest. Within this vast territory are scattered tall trees, rolling hills, flora and fauna of innumerable species, too many deer, one alleged mountain lion, beautiful beaches, and rocky bluffs that could easily challenge the spectacle of those White Cliffs of Dover. Victorian mansions with sprawling porches greet visitors disembarking the ferry at Old Harbor. These mansions, once private residences of New England's elite, had long ago been converted into high priced hotels. During the summer months, when the thin streets of Tyle Island are littered with tourists, the hotel porches bulge with preppie visitors sipping pink frosty drinks and chomping on the trendiest version of nachos to invade east coast cuisine. Elsewhere on the Island are scattered small, summer bungalows, restored B&Bs and year round residences of humble size adorned with weathered clapboard and blue gray shutters that are forever in need of painting. Clothes lines dot the landscape, small herds of cattle roam the hillsides, and roosters can be heard crowing from many a yard. There are a handful of million-dollar vacation compounds nestled into out-of-the-way hollows and coves, but the owners, most of who purchased on Tyle Island for its privacy, were obliged to be respectful of Island standards when constructing. You see, every structure built on Tyle Island must meet Conservancy Council Code - "Nothing fancy. Nothing gaudy. Nothing that would look out of place." In essence, "nothing we don't like." Only once had a developer come to Tyle Island with the intention of building modern beachfront condominiums.

The Islanders convinced him, in their own special way, that such a project would be a mistake.

Two short stretches of tarmac and one small shed act as the Tyle Island Airport. From there two, four and six seat planes make several runs a day, weather permitting, to carry over travelers who prefer flying to ferrying. There is one school on the Island that services grades K thru 12, one doctor, one grocery store and two restaurants that remain open year round. The balance of the establishments where one could wine and dine or waste money on touristy tchackas of little or no value open up Memorial Day weekend and close November first. This five month stretch is affectionately called HELL by the residents; however, they tolerate the chaos as the seven month off-season is the most peaceful to be found. Tyle Island, in the words of Owen Brady, the eighty-five year old Mayor who served thirty years in office, "is heaven on earth, which I need, as the life I've lived will surely bar me from the ever-after."

Now, imagine if you will, being one of the fortunate 512 soon to be 515 who spend every day on Tyle Island. You awake one brisk spring morning, bicycle to the one grocery store and purchase a Boston Globe plucked from a bundle just tossed off the seven a.m. ferry. You walk across the street to Clara's Diner, take your usual seat at the counter and order a breakfast of two eggs sunny side up, a side of Clara's secret recipe corned beef hash, and an English muffin oozing with butter. You help yourself to a steaming cup of real coffee, not the designer hazelnut crap, open the newspaper to page two and find a headline that reads "GAMBLING COMES TO TYLE ISLAND." Naturally you choke on your coffee, spitting a mouthful onto the counter. Clara whizzes by to scold your sloppiness and wipe up the mess. Still speechless, you push the newspaper in front of her and point to the headline. She reads the first paragraph of the article that reports of Massachusetts Governor Hardy's controversial granting of a gaming license to a man from New Jersey whose name is difficult to pronounce but ends in an "i". Clara drops her spatula, picks up the telephone, dials, then, after a short pause asks, "did you read it?" She turns her back on you but can be heard whispering above the sizzle of sausages bursting on the grill, "this one ain't going to be as easy as that condo guy."

Now if that fortunate resident was you, you're curiosity would be more than peaked, wouldn't it?

Chapter 3

The curious resident was Bob Kelly. Just six months prior Bob Kelly had been one hell of a mystery writer. More recently Bob Kelly had become one hell of a drunk. Lest you feel a twinge of sympathy for the creative soul turned lush, fear not, for in Kelly's case the transition had been intentional. Unlike his trademark main character, the loveable yet drunken PI who graced the pages of each of his crime novels, inner demons were not responsible for his over-indulgences. He did not blame the emotional torment of a writer for his drinking - words came easily. He hadn't suffered years of mistreatment by critics - his novels were praised. There had been no financial abuses by shady publishers - he was well compensated for his work. And there was no lack of appreciation by an ungrateful public - Kelly authored one best seller after another. Bob Kelly candidly attributed his alcohol dependency to nothing more than his passion for the seductive taste of Single Malt Scotch.

The love affair began during his freshman year at NYU; he was smitten after one brief sip from a half-filled highball glass snatched off of a table at an otherwise uneventful faculty-student social. The gentle burn of the amber liquor stole his heart away. It was the late '70's however, a bottle of quality scotch did not come cheap, and he, the son of a fisherman, wasn't rolling in dough. He had also witnessed too many of his father's Island cronies drink themselves into the poorhouse, a prospect which he did not hold in high regard. Bob Kelly hadn't studied his way off of Tyle Island and into NYU only to end up on skid row. Bob Kelly was smarter than that. Bob Kelly came up with a plan. Bob Kelly became a novelist.

For the next twenty years Kelly denied himself his one true love and focused entirely his on work. He churned out one best seller a year, every year, and wisely invested the profits. Then, on his fortieth birthday, he wished his editor, publisher, agent and two known friends farewell and returned to the place of his birth, Tyle Island, Massachusetts, lugging one duffle bag, a case of Single Malt Scotch and the small fortune he had amassed for the sole purpose of bankrolling an uncomplicated lifestyle of leisure and insobriety.

Kelly's needs were basic: food, clothing, shelter and scotch. Food was served up at Clara's Diner, the clothing was shipped to him courtesy of L.L. Bean, he sought shelter in his childhood home which he now shared with his younger brother Dan and his brother's son Pete, and his scotch sailed ashore every Wednesday on the ten o'clock ferry. Bob Kelly was forty years old, single, handsome, an alcoholic, and content.

And on that April morning, seated at the counter of Clara's Diner, Bob Kelly was curious. A slight twinge in his stomach at first alarmed him. An unsettled nagging in the back of his brain as he strained to decipher Clara's hushed words was bothersome. As Clara ended her phone call and returned to her griddle, Kelly continued to stare at the telephone, wondering whom it was that she had dialed. He pulled back the newspaper and read the article. When finished, he realized that the slight twinge and unsettled nagging signaled intrigue. This was a problem. Kelly had sworn off intrigue the day he landed on Tyle Island. When his worn out loafer hit the wooden boards of the Old Harbor dock he vowed to never again think a deep thought, proffer a philosophical theory or partake in any conversation that would require the use of a complex sentence. Such distractions would interfere with his devotion to scotch.

Clara served Kelly his breakfast. He ate quickly, paid his bill leaving a large tip as was his custom, tucked the newspaper under his arm, left the diner and hopped back onto his bike. A mile and a half of hard pedaling later, he dropped his bicycle on his front lawn, took the three porch steps in one giant stride, entered the house and came across his brother's son eating breakfast. Kelly ignored the young man and hurried upstairs to locate Dan. After a few minutes of unsuccessful searching he came back downstairs and though it pained him to do so he addressed the teen-ager. "Where's Dan?"

"Alaska," Pete Kelly answered, never raising his eyes from an overflowing bowl of Capt'n Crunch.

"Excuse me?"

"He left two days ago. We had a party." The just turned seventeen year old looked up at his uncle, "you were there."

"Oh. Right. Alaska."

Pete pushed his long dark hair behind his ears, "he's bush piloting. He'll be gone two months." Pete paused to pop a crunch-berry and noticed that his Uncle still looked confused. "I'll make it simple for you Bob, at a bottle a day, seven days a week for eight weeks; he'll be back in roughly 54 bottles."

Kelly was too distracted by casino related thoughts to acknowledge the personal attack. Pete awaited the customary growl, which, except for this latest verbal exchange, had been the extent of their communication since his uncle had moved in. When Kelly failed to grace him with so much as a sneer Pete abandoned his cereal, poured a cup of coffee and left, disgusted.

Upon hearing the screen door slam shut, Kelly opened the newspaper and reread the article. He replayed Clara's words in his head, 'this one ain't going to be as easy as that condo guy'. The twinge returned. Who the hell had Clara called?

The telephone rang, temporarily ebbing Kelly's growing curiosity. He answered after three rings.

"Hello."

"Is Pete there?"

"No."

"Is this Bob Kelly?"

"Yes. Who's this?"

"Chief Tatum."

"What did the boy do?"

"Nothing wrong Kelly, Pete's a good kid. I need him to fix my computer, can't get the damn thing to print. I'll try him at the school."

"Hey, Chief," Kelly spoke up before Chief Tatum could end the call, "I read the article in the Globe concerning gambling coming to the Island." The Police Chief did not respond. "Any truth to it?"

"The paper is standing by the story. I can't get through to the Capital for an explanation and I've got a mob forming down here demanding answers, so I wrote a letter to fax over to the Governor's office, but like I said..."

"You can't get the damn thing to print," Kelly finished the Police Chief's thought. Then, as if possessed by the ghost of Bob Kelly past, he added, "Well Chief rather than bother the kid at school, why don't I come down there and take a look at her for you?"

Silence.

"Chief?"

"I'm here." Silence. "It's just." More silence. "You're not usually one to volunteer."

Kelly let the second personal attack of his morning slide. He stared at the scotch bottle poised on the counter waiting patiently for his warm hand to gently caress it and pour. Then he stared at the headline written across page two of the Globe. The twinge returned. He checked his watch, 9:15; he had plenty of time to kill before the clock would strike noon signaling his legal drinking hour. He took a deep breath and informed the Chief of Police, "I'll be right down." Kelly hung up the phone, grabbed the keys to his brother's pick-up, and headed outside figuring that a little off hours intrigue wouldn't kill him.

Ironically it almost did. Absorbed in theories regarding the recipient of Clara's call, he didn't pay attention as he backed out of the driveway. Didn't pay attention is a nice way of saying that he did not look to see if anyone was coming down the road. Someone was. A dark green Jeep Wrangler that was in desperate need of a washing slammed on its brakes and careened off the road and into Bob Kelly's front yard. Before Kelly had a chance to climb out of his truck to check the condition of the driver, and more importantly his lawn, an irate young woman leapt from the Jeep, stormed up to him and spewed the longest line of "shits, damns and assholes" that Bob Kelly had heard since his cab ride out of Manhattan.

He smiled at the woman who wore a fresh cup of coffee, hazelnut from the smell, down the front of her sweater and waited for her tirade to fade naturally away. When she paused to take a breath Kelly calmly asked, "Are you alright miss?"

The relaxed tone of his question broke her stride. "I suppose," her response was less hostile however, a dash of wariness remained.

"Good," Kelly smiled a little too warmly, "I apologize. This was clearly my fault. I was preoccupied." He stepped out of his truck and politely, yet hurriedly, escorted the woman back to her Jeep. He opened her door for her and while doing so noticed that the back seat was piled high with luggage and over-stuffed brown paper bags. A laptop computer sat on the passenger seat; a case of wine took up the floor beneath. "You're not a local," he declared.

"How would you know?" the coffee soaked young woman asked as she climbed in behind the wheel.

"I'm a local. There aren't many of us. I see you're hauling a lot of cargo there."

"Not really."

"Planning on staying a while?"

"That depends."

"On?"

"Are you observant," the stranger flashed an icy grin, "or just nosey?"

"I assure you that I'm the least nosey person you will encounter on this Island Miss..."

"O'Neal," she held out a hand for shaking, "Abbie O'Neal."

Kelly kept his identity and his shaking hand to himself. "Miss O'Neal, is your visit to our fair Island in anyway affiliated with the casino?"

"What casino?"

No blinking, eyes straight ahead, Kelly concluded that her ignorance was sincere. "It's nothing, now if you'll excuse me," he leaned into the Jeep and turned the key to start the car, "I have to go."

The woman made no move to put the Jeep in gear.

"Is there a problem?" Kelly asked.

"Yeah, there's a problem," the young woman appeared to be revving up for tirade number two.

Kelly looked at her blankly. "You said you were ok. I said I was sorry and that this mishap was my fault. What more do you want from me, driving lessons?"

Abbie closed her eyes, recalled what Jack had told her about the many eccentricities of the common Tyle Islander, then took a deep breath to compose herself, and smiled. "You're right. I over-reacted. I'll be leaving now."

"I knew you'd see it my way," Kelly grinned as he stepped away from the Jeep.

Abbie closed her eyes once more as she contemplated the thin line that separates an eccentric from an asshole. This guy had definitely crossed that line. She gave the stranger a neighborly nod then slammed her Jeep into gear and hit the gas pedal, leaving a thick set of tire tracks across the man's nicely manicured front lawn. She pulled up about ten feet, stopped, leaned out the window and hollered, "Sorry! My fault!" before driving out of the yard and back onto the road.

Kelly stared down at the deep ruts embedded in his green lawn then looked up to see Abbie O'Neal waving to him out the window as she drove out of sight. A twinge hit his stomach; this bit of intrigue he chose to ignore.

## Chapter 4

Bob Kelly found a place to park between a rusted out Volkswagen Van and a Gremlin whose windshield was caked with salt and sand. The Gremlin, Kelly knew, belonged to Mayor Brady, which meant that the mob forming at the Police Station included some of the Island's heavy hitters. He jogged across the street to Clara's for a cup of coffee but found a CLOSED sign hanging on the door; a lot of heavy hitters. A pang struck Bob Kelly's stomach. As familiar as the curiosity twinge, Kelly hadn't felt this particular discomfort since typing THE END on his last novel. This pang signaled excitement. Everything that the new Bob Kelly stood for told him to turn right around, drive home, break his noon legal drinking rule, and get drunk. Excitement would only lead to involvement, which would lead to complications and complications were not good. However, everything that the old Bob Kelly stood for told him that there was a story brewing inside the Police Station that could prove interesting. And after all, he had nothing better to do than turn around, drive home, break his noon legal drinking rule and get drunk which he could easily do after he fixed the Chief's computer. Twenty years as a mystery writer outweighed six months as a drunk. Bob Kelly walked down the street, swung open the doors to the Tyle Island Police Station and got involved.

There were neighborly greetings from each of the locals, all of who clutched the morning edition of the Boston Globe in balled fists that were white with rage. Kelly hadn't expected such a turnout; he was surprised to find his fellow Islanders such a literate group. A few of the fisherman whom he knew well from shared evenings of drunkenness at The Nest gave him friendly pats on the back as he squeezed through the crowd in the cramped station and headed toward Chief Tatum's office. The Chief's secretary, Mabel, spotted his head towering above the rest and began ordering the others to move aside and let Bob Kelly through. "He's going to fix the computer so we can clear up this mess," she announced in a shrill voice that made Kelly wince. He forced a smile despite the ringing in his ears and touched the brim of his Yankees cap in a show of polite appreciation for clearing his path. Mabel blushed. He knocked twice on Chief Tatum's door then entered. Inside the office sat the Chief, Clara, Mayor Brady, The Harbor Master John Beale and Doctor Gnocuchuk (Doc Gno for short). Their conversation halted when Kelly stepped into the room.

"Thanks for coming," the Chief rose from his chair granting Kelly access to his malfunctioning Dell. "I've tried everything, hope you have better luck."

Kelly sat and instinctively scanned the desktop for bits of off-the-record information that might pertain to the casino. It was clean. "What's the file named Chief?" he asked.

"Hardy," the Chief replied having named the file after the Governor.

Kelly nodded and began pecking at buttons and clicking the mouse. "This might take some time," he commented, "feel free to go about your business." The silence that began when Kelly entered the room continued. Then Clara suggested that the meeting move to the diner. As the others filed out, Chief Tatum asked Kelly to have Mabel call the diner once the computer was repaired. Kelly assured Chief Tatum that he would, then mindlessly clicked on insignificant icons until the others had left and the door had shut behind them.

With the software glitch quickly resolved, Kelly pulled the keyboard closer to him, typed HARDY and watched Chief Tatum's letter to the Governor appear before his eyes. He fought the urge to correct the errors in sentence structure as he scanned the correspondence. There was no doubting the sincerity of Chief Tatum's wrath; too bad, a phony letter could have proved interesting. Kelly noticed that the Chief had "cc'd" Mayor Brady and the five residents that comprised the Tyle Island Conservancy Council. Something about the list gnawed at his stomach. This was a gnawing, not a twinge, nagging or pang. Gnaws weren't good. Gnaws needed to be ignored. Kelly struck the appropriate keys and printed the file named HARDY. As he removed the letter from the printer the gnawing again made its troublesome presence known. Its difficult for anyone to truly ignore a gnaw, much less a recently retired mystery writer, so Bob Kelly spun in Chief Tatum's comfy leather chair, placed the letter on the antiquated Xerox and shot off a copy. He put the photocopy into his jacket pocket then left the office, stopping to inform Mabel that the situation was rectified and that she should telephone the Chief at the diner to inform him of the success. Kelly then squeezed his way through the office, this time receiving celebratory pats on the back; the locals all pleased that Bob Kelly had fixed the Chief's computer.

Chapter 5

Abbie O'Neal stood on the deck of the vacation house owned by her future in-laws. Her mouth hung open as she took in the view, then an "I'll be damned," escaped her lips as she walked to the edge of the deck and stared down at the rocky beach and waves gently breaking some thirty feet below her. She glanced around to make sure that no one was watching her, how could there be, there was no other house in sight, then broke into a "life is good" dance. After giving the hot tub a quick once over she regained her composure and took a long, hard look at her new digs, a converted Coast Guard Boat House whose entire ocean facing side was a two story pane of glass. Any doubts she may have had regarding her impending marriage to Jack West immediately vanished.

Ok, Abbie said to herself, Abbie often spoke to herself, the key will be under the marigold pot. She looked at the countless number of flowerpots that lined the deck and wondered what a marigold looked like. She probably should have researched that detail prior to leaving New York. Screw it, she said aloud, as she often did, and one by one she picked up each of the flowerpots and took a peek underneath. Pot number seven hid the key. Abbie let herself in, drew the curtains and sighed. She spent a few more minutes staring out at the endless horizon then tore herself away and went to work.

Abbie's future mother-in-law had instructed her to check the fax machine in the library upon her arrival at the house. She located the library, it looked more like a den to her, found the fax and quickly scanned the three sheet list of dos, don'ts, helpful hints and friendly reminders that her future mother-in-law had been kind enough, or paranoid enough depending on your perspective, to send. The caretaker had been by to remove the window guards. He had also washed the windows, turned on the electric and made sure the propane tanks were filled and operational. He should have cut the lawn (let me know if he didn't - I paid him for it!!!) her future mother-in-law had added in bold block print. Abbie's doubts regarding marriage to Jack began to filter back in. Her future mother-in-law referred Abbie to the family phone book in the top desk drawer which listed the names of places to shop and eat, emergency phone numbers, and numbers of their friends who might or might not be on the Island and checking in. Checking up, Abbie snickered, as the wave of doubt grew bigger. Then the final note, "please don't use the crystal or china, they're family heirlooms and I wouldn't want them mishandled" - woosh the tidal wave of doubt struck shore.

    Abbie left the fax on the desk and examined the shelves filled with books, most of them leather bound and from the condition of the bindings, unread. She then gave herself the nickel tour of the house ending with the master bedroom suite that occupied half of the second floor. She collapsed onto the king sized four-poster bed that was draped with sheer, white linen and congratulated herself for her good fortune. For the next eight weeks this summer hideaway would be all hers; the ideal setting to jar her writer's block. She had given herself two months to complete the "great American novel" that she had begun years earlier. If she couldn't finish with this effort she would sign on the dotted line, committing herself to five more years at her current career - head writer for The Darkest Hour, television's highest rated daytime drama. God, Abbie said aloud, if I have to write one more scene where Dr. Jasper Black and trusty Nurse Rhonda get caught screwing in ICU, I won't need a bitchy mother-in-law to destroy me, I'll do it myself. With that said, said Abbie, I think I'll unload the Jeep.

Less than an hour later she was unpacked and for the most part settled into her home away from home. Time to call Jack, she said aloud as she took the cordless from its mount, walked out to the deck and telephoned her fiancé. Four rings and she got the answering machine; her own voice instructed her to leave a message following the tone. "Just me checking in. Made it here safe and sound. I'm heading out to do some exploring. Call you later. Bye." She hung up.

"Damn" she said aloud, "I probably should have said I love you." She redialed, listened to her voice again and after the tone added, "I love you." Abbie then went out to the Wrangler, removed the doors to give her outing a more adventurous feel, and drove off to see what Tyle Island secrets she could uncover.


"So that's Abbie," Jack's latest lover, a very unnatural blonde, giggled as she unbuttoned her blouse, "you should have let me say hi."

"Leave Abbie out of this," Jack ordered as he uncorked a bottle of wine, "I love her."

"Then why are you with me?" his latest lover asked as she let her blouse fall onto Abbie's newly washed kitchen floor.

"Rehearsal. Grab that script."

The blonde lifted the binder off the counter and leafed through the first few pages. "So this is the shit she writes for you."

"It's not shit. Nobody writes better daytime than my Abbie." Jack removed two crystal wine glasses from a cupboard, engagement gifts from one of the show's producers. "Come on, I've got two scenes with Nurse Rhonda tomorrow and I need to rehearse."

The blonde unhooked her Wonder Bra, "you know you're a pervert Jack."

"No, I'm a perfectionist. And please, call me Dr. Black.

The salty air and smogless sunshine of Tyle Island triggered Abbie's appetite so she cut her outing short and headed for town. She idled down Water Street examining darkened storefronts and looking for a place to park. It's awfully crowded, Abbie said aloud, as she searched for a spot in which to leave the Jeep. Two short blocks out of town she found a space in a sandy lot that may or may not have been legal, considered looking further then decided to chance a ticket. She was starving after all, and had noticed Clara's Diner on the right hand side of the road. Her future mother-in-law's phonebook had instructed her to avoid Clara's Diner - "local hangout, cheap, greasy" were the notes the evil one had made. To Abbie, Clara's sounded ideal.

Unfortunately, when she approached the diner she found a CLOSED sign hanging on the door. Oh well, Abbie said to herself, as she walked across the street to a small barn-like structure bearing a weathered, wooden sign that read GROCERY, a sandwich will do. She entered, found a lone employee standing behind a lone cash register and asked if she could purchase some lunchmeats.

"Everybody's down at the Station," the gum-chewing girl with big blue eyes and purple barrettes in her hair informed Abbie the stranger, "but if you know how to work the slicer, you can help yourself." Abbie shrugged, that seemed fair, and having grown up in Manhattan, the deli capital of North America, she knew how to work the slicer.

Abbie cut a half of a pound each of ham, salami, bologna and provolone. Her conscience had requested turkey breast but her stomach over-ruled. She made a mental note to wash down the sandwich with a glass or two of blood-thinning red wine in order to counteract the adverse effects of her non-heart healthy lunch. Her conscience was appeased. She was wiping the slicer clean when she heard a man's voice order a pound of rare roast beef, sliced thin. She looked up to find the man who had earlier run her off the road standing at the counter.

"Sorry," she forced a smile, "but I don't work here."

"So cleaning deli slicers is just a hobby?" he looked at her quizzically.

"More of a fetish," she replied, then, thinking better of further antagonizing a local, went on to politely explain that "they're shorthanded, the girl up front told me to help myself." Abbie put her cold cuts into a brown paper bag, "I'm sure you could do the same."

"I could," said the man, "but I would most likely sever a limb. Abbie is it?"

Abbie nodded.

"Would you?"

Abbie stared at the man while contemplating his request. There was something vaguely familiar about him. He added a "please," along with a Cary Grant raise of an eyebrow.

She sliced a pound of rare roast beef, paper-thin. He complimented her on her technique. "Never has there been so proficient a deli slicer on Tyle Island. You should apply for the job."

"I've got a job."

"Where do you work?"

"Back home."

"And home would be?"

"Manhattan."

"Ah, Gotham City. That explains your ability to properly slice deli."

Abbie placed his package of rare roast beef on the countertop and handed a roll of paper towels to the very nosey man, "it's your turn to clean the slicer." She focused on his Yankee cap, an odd choice of apparel for a New Englander, and added, "I'm sorry but we've met twice now and I have yet to get your name."

He considered an alias but instead answered, "Bob Kelly."

"Pleased to meet you Bob,"

"I prefer Kelly."

"I'm sure you do. So Bob," she smiled, "do you have the correct time?"

He checked his watch and looked suddenly alarmed. "its 11:45 and I'm sorry Abbie but you're going to have to satisfy your slicer fetish without me. I have a noon rendezvous and it seems I'm running late." Kelly placed the roll of paper towels back on the deli counter and hurried away. He dropped a twenty at the cash register and commented to the gum-chewing girl with the purple barrettes, "She slices deli meats better than she drives." He then rushed out of the store without waiting for change, leaving Abbie O'Neal to clean up.

Chapter 6

Tuesday morning Bob Kelly awoke a little after ten, popped four aspirin, took a quick shower, then jumped on his bicycle and rode to Clara's for breakfast. He took his usual seat at the counter, ordered two eggs sunny-side up, a side of Clara's secret recipe corned beef hash and an English muffin oozing with butter. It wasn't until he was helping himself to coffee that he noticed Abbie O'Neal seated at a corner booth, absorbed in the New York Times. He called out "hello Abbie O'Neal," as he took his seat at the counter.

"Hello Bob Kelly," Abbie called back.

"How's the dirty Jeep this morning?"

"Fine. And how's the lawn?"

Kelly snickered and turned his attention to the place setting that Clara was arranging in front of him. "Any news on the casino Clara?"

"Not a damn thing," she appeared noticeably flushed, more so than could be attributed to the heat from the griddles.

"No response from the Governor?"

"That bastard left yesterday for a conference. Ask me where."

"Where?"

"Vegas."

"No."

"The timing's a little too coincidental for my taste."

"What did the Mayor have to say?"

Clara placed a bottle of Tabasco and a small wooden bowl filled with creamers on the counter, "I'm worried about Owen. He's not well. The shock of this damn near killed him."

Secrets are hard to keep on a small Island. Actually secrets are nearly impossible to keep on a small island where, besides fishing and boating, gossip is the major form of entertainment, so every Islander was privy to the fact that Clara and Mayor Owen Brady, nearly forty years her senior, had recently become an item. If anything was going to kill Owen Brady it would be a night of passion with a buxomly redhead half his age, not the threat of casino development, but Bob Kelly kept this thought to himself and simply asked, "how's that?"

She leaned in close, "I shouldn't be telling you this Kelly, but I figure I can trust you. You got a few flaws but loose lips aren't one of them." This was high praise; Kelly was sincerely touched by the sentiment. Clara made sure no one was listening then whispered, "A few of us got to digging last night. Doc Gno pulled the minutes from the last town meeting and guess what was on the agenda."

"Gambling?"

"Written right there in Hyacinth Poole's own hand. Said the Council approved the motion to allow gambling on the Island unanimously, and granted Barron's Hollow for the site."

"That's got to be a mistake." A gnawing began to eat a Bob Kelly's stomach that wasn't caused by the lack of breakfast. "Barron's Hollow is Hyacinth Poole's baby. Isn't she the one that donated that land to the Island in the first place?"

"She did, and it looks like she took it back. And as far as the council vote goes, I was at that meeting and no one ever mentioned building a casino. Those minutes were monkeyed with."

"What did the Widow Poole and the other Council members have to say about the discrepancy?"

"It was late and no one was answering their phones. Owen and Chief Tatum met first thing this morning to go to their houses and confront them in person. I'm still waiting to hear back."

"The eggs Clara," Kelly pointed to the griddle, which was beginning to smoke.

"Goddammit," she rushed to save his breakfast, "this casino is going to be the death of us all."

Kelly pictured the Chief's letter to the Governor and the cc's typed below. After disposing of the eggs, which had gone from sunny side up to total eclipse, Clara returned to the counter. "Sorry Kelly. I'll start you up another batch."

There was something familiar about those ccs. Too familiar. "Put breakfast on hold," Kelly didn't like what he was thinking, "I've got to run. But save my stool, I'll be back in ten."

And run he did, which wasn't easy for a forty year old, hung-over alcoholic wearing a pair of loafers that had one sole coming loose. Kelly ran the two blocks into town, turned right and came to a dead stop in front of Island Realty. The real estate agency was located next to the liquor store; Kelly had made a ritual of browsing the housing market every Wednesday before picking up his weekly delivery of scotch. This allowed him to keep current on the value of his own place. Kelly entered the agency and to the ear-shattering objections of Lila, one of only two realtors operating on the Island, rifled through her desk until he found a file marked New Listings. Kelly ignored Lila's threats of calling the police, after all, Chief Tatum owed him one, and flipped open the folder. Sure enough three of the addresses that the Chief had cc'd were listed FOR SALE, including Hyacinth Poole's. Kelly dropped the folder and resumed his run, leaving Lila kneeling in the middle of her office gathering up stray papers and ranting about a lawsuit. He turned left onto High Road and jogged in the direction of T.I. Realty. A sharp pain hit his side as he crested the hill, but adrenaline kept him moving. And what did he find being placed in the front window of the agency for all of an unsuspecting Tyle Island to see, but photographs of the two remaining Conservancy Council member's houses, also listed FOR SALE.

Kelly turned and headed back toward Clara's. He took the liberty of a shortcut through a few backyards belonging to people whom he knew did not own fierce dogs, and made it back to the diner in eleven minutes flat. He ran through the door, collapsed onto his stool and through a wheeze disguised as breathing begged Clara for a glass of water.

"Jesus, Mary and Joseph, Kelly," Clara hollered, alarmed by the condition of her biggest tipper, "what the hell is wrong with you?"

"Call everyone Clara."

"Everyone who?"

"Everyone who wants to keep Tyle Island away from the guy from New Jersey with the last name ending in "I"." Bob Kelly guzzled his glass of water then burped.

"You're not making sense Kelly."

"Their houses are for sale."

"Whose houses?"

"The Conservancy Council," he managed to gasp before falling off of his stool and drifting off into a not so friendly fog.

When Kelly came to he was curled up on his living room sofa, a blurry face looked down at him. He heard a gentle voice ask, "Would you like some scotch?"

I've died and gone to heaven Kelly thought. "Are you an angel?" he asked.

"No," the blurry figure smiled, "it's just me, Abbie."

Kelly rubbed his vision clear, looked up at Abbie O'Neal, who, upon closer inspection, really did have the face of an angel, quickly dispelled that last thought and took from her outstretched hand a glass of scotch. He sat up, sipped his beloved Single Malt then screamed, "What the hell is this?"

"Scotch."

"What did you do to it?"

"What do you mean?"

"It's wrong. It tastes all wrong."

She took the glass from him and sipped. "No Bob, that's what scotch is supposed to taste like."

Kelly's fatigued body was ravaged by fear. Had his misguided burst of energy destroyed his palate? Did goddamn intrigue cause his one true love to leave him forever in despair?

"Could you mean the water?"

"What water?"

"The water in the scotch."

"Why is there water in my Single Malt Scotch?"

"That's how you're supposed to drink it."

"Says who?"

"Scotland."

Kelly's glare said more than any string of expletives could have.

"I'm sorry Bob, but the correct way to drink scotch is with a pour of water, room temperature, not cold." Again his glare spoke volumes. "It releases the flavors."

"It ruins it," Kelly grumbled.

"Fine, I'll get you another." Abbie placed the glass on the coffee table and walked across the room to fix his drink. Kelly stared at the liquor, trying to recall the taste on his tongue. Perhaps it hadn't been all that bad. Perhaps he was over-reacting. When Abbie handed him a fresh scotch, this one slightly darker in color signaling the absence of H2O, Kelly kindly accepted and apologized for his behavior.

"It's ok, you've had a rough morning."

Kelly took a brain clearing sip then finally thought to ask, "Why are you here?"

"Someone had to bring you home."

"Where's Doc Gno?"

"With the others I guess."

"Where?"

"I don't know for sure. You had just fallen off your stool and were lying on the floor with the oddest little smirk on your face; I can't imagine what you were dreaming. Clara called an emergency Island meeting. There were four other locals in the diner, besides you and Clara of course, they all marched out and left you with me."

"They just left me?"

"Yes. So I ran after them."

"Leaving me unconscious and totally alone?"

"Well yes, I suppose. But just for a minute. I asked if they would contact a doctor. They told me not to worry, that this had happened before and Doc Gno would be needed at the meeting. Clara diagnosed you as suffering from dehydration, symptomatic of extreme hangover probably exacerbated by the strain of your run."

"Clara said all that?"

"Well no. Clara's words were, 'he must have tied a good one on last night. Could you get him home for us honey, we're busy?' So Bob, here we are."

"Has anyone ever told you that you're very wordy?"

"Often," Abbie sipped the scotch and water. She closed her eyes and smiled, "you do drink the good stuff." He acknowledged her compliment with a raise of his glass. "And speaking of wordy, you didn't tell me which wordy Bob Kelly you are."

Kelly squinted, "was that English?"

Abbie stood and walked back toward the bar where a bookshelf was stacked high with Bob Kelly novels. She pulled a book off the shelf, opened to the back jacket and pointed to the photo of the author. "You."

"Yes, me." He sipped his scotch, savoring its recuperative powers.

"I can't believe I didn't recognize you. I'm a big fan."

"I'm touched. You can leave now."

Abbie returned the book to its rightful place on the shelf and answered, "No I can't."

"Trust me, you're free to go."

"I have to stay until Pete gets home from school. Clara said so."

"Who is Pete?"

"I was told that he's your nephew."

Kelly waved a dismissive hand as he attempted to stand but found that his legs were still a bit shaky. Abbie saw him falter.

"What you need is food, and a liquid other than scotch. Some of that perfectly sliced roast beef is in the fridge, would you like a sandwich?" She disappeared into the kitchen without waiting for a response. "Do you use mayo?" she called out from the next room.

"Just a touch, and salt and pepper please." What the hell am I doing, Kelly asked himself. Salt and pepper please? He took a large mouthful of scotch and felt the liquor sting his tongue. Somewhat revitalized he made another effort at standing. Successful on the second try, he shuffled the four feet to the television, grabbed the remote control, and hit the power button. He then shuffled back to his favorite sofa, pulled an afghan over his shoulders and rewarded his progress with another satisfying swig.

Abbie came back into the room carrying a large glass of water and a roast beef sandwich that made the fare at the Carnegie Deli look like finger food. When Abbie realized what was on television she nearly dropped both. She stared at the screen. Kelly followed her frightened gaze. "It's The Darkest Hour. Haven't you ever seen it?"

"No," a loud drum began to beat in Abbie's head, "I don't have much time for television." She forced a smile despite the fact that panic was setting in. "Is it good?" she asked.

"Good?" Bob Kelly guffawed as he took a giant bite out of his sandwich. Lettuce hung out the corner of his mouth as he declared, "its unadulterated crap." Abbie swallowed hard. "But it's addicting as all hell. You see Abbie, every Monday through Friday a cast of inane characters prowl the streets of Benton Springs inventing new ways to murder, cheat, steal and screw."

Speaking of screwing, a giant 'well screw you, you elitist shit. Not all of us get paid millions of dollars to write novels' almost spewed from Abbie's tightly pursed lips, but she squelched her tirade and simply asked, "I've heard the acting on these things can be cheesy but it's well written... right?"

"Are you kidding, I could write this crap with my toes."

Knife to the heart. "So then why don't you just turn it off?"

"Like I said, it's addictive."

Abbie glanced at the screen just in time to catch a tight close-up of her remarkably handsome fiancé Jack West a.k.a. Dr. Jasper Black. The drums began to beat louder. "You now Bob, you seem to be doing much better. I'm going to take off after all."

"No, stay," he patted the sofa beside him, "we can pretend we're in college and drink every time Doctor Black and Nurse Rhonda have sex."

"Oh, no, no, no, I don't think so. I've got work to do." Abbie edged her way out of the room. "You take care of yourself Bob."

"Will do Abbie."

"See you around." She rushed down the hallway, ran out the door, climbed into the Jeep, sped home, opened a bottle of Beaujolais, sat on the deck, and cried.

Chapter 7

Three days later, after continuous writing, rewriting and then rewriting again, Abbie's novel had turned from a pile of crap into a festering pile of crap. She closed her laptop, realized that it was Friday, and decided that seventy-two hours of personal torture were enough. There had to be a Happy Hour somewhere on Tyle Island.

Bob Kelly spent those same three days on one hell-of-a binge. He couldn't quite put his finger on what had set him off, but after Abbie O'Neal bolted from his house and he finished watching The Darkest Hour, he starting drinking and didn't stop until Thursday evening around 7 p.m. That's when Clara telephoned and his brother's son refused to cover for his drunken Uncle. Kelly had put the receiver ever so gingerly to his ear and listened to Clara carry on about the situation on the Island. Desperate for peace and quiet, he promised to meet with a group of Islanders at The Nest the following afternoon at four.

During those same three days, the people of Tyle Island had stirred themselves into quite a frenzy.

Abbie looked at herself in her future mother-in-law's full-length mirror and smiled at her reflection. An hour-long soak in a jasmine scented bubble bath had done wonders for her state of mind. She put on her favorite pair of faded Levis, the ones with the slightly worn ass, and a pale pink oxford that she had stolen from a college boyfriend some ten years prior. She applied just a hint of make-up around her eyes and a squirt of Chanel at her neck. Her once white, now pale gray tennis shoes that had long ago lost their laces completed her beer-drinking ensemble. Abbie O'Neal was ready to toss back a few pints with a rowdy bunch of Islanders. The thought made her smile wider.

Bob Kelly took a thirty minute shower which would have lasted longer had his brother's son not intentionally flushed the toilet, scalding his Uncle and hurrying him from the bathroom. They growled at one another as they passed in the hallway, then, for some inexplicable reason, Kelly stopped and asked, "Where are you going tonight?"

Pete wasn't quite sure how to respond to a direct question from his Uncle, nonetheless one that implied interest in his life. He hesitated then answered, "Out?" Kelly nodded then walked into his bedroom and shut the door. Pete proceeded into the bathroom, glanced back at his Uncle's room, shook his head and closed the door behind him.

Kelly dressed in his one non-wrinkled pair of khakis, the braided leather belt he had worn since college which he was pleased to find still fit, and a hunter green Henley which had just been delivered by his friends at L.L. Bean. He reached for his favorite pair of loafers, the ones with the left sole falling off, then changed his mind and opted for newer, cleaner boat shoes. He nodded at himself in the mirror, amazed to see that after six months of concentrated insobriety, he could still clean up nicely. He then trotted down the staircase; something he hadn't recalled ever doing, paused at the first floor bathroom, debated his next action, then entered and flushed. He heard Pete scream. Kelly chuckled as he wheeled his bicycle out of the hallway and onto the porch; a civic-minded drunk he never drove a vehicle when partaking in the scotch. He breathed in the fresh Island air and just when he thought life couldn't get any better, the green Jeep that still needed washing, pulled into his driveway. Kelly started to smile then stopped himself.

"Hi Bob," Abbie waved to him out the window.

"Abbie," he nodded hello as he carried his twelve-speed down the three porch steps taking care not to soil his freshly laundered pants.

"Sorry to bother you, but I was wondering where it is that I could possibly go for a cold beer and perhaps a burger. I figured you would know."

Again Kelly started to smile; again he stopped himself. "You are an excessively wordy person Abbie, but if you're looking for a beer your only choices are The Nest, or, The Nest. It's the only bar that's open off-season. And since you're on an island, I recommend passing on the burger and ordering fish and chips instead."

"Sounds good. The Nest, that's the place near the docks in town?"

"That's correct." He paused...then added, "I'm heading there myself."

"Great." She paused...then added. "I see you were planning on biking to the bar. Would you like a ride?"

"I'm meeting some people, we might be staying late."

"Throw the bike in the back. You can pedal home whenever you want."

Kelly considered her proposition as he fought back smile number three. "All right Abbie O'Neal, you may chauffeur me."

The first twenty seconds of driving felt like ten minutes. Kelly broke the uncomfortable silence by asking, "So where are you staying?"

"The house on Madonna's Cove."

"The Boat House?"

"Yep," Abbie answered as she slowed down to let a family of deer cross the road.

"Ah ha."

"Ah ha what?"

"Ah hah you're wealthy."

"Ah ha I'm not," Abbie accelerated as the final deer scampered by. "The house belongs to Stewart and Madeline West, my future in-laws."

Kelly glanced over, trying not to be too conspicuous, and saw that sure enough Abbie wore a diamond on her left ring finger. A large diamond. He hadn't noticed that before. Wonder why not. The silence suddenly felt even more awkward. He struggled to make conversation. "Stewart West, the Manhattan attorney and mayoral hopeful?" Abbie nodded confirmation. More awkward silence. "I haven't been in that place since I was a teenager. The previous owners used to throw a damn fine party."

"Well I doubt my in-laws would know a damn fine party if one bit them on the ass, but feel free to stop by any time. The deck is a great setting for sipping cocktails." More awkward silence.

"Hey Bob, you're an Islander."

"Guilty," he replied.

"Then maybe you could tell me how Madonna's Cove got its name?"

"Old sailor's legend."

Short on words he needed prodding so she prodded, "go on."

"Sailors coming around the west side, which is our side of the Island, used to spin yarn about a vision of the Madonna that would appear late at night as they passed off the coast. They talked about seeing the image of the Virgin Mary framed in soft light with a flowing veil trailing her as she slowly walked the beach. Some of the old-timers got to calling it Virgin Cove, but that didn't sit well with the ladies. After some debate Madonna's Cove was deemed politically correct and stuck."

"It's a fine story, but I surmise from your tone that you don't buy it."

"Nah." Kelly shook his head. "I'm not the believing type. Islanders love the legend though. You see Abbie, after witnessing a visitation by the Virgin Mother a potentially rowdy bunch of sailors would behave like choirboys. Fewer bar stools crashed through plate glass windows following a sighting."

"Any of the locals ever claim to spot Mary walking my beach?"

"One or two, but mostly after a hard night of drinking. You can safely write the Madonna's Cove legend off as fog mixing with ocean spray mixing with starlight mixing with the imaginations of men who spend too much time at sea."

With that said, Abbie pulled into a parking spot behind The Nest. The two walked into the bar together; Kelly held the thick wooden door open as Abbie squeezed through. Kelly was immediately summoned by the group of locals that were congregating around several tables at the rear of the restaurant. Abbie said goodbye and took a seat at the long mahogany bar, ordered a pint of Harp and stared out the large window that overlooked the harbor. With each sip she felt more and more at home.


"What's wrong Jack?" his latest lover, this time a brunette, asked as she tied the belt on Abbie's new silk robe, an engagement gift from a producer, and sat beside Jack on Abbie's leather couch.

"Monday's script," his voice was hurried, "I'm not in it."

"Great babe," the brunette answered, "you get the day off."

"Yeah. I suppose." He looked at her through pouty eyes, "but I wanted to rehearse all weekend."

The brunette stood and loosened the belt that she had just cinched tight. "Why don't we forget about rehearsal and concentrate on fun?"

"What do you mean?"

"I'm here. And you're here."

"Yeah..."

"And we're both practically naked."

"I can't cheat on Abbie!"

"What do you call what you did last night?" The brunette opened the robe, "and twice this morning?"

"Rehearsal. For my scene today with Nurse Rhonda."

"And how did the scene go?"

"Great. Because of the rehearsal."

The brunette stood and let Abbie's robe fall to her feet. "But Jack baby, was it perfect?"

He looked up at her, a hint of a twinkle returning to his sad eyes.

"You know Jack honey, I laid here all day thinking about that scene," she knelt down and tapped her chin with an index finger topped by a long red nail, "and I think I've come up with a way that you could have done it just a little bit better."

"Really?"

"Really Jack. Shall I show you?"

"Yes. But remember, call me Jasper."


Abbie was into her third pint when her dinner of fish and chips arrived. She had been joined by a young couple that had sailed in from Newport and a pair of college seniors who had ferried over from the mainland to apply for summer jobs. A round of tequila shots had just been ordered by the collegians when a very loud "NO FUCKING WAY!" disrupted the tranquility of the bar. Abbie and her four new friends stared back at the group of locals and witnessed Bob Kelly pounding on the table. Then he flailed his arms. Then he slammed a chair. Then he turned and stormed out of the bar. "Excuse me," Abbie downed her tequila, ignoring the lime; "I'll be back in a sec."


"What the hell happened in there?" Abbie slurred as she watched Bob Kelly trying to disengage his bicycle from the back of her Wrangler.

"Go back inside Abbie."

"I intend to. But first you have to tell me what has you so worked up."

"It's none of your business."

"I'm sure its not, but I'm curious as all hell and just a wee bit drunk so I'd really like to know."

"Curiosity is dangerous on this Island," Kelly finally detached his bike, "I advise you to get home early, pack your things and drive your dirty green Jeep onto the first ferry tomorrow morning. When you dock on the mainland, drive off quickly and don't stop until you hit the Tappan Zee."

"I'm intrigued."

"Don't be. It's not worth it."

Even a wee bit drunk, Abbie could tell that Bob Kelly was sincerely upset. "Look Bob, I don't think that I'm the only one who has had too much to drink."

"I haven't had a drop."

"Bullshit."

"Smell me," Kelly breathed in Abbie's face. "See. No scotch, straight, watered-down or otherwise. He pointed a fatherly finger at her, "you seem like a nice girl. Go home, and by home I don't mean the Coast Guard Boat House at the end of Madonna's Cove." Kelly mounted his bicycle and stared into the slightly dilated eyes of Abbie O'Neal's angelic face.

"Would you do me one favor Bob?" she asked

"What?"

"Could you take the Jeep and leave me the bike? I'm not fit to operate anything with an engine."

He stared at her. "You'll leave the Island tomorrow?"

"Absolutely."

Kelly left his bicycle and drove off in the Jeep. Abbie went back inside and ordered a second round of tequila shots for her new friends. She glanced back at the group still huddled in the rear of the bar and wondered what on earth could be so unsettling as to warrant Bob Kelly staying sober.

Chapter 8

What Abbie O'Neal had been dying to hear, and what Bob Kelly wished he hadn't, was the Islander's plan for keeping gambling off of Tyle Island. Clara stood at the head of a long table in the rear of The Nest and raised the motion that "we devise a plan to off the little casino bastard." Mayor Brady and Doctor Gno simultaneously seconded the motion. Kelly sat at the table staring down at a petrified catsup stain and wondering if he had heard correctly. He couldn't have.

"How would we go about it?" John Beale, the Harbor Master, asked.

"We haven't decided yet. But," Clara smiled down at Bob Kelly with pride, "I've invited an expert in the field to join us this evening who might be able to make some suggestions."

Kelly looked around the table wondering which one of his companions was this so-called expert. Besides the Chief, Doc Gno, Clara and the Harbor Master, all he saw were fishermen, the Postmaster, the bank teller, and an artist who specialized in landscape photography.

"Say something," Clara poked Kelly in the ribs.

"I'm waiting for your expert."

"You are our expert."

"Pardon."

"Don't be bashful."

"I'm not bashful Clara, I'm confused."

"Oh Kelly, really. Think about it, you've written all those books where your Private Investigator, with barely a shred of evidence, solves crime after crime. He's brilliant."

"He's make-believe. He's a fictional character in fictional stories."

"True," countered Doc Gno, "but you created him. Your words are his words. Your thoughts are his thoughts. So in essence, he's real and he's you."

Kelly was speechless.

"Come now Kelly," Mayor Brady chimed in, "we've all read your stories. That PI of yours always figures out the crimes before any of us can." Kelly stared helplessly at the Mayor, not quite sure what bizarre proposition was about to escape his wrinkly little lips. "So we were thinking that if your Private I can work in reverse by solving a crime, he'd be twice as good at working forward and planning one."

Kelly's lips parted but nothing came out.

"So have you got any ideas?" the Harbor Master asked.

Kelly cradled his head in his hands. He could have been at home, on his comfy sofa, sipping, correction chugging scotch, but instead he was being implicated in a plot to kill a man who was rumored to be the head of the Atlantic City Mob.

"Doc," Bob Kelly pleaded with his contemporary, hoping that the one non-Islander present would provide a voice of reason, "do you honestly agree with this?"

Doctor Gnocuchuk leaned back in his chair and scratched at the damp label on his bottle of beer. Doc had come to Tyle Island in the mid-eighties after completing an internship at Boston General. His plan was to spend his first summer as a licensed physician practicing family medicine, researching Lyme Tick disease, which was rampant on the small deer infested island, and fishing. It took a while for the rather sheltered Tyle Islanders to warm up to the young Native-American, but after he successfully relieved Mary Riley's chronic arthritis with a combination of herbal medicines and an experimental drug no Islander and few doctors had ever heard of, the progressive young medicine man was welcomed with open arms. At the end of the summer, despite countless job offers from prominent research labs across the nation, Doc Gno decided to stick around for a while. Then he never bothered to leave. An adopted Islander, Doc had won the chowder cook-off five years running and was founder of the popular Tyle Island Anti-Columbus Day Parade.

After a moment of serious consideration he answered Kelly's question. "I've given this matter serious thought, and while both my culture and my profession forbid the careless destruction of life, my heart says go with offing the guy."

"We're not talking flu shots Doc, we're talking murder." Kelly rebutted. "How is it that you, a man of science, devoted to healing is asking me to act as a consultant in a murder scheme." Kelly laughed and added, "Hell, with your medical background, wouldn't you be better at handling the details of a death than I?"

"Scientifically speaking I don't need your help. Unfortunately, while I'm a skilled doctor, I'm not blessed with your creative flair. And to be totally honest Bob, I think you're getting worked up over nothing. No one has asked you to commit a murder. We're merely asking you to provide us with an imaginative, yet feasible method to go about committing a murder."

Kelly's head was spinning and his throat was in need of a scotch. "Clara," he asked, "that morning in the Diner when I showed you the newspaper article, who did you call?"

"She called me," Mayor Brady answered.

Kelly turned his chair to address the Mayor. "Clara's exact words to you were 'this one ain't going to be as easy as that condo guy'. What did she mean?"

"A few years back we convinced a condominium developer not to build here," the Mayor replied matter-of-factly.

"How?"

"We threatened him."

"With what?" Kelly dreaded the answer. "Boycotting...picketing...negative publicity?"

"Bodily harm," said John Beale.

"NO FUCKIN WAY!" That's when Kelly stood and

pounded the table. "You people have no idea what you're messing with. Threatening some two bit condo schmuck is one thing, but you threaten a casino developer and you'll all end up dead."

"We know that Kelly, that's why we need you," said Clara, "to provide the tact needed for our mission to succeed."

That's when Bob Kelly flailed his arms. "Tact. You don't need tact you need a miracle. Look, I wish there was something I could do, but your best bet is to go through the proper legal channels. Hire a lawyer. We all know that the vote to allow gambling was fraudulent. The Conservancy Council had to have broken countless laws. Those are the avenues you must pursue, not threats of injury."

"You still don't get it Kelly," insisted Mayor Brady, "we don't want him injured. We want him dead."

And that's when Bob Kelly threw his chair and stormed out of the bar.

## Chapter 9

When swapping rides, Abbie failed to consider that the first ninety percent of her bike ride would be a slow, gradual uphill. Or that the last ten percent would be a radical downgrade...in the dark...while drunk. With gravity at the helm Abbie was out of control and unable to stop her legs from pedaling, even when she rode onto Bob Kelly's front lawn, hit the rut that she had created days earlier and flew over the handle bars. Thud.

"Nice move," she heard a voice say as she lay on her back staring up at the multitude of stars that lit the night sky.

"Thanks," she moaned.

"Can you move?" the voice asked her.

"Doubt it," she answered.

Abbie heard footsteps coming toward her. She began to giggle. Then she realized that it was probably Bob Kelly ambling over to assist her. Then she wondered what she looked like. Then she wondered why she wondered what she looked like. Before she had another chance to wonder, she felt a set of strong arms take her from under her knees and arms and lift her off the ground. She recalled saying "wheeeee," just prior to passing out.

Abbie awoke in her mother-in-law's king sized bed; the drapes were pulled wide open allowing the evil sunshine to pour in, and the heavenly smell of coffee was whafting up the stairs. Abbie checked under the blanket to verify that she was clothed, thanked God that she was, climbed out of bed, crawled to the bathroom and puked in her mother-in-law's pretty mauve toilet bowl. Renewed by the purging, she undressed, put on sweats and though sore and swollen from the previous night's tumble, she managed to hobble downstairs to investigate who might have invaded her kitchen and set the coffee to brewing.

After filling a mug with the much-needed caffeine, Abbie peered out the sliding glass doors at the large framed, long haired stranger who had presumably made said coffee and was currently admiring her view. She considered being frightened but found herself too hungover to be truly concerned by the presence of this unknown man. She felt like death; he'd be doing her a favor if he offered to put an end to her suffering.

Abbie stepped out onto the deck. "Hello," she hesitated, "may I help you?" When the stranger turned to acknowledge her, Abbie was surprised to see the youthful face of a teen-ager on the body of the man.

"Hi," he extended his hand for shaking, "I'm Pete Kelly."

Nothing registered.

"Bob Kelly is my Uncle."

"Oh. Yeah. Hello Pete. I'm Abbie O'Neal." Abbie took his hand, "pleased to meet you. I've heard a lot about you."

"Really?" Pete looked skeptical.

"Actually no," she shook her hungover head and cringed at the discomfort brought on by the sudden movement, "but Clara told me you existed and you made coffee so I'm trying to be polite."

"Sorry if I scared you."

"I wasn't scared. I no longer possess the adequate number of brain cells to properly register fright. I was, perhaps, mildly concerned as to who you might be."

Damn she's wordy Pete thought as he explained, "Anyway, you were pretty out of it last night. I didn't want you getting sick in your sleep, being alone and all, so I put you to bed and stuck around."

"You're kidding?"

"Nope."

"Are you sure you're Bob Kelly's nephew?"

"I'm sure, like it or not," Pete shrugged, "I'm also hungry. I saw some eggs in the fridge, are you up for some food?"

"I still have too much liquor pumping through my system to go anywhere near a pilot light," Abbie declared.

"I think I can handle it."

"You cook?"

"Three men, one house, someone had to learn. I was nominated."

"So you live with your Uncle?"

"And my dad. He's away for a couple of months."

"No women in the house?" Abbie's interest was peaked.

"Nope."

"What about your mother?"

"Never met her."

"I'm sorry," Abbie winced as she made a mental note to kick herself once she felt stable enough to raise a leg, "that must be rough."

"Not really. You don't miss what you never had. So," Pete Kelly pushed his long hair behind his ears, "are you hungry or not?"

They adjourned to the kitchen and raided the fridge. Abbie leaned on the counter and drank her coffee while Pete whipped up a six-egg omelet accompanied by a towering stack of perfectly browned toast. They brought the plate of food and two forks back outside where they settled into deck chairs and silently devoured every bite.

"Delicious," Abbie declared as she wiped her mouth with the sleeve of her sweatshirt.

Pete rose to clear the plate, "I should go."

"No, please stay." Abbie gestured to the chair beside her. "It gets lonely around here, I'd appreciate the company." Pete went back inside and returned with the pot of coffee. He refilled both of their mugs then collapsed obediently in the chair. "So tell me about yourself Pete Kelly."

"Not much to tell."

"Got a girlfriend?"

"No, but you just reminded me," he sat up in his chair, shoved a hand in the front pocket of his jeans and pulled out a small shiny object, "here's your ring."

Abbie looked at the ring finger of her left hand and noticed for the first time that her two-carat solitaire was missing. "Ummm. Pete. Where did you get that?" she asked, taking the ring from him and slipping it back on.

"I found it last night."

"Found it where?"

He pointed out and down, "on the beach. Where you threw it."

"I threw my engagement ring onto the beach?"

"Sure did," he grinned. Abbie noticed that Pete looked just like his Uncle. "It was during a brief moment of consciousness. You were trying for the ocean, but the wind was blowing inland." Abbie's aching head dropped to her aching knees that she had pulled to her chest and was now hugging in a seated fetal position. "You know Abbie, some people might take that sort of behavior as a sign."

"Oh God," she said to her knees.

"Latent hostility. Perhaps cold feet."

"Hey Dr. Phil," Abbie looked up, "while I appreciate the diagnosis, rest assured that a very well paid shrink has been trying to thaw my icy toes for a year now." She tried to rub the weariness from her eyes. "How old are you Pete?"

"Just turned seventeen."

"Happy birthday."

"Thanks."

"Allow me to give you some friendly advice."

"Shoot."

Abbie examined her engagement ring, picking out tiny sand particles that had become wedged in the setting.

"Don't date. Don't fall in love. And most importantly, are you listening Pete?"

"Yes ma'am."

"Don't have sex."

He laughed. "I'm seventeen. I live on an Island. Besides fishing and sailing there's not a whole hell of a lot to do here besides sex."

"Then stick to fishing. Sex is bad. Good sex is disastrous." She looked up at her young guest, "am I being too forward?" He shook his head and sipped his coffee. "Good." Abbie returned her head to her knees and continued her lecture, "sex makes you stupid. Granted, the physical pleasure of sex can take you to places that one could hardly imagine, but, and this is a big but Pete, it also dulls your every sensibility. Rational thought, gone. Emotional stability, history. Trust me, one night of too much wine and fantastic food followed by hours of earth-shattering sex and poof, you're a slave to a putz."

"Are you speaking autobiographically?"

Abbie looked up at the young man who, long hair aside, was a dead ringer for Bob Kelly, "now you sound like your Uncle."

"He wouldn't think so."

Abbie wanted to pursue the obviously tepid relationship between the Kelly men but a new bout of nausea struck before she could pounce. "You know Pete, as wonderful as those eggs were, I don't think they're going to be sticking with me for very much longer."

"I'll let myself out, you go puke."

"Right," she stood, "and Pete, don't be a stranger."

"You just want me for my coffee."

"I've had people for worse reasons," she forced a smile despite the onset of lightheadedness, "but please don't repeat that, it makes me sound like a tramp." Pete crossed his heart. "Thank you for taking care of me," Abbie tiptoed and kissed Pete Kelly on the cheek.

"You're a good kid. Forget everything I said. Have sex. Go wild. Knock yourself out."

"I'll try coach."

Abbie was headed straight for the nearest toilet when she noticed that the only vehicle parked in her driveway was her Jeep, apparently driven there the night before by her young Kelly in shining armor.

"How are you getting home?" she asked.

"I'll walk."

"Take the Jeep. Trust me, I'm not going anywhere. I'll come for it later."

"How much later?"

"Why?"

"In the absence of too much wine and fantastic food, that Jeep could get me laid." He raised a devilish eyebrow. Damn, Abbie thought, the resemblance between Pete and his Uncle was uncanny.

"You can have the Jeep until tomorrow on one condition." Pete awaited her 'only if.' "Only if you tell Bob where you were last night."

"You want me to tell my Uncle that I found you lying on our front lawn so I took you home and babysat you all night long so that you wouldn't throw-up in your sleep, choke and die?"

"No need to be so graphic. Just tell him that you spent the night with Abbie O'Neal. Then report back to me on his reaction."


Bob Kelly awoke with every intention of repairing his damaged lawn. Such busy work would keep his mind off the prior evening at The Nest, a conversation that even half a bottle of scotch had not allowed him to forget. He was just heading out the front door when Abbie O'Neal's Jeep pulled into the driveway. A little smile started to curl at the corner of his mouth then abruptly stopped when he saw not Abbie, but his brother's son seated behind the wheel. The smiled turned downward. Kelly watched Pete hop out of the Jeep, pat the hood, push his long hair behind his ears and move in a manner that resembled skipping toward the porch. Though it pained him to do so, Kelly asked, "What are you doing with Abbie O'Neal's Jeep?"

Pete jumped up the three steps and landed with a heavy thud just inches from his Uncle. "Needed a way to get home this morning."

"From?" Bob Kelly asked.

"Abbie's," Pete's grin grew wider.

"Excuse me?"

Pete Kelly patted his Uncle on the shoulder and winked, "I spent the night." Bob Kelly's chin and coffee cup simultaneously hit the porch.

## Chapter 10

Abbie spent the remainder of her Saturday asleep, but awoke bright and early Sunday feeling one hundred percent better than the day before. She dialed New York City and got a hold of Jack whom she caught in mid-rehearsal. They spoke for just a minute; Jack promised to call back at a more convenient time. Abbie then climbed out of the king sized bed, showered, wrapped herself in a fluffy bath towel, snuck outside and slid into the hot tub for a bubbly soak. Life doesn't get much better than this she said to herself as she slipped lower into the churning water. She passed the time watching seagulls dive into the waves and a bright white sailboat drift by against a backdrop of dark gray storm clouds that were assembling off the coast. Abbie closed her eyes and listened to the waves crashing on the beach below; the bell buoy clanged as it rose with every swell. Her tranquility was briefly interrupted by the thought of her laptop and the crappy novel stored within. Oh hell, she said to herself as she sunk to chin level, I've still got seven weeks.

Mayor Brady dragged his eighty-five year old naked body out of Clara's waterbed, slipped on his boxers and Clara's pink bathrobe and hobbled to the kitchen, stopping every few steps to work out the early morning kinks that plagued his aging body. After brewing a cup of tea, he opened the front door and slowly leaned down to pick up the Boston Globe that the Carley kid delivered every Sunday morning, always an hour late. He then returned to the kitchen, spread the newspaper out on the table and with teacup in hand began to scan the pages for news regarding the casino. Page three showed a picture of Governor Hardy disembarking a plane at Logan International Airport while waving to a welcoming crowd. The bullet under the photo read "Gov. Hardy greeted by pro-gambling public." The story detailed the Governor's trip to Las Vegas and mentioned several meetings held with Nevada Gaming Officials during his stay. It then stated that the Governor, exhausted from his grueling schedule, was heading off for a relaxing weekend at his vacation house in Wakefield. Mayor Brady dropped his teacup and, ignoring the tugging feeling in his chest, hurried into the bedroom where he traded Clara's pink bathrobe for his own work pants and flannel shirt. He then warmed up the Gremlin and, after stalling out twice, sped out of town.

Harbor Master John Beale walked into the Diner, his face paler than the whites of the eggs being fried.

"What's wrong?" asked Clara, fully expecting his lack of color to be related, in some way, to the casino.

John Beale lowered his barrel shaped six foot plus frame onto a rickety wooden stool. "I got a call late yesterday from a shipping company out of Port Elizabeth, New Jersey. Wanted to know if the harbor could handle a freighter loaded with machinery, lumber and building supplies. I told him no way. Any supplies that come to this Island come aboard trucks. And the only trucks that come to this Island sail here on the Ferry."

"Good for you John," Clara poured a cup of coffee for her friend.

He leaned in closer and lowered his voice, "the man offered me a bride. Told me that if I let their freighter enter the harbor there might be something extra in it for me."

"Did you tell him to screw off?" Clara's voice was loud and her language questionable, especially for a Sunday morning. Half a dozen locals paused in mid chew at the outburst. She apologized. They all nodded and returned to breakfast.

"I figured I'd be better off stalling them, so I held my temper and told him to fax me the specs on the ship and let me know when they'd be expecting to pull in. I'd see what I could do. Of course I got no intention of letting their goddamn ship into my port, but this way we know just what to expect and when to expect them."

"That was brilliant of you John. When did you get to be so clever?"

The Harbor Master blushed. "I checked a few of Bob Kelly's books out of the library. Stayed up late every night this week reading them. I'm getting a feel for this crime stuff Clara."

"We're lucky to have you on our side. Make yourself comfortable John, breakfast is on the house."


Mayor Brady and his Gremlin barely made it to Chief Tatum's house. By the time the Mayor pulled onto the Chief's side lawn the Gremlin was smoking and the Mayor had broken into a sweat. He marched up to Chief Tatum's back door and began pounding. When the Chief finally answered, the Mayor shoved the newspaper in front of his face. "Have you read it Tatum? Have you read what they're saying?"

"What time is it Owen?"

"Have you read it? Have you?"

"I just woke up Owen. Now calm down. Come inside."

"I don't want to calm down and I don't want to come inside," Mayor Brady struggled to catch his breath, "I'm sick and tired of everybody on this Island dragging their asses and prayin' for this goddamn casino to go away. Prayin's for women and pussies Chief, I'm neither."

"I know you're not Owen. Now please come inside, you look like hell."

"I've looked like hell for twenty years and let me tell you, twenty years ago this casino bastard would have already been six feet under, my woman wouldn't be crying herself to sleep at night, and I wouldn't have to be waking the Chief of Police in order to get him to do his goddamn job!" The Mayor gasped for breath.

Chief Tatum took the Mayor by the arm, "I'm calling Doc Gno."

"Not until you promise me some action. Some old fashioned Tyle Island action."

"I promise Owen. One way or another we're going to keep that casino from being built."

"You swear?"

"I swear."


"You swear?"

"I swear," Abbie stood on her deck holding a fluffy white towel firmly around herself, "I did not deflower your young, albeit handsome nephew." Abbie was dripping wet, having stepped out of the hot tub just moments before the Kelly men had unexpectedly arrived. Wouldn't that have made for quite the moment, Abbie smirked, being accused of moral indecency while soaking buck naked in a hot tub. Abbie choked back a giggle as she tried to sound offended by Kelly's accusation.

"I want to know what happened between the two of you."

Abbie wiped a droplet of water from her nose, "I rode your bicycle to your place Friday night, bumped into your nephew, and after all the drinking I had done I just sort of ...crashed. Pete merely saw to it that I made it home safely."

Pete stood a few feet behind his uncle; tears were forming in his eyes as he, like Abbie, forced back a guffaw. Kelly turned to address his brother's son; Pete stood a little straighter and looked down at his feet. "You said you spent the night."

"Yeah, but I sure as hell didn't say that I had sex with her."

"You implied..."

"No, you inferred."

Kelly grimaced. "Why'd you look so happy?"

"She loaned me the Jeep. You know what that means."

"Yeah, yeah," Kelly appeared defeated, "you'd probably get laid."

"By someone other than me," Abbie added. "Now if you're through slandering me Mr. Kelly, I've got work to do." Abbie stormed inside, slamming the sliding glass door closed for effect.

"I told you, you were making a big mistake."

"What else was I to think?' Kelly stared at the still vibrating glass door, not exactly sure how to proceed.

"I'm actually flattered," said Pete, "she's smart and hot and you thought she would screw me." Kelly glared. Pete raised his hands in an "I give" gesture. "When you go in to apologize, tell Abbie that the keys are in the Jeep and thank her for me. It was a successful Saturday night," he winked at his Uncle, "for one of us."

Kelly snarled. Pete laughed and trotted down the dirt road toward home.


Bob Kelly stood in Abbie O'Neal's driveway feeling like the world's biggest ass. She had every right to be offended, hell, she had every right to hate him. He had just accused her of statutory rape and he couldn't even blame insobriety for his lack of good judgment. What was bothering Kelly the most; however, was why it mattered? Plenty of people hated him. What was the big deal about one more? His preoccupation with getting back into Abbie's good graces could have had something to do with the towel she was wearing, and by the way she was clutching it so tightly, the lack of anything being worn underneath. Kelly pictured the diamond ring and pushed the preceding thought out of his mind. He had serious matters to address. Tyle Island was prepping for a battle it could never win and he needed to hear from a voice of reason. Why he thought that the angel faced, towel clad Abbie O'Neal would be rational God only knows; but he did know that she came from New York City. If not rational, she would at least provide the dose of cynicism needed to keep him from marching into the diner and outlining the plan to save Tyle Island that he had stayed up half the night concocting. A plan he knew would most likely get them all killed. The writer needed an editor. Someone to say, "What are you kidding me? Are you out of your frigging mind?" Abbie O'Neal seemed well suited for the job.

He took a deep breath, climbed the steps to the deck and knocked on the sliding glass door. She didn't answer. "Come on Abbie," he called out, "answer the door or I'm coming in."

She yelled back from somewhere inside, "you do and I'll call the police. I'll tell them that there's a pervert at my door. I'm sure on this Island I'd be justified in shooting you."

"As a matter of fact you would." He peered through the glass and wondered where she was hiding. "And ironically, it's just that sort of vigilantism that I need to speak with you about."

Hmmm. Abbie figured that Kelly had suffered enough embarrassment and his last comment was too intriguing to easily dismiss, so she walked out of the kitchen, slid open the door and allowed him to enter.

"Thank you," Kelly checked out the up-scale decor, "this place has certainly changed."

"Doesn't suck huh?"

"That's one way of putting it. And by the way, I'm sorry. I have no idea what came over me. If it is at all possible to forget the past half hour, please, I beg you to do so." Abbie stared at him while she processed his request. He raised the Cray Grant eyebrow and added, "please."

Abbie relented. Actually Abbie melted. "You're forgiven, but only because Pete is such a doll."

"He's not that great," Kelly groaned.

"Yes he is. If he came in an adult model I'd snatch him right up."

"What would your fiancé say?"

"Wouldn't matter, but anyway, there's no grown up version now is there?" Abbie smiled, "so what can I do for you?"

"I could use a drink."

"Sorry, no scotch."

"I was thinking of something softer."

"Pepsi?"

"Perfect."

"Help yourself, it's in the fridge. I have a quick call to make and I really should get dressed."

Kelly watched Abbie run up the steps and muttered, "Not on my account."


Abbie picked up the telephone, dialed her number back in New York and thank God, heard her fiancé say hello.

"Hey Jack it's me."

"Look Babe I'm still rehearsing. I'm going to have to call you back."

"How can you still be rehearsing? I wrote your lines. You don't have that many."

"Calm down Babe, you're sounding crazy. What's wrong? Is that little Island getting to you already?"

No, Abbie wanted to shout, but one little Islander is and I need to feel some sort of bond with you right now you frigging moron so that I don't go and do something that I know I will definitely regret. Instead Abbie answered, "I don't know. Maybe."

"I miss you Ab."

"Me too," she walked over to the window and stared out at the stormy sea.

"Look Babe, I'm struggling with this one scene."

"Which one, I'll help you out."

"Thanks for the offer but I need to do this on my own."

"You sure?"

"Trust me, a few more hours of uninterrupted rehearsal and it'll be perfect."

"All right Jack, but don't overdo it. You want some spontaneity in your performance."

"I'll keep that in mind. Call you tonight. Ciao." Jack hung up the phone and went back to rehearsing, this time with a redhead.

Abbie went back downstairs with her still damp brown hair pulled back in a short ponytail. She wore an NYU sweatshirt and a pair of faded jeans. "So Bob, what's going on?"

"Do you mind if we walk and talk? I could use the air."

Abbie grabbed a soda and they headed for the beach.

## Chapter 11

"Wow."
"Yep."
"Wow."
"I know."
"Wow."
"I was hoping for a more insightful response."
"Sorry. Wow."
Kelly took a seat on a large piece of driftwood and waited for Abbie to finish processing his information.

"So," she picked up a long abandoned snail shell and tossed it into the sea, "you're telling me that the Islanders want to do away with a casino developer who is probably connected to the Mob, and they want you to tell them how to go about it?" Kelly nodded. "Well it's clear to me," she picked a small flat rock out of the sand, "they are insane."

"That was my first thought."

Abbie side-armed the pebble into the ocean and watched it skip, skip, plunk, then realized what Kelly had just said. "What do you mean first thought? First thought implies that a second thought followed." He did not respond. "Excuse me, but are you actually considering leading these people on some misguided quest to get themselves killed? Are you kidding me? Are you out of your frigging mind?"

"No," he countered, "I'm just saying that these people are desperate not crazy."

"Mere semantics. Crazy or desperate, the end result, death, will be the same."

Kelly was warming up to the banter. "You've spent less than one week on Tyle Island, and sooner or later you're going to pack up your dirty green Jeep and drive back to New York. According to our conversation of Friday evening you should have already been well on your way; however, I'm willing to forgive your lie regarding your ETD partly because I accused you of having sex with a minor and partly because I now need your help."

And he thinks I'm wordy, Abbie muttered.

"To an Islander this place isn't some must see vacation spot; a pretty place to spend a week or two every summer. It's our home and we don't want to see our home destroyed."

"I know this might sound too main stream for you Islanders but what about turning this problem over to the law?"

"The Conservancy Council members, all of whom have taken off without leaving so much as a forwarding address, did a pretty thorough job of covering their tracks. According to Chief Tatum, the paperwork looks legit."

"You can file suit. Claim fraud. Property that's under litigation can't be developed. Granted it's not a solution but at least it's a delay."

"Are you an attorney?" Kelly asked.

"No. My former roommate is. I used to assist her with briefs."

"So you write?"

"Not really. Let's get back to Tyle Island."

"Right. For the record, prior to becoming emotionally involved, I did suggest that the locals seek legal advice. I even called my own lawyer back in New York which I swore I'd never do, but considering my recent change in lifestyle and the subsequent reduction of his income, he's not exactly taking my calls."

"Mine will."

Kelly smiled. "I was hoping you'd say that."

They slowly retraced their steps in the sand, neither in any great hurry to get where they were going, until Pete appeared a hundred or so yards up the beach. He started to run toward them. "This can't be good," said Kelly as he picked up the pace.

When they were no more than twenty yards apart Pete stopped and yelled "Mayor Brady had a heart attack. Clara's been trying to get a hold of you. She said the old man won't let them fly him off Island until he talks to you."

"Crazy bastard," Kelly forgot about his recent exertion-induced collapse and began to run.

"I brought the pickup. I'll drive you to the airport."

"The storm's rolling in," Kelly looked up at the sky as he hopped the stone wall into Abbie's yard, "I don't know if they can fly in this weather."

"They're gonna have to," said Pete, "or Mayor Brady's gonna die."

Abbie stayed behind, poured herself a glass of sauvignon blanc and dialed her ex-roommate/best friend/attorney. When she heard the familiar voice answer, she immediately blurted out, "Meg it's me, please don't hang up."

"Is this Abigail O'Neal?"

"Yes Meg."

"Is this the Abigail O'Neal who is soon to become Mrs. Jack 'I'm a total ass but I'm an actor so adore me' West?"

"Yes Meg."

"So you're not calling to inform me that the nuptials have been cancelled?"

"No Meg."

"And you still want me to wear an unflattering dress and stand beside you at the altar pretending to approve of this farce which you refer to as a marriage?"

"Yes Meg."

"Then I have nothing more to say." Click.

Abbie whispered 'bitch' and hit redial.

"Do not hang up on me again Megan. I need your help."

"Well isn't that just lovely. You don't call me for close to a month, and when you finally do it's because you need something."

"I didn't call you for a month because the last time we spoke you told me that, if I remember your words correctly, I was an emotional child who was marrying the world's biggest dick because he has the world's biggest dick."

"Those were my words, and I stand by them."

"You now I love him Meg."

"I know you can't tell me why."

"Megan."

"Yes Abigail."

"I know what I'm doing. You're my best friend. Please trust my judgment."

"I know you too well to trust your judgment, but I'm getting bored with this conversation so I will change the subject. How's the little retreat to Tyle Island going? Did you notice that I did not call it an escape, thereby characterizing your jaunt to New England as a running away?"

"I noticed."

"Good. So is Tyle Island everything you hoped it would be?"

"Oh yeah Meg, and more."

"OH MY GOD!"

"What?"

"You met a man."

"What?"

"You met a man. I can hear it in your voice. Saints be praised, Abbie met a man."

"What the hell are you taking about? All I said was 'yeah Meg and more'."

"No, you said "oh yeah" and your voice was all deep and breathy when you said it."

"Well Megan, if we're being literal yes, I've come to know several men, but none in the biblical sense as you would have it sound, just, just friendly men, the kind that you can innocently have a scotch or maybe a beer with, no, no thought of sex, love, commitment or anything else that would complicate ones life and upcoming wedding."

"You're fumbling Abigail. You only fumble when you're nervous, and the only reason you have to be nervous is that I'm right and that you met a man."

"Let it go Megan."

"All right. So, is he cute?"

"Drop it or I'll elope tomorrow."

"Fine, I give. So what do you need from me?"

"Legal advice."

"I'm listening."

"You see I met this man..."

"I told you!"

"No. No. No. Not like that. This man is Bob Kelly, the writer."

"Damn."

"What's wrong now?"

"You were telling the truth. Abbie I was truly hoping that you had made a love connection, but if the man is Bob Kelly then you were right, it's strictly platonic. So go ahead, you met Bob Kelly and..."

"Why would you assume that any relationship between Bob Kelly and me would have to be strictly platonic?"

"He's handsome, talented and literate."

"So."

"He's not your type."

"Excuse me?"

"Nothing Ab, forget I said anything. And besides, you're engaged to Jack West, the mono-syllabic stud of daytime drama, whatever would you want with a dashing member of the literary world?"

"I hate you Megan."

"Now about your legal problem?"

Abbie filled her ex-roommate/best friend/attorney in on the details of the fraudulent vote to bring gambling to

Tyle Island and Governor Hardy's noticeably intimate involvement with the cause. Megan listened intently then offered, "Why don't you call in the press? The media would get a hard-on over a story involving a small group of downtrodden islanders being sold out to the mafia by a corrupt government official. Its real heartstrings crap."

"Allegedly corrupt official," Abbie corrected as she pictured the headline TYLE ISLANDERS PLOT TO MURDER MAFIA DON. "I don't think publicity will help at this stage." She downed her glass of wine. "What can we do legally?"

"Honestly?"

"Of course."

"Very little if your intention is to keep the fight hush-hush. Any documents you file in court would be a matter of public record. They'll pass through the hands of some string reporter, and before you know it you'll be swamped by the press."

"So there's nothing we can do?"

"I didn't say that. Do you have access to the records in question?"

"I could probably get my hands on them."

"Good. You have to find a flaw, something that was missed. A "t" not crossed, an "i" not dotted, anything that would render the vote null and void. If you get a copy to me I'll look them over."

"Thanks Meg."

"Don't thank me yet. If you really are dealing with a mix of mafia and politics those records will be squeaky clean."

"Then what do we do?"

"How far are you prepared to go?"

"What are you asking me?"

"What any self respecting Upper East-Sider with Esq. at the end of her name would say. If you can't fight fair, fight dirty."

"I'm listening."

"You'll have to prove your hunch that the Governor is in bed with the bad guys. In your case the bad guys are (a) the M.I.A. Council members, as well as (b) the mob. If you can prove collusion with either, especially the latter of the two, then with one quick visit to the state capital and a brief meeting with the Gov, evidence in hand and Mike Wallace's telephone number on speed dial, your Island will be free of slot machines for ever and ever Amen."

"You're brilliant Megan."

"I know. There is one more possibility that you'll have to consider."

"What's that?"

"What if you can't prove that the Governor has been screwing around?"

"I don't want to think about it."

"Well you better start."

"Got any suggestions?"

"Abigail, you're the Hemingway of daytime drama. Just pretend that these people live in Benton Springs, and write yourself a happy ending."

"Fictionalize, now that I can do."

"Might even be fun. Get the documents to me and keep me up to date."

"Will do. Thanks Meg." Abbie hung up the telephone and ran upstairs to retrieve her laptop. The rain had begun and she could hear the distant clap of thunder. She tossed the computer disk containing her crappy novel on her bed and pulled a fresh disk from her backpack. She carried the laptop downstairs, settled onto the sofa, put her feet up on the coffee table and stared out the huge window. A bolt of lightening touched the ocean far out at sea. Abbie began typing.

Chapter 12

Clara spent the ferry ride quietly cradling the cookie tin that held the remains of Owen Brady. Doc Gno sat at her side. He had accompanied her to the mainland to retrieve the Mayor's ashes and bring them home for a proper Tyle Island funeral.

Abbie arrived at the Kelly house just before ten on the morning of the service. A cold front had moved in, dropping the seasonal temperature of sixty degrees to near freezing, and creating an eerie fog that blanketed the Island. Abbie and the Kellys drove in silence to the North Light House and parked among the hundred or so other vehicles that had already jammed the narrow dirt access road. Kelly handed a silver flask to Pete who then headed off to join his friends. Abbie and Bob made their way along the sandy footpath bordered by sea-grass and wildflowers toward the site of the memorial.

The now 511 soon to be 514 Islanders assembled at the base of the lighthouse. With angry waves crashing onto the rocky cliffs below, first Chief Tatum then Clara stood before their fellow Islanders and eulogized their departed friend. Doc Gno recited a Native American burial prayer in honor of his non-denominational friend. When all of the kind words were completed, Clara climbed the stairs to the top of the lighthouse, opened her cookie tin and cast Owen Brady into the wind. As his ashes took flight every Islander lifted his or her bottle or flask and drank a toast. Milo Donoghue stood alone on the beach below and played a mournful Danny Boy on his bagpipes. After the cry of the pipes quieted, the citizens of Tyle Islander slowly made their way back to their cars.

"What did you think?" Kelly asked.

"It was beautiful," Abbie hesitated, "but bizarre."

"That's Tyle Island."
"So what's next?"
"We go to The Nest."
"Is there a reception?"
"You could call it that."


Once in town it was time to party. The first person to enter The Nest was Chief Tatum, and his first act was to remove the sign declaring the bar's maximum occupancy of 200 from the wall. With the legal notice stashed behind the cigarette machine, the taps were opened. An accordion and a kaylee joined Milo Donoghue's bagpipes as Islanders belted out off-key renditions of the Mayor's old Irish favorites. Stories, some touching, most tawdry, recounting Owen Brady's full life flowed as freely as the Jamesons. Abbie stuck with pints of Harp while Bob Kelly nursed a Single Malt for the duration of the funeral bash. As the revelry, entering its fifth hour, started to subside and drunken bodies stumbled out onto the streets, Chief Tatum pulled Kelly aside. The two men exchanged heated words and for the second time in less than a week Kelly stormed out of the bar. Abbie watched Chief Tatum shake his head in apparent disgust, then walk into the kitchen, followed by Clara, Doc Gno and the Harbor Master. She climbed over the bar, pried a bottle of Wild Turkey from the hand of the bartender who had passed out several hours earlier and poured herself a shot. After downing the whiskey she took a deep breath and marched into the kitchen where she encountered a cook curled up on the greasy floor and Doc Gno, Chief Tatum, Clara and John Beale huddled together in conference.

"Can we help you dear?" Clara asked.

"No Clara," Abbie answered, "but I may be able to help you."

Chapter 13

Abbie awoke at the crack of dawn and headed to Clara's for breakfast with Doc Gno, John Beale and the Chief. Clara had insisted that they start their day with a hot breakfast; detective work could not be done on an empty stomach. When Abbie's phone began ringing at six thirty a.m. and she was not there to answer it, her fiancé on the other end became just a wee bit suspicious.

Bob Kelly also awoke early, after sleeping little. He brewed a pot of coffee then went back to work at Pete's computer which he had confiscated the night before. Kelly stared at the monitor, re-reading what he had outlined. His own plan for saving Tyle Island sounded crazier than the murder scheme proposed at the Nest. There were just a few details that needed polishing before going public; Kelly set a three o'clock deadline. He would then run by Abbie's for some editorial input and offer to buy her dinner as a way of saying thanks.

Jack West arrived early at the set of The Darkest hour. He informed the producers that Abbie was ill and needed him on Tyle Island. After a little creative rescheduling and a promise to be back on the set Monday morning at nine o'clock sharp Jack was on his way to pay his fiancé a surprise visit. The one o'clock ferry would land him on Tyle Island before two thirty. He'd be standing on his parent's deck by three o'clock sharp.

Abbie picked at a large plate of blueberry pancakes while she listened to John Beale's update regarding the palm greaser from Port Elizabeth and his oversized freighter.

A fax listing the specs of the vessel had come in during Mayor Brady's funeral party. Had it not been for the overwhelming need to pee which had struck John as he stumbled past his office, combined with his desire not to soil the memory of Owen Brady by relieving himself by the side of the road, he never would have seen the fax until this morning, when sober. Fortunately, he read the fax when his inhibitions were at an all time low, and after laughing out loud then pausing to pee, he dialed the shipping company in New Jersey and asked to speak with the little palm greaser. Their conversation was candid.

Harbor Master John Beale informed the palm greaser that his ship was simply too big to dock in the harbor of Tyle Island, and taking a look at the depth of its hull, his ship could not safely come within a half mile of the Island without risking severe damage to its underbelly. The palm greaser didn't buy it so John Beale let it be known that he didn't care if the little palm greaser believed him or not, the ship was not docking. Then, following a terse exchange of colorful language, the palm greaser from New Jersey informed the Tyle Island Harbor Master that his freighter would anchor any place it pleased and his crew would transport his load whether he liked it or not. John Beale laughed even harder and invited the man from New Jersey to do just that. He was even kind enough to offer some logistical assistance. He explained that the only place a ship as large as his could anchor anywhere near Tyle Island was on the north side, just below the infamous cliffs. John Beale then referred the palm greaser to a book entitled "Great Wrecks of the Atlantic" and asked him to please read pages 130 through 210 which detailed the many shipwrecks that had occurred due to the wild tides and rocky underwater terrain off the very same cliffs by which he would be parking his very expensive vessel. He then asked the palm greaser if he would be so kind as to advise him, prior to setting off on his voyage north, of the number of crew members traveling aboard the freighter. This would allow the Island doctor ample time to requisition the appropriate number of toe tags and body bags needed for the failed rescue. He then pointed out that the rescue was sure to fail, for not only was he the Harbor Master, he was also the President of the Tyle Island Emergency Squad. As such, it was his responsibility to supervise all water rescues, and he sure as hell was not going to dip a toe in the chilly Atlantic water for some son of a bitch who dared to question his authority. He informed the palm greaser that if he would like to make ferry reservations for the purpose of transporting his equipment and supplies, he should call the office of Tyle Island Navigation Monday through Friday between nine a.m. and three p.m. John Beale then hung up the telephone and dialed Marcy, the ferry reservations clerk, and gave her the week off.

Doc Gno patted John Beale on the back, "you've given them something to think about."

"You've given them something to stew about," Chief Tatum corrected, "and you've made a dangerous enemy."

"Don't you worry about me Chief," John Beale's face showed no fear, "he may be dangerous in New Jersey, but I'm dangerous here." He then handed a fax to Abbie, "I got their schedule. They planned on coming into port a week from today."

"Having to ferry over their equipment will delay the start of construction," Clara seemed pleased by this glimmer of hope.

"Problem is, before they construct, they must destruct," Abbie added less optimistically.

"She's right," agreed Doc Gno, "and they don't need heavy machinery to clear that land. Besides a few trees, Barron's Hollow is mostly small brush and wildflowers. All the developer needs to get started are some able bodies with shovels and picks. That could begin tomorrow for all we know."

"So our primary goal is to protect the land." Abbie took charge. "Chief, you've got the most pull around here, is there any way you can rustle up a few of the more intimidating Islanders for guard duty?"

"I'll hit the docks and deputize some of the fellas. Trust me Abbie, no stranger will step foot on this Island, let alone get within fifty yards of the Hollow, without us knowing about it."

"Good," Abbie pushed aside her half eaten plate of pancakes, "we already know that no Islander will hire on with these people, correct?" The others nodded, "so the crew will have to be brought in from outside."

"We can't stop them from bringing a work force from the mainland," Chief Tatum replied.

"True," said Abbie, "but unless those workers want to start every day with an hour and a half ferry ride over here and finish every day with an hour and a half ferry ride home, they're going to need beds to sleep in and food to eat."

"I hear what you're saying," answered Clara, "and I think food and lodging are areas that I can cover quite nicely."

Abbie scribbled notes on a paper placemat. She asked the Chief, "What sort of building and work permits will be required in order to begin construction?"

"Lots of complicated ones?" he answered.

"Way lots Chief," said Abbie, "and everything has to be approved by the Tyle Island Building Inspector. Who is you building inspector?"

"He moved off Island in February, we haven't gotten around to replacing him," answered John Beale.

"Perfect. Is his name still on his office door?"

John Beale nodded.

"Good. Hook up an answering machine. We'll consider him unreachable for now and deal with a replacement when the time comes. Has anyone had any luck tracking down the Conservancy Council members?"

"Nope," answered the Chief, "it's as if they've all vanished. Lila over at Island Realty hasn't been any help. She's selling Hyacinth Poole's house as well as two others, so she has to know how to get a hold of them, but she's not talking."

"That Lila has been a bad seed since kindergarten," Clara declared.

"Yeah, well," Abbie was unsure how to properly voice her next concern, "it's the possibility of additional Lila's surfacing that poses a major problem."

"Meaning?" asked Doc Gno.

Abbie chose her words carefully, "from what I have observed Tyle Island is made up of predominantly middle to lower middle class people."

"A fact we're not ashamed of," Clara's Irish was rising,

"And you shouldn't be. My point is there is a potential for some serious money to be made here. Land values will skyrocket if this casino deal gets off the ground. Clearly Lila has already seized the opportunity."

"And you want to know how long it will take the rest of us to give in to the pressure of the almighty dollar?" John Beale did not like the direction Abbie was going.

"Please don't misunderstand me, I'm not questioning any of you, I'm just suggesting that you put some thought into who might not share your loyalty."

"You don't know the people of this Island Abbie," Clara was on the attack until Chief Tatum interrupted.

"How well did we all know Hyacinth? How many egg white omelets did you cook for her, Clara? John, how many Sherries did you drink on her front porch? Doc, she made you dinner at least once a week for as long as I can remember. No one was as staunch in their support of land preservation, but can anyone tell me where she is right now?"

Silence.

The point was made so Abbie quickly moved on. "Hyacinth is the key to this story. She signed those minutes, I need to know why." She looked to Chief Tatum, "I need to get a hold of her personal records."

"Say no more to me Abbie, I'm still the law on this Island. Hyacinth holds an elected position and is under suspicion of official misconduct so her office in town hall is open to investigation, but her personal records are another matter."

"There's nothing you can do?" Abbie pleaded.

He paused, then, "Be at The Nest at eleven thirty."

"And?"

"Just be at The Nest."


Abbie spent the morning searching Hyacinth Poole's office. Besides an unmarked computer disc that appeared innocent, Abbie had come up dry. At just before eleven thirty she pocketed the disc, walked down to The Nest, took a seat at the bar and casually sipped a soda while watching hung-over employees attempting to repair the devastation caused by Mayor Brady's funeral fest. She offered to assist with the cleanup but the man replenishing the supply of liquor bottles wouldn't hear of it.

"You've got more important business to tend to Abbie," he told her.

Abbie hadn't recalled introducing herself so his knowledge of her name was unsettling, as was the curious wink that had accompanied his statement. She didn't have much time to worry about the bartender's inside information; however, for as she sipped her soda two young men entered the bar and occupied the stools on either side of her. Abbie noted that the men were twins, from where she sat, identical, and from their scent, fishermen by trade. The twin on her left asked the bartender for two mugs of Bud. The bartender poured them, placed them on the bar, told the twins that they were on the house, and again winked suspiciously at Abbie.

"You Abbie?" the twin on her left asked.

"Yes," she hesitated, "who are you?"

"Not important," said the twin on her right.

"Allrighty then," said Abbie as she lifted her soda and began to chew nervously on the straw.

The twins downed their mugs of Bud then stood and headed for the door. "You comin?" one twin asked, but since they were no longer seated Abbie didn't know which one had made the inquiry.

"Coming where?" she asked

"We're taking you where you want to go. Come on."

Abbie's confusion was akin to Kevin Costner's in 'A Field of Dreams'. She knew that what she was about to do was foolhardy, and could very well be the biggest mistake of her life, yet she found herself compelled to do it anyway. Abbie left The Nest with the twins, climbed into the front seat of their pick-up truck and was joined on either side by either twin.

"Couldn't talk inside," said the twin now seated to her right.

"Too risky," added the twin driving.

"Uncle Owen was a good man," said the twin on her right.

"Oh," Abbie finally let out the breath she had inhaled upon entering the truck, "the Mayor was your Uncle."

"Great-Uncle. He loaned us the money to buy our first boat. We owe him this."

"Owe him what exactly, if you don't mind me asking?"

"Helping you."

"Helping me do what?"

The twin driving leaned forward in his seat and addressed his brother. "Didn't Tatum say she was smart?"

"Yep," the twin to Abbie's right answered.

"We'll see," said the twin who was driving. They drove on for several minutes then pulled off to the side of the road. The twin to her right stepped out of the truck, then helped Abbie out and lifted her over a puddle cautioning, "Careful, it's muddy."

"Thanks," Abbie forced a smile as she wondered which direction would be best to run screaming for help.

"Come on," said the twin who had been driving. The three of them walked up to a stone wall in which a sign was carved that read BARRON'S HOLLOW - NATURE REFUGE. Below it was a notice stating - NO MOPEDS OR BICYCLES ALLOWED. They hiked in silence for close to a quarter mile until they came to the crest of a steep hill.

"Holy Mother of...." said Abbie as she took in the view; Tyle Island's rustic beauty in three hundred and sixty degree panorama.

"Pretty, huh?"

"It's amazing," replied Abbie as she watched birds of every color sail through the sky. She spun around, then around again, absorbing the breathtaking scenery that was Tyle Island's north, south, east and west.

"This is the land the Widow gave to the casino developer," the twin standing on her right informed her. Abbie felt her throat tighten as she looked up at the twin and saw tears in his eyes. "Thought you oughta see this before we go do what we gotta do. Come on."

What they went to do was break into Hyacinth Poole's house. The twins told Abbie to stay back as they walked up to the back porch door and gently rapped on the door. "Widow Poole," the twin on the right called out quietly, "you home Widow Poole?" No answer. "Doesn't look like she's home," one twin said to the other. "Nope it doesn't. We should go." "Wait. Do you smell propane?" Sniff, sniff. "I think I smell propane."

"I don't smell anything," Abbie commented.

Both twins glared. She got their point. They carried on. "That could be dangerous. Maybe we should check it out." "Maybe." One twin, using his elbow protected by the bulk of his coat, broke a pane of glass in the porch door. "Look, it's broken," said one twin. "Yeah I see," said the other. One twin reached inside and unlocked the door handle, "and look, the door is open." "Sure is. We should probably check it out." "It would be the neighborly thing to do," the twin agreed with his brother. The first twin entered, the second twin looked back at Abbie and asked, "You comin?"

Abbie pictured the beauty of Barron's Hollow that would soon become home to high rollers rather than rolling hills and answered, "Yeah, I'm comin."


Clara's first three visits to Hotel and Bed & Breakfast owners were successful; no rooms would be rented to anyone associated with the building of the casino. Granted, she had taken a liberty or two in order to guarantee Island unity, such as suggesting that the casino complex would no doubt include a luxury hotel, and pointing out that a luxury hotel would greatly contrast the charming B&B's and Inns currently operating on the Island, then implying that gamblers generally prefer luxury to charm, then speculating that raucous gamblers would drive away the more civilized vacationer who preferred charm to luxury and who currently filled their quaint rooms every season, which would lead to vacancies, which would lead to debt, which would lead to bankruptcy, which would lead to minimum wage jobs at the luxury hotel that had put their own establishment out of business in the first place.

Her next stop didn't go so well. According to the personal secretary of Robert J. Prescott III, owner of The Water Lily, the largest of the three hotels overlooking The

Old Harbor, 'Mister Prescott is off-Island and under no circumstances can he be reached'.

Clara, who longed to tell the uppity little west coast bitch exactly where she could get off, instead remained calm and politely asked the young woman if she would please confirm if any rooms had been rented to anyone associated with the much publicized casino deal. The personal assistant refused to confirm, which, to Clara, confirmed.

"Dirty foreign bastard," she muttered as she stormed out of the hotel, "I should have known that a damn Brit would betray us." Pissed off but otherwise undaunted, Clara marched next door to meet with Taloy Jobbs, the off the boat Irishman, free spirit, and owner of the other two Victorian hotels overlooking the Island's Old Harbor.

Over a lunch of Bloody Marys, Clara and Taloy casually debated the pros and cons of having a casino on Tyle Island. Clara knew that Taloy was too shrewd a businessman to be conned by her insinuations of pending financial doom, but she also knew that he had more money than God and loved the laid back lifestyle of off-season Tyle Island. They chatted about the increase in property values not to mention profit margins that would accompany year round tourism. They discussed the overcrowding, the Island's already inadequate infrastructure and the potential strain that a building of a casino's magnitude would have on utilities and waste management. Clara sensed that despite Taloy's love of the Island, he was balanced precariously on the pro-casino fence, so she played a hunch and informed the Irishman that the Brit next door had already agreed to cooperate with the enemy.

A devilish chuckle escaped the thin lips of the giddy Irishman. He added a shake of pepper to his Bloody Mary then, through a thick brogue that was barely discernable, Taloy suggested that it might be the perfect time to start a rumor. Tyle Island rumors have been known to arise on the north side at seven a.m. and be settling in at the southern tip by seven-ten. Taloy glanced about to make sure they would not be overheard, then suggested that perhaps, just perhaps, he had a meeting scheduled with a certain Bostonian with the last name of, lets say, Kennedy, to discuss the rental of one of his hotels for a fast approaching and very hush-hush wedding. Taloy assured Clara that Prescott would surface to steal his high profile client; blue-collar construction workers would surely take a backseat to Teddy and the boys. Clara thought Taloy's idea inspired so when he offered his services in supplying a fictitious Kennedy and handling the details of the deception himself, Clara graciously accepted. Granted, in two or three weeks time there would be no wedding and the rooms of The Water Lily would be freed, but two or three weeks was a sufficient band-aid for their currently gaping wound.

    Clara left Taloy planning his sting while she concentrated on the next hurdle - food. None of the hotel kitchens operated off-season so unless catering was to be brought from the mainland, food would have to be supplied by either of the two eateries currently serving on the Island; her own Diner or The Nest. Fortunately unlike the rivalry in the hotel department, the purveyors of food and drink on Tyle Island were a close-knit bunch. A lack of cooperation on her own part was a given, and just as she had expected, the owner of The Nest, a long-ago escapee of Los Angeles crowds, agreed to refuse burgers and beers to anyone affiliated with the casino.

    The grocery and liquor stores were less receptive to an out-and-out boycott, but did agree to gouge prices of items sold to construction workers to points well beyond obscene. Prices would remain the already inflated yet tolerable status for Islanders, all of whom were known by face and name, and most of who had accounts at both establishments, allowing the price hike could take place on the QT.

Pleased with her progress, Clara headed to Doc Gno's office, where he had been detained all morning treating several nasty cases of the flu.

On a hunch that his palm-greasing pal from New Jersey might have a trick or two up his sleeve, John Beale took it upon himself to cover his ass.

Tyle Island has two harbors that handle all boat activity, Old Harbor and New Harbor. The Old Harbor, the hub of island activity, services the ferries, the commercial fisherman, many of the boat owning islanders and a handful of wealthy yachtsmen who pay dearly to have slips available just in case they feel the urge to sail in once or twice seasonally. There was no available dock space, therefore no concern for having the palm greaser pull a fast one via the Old Harbor route.

The New Harbor landing was another story. New Harbor slips, while less conveniently located a mile or so out of town, are rented on a daily, weekly or monthly basis and, as it was still April, most were available. Sensing that the palm greaser might try to bypass the hour plus ferry ride with shorter trips made by smaller, faster vessels that could easily dock at New Harbor, John Beale wielded his power and cut them off at the pass. He declared all four piers at the New Harbor unsafe and off limits until repairs were completed. Granted the docks needed nothing more than a fresh coat of Thompsons; however, John Beale saw little difference between a sign reading "wet paint" and one stating "condemned."

It was as if Abbie had stepped back in time. She entered Hyacinth Poole's doily and Depression glass filled cherry wood kitchen and felt as if she was standing in her own grandmother's house. A small round table tucked unobtrusively in the corner of the room was covered with a crisply laundered linen, a crystal vase centerpiece filled with flowers that had dropped all but the most stubborn of buds, and the perpetual place setting of Royal Dalton China standing ready to serve Hyacinth's afternoon tea. Abbie had never understood her own grandmother's similar obsession with order and propriety, but following every holiday dinner they would wash the dishes, change the tablecloth and reset the table. Abbie, who at the time considered the ritual a nuisance, suddenly longed to be back at her grandmother's house with a damp dishcloth slung over her shoulder and a plastic apron tied around her waist. She would have remained lost in her trip down memory lane if one twin hadn't offered her an oatmeal cookie plucked from a cat shaped ceramic cookie jar, while the other twin asked "so what are we looking for?"

Abbie took a pass on the cookie, although it looked tempting - home made, loaded with raisins - and instructed the twins to bring her anything they could find that mentioned Barron's Hollow, the casino development or Governor Hardy.

Abbie was on pins and needles as she searched the house, expecting Lila the Realtor to barge through the front door with prospective buyers while she had the contents of Hyacinth Poole's cadenza drawers strewn across the oriental carpet that covered her living room floor. After a full hour of snooping they had found nothing that could link the Widow Poole to the bogus vote.

"How about the basement?" one twin offered. The three marched downstairs where, besides uncovering a lifetime's worth of Christmas, Easter and Thanksgiving decorations, they turned up naught.

"Shit!" Abbie yelled in frustration.

"You kiss your mother with that mouth?" one twin asked as the other placed his hands mockingly over his ears.

"Sorry," Abbie collapsed onto a cardboard box stenciled with the word SNOWMEN and apologized for the vulgarity. "We needed to find some sort of link between Hyacinth and the casino. The Widow Poole is smarter than I gave her credit for."

Twin number one was busy untangling a string of Christmas lights while twin number two sat on a carton stenciled ELVES and thumbed through a box filled with colorful Yule Tide greetings.

"We should get out of here," Abbie stood, "we're pushing our luck."

The one twin put down the string of lights and joined Abbie at the base of the stairs. The second twin stared at one of the more elaborate Christmas cards whose gold trim and fancy red ribbon had caught his eye. He opened the card and read the message. "Abbie?"

"Yes?" Abbie felt awkward as she had yet to learn the name of either twin.

"What's Governor Hardy's first name?"

"Patrick. Why?"

"You know his wife's name?"

"No," she snapped, short on patience due to the duration of their illegal stay, "I'm from New York, you're the home town boys." Then, feeling badly about her snippiness added a kinder "why do you ask?"

"Well," the twin stood and held out the Christmas card, "if the wife's name is Priscilla and their kids are Todd and Amy, then the Widow Poole is Governor Hardy's Aunt."

Abbie took the Christmas card, opened it and read the professionally inscribed gold lettering, "Happy Holidays, Love, The Hardys - Patrick, Priscilla, Amy and Todd." At the top of the card in flowing script was written "Dearest Aunt Hyacinth."

Chapter 14

   After re-ransacking Hyacinth Poole's house, Abbie and the twins tossed four photo albums filled with black and white snapshots, the box of Christmas cards and an old address book excavated from the depths of a kitchen drawer into the bed of the truck. With their felony completed they headed to The Nest for a celebratory beer. While the twins transferred their booty to the Jeep Abbie went inside and ordered two mugs of Bud and a pint of Harp; she was buying. By the second round they were joined by Clara and Doc Gno who had spotted the Jeep and stopped in for a progress report. Abbie was leery of publicly discussing her brush with B&E, so she suggested that the group meet at her place in an hour for cocktails and an update. Clara hurried off to pick up lobsters to steam for dinner and pass on their plans to John Beale and the Chief. Doc Gno headed out on a house call, but promised to be at Madonna's Cove by four.
   The twin to Abbie's right stood, "gotta go. It's been real." His brother stood and gave Abbie a short salute.
   "Will I see you tomorrow?" Abbie looked around to make sure no one was in earshot, "we might have a few more houses to hit."
   "We'll find you when we need to," answered one twin. The other asked, "Are you through with the Widow's place?"
   "I think so?"
   "Are you sure?"
   Abbie thought a moment then nodded, "yeah, I'm sure. All we have to do is return what we took once I'm through with it."
   The twins smiled at each other and left. Abbie downed her beer, checked her watch and realized that it was already three o'clock. She had a few groceries to pick up before making a quick detour to Kelly's to invite him to

the evenings swarre'; today's development was big and she needed him, professionally speaking of course.

Buying elegant hors d'oeuvres off-season on Tyle Island is impossible. This Abbie discovered as she perused the five-foot long frozen food case that comprised the 'refrigerated aisle' of the grocery store. She was in search of something for her guests to nibble on before dinner. After ten minutes of staring at Velveeta cheese blocks and canned sardines, she selected a box of whole-wheat crackers, a crock of port wine cheese spread, and a jar of creamed herring. Screw it, Abbie said to herself, maybe it'll taste better if I serve it on the heirloom china.

Abbie turned into the Kelly driveway and was greeted by Pete, who looked none too happy.
"You know where Bob went?" he asked her.
"Nope, I'm looking for him myself."
"He took off in my dad's pick-up," Pete complained. "Last night he stole my computer and now the truck. I liked him better when he was an unmotivated drunk."
"He stole your computer?" Abbie was intrigued. "Get in. I'll take you to my place. You can have the Jeep, just make sure you return it tonight, I'll need it in the morning." A few minutes later they pulled into Abbie's driveway and parked behind a black Ford F150.
"We found Bob," Pete pointed to the truck, "that's my dad's."
"And my lights are on, which means your presumptuous Uncle has made himself at home."
As Abbie climbed out of the Jeep, the warning drums began to play in her head. She noticed two figures, not one, seated on her deck. She squinted, shit, two familiar figures. Abbie looked to Pete and asked, "you think we can get away unnoticed?"

"What's wrong?"
"It appears that your Uncle is entertaining my fiancé."
"The guy whose ring you tossed?"
"Uh huh."
"Oh, this should be good." Pete jogged ahead as Abbie swallowed hard, whispered shit, shit, shit, fixed her hair and forced a smile.
"Hi guys," her voice cracked as she called out to the men standing on her deck, "what a pleasant surprise."


Kelly thought he was catching a burglar in mid-burgle, but then realized that the man standing on Abbie's deck hadn't tried to take-off when he saw the pick-up drive up to the house. He then noticed that the man standing on Abbie's deck looked familiar. Although he couldn't quite place the face, he was sure he had seen him before.
"May I help you?" Kelly asked as he climbed the steps.
"I sure hope so," the stranger introduced himself as Jack West, Abbie's fiancé.
"Pleased to meet you Jack," Kelly took the man's hand and gave it an overly firm shake, "I'm Bob Kelly. I live down the road. I just stopped in to see Abbie."
Jack West looked at Kelly suspiciously until he glanced down at the papers in Kelly's left hand. "Oh, I get it, you're working with Abbie on the book."
"The book?" Kelly tried not to sound ignorant.
"Abbie's novel. The reason she's here."
"Oh. Of course. The book." Kelly placed a hand on Jack West's shoulder and directed him to a deck chair. Both men sat. "I'm a writer myself. I stopped by to discuss my latest thoughts, but," Kelly looked around, "no Abbie."
"I know. I'm worried about her. I've been trying to reach her since six thirty this morning, but like you said, no Abbie. Do you think she's all right?"

"Oh. I'm sure she's just fine," although she won't be after I get a hold of her Kelly thought as he explained, "Abbie has embraced Tyle Island and its people. I'm sure that she's sitting on the beach right now pouring her thoughts out onto paper."

"She uses a laptop," Jack corrected.

Kelly smiled and again wondered from where he knew this too young, too handsome, and from his last statement, too stupid man. He debated explaining to Abbie's less-than-mensa fiancé that he too, like most writers of the late twentieth century used a computer. Then Kelly took a closer look at Jack West and decided not to waste his time. Instead he leaned forward in his chair and asked, "Have we met before? You look very familiar."

And then it happened. Jack flashed his daytime drama studly smile. The blinding reflection off his perfectly aligned pearly whites triggered Kelly's memory and, oh dear God, Kelly said to himself, it's him, just as Abbie O'Neal's future husband announced "you may have seen me on television. I'm Doctor Jasper Black on The Darkest Hour."

Now Kelly was in a real quandary, for he distinctly recalled Abbie telling him that she had never seen The Darkest Hour which clearly could not be the truth if she was engaged to the show's leading man, which clearly she was because he was sitting on her deck. This obviously meant that either Abbie was too embarrassed by her future husband's career choice to admit her knowledge of the show, or was too embarrassed by her choice of future husband, which was easily surmised if one was a viewer and confirmed upon meeting him.

"I'm surprised Abbie didn't tell you," Jack West a.k.a. Jasper Black, appeared slightly annoyed.

This called for a quick volley, "mine and Abbie's is a professional relationship. We don't discuss personal matters."

"I understand Bob," Jack rose from his chair. Kelly noticed that the man seemed to be flexing his muscles but for whose benefit Kelly hadn't a clue. "But the Darkest Hour is Abbie's profession."

"Excuse me," Kelly didn't understand, "I thought she was a novelist."

Jack West circled Kelly, studying him. His contact lens enhanced blue eyes squinted as if his small brain was attempting to churn out a big thought. Then suddenly his flexed muscles relaxed.

"Oh I get it," his stupid smile returned to his perfect face, "my Abbie is so thoughtful. She probably didn't want you to feel bad, seeing as how you're a struggling writer and she's such a success."

"Success at what?" Kelly was now totally confused.

"The Darkest Hour."

Bob Kelly's blank stare signified the depth of said confusion.

"Abbie is the head writer for The Darkest Hour. All those brilliant things I say and do on the show, Abbie writes them."

Holy mother fucker almost spilled out of Kelly's mouth, recalling not only Abbie's denial of any knowledge of the Darkest Hour, but his own critique of the show during which he commented that he could write the inane crap with his toes. This meant that Abbie wasn't embarrassed by her choice of fiancé, although she should be, but rather by her choice of careers. And what had he done? He had told the young woman with the face of an angel that her life's work was garbage just moments after she had revealed to him that she was one of his biggest fans. The Bob Kelly, who minutes before wanted to stick it to Abbie for lying about not being a writer, now wanted to retreat to safety, thus salvaging the last shred of Abbie O'Neal's delicate dignity.

The Jeep pulled up. Too late.

"Hi guys!" Kelly heard Abbie's voice crack as his brother's son bounded up onto the deck wearing a grin that could only be described as shit eating. He introduced himself to Abbie's fiancé.

Jack flashed his pricey smile, "So you two are related?"

"He's my brother's son," Kelly responded dryly.

"If you'll excuse me," Jack winked, "I'd like to say hello to Abbie." He sauntered down the steps and out to the Jeep where Abbie was removing a grocery bag and stalling for time.

"Do we know him?" asked Pete.

"No."

"I swear I know that guy."

"You don't."

"I do. I'll ask him."

"You do and you die."

"What's the big deal? I'll just ask where he's from."

"Yes you know him," panic was setting in, "from television. He plays Doctor Jasper Black on The Darkest Hour, now let's get out of here."

"Wow you're right. I gotta ask him about Nurse Rhonda."

Bob looked at Pete whom he noticed was just shy of his own 6'2", "you won't ask him anything, you won't say another word, we're leaving."

"Why?"

"Because I said so."

"Not good enough."

"Abbie will be embarrassed if we stay. Do you want that?"

"No." The awe of meeting a TV star subsided and the memory of a drunken Abbie casting her engagement ring upon the waters returned, "You're right, we gotta go." Pete began to walk away.

Bob grabbed Pete by the back of his sweatshirt stopping him in mid-stride. "We can't just run away.

We need a story," he instructed the younger and less socially graced Kelly.

"Fine. You're the writer, come up with a story. And make it quick, they're coming."

The Kelly men watched Abbie walk around to the back of the Jeep and remove what looked to be photo albums, the color had yet to return to her angelic face.

"Dinner's on."

"Huh?"

"You left our dinner on the stove. We've got to get home before it burns."

"It's not even four o'clock in the afternoon."

"We'll say its stew. That cooks a while."

"Yeah it simmers for hours and it doesn't burn and if you haven't noticed Bob, it's the nineties, nobody makes stew anymore."

Kelly thought a moment, "Fine. I'll tell her that I'm not feeling well. You offer to drive me home."

Just as Abbie and Jack headed toward the deck, bundles in hand, two cars pulled down the dirt road and parked behind the Jeep that was parked behind the pick-up. Clara got out and hollered, "Bob Kelly, you're just the man I wanted to see. Sit yourself down; we have a thing or two to discuss." Too late.

## Chapter 15

Abbie uncorked a bottle of cabernet, raised it to her lips, and guzzled. After downing the equivalent of a glassful or so, she placed the bottle on the counter, wiped away the spittle that remained on the rim, walked into the dining room and began removing her soon-to-be mother in law's heirloom crystal from the breakfront. Knowing that the evil-one would someday sip out of the same glass from which the owner of Clara's 'cheap greasy' Diner downed gin brought a momentary smirk to Abbie O'Neal's angelic face. With the highball, lowball and wine glasses displayed on the coffee table along with various bottles of liquor, mixers, a decanter filled with amber colored spirits, and a bucket of ice, Abbie returned to the kitchen, banged her head on the refrigerator three times, helped herself to one more swig from the bottle of cabernet then began removing her groceries from their bag. All the while Jack West, daytime drama stud, was surrounded by four adoring fans who, unlike the Kelly men, had recognized him at first sight.

Abbie peeled the protective plastic covering off of her package of port wine cheese spread, ran a knife around its edge and turned it over onto a piece of fine china. She peeked to make sure that the two hundred dollar dish hadn't rejected the three dollar processed cheese food. Once satisfied that the plate would not self-destruct, she stuck a sterling silver serving knife into the mound of pinkish goop and placed the plate on the coffee table beside the decanter. She then went back to the kitchen, allowed herself another swig of wine, and uncapped the jar of creamed herring. As she dumped the dead little fishes into a small china bowl, Bob Kelly entered the room. Without looking up from the sad fish floating in their tasteless pool of cream sauce Abbie said, "Shut up."

"I didn't say anything," Kelly replied.

"You were about to," Abbie thunked a miniature serving spoon into the bowl of lumpy, grayish gunk.

"I just came in to see if you needed a hand," Kelly's voice was an octave above normal.

"A hand at what exactly? Preparing shitty hors d'oeuvres?"

Kelly assumed that Abbie's question was rhetorical and wisely chose not to answer.

"I may not know you all that well Bob Kelly, but taking into account the quality time that we've spent together, I can safely say that you did not stroll into my kitchen to assist with the food." Abbie grabbed her bottle of wine and downed a big gulp.

"I don't know what you're talking about," Kelly's performance was less than convincing.

She pointed out the window at the group assembled on the deck and flashed the same icy grin that she had given him the first day they met, "so now you know."

"Now I know what?" Kelly feigned ignorance.

"That I'm engaged to a Ken doll," Abbie opened her arms, "go ahead Kelly, take your best shot."

"Jack seems like a nice guy," the sentence sounded more like a question then the supportive statement it was meant to be.

"Oh that was low."

"I'm sorry."

"Don't apologize to me."

Kelly lowered his head and shoved his hands in his pockets; his stature resembled a schoolboy being reprimanded by a seven feet tall nun named Sister Rocco. "The other day when I passed out and you took me home I insulted you by belittling the Darkest Hour. Had I known that you were the writer I never would have..."

"What did you say?"

Kelly peeked up at her, "I said that had I known you were the writer."

"I heard you the first time. How did you come to discover that I write The Darkest Hour?"

"Jack told me?"

Abbie guzzled. Then guzzled more. Kelly felt the need to break the silence so, unlike earlier when he wisely remained quiet, this time he spoke. "I can't pretend that I didn't hurt your feelings."

"Yes you can," she wiped away the cabernet that was dripping from her chin.

Kelly's attempt at a friendly smile looked more like a cringe brought on by pain. "What do I know about television anyway? I'm sure it takes a lot of talent to do what you do."

"Don't patronize me Kelly."

This was not going as planned. Kelly considered a retreat to the deck, safety in numbers and all, but he just couldn't make himself leave Abbie alone in the kitchen; after all, there were sharp knives everywhere. He stared down at his favorite pair of loafers and mumbled, "Please just tell me what I can say or do to get back in your good graces." He awaited a response but got none. The growing level of tension caused the typically eloquent author to babble. "Trust me Abbie, the minute I recognized Jack I tried to leave but it was too late. I knew you'd be embarrassed, and I didn't want you to be, and you really shouldn't be, and I'm sorry I should stop speaking, shouldn't I?" Kelly looked up to see a tear roll down Abbie's cheek. "Oh God, that's not because of me is it?" Abbie sniffled and chugged more wine. "Do you want me to leave? I'll leave and take the others with me. You'll never have to see any of us again. I'll do whatever it takes, but please Abbie, do not cry."

Abbie put down the bottle and wiped away her tears. "I don't want you to leave," her glassy eyes met his and stayed there a moment too long. She took the bowl of grayish gunk in one hand and her bottle of wine in the other and ordered, "Grab the Wheat Thins." Kelly picked up the basket of crackers, afraid to do otherwise, and followed Abbie into the living room. She took a hit from her quickly approaching empty bottle of wine and asked, "Care to join me?"

"You don't carry my brand," Kelly answered, relieved to see that her tears had subsided.

"Surprise," she said as she placed the bowl of herring on the table by the pink pile of cheese and pointed to the decanter. She looked up at Kelly; again their eyes met, and again stayed a moment too long. "I had to special order, but hey," she shrugged, "what are friends for?" Abbie opened the sliding glass door, stepped outside, turned off the sadness and turned on the charm.

After passing out cocktails to her enthralled friends, Abbie sat on the edge of the hot tub, hugged her wine bottle and tried to figure out what had taken place in the past hour to transform her from Wonder Woman into Emotional Wreck. Her fiancé had come for a surprise visit. A generally accepted reaction to such spontaneity by a lover would be 'oh Honey', hers had been 'oh shit.' That was not a good sign. Then there was the ring toss of the prior weekend, not to mention the third postponement of her pending nuptials, this time under the guise of completing her novel, which by the way she hadn't touched but once this week. Abbie studied Jack, whose perfect smile and dopey charm were wooing the Islanders. He really is a sweet man, she thought. Granted he's no rocket scientist, but who ever said a husband had to be smart. Or funny. Or sincere. Guzzle, guzzle. Well, thought Abbie, Jack might not be a stimulating conversationalist but he is attentive, and as loyal as a puppy dog. Abbie began to feel warm inside. Maybe she was just feeling out of sorts because of their recent separation. They hadn't seen each other in nearly two weeks and had barely spoken due to Jack's constant rehearsals. A cool reception on her part was probably the norm. Hmmm. Abbie couldn't forget the fact that Jack had been generous enough to grant her this two month sabbatical in order to pursue her dream of completing her novel; how many single, straight, attractive men would be that unselfish? The warmth inside Abbie grew. Perhaps her initial 'oh shit' was merely a territorial response. Tyle Island had become her world away from reality and seeing Jack standing on the deck of her castle brought back all the complications surrounding her life in New York. Hmmm. Abbie liked the sound of these rationalizations. If she was merely acting out a manifestation of insecurity due to time spent apart and protectionism of her new, albeit temporary world, then maybe, just maybe, she really did still love him. Only true love could give me such a feeling of warmth, she told herself. Then Jack tossed his head, mussed his hair, and did his subliminal muscle flex that made the baby hairs on the back of her neck stand on end. Then again, she stared at the stained label on her bottle of cabernet; it could just be the wine.

As Jack West spun tales regarding stardom to the awe stuck Doctor, Diner Owner, Harbor Master and Chief, Abbie took the opportunity to pull Bob Kelly aside.

"I need to speak with you," she gently touched his arm, "in private."

Kelly, pleased to escape Jack's next line of BS, followed her inside.

"You need a refill," Abbie poured scotch from the decanter into Kelly's glass. She sat on the sofa, took a drink of wine while still ignoring the concept of using a glass, and declared, "I have a confession to make."

Kelly sat beside Abbie; a little too close, sipped his scotch and felt his stomach twist into a knot. This was not a twinge or a gnaw, this was a knot, and Bob Kelly had never before felt a knot quite like this one.

"You can tell me anything," he smiled crookedly.

Abbie looked into Kelly's face which was for some reason becoming blurry, and wondered what the strange grin was for. It was the same smirk he wore that day when he was lying on the floor of Clara's Diner. Abbie ignored the stupid smile and said, "please don't be angry with me for what I'm about to say to you."

"I won't be angry," Kelly assured the angel face.

"I value our friendship and I don't want to do anything to jeopardize it."

"I won't be angry," he repeated.

"You promise?" Abbie squinted. Kelly took Abbie's squint as coyness when in reality she was trying to focus despite experiencing double vision brought on by rapidly ingesting a bottle of wine.

"I promise."

"Good," Abbie polished off the last drop from the bottle, "then I'm just going to come right out and say what I have to say."

"Go ahead."

"Bob," she placed a hand on his knee to steady herself.

"Yes," the knot tightened.

"I."

"Yes," his mouth went dry.

"Love."

"Yes," his glass began to tremble.

Abbie took a deep breath; Kelly was holding his. "This Island and so I went and got involved with the others in trying to halt this casino deal and new information has come to light and now I think that I may be in over my head and I was hoping that perhaps you would agree to step in and help us out."

Not exactly what he had been expecting. Just as he was about to ask Abbie to repeat herself, having missed her declaration of love, lust or at least mild physical attraction, his brother's son walked in. "Pete, go home."

"Did you just call me Pete?"

"Go home."

"Why?"

"Same reason as before."

"What, the stew is burning?" Pete saw the anger on his uncle's face and announced, "I'm outta here. Can I take the truck?"

"Keys are in it."

"Everyone will have to move their cars or I'll have to drive on the lawn."

"Drive on the lawn." Kelly finished his glass of scotch then filled it again. He stood and walked to the sliding doors, collecting his thoughts while listening to the group outside laughing over Jack West's tall tales.

"I knew you'd be mad." Abbie headed straight for the wine rack, pulled out a fresh bottle, this time a merlot, and set about the complicated task of operating a wine opener while three sheets to the wind. "Please Bob," she paused, "I need you."

Kelly continued to stare out at Dr Jasper Black, "for what?"

"Well for starters," Abbie held the wine bottle between her knees and tugged at the reluctant cork, "for getting this frigging cork out of this frigging bottle of wine." Kelly walked across the room, extracted the cork and handed the bottle to Abbie. She sniffed the wine, as if the bouquet really mattered, then took a swig. "That day on the beach when I told you that you'd be crazy to get involved, I was wrong. Tyle Island is your home and these people are your friends and you have to help them."

"By getting them killed?" Kelly fought to maintain his composure.

"Well," Abbie shook a wine stained finger at the three Bob Kellys she saw standing before her, "as a matter of fact, I've worked out some of the details and you know I don't think anybody else has to die."

"Why not Abbie? Because you write The Darkest Hour?" Kelly laughed. "This is not your little soap opera my dear, this is the real world." His composure was fading. "Unlike your far fetched story lines, women on the planet earth are not cured of cancer by visiting a spa in Switzerland where they are injected with moose urine, smothered with therapeutic space mud and given a free Estee Lauder makeover with every sustained remission." Composure was fading fast. "In the real world people with no judicial background do not successfully defend themselves in the court of law simply because they look good in an Armani suit and black leather wingtips." One fragile thread of composure remained. "If I remember last week's cliffhanger correctly, a person who has been decapitated in a train wreck can not be brought back to life courtesy of a laser surgery head transplant." What composure? "And most obvious of all," Kelly pointed out to the deck, "in the real world, there would be no chance in hell that Jack West would be a brain surgeon."

"What exactly are you trying to say Kelly?"

He took a deep breath and spoke through gritted teeth. "I'm trying to say that problems such as the casino can not be solved with trite and unsubstantiated twists of plot."

"You're calling me a shitty writer."

"I'm not."

"You are."

"No. I'm not."

"You are. You're insinuating that simply because my paycheck comes from The Darkest Hour, and that the story lines I write for that television show can, on occasion, be far fetched, that the length and breadth of my talent stops with stupid. Not all of us are contracted to write novels for highly respected publishing houses Bob Kelly, but we do all have to pay the bills."

"I'm not judging you," Kelly ached for more scotch.

"Like hell you're not. You're not the least bit curious as to what I may have uncovered or may be planning simply because I'm Miss Inane Crap while you on the other hand are Mister Haughty Taughty Author Extraordinaire." Kelly opened his mouth but Abbie squelched his rebuttal. "Well Mister Big Shot Novelist let's review a thing or two." She allowed herself a brief pause to drink some wine. "You write books. I will concede that you write good books. Perhaps even brilliant books. But books are limiting. You see Bob, books such as yours have a handful of main characters, one plot, a subplot is possible but not mandatory, and every itsy bitsy little detail is dreamt up in that imaginative little brain of yours without influence from the outside, or as you would put it the 'real world'." She drank again. "Well Mr. Superior Writer, guess what I do every day? I juggle a minimum of ten to twelve story lines, involving twenty or so main characters and a dozen or so secondary characters whose public response I must continuously monitor so that I know the correct moment to thrust these characters into starring roles or kill them off in fatal car crashes. There are occasions, more often then not, where I must change a script on a moments notice at the whim of a horny producer who is looking to get laid by a Hollywood wannabe with no talent but tits the size of Mount McKinley. Now Bob Kelly, understand that these characters are not merely figments of my imagination. These characters are all connected to living, breathing, psychotic actors whose egos I get the pleasure of stroking on a daily basis. I know which of my actors can cry, and guess what, they're the ones whose lives are racked with heartbreak. I know who is capable of performing Hamlet, and who would struggle with a reading for Bay Watch, and that's the way I script them. I churn out five shows a week, fifty-two weeks a year. I've got the highest ratings in the history of daytime drama, two Emmys under my belt, and the knowledge that millions of people, you included, admit to being addicted to my inane crap. I may not be a best selling novelist Bob Kelly, but I thrive in world that would reduce you to 'see Dick run.' So Shakespeare, do not stand before me and claim superiority. Our talents are unique, but not mutually exclusive."

"What exactly are you trying to say Abbie?"

"I'm suggesting that we merge our talents and write our way out of this mess. You unhook your single malt I.V drip long enough to develop our main plot, focusing on our main players. I'll handle the subplots, secondary characters, research and organization of all of the above. I think that together we can keep gambling off of Tyle Island. We may lose a night or two of sleep in the process, but I guarantee that we will not lose another life."

Kelly pulled the pages that he had brought over for Abbie's review from his back pocket, unfolded them and handed them to her. "While you've been running around playing Nancy Drew I've been doing some work of my own. You sober enough to read?"

He nibbled on a pink cheese and whole-wheat cracker while Abbie scanned the pages. When she finished she looked over at Kelly, her bloodshot eyes filled with admiration. "This is some crazy shit."

"I know," Kelly's smile looked more like a gloat, "so Abbie O'Neal, TV phenom, what do you have for me?"

She played her trump card. "Hyacinth Poole is Governor Hardy's Aunt."

Abbie watched the look on Kelly's face change from one of amusement to one of awe. "So what do you say Bob?" she sipped her wine, "are we partners?"

## Chapter 16

Divide and conquer, that was the game plan. John Beale, Clara and Doc Gno were placed in charge of stall tactics; they were to throw every monkey wrench they could find into the plans of the man from New Jersey whose named ended in "i". Kelly impressed on them the need for creativity and stealth. The balance of the team would attack from three different angles, hoping that one would succeed. Chief Tatum's mission was to locate Hyacinth Poole and the other missing Conservancy Council members. Abbie was to focus on nailing the Governor while Kelly concentrated on the Mob.

It was nine a.m. on day one of Operation Crap Shoot. Abbie O'Neal, the hub of Tyle Island's casino fighting machine was, once again, hung-over. She slouched in a deckchair wearing dark sunglasses; a gallon of spring water and a bottle of Advil were at her side. It had been a rough night followed by an even rougher morning thanks to Jack, who had awoken her from a near coma for the sole purpose of informing her that he was heading out for a run. A note would have sufficed. Abbie scowled as she pictured her fiancé energetically springing down the winding roads of Tyle Island in his gym shorts and Nike Cross Trainers, flexing with every stride. She glanced over at the Jeep and considered taking a drive. The Island was filled with blind twists and turns. The streets were barely wide enough to allow two SUV's to squeak past one another without incurring side mirror damage. She could sneeze. It would be an accident. He would never see it coming. One well timed achoo could end it all. Abbie grabbed the jug of water and popped two more aspirin. If she was actually contemplating murder, the wedding had to be called off, but how and when and oh God her head hurt too damn much for all this introspection. The decision was made; the details would inevitably fall into place. What wasn't falling into place, however, were the details regarding the relationship between Governor Patrick Hardy and "dearest Aunt Hyacinth" Poole.

Strike one had come with the Christmas cards. Following Jack's early morning revelry, Abbie had dragged her wretched body out of bed, curled up on the bedroom floor, yanked the phone off the nightstand, and, employing every ounce of strength she could muster, dialed information. Minutes later she was speaking with a friend of a friend who was the weekend society editor for The New York Times. Following a false promise of a wedding invite and a photo of she and Jack for the friend of a friend's column, Abbie was given the maiden name of Boston's First Lady – Des Pierre – could you get any more Boston blueblood?

Armed with two family names that could link Governor Hardy to Tyle Island's missing Conservancy Council Secretary, Abbie, still weak in the knees and dreading the affects that additional altitude might have on her already throbbing brain, crawled down the staircase and sprawled out on the living room floor with the seven bundles of stolen Christmas Cards representing Hyacinth Poole's seven Christmases past. While she did manage to get three serious paper cuts and locate a missing sock that had somehow made its way under the sofa, Abbie found no additional "Happy Holidays" from the Hardy family nor anyone named Des Pierre. One Hallmark was circumstantial evidence; multiple Hallmarks would have been a noose.

Abbie paused to collect her thoughts, which wasn't an easy task considering her tender condition, then crawled onward to the kitchen, retrieving her sunglasses, the Advil and the bottle of spring water. She spent several minutes struggling with the childproof cap before giving up and using a meat cleaver to separate the bottle's bottom from its top. She then dragged herself, the medication and The Widow Poole's photo albums out onto the deck for more research and a much-needed breath of fresh air.

Which led to strike two. Utilizing the few functioning brain cells she still possessed, Abbie analyzed each of the four photo albums. The back of every photograph, spanning the years of 1940 through 1979, had been meticulously labeled with the date the photo was taken and the names of those posing. While there was no shortage of snapshots featuring attractive young men and women in varying states of celebration, family photos were nonexistent. Abbie found no pictorial evidence that Hyacinth ever had a mother, father or sibling, let alone nieces or nephews. Her hope for discovering a family portrait with a young Patrick Hardy or Priscilla Des Pierre sitting on the knee of his or her favorite Auntie Hyacinth was dashed.

She sighed. She should have known this wouldn't be easy. Kelly knew it wouldn't be easy, and boy, would he let her know that he knew. He would stand over her with hand to chin in a pose of intellectual dominance wearing his rumpled khakis and time worn t-shirt making him look all...literary...and he would lecture her on how quick fixes to intricate problems only happen in soap operas. He would make his point clearly and concisely and he would no doubt use large words...correctly. Which led Abbie to her previously mentioned thoughts regarding Jack, jogging and a fatal Jeep mishap.

She popped a few more Advil then staggered inside and rummaged through her backpack until she located the pocket sized notebook that she used when script writing; one never knew when a story idea would come to mind. She returned to the deck, gave the Jeep a second glance, hemmed, hawed then decided to once again focus on work. After chugging more water and popping another Advil, Abbie adjusted her sunglasses; it was time to get serious.

She reopened the first of the albums and removed a photo from its plastiscine page. The year was 1940. Two young men in naval uniforms stood on a boardwalk; The Cyclone towered over them in the background, Coney Island. Abbie opened her notebook, flipped past The Darkest Hour references, found a fresh page, and jotted down the names of the sailors. Any one of the people in any one of the photos could provide the link between Hyacinth and the Governor; she would not disregard any possible leads.

Abbie was midway through her project when Jack returned, smiling and flexing and eager for an island meal of raw clams and oysters on the half shell. Abbie, still unable to get past the thought of eating anything not ibuprofen based, let alone something wiggly and mucus-like, took a pass and sent him into town to appease his craving alone. A brief thought involving her fiancé and food poisoning flashed through her aching mind supporting her earlier decision to end their engagement. She checked the bottle of Advil but found, to no avail, that it was empty.

Abbie forced herself to finish with the photo albums then took a long hot shower and followed up with a perusal of Hyacinth's address book. Talk about vague. House numbers are not used on Tyle Island, so listings consisted of street and family names only. "Collins, Jim &Julia - Old Town Road" was a typical entry. The book contained only a dozen or so non-Island addresses all of which were located in the New York City area. She cross-referenced the names from the address book with the names pulled from the photo albums; only four appeared in both, all men.

Then she attempted food. Big mistake. For the second time in a week Abbie found herself hugging her future mother-in-law's pretty mauve toilet bowl. This drinking has to stop, she told herself as she examined her manicure and awaited the next dry heave. She stared at her left hand and the large diamond ring adorning it when "wait a minute," she said aloud, "where are the wedding photos?" Abbie closed her eyes and took a mental tour of Hyacinth's house. She didn't recall seeing any framed wedding pictures. She stood, flushed, brushed her teeth then ran downstairs to review the albums and list. No handsome young man with the last name of Poole. No ugly young man with the last name of Poole. No photo of anyone named Poole. She flipped to 'P' in the address book, no Poole's whatsoever. Her energy was returning. She reached for the Jeep keys only to remember that Jack had taken the truck. "I should have killed him when I had the chance," she said aloud as she hoisted her water bottle and headed out on foot, an act which proved to be her second big mistake of the day, for, by the time Abbie dragged her near lifeless body up Bob Kelly's three front steps, vertigo had taken hold. It was while she paused on the porch to catch her breath and keep from once again puking, that she noticed the distinct smell of smoke that hung in the air. There had been no odor back at her place; the ocean breeze must have kept it away. The trusty panic drum began to beat in her head, which was all she needed considering the magnitude of her migraine. Abbie knocked on the door. No one answered. She checked the driveway; the pick-up was gone. She opened the screen door, poked her head inside and called out both Kelly names. No one was home, but Bob Kelly's bicycle was leaning against the wall in the hallway.

The members of the Tyle Island Volunteer Fire Department, along with other concerned Islanders that had left their beds to lend a hand fighting the blaze, gathered at Clara's Diner. The house had been unoccupied so there was no loss of life, and fortunately, no injuries. Despite their efforts; however, the structure could not be saved. As Clara poured coffee for the crowd and announced that the first batch of scrambled eggs was up, Abbie skidded past the diner on Bob Kelly's bicycle. Pete nudged his Uncle. The two Kellys sipped coffee and watched out the picture window as Abbie attempted to climb off the bike, got her pant leg caught on the seat, pirouetted in a feeble attempt to maintain her balance, failed, and fell along with the bicycle in the middle of the road.

"She's dangerous huh?" Pete commented to his Uncle.

"You have no idea," Kelly replied.

They were silent for a moment.

"She looks like hell."

"That she does."

"Rough night?"

"For some."

Pete added half of a sugar packet to his coffee and stirred. "Don't you think you should go help her?"

"No."

"Why not?"

Kelly stared into his coffee cup. "Doctor Jasper Black should be nearby."

Pete muttered something as he started to rise. Kelly, who had heard a somewhat garbled 'she's not gonna' before the sentence trailed off into blah, blah, mumble, mumble, grabbed Pete firmly by the wrist and pulled him back into his seat. "What did you say?"

"Nothing."

"You said something." Kelly tightened his grip.

Pete stared directly into his uncle's eyes and calmly but firmly demanded, "Let go of me."

The elder Kelly noticed that the younger Kelly's biceps were larger than his own. He released his hold. Kelly cleared his throat and tried a friendlier tone. "Would you mind repeating yourself?"

Pete pushed his long hair behind his ears, "I shouldn't be telling you this."

Kelly directed Pete's attention to the burly volunteer firefighters devouring scrambled eggs at the counter, "there's a lot of things we shouldn't do Pete, but we do them anyway."

"Point taken." Pete looked out the window to verify Abbie's whereabouts. She was still lying motionless in the road. "I said she's not gonna marry the guy."

"What makes you say that?"

"Last weekend when I stayed at her place..." Pete hesitated.

"Go on."

"You won't tell her I said anything?"

"No. Go on."

Pete again checked on Abbie, she still hadn't moved. He leaned forward and whispered, "she tried throwing her engagement ring into the ocean."

"Bullshit," Kelly whispered back.

"I swear. She almost made from the deck."

"Strong arm."

"Tell me."

"What else?"

Pete snuck another nervous peek outside. There was still no movement on the Abbie front. "She talked about having cold feet then rambled on and on about how I shouldn't have sex because it'll ruin my life."

"She does tend to ramble."

"Yeah," Pete sipped his coffee, "but it works for her."

Kelly chose not to respond.

"There's one more thing you should probably know."

"I'm waiting."

"She only loaned me the Jeep on the condition that I tell you that we had spent the night together."

"Really?" It was Bob Kelly's turn to sneak a peek out the window. He saw a hand move.

"Yeah, she wanted to know your reaction."

Kelly raised an eyebrow.

"So are you gonna help her...or am I?"

Bob Kelly crossed his arms and stared down at Abbie who had managed to sit up and was now examining her injured knee. "I'm bleeding."

"I see."

"I tore my pants."

"Tough break."

"I borrowed your bike."

"That's fine."

"And crashed it."

"The important thing is that you're all right."

"Why are you being so nice?"

"Just happy I suppose."

Abbie used the sleeve of her sweatshirt to dab blood from her wound. "I didn't know you were capable of experiencing joy."

Kelly took a deep breath of fresh Island air, "it may actually be optimism."

"Would that make the scotch glass half full today?" Despite the feeling that death was imminent Abbie was able to chuckle at her own joke. She shielded her eyes from the blinding sunshine and looked up at Kelly who was wearing his all too familiar crooked grin. She noticed that it made him look, kind of, cute.

"Is Clara around?" she asked, "I need to speak with her."

"She's manning the grill. But before you go inside, there's something you should know."

"What?" Abbie asked as she picked a speck of dirt from her knee.

"The house burnt down last night."

"Whose house?"

"The Widow Poole's."

Abbie looked up. "No way."

Kelly looked down. "Yes way."

"How? Why?"

"You want the truth or what's going in the official report?"

"The truth."

"How? Arson. Why? To make a point."

"You're kidding."

"Nope."

"That's messed up."

"That's Tyle Island." Kelly waved to a fisherman who drove around them and beeped.

Abbie cringed at the noise. "Well Bob, seeing as how I'm just a city girl who isn't from these here parts; will you please explain what point was to be made by burning down The Widow Poole's house?"

Kelly sat down beside Abbie in the middle of the road and searched for the proper urban metaphor. "Lets' say that you're walking through Central Park alone at night."

"I wouldn't do that."

"Pretend you would."

"I'm not that stupid."

"Fine. Lets' say Jack is walking through Central Park alone at night. A mugger jumps him, but a cop witnesses the assault. The cop calls out to the mugger to halt but the mugger takes off so the cop shoots him, pow, dead on the spot." Kelly seemed satisfied with his explanation.

"That's it?' Abbie asked.

"Yes," Kelly answered.

"I don't get it."

"The fire was the halt."

"What?"

"The fire was a warning."

"What have you been smoking?"

"Nothing."

"Then you're losing it pal because I have no clue what you're talking about."

"Last night's fire sent a warning to every Islander that siding with the enemy, just as Hyacinth did, will not be tolerated."

"So some crazy Islander is threatening people into solidarity?"

"That's one way of putting it."

"You have another?"

"I'd say some crazy Islander is trying to guarantee a fair fight. One on one, us versus them. Not us versus them versus each other." A stray mutt wandered over to inspect the two humans lounging in the road.

Abbie had to concede that a lack of unity had been a concern of hers as well. She had raised that very issue to Clara and the others prior to meeting with the twins. The twins. Abbie recalled her conversation with the twins as they were leaving The Nest. They had asked if she was finished with the Widow's place. They had pressured her to be sure. "I know who set the fire."

"No you don't." Kelly tried to shoo the mangy dog away.

"The twi.."

"Whoa, whoa, whoa," Kelly interrupted; his sudden rise in volume caused the nervous dog to bolt. Kelly placed a brotherly arm around Abbie's shoulder, leaned close, noticed the apple scent of her shampoo, thought some very un-brotherly thoughts, and whispered, "Unless you want an angry mob to load you onto the next ferry, I wouldn't accuse any Islander of arson, especially the twins. The twins did not set that fire."

"But they said...."

"I don't care what they said, the twins are not arsonists."

"No, just burglars."

"As are you." Kelly snuck one more sniff of Abbie's hair then stood. "Now let's go inside and get you cleaned up."

"Fine," Abbie plucked a piece of gravel from out of her palm then reached her hand up to Kelly who hoisted her to her feet. "Bye the way Bob, how well do you know the Widow Poole?"

He up-righted his bicycle and wheeled it to the curb. "Not well, but I've been away for twenty years. We've had a couple of conversations since I've been back, but nothing beyond commenting on the weather or the price of bread."

"How about her husband?"

"Never met him."

"You grew up here, how could you have not met him?"

"He died before my time. Where are you going with this?"

"I went through her photo albums this morning. She didn't have any pictures of her family."

"I don't keep pictures of my family."

"Don't take this personally Bob, but I've seen you with your nephew, you're not exactly the standard by which I judge normal familial behavior. You've also never been married."

"True. Speaking of which, when is your big day?"

Abbie ignored the question. "For the sake of argument try to put yourself in Hyacinth's shoes. If your entire identity is based on being 'The Widow Poole' don't you think you should at least have a snapshot of your dearly departed lying around?"

"Yes. But what does that have to do with Governor Hardy?"

"I don't know. That's why I need to speak with Clara."

Kelly took Abbie by the arm and led her toward the diner. "Then let's go find her."

"Bob."

"Yes."

"Do you mind if I ask you one more question?"

He held the door open. "Be my guest."

"How do you know that the twins didn't set the fire?"

"Drop it Abbie."

"Yes dear."

## Chapter 17

Mildred Ahearn was seventy-nine years old, blind as a bat and destined for deafness, but Clara assured Abbie that the woman possessed a memory like a steel trap and was Hyacinth's closest friend. If anyone could supply Abbie with the lowdown on The Widow Poole's past, it would be Mildred.

Abbie approached the ramshackle cottage with caution, not quite sure how well she could communicate with a person of Mildred's description. After knocking, then banging, then pounding on the wooden screen door, her concerns regarding their meeting were validated, and then some. She peered through the torn screen and watched an ancient looking woman, whose slight stature was further reduced by the hunch of osteoporosis, shuffle slowly toward the front door carrying what appeared to be...Abbie squinted...no...It couldn't be. She took a few steps back as the old woman fumbled with the door handle, pushed her way outside and shuffled onto the porch where she teetered, balancing a shut gun on her crooked hip and sniffing the air as if sizing up her intruder by scent. Mildred wore dark wrap-around sunglasses, a yellow polka dot dressing gown, purple knee socks and black high-top sneakers. A thick coating of cherry red lipstick created an otherwise non-existent upper lip off of which hung a cigarette whose ash was an inch in length and threatening to drop at any moment. Two perfectly round splotches of orange rouge colored Mildred's gray wrinkled skin, and her hair, which was done up in curlers, appeared to have been mis-dyed a robin's egg shade of blue. When Abbie stared down the barrel of the shotgun aimed directly at her head, she questioned Mildred's blindness, and ducked.

"Mrs. Ahearn," Abbie hollered from her crouched position, "please don't shoot. My name is Abbie O'Neal. Clara sent me."

"What are you some sort of midget?" Mildred hollered back, lowering the shotgun toward the source of the voice. The cigarette remained affixed to the moist layers of lipstick.

"No."

"Then what the hell are you doing down there?"

"I was, am, trying to keep from getting shot."

"I can shoot just as good down low as up high you stupid girl. Now what do you want?" The cigarette bounced as she spoke but stayed glued to her lip.

"I need to speak with you about Hyacinth Poole."

Mildred waved the shotgun in the air, "what about Hyacinth?"

Abbie kept an eye on the barrel of the gun that poked about dangerously close to her face. She yelled even louder, "I've got some questions regarding her past. Clara thought you might have the answers."

Mildred thought a long moment then lowered the gun. She took the cigarette out of her mouth, dropped it on the porch then stomped her black high top where she thought the butt had landed. "Go on in," she ordered.

Abbie stood, squeezed past the old woman and the old woman's gun, casually stepped on the still burning cigarette and entered the small cottage that was brimming with bags, boxes and cartons of crap. She then stood aside to let Mildred enter behind her. Mildred leaned the shotgun against the wall by the door and expertly maneuvered through her crowded living room and into the kitchen. Abbie followed. Mildred slowly lowered herself onto a chair at the kitchen table and hollered, "So what do you want to know?"

Abbie displaced the calico cat that was dozing on the chair across from Mildred, sat, and yelled back, "Do you have any idea where Hyacinth may have gone?"

"Hyacinth didn't go anywhere," Mildred grumbled.

"She left the Island Mrs. Ahearn." Abbie yelled, wondering how Hyacinth's best friend could have missed that bit of information.

"Bullshit," Mildred yelled back.

"It's not bullshit Mrs. Ahearn," Abbie argued, quickly surmising that Clara had been mistaken about Mildred's investigative value, "Hyacinth has disappeared." Considering her time all but wasted, Abbie began to conjure an excuse that would allow her a speedy yet, recalling the shotgun, polite exit.

"I know Hyacinth disappeared," the old lady barked as she felt about the table for a pack of cigarettes. Abbie stood and studied the living room layout for an unobstructed get-away path. "But Hyacinth would never leave Tyle Island," Mildred lit a Pall Mall, "if Hyacinths gone then somebody took her."

Abbie raised an eyebrow; she hadn't considered that option.

"Personally," Mildred took a long drag from the cigarette, "I think she's dead."

Abbie sat. "What makes you say that?"

"Me and Hyacinth were friends for seventy years, that's a long goddamn time. You get to know a person after that long a goddamn time. Besides her five o'clock sherry, this Island was the only thing that old bitch ever loved." Abbie pulled out a pen and her notebook. "I know Doc and the others are saying that Hyacinth gave Barron's Hollow away, but trust me honey, it ain't true."

"What do you think happened?" Abbie opened to a clean page.

The old woman leaned forward in her chair, her nicotine voice dropped to a whisper while her Pall Mall trembled between two spindly fingers. "Those casino pricks forced her to sign those papers, maybe even forged her name. Then they killed her and dumped her body."

Abbie closed her notebook and put her pen away.

"Mrs. Ahearn, prior to her disappearance Hyacinth had

put her house up for sale. Why would she have planned to move off the Island if she wasn't involved in the land scam?"

Mildred tamped out her half smoked cigarette in an already overflowing ashtray, stood and slowly shuffled toward the kitchen counter. "Are you stupid girl?" she asked. Keeping in mind the shotgun leaning by the front door, Abbie ignored the insult and returned to her getaway plan. Mildred opened a cabinet and removed a box of cookies. She then shuffled back to the table, Oreos in hand. "'Cus you know honey, if you were smart I wouldn't have to tell you that if those pricks could make her sign the town meeting papers, they could make her sign the papers on her house."

Abbie fought the urge to slap the old hag and calmly replied, "It's an interesting theory, but no one is going to believe you without proof."

Mildred carefully lowered herself back into her seat. "So I'll find her body. Then you'll have proof." She bit an Oreo and asked, "You want a cookie?"

Abbie stared at Mildred's bright red lips which were now speckled with black cookie crumbs and flecks of creamy white filling. 'You want a cookie' - the words echoed in her head. "Oh shit," she whispered as she flashed back twenty-four hours to Hyacinth Poole's kitchen where either twin had offered her a cookie as Mildred had just done. She pictured the Royal Dalton china set out for afternoon tea, the vase filled with dead flowers and the crumbled petals and yellow pollen that had fallen onto the perfectly starched tablecloth. The panic drum began to beat a slow and steady rhythm. Surely a woman who carefully bundled and saved her old Christmas cards, meticulously labeled forty years worth of photographs and actually stenciled her storage boxes with their contents - SNOWMEN, ELVES - would have taken the time to put her house in order before going on the lam. Unless her departure was unplanned. Abbie closed her eyes, or unless she didn't depart at all.

"You're too damn quiet girl, what's going on?" Mildred's question jarred Abbie from her thoughts.

No longer considering her time wasted Abbie addressed the primary reason for her visit. "What do you know about Hyacinth's family?"

"I know she ain't got one."

"No family at all?"

"We met at Saint Cecilia's Home for Girls in Newark, New Jersey when we was six years old. It's an orphanage. We stayed there for ten years then took off. They wanted us to become nuns." Mildred snickered, "but we weren't cut out for that kind of work."

That explained the lack of a family portrait or any photographs predating 1940. Abbie made a few notes. "What can you tell me about the Widow Poole's husband?"

Mildred put down her cookie and reached for the cigarettes. "Hyacinth's husband you say?"

"Yes. I can't find any record of Mr. Poole."

The tall flame from Mildred's lighter nearly brushed her nose, "you can't find no record of him, "a hoarse chuckle escaped her crimson lips, "cus there never was no Mr. Poole."

"Excuse me?"

"Are you deaf dear?" Mildred took a drag, "I said there never was no Mr. Poole."

"But..." Abbie stammered, "She's a widow."

"Nah. We made that up."

Abbie reached across the table, pulled a cigarette from Mildred's pack, grabbed the antique Zippo and lit up. She leaned back in her chair, crossed her arms, took a drag and yelled, "All right Mildred, start talking."

Mildred pulled a deep breath of smoke into her lungs then slowly exhaled through her nose. "I've kept this secret for almost sixty years. But seeing as how

Hyacinth is dead and all," the old lady shrugged, "I figure, what the hell?" Mildred instructed Abbie to go into the living room and retrieve a mahogany box that she kept on the top shelf of the bookcase. She urged Abbie to be careful, that it was valuable. Abbie did as Mildred requested placing the worn box on the kitchen table. Mildred gently caressed the dark, rich wood then carefully opened the lid revealing a pile of old photographs, letters and postcards stored within. "Seeing as how I'm blind and all, you're gonna to have to help out."

"What have you got there? " Abbie asked as she moved in for a closer look.

"Memories," Mildred smiled revealing Oreo encrusted dentures, "and proof. Now where do you want me to begin?"

"The beginning is always good," Abbie replied.

"All right then, the year was 1945." Abbie closed her eyes and dropped her head to her hands, regretting her suggestion to begin at the beginning. She was about to ask Mildred to fast forward a few decades when the old lady completed her thought, "when Hyacinth made her first visit to Tyle Island. My husband just died, he was a fisherman. We were married less than a year when his boat was lost at sea. Hyacinth came up from New York City to take care of me. See I was real depressed and she was in a bad way herself."

"Bad way?" Abbie rubbed her temples and dreamed of Advil, "what do you mean?"

"It was the forties honey, not the best time to be nineteen and knocked up."

Abbie looked up, "knocked-up?"

"That's what we called it when a working girl got pregnant."

"Working girl?"

Pete Kelly sat in an uncomfortable chair in Chief Tatum's office and stared down at his scuffed Doc Martins while the Chief finished up a call. Pete had nearly died when the Chief telephoned and demanded, not requested, but demanded his presence at the Police Station a.s.a.p. He swallowed hard as the Chief hung up the phone.

"Crazy night, huh Pete," the Chief commented as he leaned back in his comfy leather chair.

"Yeah." Pete continued to stare at his boots.

"Tell me Pete, how old are you now?"

"Seventeen," he answered while studying the carpet pattern and playing with a frayed thread in the torn knee of his jeans.

Chief Tatum picked a pen up off his desk and began clicking the silver button at the end that made the nib go in and out and in and out and in and out. "So technically you're still a minor."

"Uh huh," despite his efforts to appear innocent, Pete could not make eye contact with the Chief.

"So if you broke a rule," Chief Tatum paused, "or committed a crime," he paused again, "in the eyes of the law you wouldn't be treated like an adult." Click, click, click, click.

"I suppose not." Pete forced himself to look up. His gaze made it as far as the desk calendar and remained fixed there.

"You're aware of the casino problem?" Click, click, click, click.

"I heard about it." Pete crossed then uncrossed his legs.

"Well," Chief Tatum cleared his throat, "your fellow Islanders don't think a casino is a good idea."

Pete nodded agreement, as he was too terrified to speak.

"So we're going to stop the development." Click, click, click, click. "Your Uncle and Abbie O'Neal have come up with a plan."

"Yeah?" Pete chanced a quick peek at the Chief, saw his grim expression and returned his frightened gaze to the carpet.

"Pete my boy, I've known you since the day you were born, so I think we can speak frankly. Do you agree?" Click, click, click, click.

Pete gulped hard and forced out a "sure".

"I have to track down Hyacinth Poole and the other Council members. That's a lot of work on top of maintaining the law around here." Click, click, click, click. "Especially with added trouble like we had last night." Click, click, click, click. "I figure that fire was just the beginning, more trouble is sure to follow. You got an opinion on that Pete?" Click, click, click, click.

"I, I, really couldn't say."

"Have you ever heard the saying 'idle hands are the devils workshop'?"

Pete nodded.

"Do you know what it means?"

Pete nodded again.

"Tell me what it means Pete."

"You can't cause trouble if you're busy.'

"Exactly. Guess what Pete."

"What Chief?"

"I know what happened last night."

"You do?"

"Yep. So I think we ought to keep you busy for a while."


Three hours, two packs of Pall Malls and a half bottle of Harvey's Bristol Cream later, Abbie showed up on Bob Kelly's doorstep. She knocked twice then let herself in. "Bob!" she called out, "where are you?"

"Upstairs," he called back, "end of the hall."

Abbie ran up the steps, taking two at a time and marched down the hall to Bob Kelly's bedroom. She stood in the doorway, stared at his mess and declared, "This is not at all what I had imagined."

Kelly stood knee deep in clothing, he held a sport coat in one hand, and several ties in the other. Papers were strewn everywhere and more than a few scotch glasses were placed like trophies on the desk, nightstand and dresser. "Why Abbie," Kelly grinned, "in what context have you been imagining my bedroom?"

Abbie grinned back, "Oh Kelly, the scotch glass will never be that full."

Touché. He changed the subject, "Do any of these match?"

Abbie trudged through the mounds of clothing, chose a navy blue geometric patterned tie and coordinated it with a shirt from the stack of oxfords lining the bed.

"Thank you," said Kelly as he added the outfit to the pile spilling from his bag. "So tell me Miss Marples, what insights did your visit to Mildred Ahearn's shack provide?"

"Hyacinth Poole was a hooker."

"Pardon?"

"Hyacinth Poole was a hooker."

"She's pushing eighty Abbie, I can't see how there'd be much of a demand."

"Not recently," Abbie scowled, "sixty years ago." Kelly looked skeptical. "I swear to you Kelly, Hyacinth Poole was a hooker and she had a baby when she was nineteen which she gave up for adoption and I bet you that the baby is now Governor Patrick Hardy and out of some misguided guilt over abandoning her child she signed over Barron's Hollow to her long lost son."

"Sit down," Kelly moved a mound of socks to allow Abbie room to sit. "You've been drinking again haven't you?"

She raised a hand as if taking an oath, "iced tea only. Mildred polished off a few glasses of Harvey's, but that was after she dished the dirt. I did not partake as I'm still very hung-over and do not find cream sherry at all appealing."

"So you're inability to do math is genetic rather than alcohol induced?"

"Huh?"

"If Hyacinth Poole is eighty and she had a baby at nineteen the child would now be roughly sixty years old."

"Give or take."

"Our young governor has yet to hit fifty."

Kelly tossed a pile of khakis to the floor and joined Abbie on the bed. "Didn't we already discuss the dangers involved in applying soap opera logic to real life situations?"

"But..."

"No buts," he interrupted. Abbie knew that arguing would be futile so she grabbed a handful of socks and began pairing and rolling them into balls. "We've got a lot of ground to cover in a very short amount of time. We must stay focused. Now I want you to repeat after me, 'facts are good, fantasy is bad.'"

"Screw you Kelly."

"Now look who's being optimistic. Let's stick to business. I'd like you to try applying our new mantra. You went to Mildred's to find out about Hyacinth's family. What facts did you uncover?"

Abbie tossed a navy blue sock ball into Bob Kelly's bag. "I learned the fact the Hyacinth's husband was a fantasy. There never was a Mr. Poole. Mildred and Hyacinth made him up."

Kelly laughed, "And why would they do that?"

"Because, fact number one, Hyacinth was nineteen and pregnant. Keep in mind that this all took place pre-Murphy Brown; society wasn't as hip regarding unwed motherhood as we are today. The girls saw how Mildred, a bona fide widow, was getting all sorts of emotional as well as financial support from her community, so they figured Hyacinth might as well give it a shot back in New

York. Pregnant widow evokes more sympathy than knocked-up whore. Which leads us to fact number two. Assuming the identity of "The Widow" Poole, Hyacinth returned to The Big Apple where she gave birth to fact number three and subsequently gave him or her up for adoption. Fact number four, preferring her new persona to her old, Hyacinth relocated to Tyle Island where no one but Mildred was aware of her checkered past. Facts number five, six and seven, she bought a house, never married, or should I say re-married, and lived happily ever after." Abbie paused, "perhaps facts six and seven are redundant."

"And you're absolutely sure that this storyline didn't come from The Darkest Hour?"

"I couldn't make this shit up if I tried. Anyway Mildred has the documentation to back it all up. She's got a stack of old letters and postcards written by Hyacinth at the time it was all going down. Oh and you'll love this one, Hyacinth's real name is Peters. They chose the alias "Poole" because they were swimming when they came up with the scheme."

"Unbelievable."

"There's more."

"Do tell."

"I no longer think that Hyacinth was a willing participant in the land scam."

"And the basis for this conclusion would be that an ex-hooker who abandoned a child and lied about being a widow wouldn't do such a dastardly deed?"

"No. And I'm trying to make a point here, sarcasm is not appreciated."

"I apologize. What caused your sudden change of heart?"

"Cookies."

"Cookies?"

"Yes. And china."

"Let me guess. You got a fortune cookie that said the lying ex-hooker didn't do it?"

"Not china as in the country, china as in dishes."

"I think I prefer the fortune cookie approach."

"Shut up and listen. When the twins and I broke into Hyacinth's house there were cookies in the cookie jar, dead flowers in a vase and her very valuable Royal Dalton china set at the table. My research has shown that Hyacinth Poole was way too anal retentive to just up and leave her home and belongings in such disarray. Mildred believes that Hyacinth was either forced to sign those minutes or that her signature was forged and that she is now dead."

"And she can prove this?"

"That's what I asked."

"And how did she respond?"

"She's going to find the body."

"Mildred Ahearn is totally blind, practically deaf and bent like a question mark. How is she going to find a dead body?"

"She has a keen sense of smell."

"You're kidding."

"No. She knew that I wear Chanel just from the scent that lingered on my clothes. That old lady has quite a nose."

"So she's going to sniff her way around the Island until she finds Hyacinth's dead body?"

"That's her intention."

"And you allowed this?"

"I can't tell the woman what to do with her free time. And I see the way that you're looking at me and no Kelly I'm not using soap opera logic, I don't expect her to find the body."

"Well that's a relief."

"I figure it was dumped at sea."

"Wait, wait, don't tell me. You're going to rent a boat and drag the harbor."

Abbie rolled her eyes, "Of course not. You said yourself that we're short on time. What I did do, however, was borrow some letters written by Hyacinth. I'll send samples of her writing along with the minutes of the meeting to a handwriting analyst who should be able to tell us if the documents are authentic. And before you go objecting, think about it, it will take no unusual effort on any of our parts and if Mildred is correct and the signature a forgery we'll have what we need to halt construction. So when are you heading to the city?"

"Tomorrow." Kelly resumed packing, "I'll take the ten o'clock boat and train it into Manhattan."

"Don't sweat the train. We can put the Jeep on the ferry and drive. You can stay at my place. I'll spend Monday and Tuesday tracking down some addresses and a handwriting guy and be back up here by Tuesday night at the latest."

"Aren't you forgetting something Abbie?"

"What?"

"Jack."

## Chapter 18

Robert J. Prescott III set up surveillance in a second floor guestroom of his hotel, The Water Lily. His binoculars were focused on Taloy Jobbs as he greeted the four o'clock ferry that Saturday afternoon. Prescott watched Taloy shake the hand of a husky gray haired man who strolled off the ferry, and kiss both cheeks of the attractive young brunette clinging to the gray haired man's arm. Prescott noted that both visitors were very well dressed; he was unaware however, that they were also well rehearsed.

Taloy and his guests slowly crossed the ferry parking lot, taking their time and drawing the attention of the Islanders milling about who had all gotten, and dutifully passed on, Taloy's rumor. As the threesome crossed the street directly in front of The Water Lily, Prescott observed Taloy gently take the gray haired man by the elbow in an attempt to lead him toward his own hotel. The attractive brunette stopped, removed her designer sunglasses and stared up at Prescott's grand Victorian; the Brit took a quick step back from the widow so as not to be caught spying. The gray haired man pointed to the hotel two doors down. The brunette shook her head and pointed to The Water Lily. Taloy casually glanced up at the hotel trying to determine where Prescott was hiding; he spotted a curtain flutter on the second floor. The gray haired man and his lady friend spoke briefly in private then the gray haired man returned to Taloy.

"You think he's watching?" he asked in a well-tuned Boston Irish accent.

"Second floor, third window on the left," Taloy did his best to appear deflated, "you sure you can handle this?"

The gray haired man patted Taloy on the shoulder, his brogue surfaced for just a moment as he answered, "just have a pint of Guinness waiting my friend, this pigeon won't take long." The two men shook hands and parted.

The couple headed inside to book a wedding while Taloy headed home to phone Clara.

Doc Gno held a stethoscope to the chest of five-year-old Timmy Barlow and asked him to take a deep breath. His mother sat in a plastic chair and flipped through a copy of National Geographic.
"How long has he had the fever?" Doc Gno asked the mother.
She looked up from the article she was reading on Great White sharks and answered, "Since yesterday morning."
"Any other symptoms?"
"He's been real tired and complaining about having the aches. What is it Doc, something serious?"
Doc Gno felt the boy's glands, "have you been checking him for ticks?"
"Always do, but those deer ticks are tiny buggers. I didn't notice a rash. You think he's got Lyme?"
"Probably not, but I'll run the test to make sure. I've had several similar cases this week, all came up negative."
Mrs. Barlow shook her head, "With all the damn deer around here, its no wonder Lyme disease ain't already an epidemic."
Doc Gno snapped on a rubber glove and grinned, "Remarkable isn't it."


As Clara entered Joe's Hardware and Boat Supply a bell jingled signaling the presence of a customer. Joe emerged from a back room dragging a large barrel that, from the way the burly man struggled, was very heavy.
"Evening Clara," he nodded a hello.
"Evening Joe, is that my order?"
"Sure is," he rubbed a rock solid forearm across his sweaty brow, "I got something else to show you." While

he disappeared into the back room Clara inspected the barrel filled with metal chain. The links were at least an inch in diameter; they would take forever to cut through. Moments later Joe re-emerged carrying one end of what looked to be fifteen feet of heavy duty rubber flashing laced with four inch long spikes. A younger, leaner version of Joe carried the other end. "You know my boy Clara."

"Sure do, good to see you young Joe."

"Hello ma'am."

"I hear you're heading down south to do some racing this summer."

"Yes ma'am."

"The boy's got a spot crewing on a real beauty out of Newport. They're taking her down to the Keys after race week."

Clara smiled proudly, "next stop, The America's Cup." The young man blushed. "So what have you got there Joe?"

"I rigged up some road spikes. Figure we'll make up a couple more sets."

Clara touched a finger to the sharp end of a spike. "Where do you plan on putting them?"

"We'll lay them in the brush along Westside road, that's the quickest route to the Hollow from the Harbor. When their trucks roll off the ferry we'll pull them across the road. Anything that drives over these spikes won't be driving much farther."

"Might even cause an accident," young Joe added.

"That would be a damn shame," Joe didn't sound sincere. "When do you want the chains delivered?"

"Can you bring them to the Hollow tomorrow around noon? I'll meet you after Church."

"Church, Clara?"

"Oh don't you worry, I'm still a sinner," she winked, "I won't be praying, I've got recruiting to do."

Pete Kelly moved his computer equipment into the office of The Tyle Island Conservancy Council, a ten by ten foot former bedroom in a small old Victorian just outside of town that also housed the public library, a small art gallery and the Island Historical Society. The relocation assured him that, in the event of a slip-up, his cyber-exploits would be traced back to a group of missing persons rather than to himself.

Once his system was up and running he scanned the list of information that Chief Tatum had asked him to acquire. It was a pretty straightforward hack; bank and credit card statements as well as telephone records for all of the Council members, all logical first steps in tracking down fugitives.

Police Chief Tatum slowly walked down Water Street, gazing up at the starry sky and contemplating the future of his Island. It was a typical off-season Saturday night, besides a half-filled parking lot outside the Nest, town was deserted and all was quiet except for the faint sound of Van Morrison seeping out of the bar. The Chief sighed as he sat on a wooden bench outside of an empty shop that, during the summer, housed an ice cream parlor. There would be no more leisurely Saturday night strolls if a casino were to be built. Tyle Island would never be quiet again. Several minutes passed before he heard the familiar, "evening Chief."

"Evening Teddy."

"Heading to the Nest tonight Chief?"

"In a bit Teddy."

"See you there."

Chief Tatum watched the proprietor of Tyle Island's liquor store cross the street and head down to the docks. He waited a few minutes before resuming his patrol. This night however, Chief Tatum deviated from his usual route. Rather than heading straight toward the bank, he made a right, walked a short half block and stopped in front of Island Realty. The small storefront was dark, as was the adjacent liquor store. Chief Tatum removed a thin metal nail file from his shirt pocket and let himself in.

    Robert J. Prescott III's personal assistant signed her employer's name to the correspondence he had dictated before retiring for the night. She reread the letter to check for errors. "Dear Sirs, Your failure to provide the deposit required to secure your reservations has resulted in the release of rooms previously held for your party. The Water Lily has no additional vacancies at this time. Regretfully, Robert J. Prescott III, Proprietor."
    Regretfully...if she only knew.

## Chapter 19

Kelly should have taken the train. Wedged into the backseat of a Jeep Wrangler cradling an overstuffed duffle bag for the duration of a what should have been a four hour car ride, but due to traffic lasted just over five, most of which was spent in silence because the driver a.k.a. Abbie and the passenger a.k.a. Jack were experiencing some tension in their relationship, is no way for a civilized human being to travel. One would think that Kelly would have savored the friction between the lovebirds; however, with the receiving end of a seatbelt embedded in his hind quarters and the heel of a dress shoe digging into his upper thigh, thoughts of romance were non-existent. Thoughts of scotch, on the other hand, were ever present. Conversation resumed as they hit mid-town Manhattan when Jack asked, "where can we drop you Bob?"

"Any corner will do."
"He's staying with us."
"I thought we discussed this."
"That corner looks nice."
"We did."
"And?"
"And he's staying with us."
"There goes another corner."
"So I have no say in who stays in our apartment?"
"None. And for the record, it's my apartment."
"Oh look, here comes The Plaza."
"I don't know what's happened to you in the past two weeks," Jack harrumphed loudly, "but you've changed."
"And there goes the Plaza."
"Spare me the melodrama Jack, the cameras aren't rolling."
"What do you mean by that?" The flexing began.
"I mean the heavy sighs, the misplaced inflections, the muscle flex."

"You can pull over any time."

"I'm dramatic, I'm an actor."

"I know you're an actor, but guess what Jack, you're not on the set. You're in a real car having a real argument with your real fiancé, so do me a favor; put Dr. Jasper Black away for five minutes and deal with me as Jack West."

"Right here looks fine."

Jack was quiet for a moment as he processed everything that Abbie had said. It was a lot of information. Then, "wait a second..." he turned in his seat and stared first at Kelly, then at Abbie, then back at Kelly, then back at Abbie, "the two of you aren't...?" He stopped in mid sentence; the car became eerily silent. Kelly understood Jack's implication and, recalling Abbie's tirade on the first day they met, shielded himself with his duffle bag.

She spoke as if the t's in her words were bullets - "the two of us aren't what Jack?"

"Nothing Babe."

"Don't babe me. Finish your sentence. The two of us aren't what?"

"If you'll just slow down I'll jump out."

"You're not getting out of the car," Abbie glared into the rearview mirror, "and you're not getting off the hook," Abbie glared at her fiancé, "and for Christ's sake Jack will you please stop flexing?" Kelly raised his duffle bag an inch higher while Jack released the tension in his biceps and shrunk in his seat.

'I know I have to call off the wedding,' Abbie mumbled to as she cut off a taxi and nearly sent two pedestrians to the morgue; 'however, now is not the time and fiftieth and fifth is not the place,' so she gritted her teeth and calmly explained, "there is nothing inappropriate going on between Kelly and me. We are working together. Our collaboration is no different than...than...." she was at a loss for words until a thought came to mind, "your rehearsals. Ok Jack?"

Kelly lowered his duffle bag, Abbie cut off another cab and Jack West stared out the window - that was definitely not OK.

Clara was setting up a card table outside of Saint Joseph's By the Sea when Chief Tatum walked up, stormed past her without so much as a good morning and entered the church. The Pastor was reading the Gospel of Mark, Chapter 11, Jesus throwing the money changers out of the Temple, when the Chief marched up the center aisle, stopped four rows from the front and slapped a set of handcuffs on Lila the belligerent realtor. The church fell silent as the Police Chief announced that Lila was being brought in for questioning relative to the disappearance of Hyacinth Poole. A collective gasp escaped the mouths of the congregation. The Chief then removed his hat, apologized for the interruption and began dragging Lila, kicking and screaming, out of the church.

The organist spontaneously broke into an off key rendition of "We Shall Overcome" as the worshipers, also singing off key, fell in line behind the Police Chief and his prisoner. They sang their way right out of church and right up to Clara's card table where a sign read "Volunteers Needed".

"Morning Clara," Chief Tatum winked as went by.

"Morning Chief."


Doc Gno joined a group of amateur artists for a Sunday afternoon of painting. This week's subject was the old Allen barn on the North side of the Island. Since the doctor's skills with a brush ran shy of passable paint by number he asked if rather than participate, the group wouldn't mind if he observed. They welcomed his presence.

Doc Gno casually strolled about the group of artists inspecting each of the canvases, admiring some and cringing at others. There were watercolorists whose wispy brushstrokes created a sleepy, pastoral version of the rotting barn. Nice, but not what he was looking for. There was a charcoal artist whose modernist approach was dramatic but far too abstract for Doc Gno's needs; the barn looked to be set amid a bombed out World War II battlefield rather than a quiet pasture filled with tall grass and wild flowers. A pen and ink sketch was interesting but totally inappropriate. "Whatever happened to realism?" he asked himself as he wandered toward a painter who had separated herself from the group. She was seated cross-legged on a patch of soft grass, her lap acting as her easel and a Dixie plate as her palette. Doc Gno smiled at the young artist. She smiled back revealing a set of shiny metal braces covering her teeth. He examined her canvas. There was the barn, rotting board for rotting board, wildflower for wildflower; a perfect replica. Finally.

Pete Kelly was shocked to find that the one jail cell on Tyle Island was occupied. "What's up with that?" he asked Mabel who was busy at her typewriter completing the paperwork on Lila's arrest. She moved her dime store reading glasses to the very tip of her nose and read aloud, "obstruction of justice, suspicion of kidnapping and assaulting an officer. She bit the poor Chief you know."

"I want my lawyer," Lila yelled in response to the charges.

"It's Sunday. He's gone fishing. Now hush up I've got work to do."

"Is he in?" Pete asked.

"Sure is. He's expecting you."

"This is your Uncle's fault," Lila screamed at Pete as he walked by, "damn drunk should have minded his own business. When I get a hold of him..."

Pete turned to Mabel, "that sounded like a threat."

"We'll need a restraining order," Mabel pulled a sheet of paper from her drawer, "I'll fill out the form." She stuck her tongue out at Lila and continued typing.

Pete gave Chief Tatum a run down of his progress while helping him bandage his bite wound. No large deposits had been made to the bank accounts of the Council members, no withdrawals either. The two council members who possessed credit cards had little activity in the past month, nothing since they disappeared. He hadn't yet had a chance to review the phone records.

"So what are you doing now?"

"John Beale wants me down at the docks. Marcy took some time off and he doesn't have anyone to take ferry reservations." Pete pushed his long hair behind his ears and let out an audible sigh, "he said you would want me to volunteer."

"Well Pete, you've done such a good job with this," Chief Tatum tapped his bandaged index finger on the stack of papers, "that I'll tell John you can't make it today."

"Really?" Pete envisioned a lazy Sunday afternoon spent drinking beers on the beach with his buddies.

"Oh sure. What we've got going here is much more important."

The vision faded. "What do you mean?"

Chief Tatum flipped through the pages of hacked phone records, "first you have to call all these numbers and see who answers?"

"All those numbers?"

"Yep."

"But that'll take forever."

"Pete..."

"I know Chief, I know." He rolled his eyes, "idle hands are the devils workshop."

Chief Tatum left Pete Kelly to do his dialing while he set out for the airport. His immediate goal was to determine the method that had been used to get the Conservancy Council members off of Tyle Island. John Beale had offered to question the employees of the ferry service to see if anyone had noticed Hyacinth and the others leaving for the mainland, which left Chief Tatum to cover the skies. Since FAA regulations required pilots to file flight plans, he would be able to track the comings and goings of Tyle Island's airfield. If the Council members flew off Island he'd find out when and where they'd been heading. The Chief had just turned left onto Airport Road when he drove past Mildred Ahearn standing on the side of the road with her head in the bushes and her ass in the air. He looked in his rearview mirror and wondered what on earth she could be up to. Then he realized it was most likely better that he didn't know.

Chapter 20

It was four a.m. and Jack West had yet to fall asleep. He lay in bed staring at Abbie, worrying that at any moment she might awaken and feel the need to collaborate with Bob Kelly. The thought of the two of them writhing in mid-collaboration brought on an uncontrollable bout of muscle flexing. Why would Abbie want to collaborate with that Islander anyway? He was old. And out of shape. After racking his brain for a good twenty minutes Jack came to the astute conclusion that they were probably collaborating because Bob Kelly, like Abbie, was a writer. His skewed logic suggested to him that just as he needed to rehearse with fellow actors in order to fine-tune his craft, Abbie probably needed to collaborate with a fellow writer to fine-tune hers. Then his logic skewed a touch too far when Jack West decided that if he was to successfully compete for Abbie's collaborations he too would have to write a book.

This left Jack in a real pickle since he didn't know the first thing about writing, and as a rule rarely read. He made exceptions for GQ and Soap Opera Digest, and scripts of course. Those he had to read. But the idea of reading for pure enjoyment was foreign to the actor. Abbie, on the other hand, read a lot. She had a large collection of books. She even had the heavy, hard covered kind. Beyond their use as a weapon for killing roaches, Jack had never taken an interest in them. In truth, books bored him. His thoughts drifted back a few months to the kinky chick with the body piercings that he had done a scene with for an acting class. They had rehearsed at her place. She had a lot of books too. Manuals she called them. They were filled with pictures. Interesting pictures. Those books didn't bore him. Jack was sure that he could write a book like that. Then Abbie would be so proud of him that she would never collaborate with Bob Kelly again. He rolled over and drifted off to sleep, looking forward to the prospect of becoming an author.

When one is asking for favors it is best to bring a gift, so when Abbie entered Megan's office on Monday morning she carried a large black coffee and a pumpernickel bagel slathered with cream cheese and topped with smoked salmon.

"Show me what you've got," Megan declared as she removed the plastic to-go lid from her coffee and breathed in the caffeine. Abbie handed over the folder that contained every shred of paperwork she could find that pertained to the questionable town meeting and the fraudulent vote.

"I threw in a disk that I found in the old lady's office. It didn't look suspicious to me, but I don't have your knack for seeing the illicit forest through the trees." Flattery also helps when asking favors.

"I'll take a look," Megan unwrapped her bagel, "now cut with the ass kissing and get to the point. What else do you need?"

"The name of a handwriting analyst."

Megan scanned the documents, "we've got someone on file. You want the signature on the minutes authenticated I presume."

Abbie nodded. "I included some personal letters written by Hyacinth for comparison."

"Good." Megan called in her secretary and instructed him to make two copies of the documents, send one to whomever the firm was currently using to analyze handwriting and return the other to her a.s.a.p. He obeyed. Both women watched the young man leave the room.

"He's new," Abbie commented.

"He's cute and stupid. What do you think he aspires to be?"

"I have no idea."

"An actor." Megan grinned then quickly moved on.
"So you think that the minutes were forged?"
"No, but it would make my job easier."
"It would, so don't count on it. What else have you got?"
Abbie showed Megan the Christmas card. Megan whistled. "Don't get excited, it's not as promising as it looks. Hyacinth Poole was an orphan. According to an old friend she had no family except for an illegitimate child whom she gave away at birth. And as an added bonus, Hyacinth was a hooker at the time. I can only assume that the child may have been conceived through a business relationship."
"Don't assume anything. And by the way, do you realize that you're speaking of the missing person in the past tense?" Megan asked.
"I know." Abbie took a bite of Megan's bagel and spoke with a full mouth, "I think she's dead."
"Why?"
"Call it a gut feeling."
"So your gut says the old bag is history. You've got a Christmas Card which seems to be from the Governor referring to your dead friend as "dearest Aunt" but no other proof to substantiate a relationship between Hardy and the dearly departed."
Abbie swallowed, "correct."
Megan sat back and sipped her coffee. "You know Ab, some people address close family friends as "aunt" or "uncle.""
"I considered that. I pulled some names from Hyacinth's address book and photo albums. They're all here in the city so I'll do some digging before heading back to Tyle Island."
"I'd feel better if you hired a Dick to do the legwork. "
"My legs work just fine."
"It's your call. And speaking of dicks, how's Jack?"

Abbie took a deep breath as she prepared to say the words aloud for the very first time. "I'm not marrying him."

Megan put down her coffee. "Don't mess with me Abbie."

"I'm not messing with you."

"You swear?"

"Cross my heart."

"I can burn the ugly dress?"

"You may."

"It's the author isn't it?"

"No."

"Abbie?"

"Truthfully Meg, it's not."

"Then what happened to change your mind?"

Abbie paused to consider the question. "Tyle Island happened."

"Meaning?"

"It's complicated, but suffice it to say that Jack and I spent some much needed time apart."

"So absence didn't make the heart grow fonder?"

"Not even close."

"If you'll forgive another cliché, while the cat was away did the mouse play with the writer, even just a teeny bit?"

"Nope."

"Did the mouse consider playing?"

"It did, but it's not gonna happen. I'm not getting out of one dysfunctional relationship with an ego maniac just to jump into another with an alcoholic who, by the way, isn't short on ego himself."

"You're sure?"

"Positive."

"Good. Then introduce me to Bob Kelly."

"No."

"Why not?"

"I may change my mind." Abbie stood to leave. "And do me a favor, keep the me and Jack thing to yourself."

"You haven't told your families yet?"

"I haven't told Jack yet."

Bob Kelly stepped off the elevator on the eighteenth floor of the Heck Building, which housed the offices of Heart Publishing. He walked directly past the receptionist slowing down just to say "good morning Amy."

"Morning Kelly," the young woman responded without taking her eyes off the pages of the paperback in which she was immersed. "Kelly?" she looked up from the book, "Kelly," she hollered as he turned the corner, "you can't go in there, Kelly!" She pushed the intercom button to warn her boss, but was too late.

"Amy!" Sam Heart's voice boomed through the speaker on her phone, "Call security Amy!!!"

"Don't call security Amy," Kelly sounded amused, "Sam doesn't really want me thrown out."

"Like hell I don't"

"Come on Sam, you wouldn't toss out your bestselling author."

"Former bestselling author."

"And future."

"What happened to retirement? You run out of scotch?"

"No Sam, I ran into a story."

"Shall I call security Mr. Heart?" Amy asked.

There was a long silence then, "No, but stay by the phone just in case."

"Yes sir."

"Bye Amy."

"Bye Kelly."

Kelly left the office of Heart Publishing two hours later with a twenty thousand dollar advance and the promise of Sam Heart's personal backing. The money was a nice perk but didn't really matter; it was Sam's support that Kelly needed to legitimize his scheme. Sam hadn't wanted to play along at first, thinking that Kelly's hairbrained idea to tangle with the Mob would get him killed, but then Kelly pointed out that Sam had been wishing him dead for the past six months as it was, so what was the big deal? Sam conceded that Kelly had a point, so the men struck a deal. If Kelly actually pulled off his ploy and survived a meeting with the Mob he would write one more novel at the drastically discounted cost of one hundred grand. In exchange, Sam promised to confirm to any and all inquiring parties that Kelly was currently under contract with Heart Publishing to ghostwrite the tell all autobiography of one Nicky "The Ax" Scarpelli, a former mafia enforcer from New Jersey who found God and moved to the woods of the American Northwest to write an operetta for the harpsichord and raise wolves.

Nicky "the Ax" was, of course, pure fiction.

Chapter 21

Twelve-year-old Lindsey Mott blended one part rosewood with one part pink and one part dove white on her Dixie plate palette. She then placed the book Doc Gno had given her on the examination table and prepared her brushes.

"I'm all set."

Doc Gno opened the door and called in his first patient. Taloy Jobbs walked in and shook hands with the Doctor who instructed him to remove his left shoe and sock and roll up his pant leg. Doc cleaned an area above the ankle with alcohol and thoroughly dried it with cotton swabs. Then Lindsey took over. Using the medical book as a guide, she painted a Lyme Tick rash on Taloy's freckled calf that was so lifelike it could have hung in the Met.

"Damn fine likeness Lindsey," Taloy admired the artwork while Doc Gno took a Polaroid for his records. As soon as he was satisfied with the clarity of the picture he removed the paint from the Irishman's leg and called in the next patient.

Clara's Diner was filled with the volunteers who had signed up for Tree Hugging Duty. One by one each Islander stepped forward and made a mark on an aerial map of Tyle Island showing his residence and place of business in relation to Barron's Hollow. Clara would use the information to set up a fast response telephone relay that would be set in motion when word came down that the construction crews had boarded the ferry. She was thrilled to see that both pregnant Islanders had signed up to be a part of her crew. "Alrighty then", Clara announced to the twenty or so volunteers, "I've got leg and hand shackles for each of you, step on up and take a set, and then we'll head up to the hollow for chaining practice."

John Beale ferried to the mainland to meet with Michael Patrick O'Shaunassey, the head of the local Dock Workers Union, who also happened to be his second cousin on his mother's side. The men sat at O'Shaunassey's kitchen table playing backgammon and discussing viable methods for disrupting the peaceful transport of building equipment and workers to Tyle Island. After two pots of coffee and countless backgammons, the men agreed that the most effective method would be a strike. Any construction worker in his right mind, unionized or not, knew that crossing a Teamster picket line was not a wise, nor a healthy thing to do.

Chief Tatum sat at his desk studying the flight information he had taken from the airport. When Pete Kelly entered his office, he quickly covered the document with the morning copy of The Globe.
"What can I do for you Pete?" Chief Tatum asked.
"Where's Lila?" Pete asked, "You set her free already?"
"Her lawyer finally showed up, and seeing as how I didn't really have anything on her, I had to let her go."
"If you didn't have anything on her, why did you arrest her in the first place?"
"She was pissing me off. I know she's involved, I just can't prove it."
"Did you search her office?"
"Yeah, but without a warrant, so keep that one to yourself."
"And you didn't find anything?"
"She's smarter than she looks. After your Uncle ransacked her place she moved all her files."
"They're probably at her house."
"Probably," Chief Tatum concurred.

"So why don't we just go over there and have a look around?"

"I have a better idea Pete, why don't you just tell me what brings you here this morning?"

"I finished making the calls," Pete handed a folder filled with information over to the Chief; "it looks like Old Lady Harper was addicted to one of those psychic hotlines."

"No kidding," Chief Tatum opened the folder and glanced inside, "did they tell you your future while they had you on the line?"

Pete laughed, "Yeah, some spooky sounding chick calling herself Destiny said that I will soon experience some radical changes in my life."

"Really?" the Chief looked up from the file.

"Like that was a tough one. What seventeen-year-old doesn't experience radical changes? The whole things a joke."

"Yeah," Chief Tatum hesitated, "they're all crackpots." He paused then asked, "What else did she say?"

"Typical love-life bullshit. She even said I'd cut my hair for a woman, like that'll ever happen. So what's next?" Pete asked.

Chief Tatum leafed through the phone records before answering, "English."

"What?"

"It's Monday, go to school."

"Look Chief, I know I complain and all, but detective work beats Trig any day."

"School. Now. I'll call you when I need you." Pete shrugged and walked out the door. Chief Tatum waited until he heard Mabel say goodbye before moving The Globe aside and revealing the copy of a flight plan showing that a Cessna carrying five passengers took off two days before the casino deal hit the newspapers. Its destination was Allaire Airport in Ocean County, New

Jersey. The pilot was Dan Kelly. Radical changes, it looked like Destiny had hit the nail on the head.

## Chapter 22

Clearly Hyacinth's address book was in need of updating. The first three addresses led Abbie to a parking garage, an abandoned apartment building and PS 140 respectively. She was about to give up when she noticed that the last address was in the same neighborhood as one of her favorite Italian restaurants, and seeing how she had gone three weeks without a quality dose of putanesca sauce, Abbie decided to take a shot at locating Mr. Eddie Steele before stopping in for a much needed pasta fix.

She stepped out of a taxi in front of a brownstone that any New Yorker, she included, would have given her eyeteeth for. She climbed the front steps, rang the bell and waited for someone to answer. And she waited. And waited. She was about to head off for a bowl of penne when a voice called out from the stoop next door, "May I help you Miss?"

New Yorkers are, by all rights, wary of unfamiliar voices offering assistance, so Abbie hesitated before chancing a glance at the source of the inquiry. She was relieved to find that the voice belonged to a silver haired man who was dressed from head to toe in black but for the white Roman Catholic collar encircling his neck. This was a man who could offer assistance.

"I'm looking for Mr. Eddie Steele. I show this as his last known address."

"Are you are relative?" The priest seemed a touch wary himself.

He knows of Eddie, that's a good sign, Abbie thought as she explained, "No, I'm a friend of a friend."

"Well I'm sorry Miss, but Eddie passed away six months ago."

"Son of a bitch," she muttered a little too loudly.

"You seem disappointed," the priest smirked.

"I'm sorry Father; I've had a long and unproductive day. I'm trying to track down someone that Mr. Steele knew a long time ago, and I had a lot riding on being able to speak with him, and I don't know why I'm burdening you with all of this." she began to walk down the steps, "Thank you for your help, I'm sorry to have bothered you."

"I'm here to visit with my father," the priest called out after her. "He and Eddie were like brothers. Perhaps he has some information that might help you find your friend."

Abbie's first thought was 'why is this guy being so nice', and then she took another look at the collar and realized that kindness was in the job description. "If it's not an inconvenience," Abbie made a mental note to go to church on Sunday and throw a fifty in the collection basket, "that would be great."

"Come on in."

Abbie trotted up the steps to the adjacent brownstone and introduced herself, "I'm Abbie O'Neal."

The priest smiled, "I'm George."

"Pleased to meet you Father George."

"George is fine."

"I had twelve years of Catholic education; I don't think I'm capable of being on a first name basis with a priest."

"Please try."

"I'll do my best."

Father George opened the front door and the two stepped into a world that Abbie had only experienced in Francis Ford Coppola movies. The panic drums should have been beating, but a cloud of garlic and tomato that seemed to envelope the house was asphyxiating her brain.

"I'm sorry if I seemed suspicious regarding your relationship with Eddie," the priest apologized as he hung his overcoat on a hook by the door, "he was a wealthy man, which has sadly caused some problems with the settlement of his estate."

Two slickly dressed men, one heavy and one thin, rose from their chairs that were stationed in the hallway, to greet Father George.

"Gentlemen this is a friend of mine. We'll be going up to see my father once we investigate the slice of heaven Isabella is creating in the kitchen."

The gentlemen returned to their seats. Father George led Abbie down a narrow hallway into a large kitchen where a fireplug of a woman stood on a small wooden stool stirring an enormous pot filled to the rim with meatballs and gravy. Father George snuck a taste, kissed his fingertips and told the fireplug that only an angel could create such flavors. He then dragged a salivating Abbie out of the kitchen, assuring her that they would return for a plate when they finished visiting with his father.

"My father looks frail but he's as tough as nails," Father George explained as they climbed a staircase to the second floor. "His thoughts can drift from time to time but besides the occasional bout of confusion he still has a very firm grip on reality." He knocked on an elaborately carved wooden door, and entered.

"You are late Giuseppe," a strong voice scolded as the priest entered the room, "my shows are over an hour already, where you been?"

"I'm sorry Papa," Father George crossed the room and kissed his father on both cheeks, "I was held up at the prison."

Prison? Abbie wasn't sure she had heard correctly. Did he say prison? She found herself frozen in the doorway.

"I'd like you to meet a friend of mine papa," Father George urged Abbie to come in.

He said prison, didn't he? She eyed the staircase, and though her brain was yelling run, run, run, she couldn't get her feet to obey.

The old man in the wheelchair squinted through his thick eyeglasses, "she's a pretty one Giuseppe, but I don't think she can walk."

The old man's playful chiding lightened the moment; Abbie laughed as she realized that her behavior was ridiculous. She was with a priest who was probably just a prison Chaplin and an adorable old man in a wheelchair, what possible danger could she be in? She entered the room and approached the two men.

"What you doing with such a pretty girl Giuseppe, you still a priest?"

"Yes Papa, I'm still a priest."

"You got a name little girl?" the old man asked. Abbie nodded. "First she don't walk, now she don't talk?"

"Don't tease her Papa." Father George made the introductions. "Abbie O'Neal I'd like you to meet my father, Vincent Gianninni."

Abbie's knees buckled under her - Gianninni - difficult to pronounce but ends in an "i".

Jack West left the set of The Darkest Hour and stopped at a stationary store where he purchased a composition book, a Polaroid Camera and film. Following two rather lackluster scenes with Nurse Rhonda, the failure of which he attributed to his lack of a thorough rehearsal, Jack had been struck with a brilliant idea for the subject of his book. The title would be "An Actor's Guide to Rehearsing." He was sure that other actors could use his advice on how to prepare for demanding love scenes. Like the manuals, he would use the Polaroids to help get his point across.

Abbie opened her eyes to find Father George kneeling beside her, calling her name. She sat up.

"What happened?" she asked the priest.

"You fainted. Are you ill?"

"You sure can pick 'em Giuseppe. She can't walk, she can't talk, she's probably got the AIDS." The old man had wheeled himself over to get a closer look at the young woman lying on his floor.

"I'm fine Father," Abbie stammered, "it's just that I, I haven't eaten today. Please forgive me. I'll be on my way."

"You'll do no such thing. Sit down here," Father George helped Abbie to her feet and led her to a chair, "I'll get you a plate of Isabella's meatballs."

"And bring some Chianti Giuseppe. I haven't had a pretty girl on her back in my bedroom since your Momma died, we should celebrate."

"There's no need for such a fuss," Abbie stood, "I'm imposing."

"Sit," Vincent demanded. Abbie gulped hard and sat. "Go get the food and wine Giuseppe. I will take care of pretty Abbie."

What the hell does he mean by "take care of" Abbie wondered as she longed to have Bob Kelly by her side. He would know exactly what to do. She was just a soap opera writer for Christ sakes. A soap opera writer who was stuck in the bedroom of a retired Mafioso who just happened to have a son who owned casinos and was believed by every living, breathing Fed to have followed in his father's footsteps. Abbie tried to calm herself and think of what Kelly would do if he found himself in her position.

"When you was laying there like a dead mackerel," Vincent grinned, "Giuseppe told me you was looking for Eddie Steele. What you need Eddie for?"

Abbie decided that Kelly would do whatever needed to be done, and considering the circumstances, he would do it quickly. Unsure of her ability to speak she cleared her throat then said, "I'm trying to track down an old acquaintance of Eddie's."

"Who?"

"Hyacinth Poole."

The old man thought a moment, "never heard of her."

"You would have known her as Hyacinth Peters." Still he looked bewildered. "I have an old photograph of Hyacinth with Eddie. May I show it to you?" Abbie pulled the snapshot out of her backpack and crossed the room. She knelt in front of Vincent Gianninni and handed him the photo; she stared into his eyes as he looked at the picture.

He was quiet for a moment, then whispered, "Never seen her before."

His lips said no, but his eyes said...ah Hyacinth. He handed back the photograph and turned his attention to the television that was tuned to Judge Judy.

"Does the name Mildred Ahearn ring a bell?" Abbie asked, again looking for a reaction in the old man's face. "She was a friend a Hyacinth's at the time this photo was taken."

"Why you looking for this Hyacinth?" Vincent asked, still staring at the television screen.

"I'm concerned for her safety. She's disappeared."

"Disappeared from where?"

"Her home."

"Where she live?"

"Up north," Abbie was intentionally vague, "Massachusetts."

"How long she live up there?"

"Close to sixty years." Surprise flashed across the old man's face. "I was going to ask Mr. Steele if he knew the whereabouts of Hyacinth's child." Abbie held his fragile hands in hers and whispered, "It's very important."

Vincent's eyes darted from Abbie to Judge Judy and back again. "Did you know that Chelsea Castle slept with Marco today?" he asked, his voice filled with excitement, "and Virginia is blackmailing Constance because she knows that Astor isn't Miles' real father."

Father George returned in the middle of the old man's rambling. "I'm sorry," he put down the tray of food and went to his father's side. "When my father gets troubled he escapes into this fantasy world. Speaking of Eddie must have stirred up some emotions. He's had a difficult time dealing with his death." He stroked his father's hair as Vincent muttered how Harley was going to the Benton Springs Hospital Ball with that troublemaker Reb, "as you can see, my father has quite an imagination."

Abbie released the old man's hands and stood. "You'd be amazed how many people escape into worlds just like your father's," she smiled supportively and thought - every afternoon from 1 to 2 pm. Abbie thanked Father George for his kindness and left him her phone number on Tyle Island just in case Vincent remembered anything. She then went out to the street, hailed a cab and headed straight for The Darkest Hour studios. The pasta would have to wait; tomorrow's script needed revising.

Kelly settled into a suite at The Rio, studied the contents of the honor bar and was dismayed to find that scotch was unaccounted for. He had experienced a range of emotions during the drive to Atlantic City, beginning with determination and culminating with dread. It seemed that the greater the mileage between he and Tyle Island, the more ridiculous this plan of his seemed. What the hell was he doing here? If he wanted to live the life of a drunken recluse he didn't need to do it on Tyle Island. He was rich. He could move to Nantucket. And sure Abbie was cute, but she was a little high maintenance and even a little more engaged; other women were sure to come his way. So, Kelly wondered, why exactly was he sitting in a hotel room in Atlantic City, New Jersey, preparing to blackmail an alleged Mobster? It was an excellent question, and one that called for serious contemplation.

Kelly lay back on the bed and stared up at the ceiling. A half hour passed but no answer came. He took a long hot shower but there was still no enlightenment. He studied the "escape route in case of fire sign" that hung on the back of his door, using his index finger to trace the path he would take if the high rise was to go up in flames, and concluding that survival wouldn't be worth the energy expenditure that running down twenty flights of stairs would involve.

"If a fire starts," Kelly announced to the door, "I will simply make myself comfortable and die gracefully. After all," he let out an uncharacteristically whiney sigh, "it's not like I'd be missed."

Kelly then pictured his lifeless body, slightly charred and smelling of smoke, lying unclaimed in a sterile metal drawer in the basement of the Atlantic City morgue. Eventually his death would be discovered and a small obituary would run in the Times - Novelist Robert Kelly, dead at forty. There would be no Memorial Service at the North Light, no party at The Nest. No bagpipes would play in his honor, and certainly no tears would be shed. How would the stories of his life go? Would fishermen sit around a bar and reminisce about how Bob Kelly woke up one morning, mowed the lawn and then got drunk. How about the time he woke up, ate breakfast, did a load of laundry and then got drunk. How pathetic.

Kelly grabbed a diet soda out of the honor bar then telephoned down to the front desk and asked for Mr. Antonio Gianninni. He butted heads with a receptionist who refused to put him through, but instead transferred him to Gianninni's administrative assistant. The assistant made it clear that no one speaks with her employer unless she knows the source and the subject of the phone call.

"My name is Robert Kelly," he announced, "Heart Publishing has contracted me to ghostwrite the autobiography of one Nicky Scarpelli. You might remember him affectionately as "The Ax". Mr. Scarpelli has made some very interesting allegations regarding Mr. Gianninni's business as well as personal affairs, and has supplied me with concrete evidence to support his claims. I am in town until tomorrow and would like to get Mr. Gianninni's response to these accusations. If you prefer not to bother him with my phone call, I'll simply submit my manuscript with a foreword stating that I contacted Mr. Gianninni regarding the allegations but was advised by his secretary that he had no comment."

"Hold."

Kelly rifled through his duffle bag while awaiting a voice on the other end. The secretary came back on the line.

"Mr. Gianninni will meet with you tomorrow morning at ten. Don't' be late. His offices are on the penthouse floor of The Rio, a pass will be waiting for you at the front desk." Click.

Kelly put down the phone and found the envelope wedged between a pair of khakis and Abbie's laptop, which he had borrowed for the trip. He removed the contents and examined Nicky "The Ax's" proof, still amazed at what some file photos, a quality scanner and a high definition printer could create.

# Chapter 23

Antonio Gianninni was, in essence, the anti-Corleone. One hundred sit-ups every morning assured that his body would not develop the paunch ordinarily associated with sixty-year-old Mafiosos, like himself. His silver-gray hair was cut fashionably short, and wire-rimmed glasses framed his hazel eyes, giving him the look of an academic rather than that of a Don. He was well educated, Columbia University, and as a result well spoken; these, those and them were not pronounced dees, dos, and dem. He owned a casino but did not gamble, ran the Mob but did not associate with mobsters and, unlike many of his contemporaries from other families, shied away from the limelight, preferring to focus on expanding his rather quirky art collection rather than his notoriety. The one characteristic of Antonio Gianninni hinted that he was "connected" was his wardrobe. Every day, rain or shine, summer or snow, he dressed in a black Armani suit, hand sewn black dress shirt, black leather loafers and a snow-white silk necktie.

Like his persona, the decor of his office was, in a word, atypical. Behind his sleek, black marble desk was a huge stained glass window through which the morning sunlight streamed, casting brilliant rainbows of color across his office walls. Religious artifacts adorned the walls and a salvaged church pew was the only seating which was why, on this particular morning, an enormous man in a poorly fitting Armani knockoff had chosen to stand during his meeting with the Boss.

"Ummm," the giant goon scratched his head, "where did you say you wanted me to go?"

"I didn't say that I wanted you to go anywhere Dino," Antonio Gianninni's voice was gentle yet firm. "I said that you are going to Tyle Island, Massachusetts."

"Yes sir. Tyle Island, Massachusetts. What's in Tyle Island, Massachusetts?"

"A thorn in my side," Gianninni picked up the letter that he had received that morning and skimmed down to the signature, "named Prescott."

"So you want that I should get rid of the problem?"

Gianninni closed his eyes and sighed at Dino's butchering of the English language. "No Dino, I do not want you to get rid of the problem. I merely want you to let this Prescott know that he made a mistake when double crossing me."

"Someone goddamn double crossed you Boss!" the big man boomed.

Gianninni pinched the bridge of his nose, "Dino, what have I told you about using the Lord's name in vain?"

"I know Boss, I'm sorry." The goon lowered his monstrous head in shame. "It's just that I get mad when you're disrespected."

"You get angry when I'm disrespected, not mad. And I get angry when the Lord is disrespected. You don't want to make me angry, do you Dino?"

"No Boss."

"Good. Now listen to me very carefully."

"Yes sir."

"I want you to gather up your wife and children and take them on a vacation."

"Angie would like that."

"When you get to Tyle Island, go to a hotel named The Water Lily and ask for Robert Prescott."

"The thorn?"

"Yes Dino, the thorn. Let him know how disappointed I am in his behavior. Be firm, but do not get rid of the problem. Do you understand?"

"I understand Boss."

"I've got a project starting up there next week which might meet with some protest by the local residents. Land needs to be cleared before construction can begin. I want you to oversee the progress, make sure that everything goes smoothly. My man in charge will contact you when he arrives on the island. See Theresa on your way out, she has all the details. Any questions?"

Dino had a million but he answered, "No Boss."

"I don't understand," Jack stood in Abbie's office holding the pages of the day's script in one hand and a Starbucks latte in the other. "Who's Mr. G?"

"He's a patient. A patient suffering from amnesia who you cure on page three."

"But why?"

"Because Dr. Black is a brain surgeon."

"I know but…"

"Jack," Abbie laid her head on her cluttered desk, "please don't make this difficult. I was up all night rewriting the script so that I could fit this scene. It's a two-minute clip. It's very important to me. I need it in tomorrow's episode, so please just do it."

"Did you know my scene with Rhonda was cut?"

"Yes Jack, I cut it."

"Why?"

"The new scene is more important."

"But after you called last night and told me you wouldn't be coming home, I rehearsed."

"Why are you making this so difficult? It's one lousy scene?"

"You never cut my scenes before."

"I never had to before. And if you take a closer look at the changes you'll see that you've got more screen time by doing the amnesia bit than the sex in the O.R. bit, and as an added bonus you get to use the medical equipment."

"But…"

Abbie's cell phone began to ring. "No buts Jack," she fished through her backpack trying to locate the phone, "you're doing the scene. The actor who's playing Mr. G is in make-up. If you're worried about your performance go down there and grab some rehearsal time. You can't miss him, he's the only bald, old man in a wheelchair."

Jack looked thoroughly disgusted. "I'll do the scene Abbie," he headed out the door, "but I'm sure as hell not going to rehearse with him."

She finally located the phone, flipped it open and said, "What!?"

"Abbie?"

"Yes?"

"It's Chief Tatum."

"Oh. Chief. Hi."

"Sorry to bother you, but you gave me this number in case there was an emergency."

Abbie closed her eyes, just what she needed, an emergency. "What's wrong Chief?"

"Can we speak confidentially?"

"Sure."

"It's about Dan Kelly."

"Who?"

"Bob's brother. Pete's dad."

"Oh right. He's in Alaska isn't he?"

"I'm not so sure about that."

"What do you mean?"

"Are you coming back today?"

"Yeah, I'm on the four o'clock ferry."

"How far are you from Ocean County, New Jersey?" he asked.

"An hour or two tops, why?"

"Do you have time to make a detour to Allaire Airport, it's in Ocean County."

"I know where it is, but you have to tell me what's going on."

"I need you to get a copy of a flight plan and bring it to me."

"Chief what the hell is going on?"

"Abbie," he paused, "I think Dan Kelly may be involved."

As he was getting off the elevator on the penthouse floor of The Rio, Bob Kelly passed an enormous Italian man who was scratching his head and staring at a map. Kelly chuckled, thinking that the guy looked like the stereotypical hit man. Then he remembered where he was and who he was meeting with and stopped chuckling. Just as he was about to hop back onto the elevator, ride down to the lobby, hit the first bar he could find and order a bottle of scotch, the receptionist asked, "Are you Mr. Kelly?"

He considered saying no. Then he thought about what Abbie would do in his position. She wouldn't run away and hide in the bottom of a bottle. She would march into Antonio Gianninni's office and give the mobster a piece of her mind. He couldn't let Abbie down. Not if he wanted her to cry at his funeral.

"Yes," he answered, "I have a ten o'clock with Mr. Gianninni."

"I'm sorry but Mr. Gianninni had some unexpected business matters arise this morning that needed his personal attention. He asked me to extend his apologies and reschedule for this evening."

"I'm working on a deadline."

"As is Mr. Gianninni. I'll put you down for seven o'clock. Good-bye Mr. Kelly."

Kelly turned to leave. He had an inkling that Gianninni's unexpected business matters had something to do with Tyle Island, so he headed back to his room to contact Abbie and see what sort of trouble she and his fellow Islanders were brewing.

Abbie hadn't even made it to the parking garage before her cell phone started to ring. She dug through her backpack while mumbling how she hated that goddamn phone, finally found it, flipped it open and answered, "What?"

"Good morning to you too."

"Kelly?"

"Yes."

"What's going on? Are you in A.C.?" She entered the garage and gave her ticket to the attendant.

"I have a beautiful room at the Rio, you should see this place."

"Was that an invitation?"

"If only I wasn't meeting with a mobster."

"I met a mobster."

"Pardon?"

"Actually retired-mobster would be a more accurate moniker. I fainted in Vincent Gianninni's bedroom."

"Vincent Gianninni the father of Antonio Gianninni?"

"That would be him. Antonio has a brother, correct?"

"Yeah. His name is Giuseppe. He's a..."

"Priest. I know. Hold on a sec," the attendant pulled up in the Jeep, Abbie tipped him, got in, tossed her backpack on the floor and pulled out onto the street. "Sorry about that. His name is Giuseppe but he goes by Father George. He's a real sweetheart." There was silence on the other end. "You still there Kelly?"

"I'm here," he responded, "what exactly were you doing in Vincent Gianninni's bedroom?"

"You mean besides fainting?"

"Yes, besides fainting."

"Investigating. It was purely accidental." Abbie nearly sideswiped a cross-town bus. "So have you met with Antonio yet?"

"I had a ten o'clock appointment but he cancelled. We're rescheduled for tonight."

"What have you got going today?"

"Nothing until seven."

"Good meet me at the rest stop on the Garden State Parkway, the one around exit 100. I should be there by one o'clock."

"I thought you were supposed to be going home this afternoon."

Abbie liked the way that Kelly referred to Tyle Island as home. "I have a detour to make in Jersey so I switched my ferry reservation to the seven o'clock. You can buy me lunch before I head north."

"Abbie, what are you getting yourself into?"

"Relax Kelly," she hooked a left from the middle lane of Broadway nearly taking out two cabs in the process; Kelly could hear the car horns blaring over the phone, "I've got everything under control."


Dina DeLuca filled the trunk of his Lincoln Towncar with imitation Bendel luggage. "Move your ass Angie," he yelled, "we're gunna miss the fucking ferry."

Angie teetered out of the house on five inch, fire engine red, stilettos dragging a chubby, brown haired girl by the arm and an even chubbier, brown haired boy by the ear. "Let's go Ma," she yelled.

"What the fuck is this?" Dino held up a blue and white rectangular piece of foam plastic.

"It's a fucking boogie board. It's for Pasquale to use at the beach."

"It ain't fucking August Angie. The beach is gunna be fucking cold."

"This is the first vacation we've gone on in five fucking years Dino. We ain't going to no fucking island without going to the fucking beach. You got me?"

"Yeah, yeah I got yuh," Dino muttered as he jammed the boogie board into the trunk and slammed it closed.

"Ma! Where the hell are you Ma?" Angie yelled as she put the kids in the back seat of the car. "Buckle em in Dino."

"Why don't you buckle em in?"

"I just got my fucking nails done. You want me to chip my polish and waste twenty bucks? Ma!"

Dino buckled his chubby children in place, got into the car and watched his mother-in-law walk out of the house, approach the car and remove a bottle of holy water from her purse. She made the sign of the cross then doused the windshield. Dino turned on the wipers in response to the blessing. The old lady kept sprinkling, Dino kept wiping. Angie got out of the car teetered back to the front door, locked the house, put her mother in the back seat with the chubby children, got back into the car and announced, "Ready!"

Dino backed out of the driveway and headed for Tyle Island.

## Chapter 24

It was a quiet morning on Tyle Island, the proverbial calm before the storm.

Doc Gno sat on his bedroom floor sipping green tea and stapling the photos of Lindsey Mott's artwork to blood tests results that he had masterfully falsified. It appeared that Tyle Island was in the midst of a Lyme Tick epidemic, and in his professional opinion, quarantine was required until the outbreak could be controlled.

Clara sat with Taloy Jobbs on the porch of his grand hotel, sipping a Bloody Mary and watching the caretaker of The Water Lily scrub all one hundred windows of the old Victorian in preparation for a Kennedy Wedding.

John Beale circled the Island in his speedboat keeping an eye out for any suspicious vessels that might attempt to invade Tyle Island waters.

Chief Tatum performed a brief ceremony in his office during which he deputized six of the Island's most intimidating fishermen, and set about scheduling them for patrol and sentry duties.

Pete Kelly skipped school and headed to Lila's house.

Chapter 25

Abbie slipped the flight plan into her backpack when she saw Kelly approach.
"Hi Bob," she waved hello.
"Abbie." Kelly stopped about two feet away from her. He stood for an awkward moment during which each tried to decide how to appropriately greet the other. Had they progressed to the kiss on the cheek stage, or were they still floundering in smile and nod territory? Both hesitated, then smiled and nodded.
"You hungry?" Kelly asked.
"I'm always hungry," Abbie answered.

Jack West finished taping his scene with Mr. G. It went well. He liked using the stethoscope. Abbie had left a note in his dressing room informing him that she was off to Tyle Island and would call after she arrived. The apartment was empty. He thought of the brunette from last week. She was a very good actress and a very enthusiastic rehearser. She was probably very photogenic too. He decided to call her and see if she was free for the afternoon.

"Chianti?"
"Yes."
"You drank Chianti with Vincent Gianninni?"
"Actually, no." Abbie took a bite of her cheeseburger.
"Well that's good."
She chewed then swallowed. "He went nuts before we had a chance to toast."
"Nuts?" Kelly stole one of Abbie's fries, "is that a clinical term?"
"It was when Father George left us alone to get the wine and meatballs..."

"Did you say meatballs?"

"Yes. As I was saying, while Father George was gone I pressured the old man about Hyacinth. At first he was adamant that he didn't know her, but then I showed him a photograph of her with his old friend Eddie and bingo, something clicked."

"He admitted to knowing who she is?"

"No. But the look in his eyes told me that he once knew Hyacinth very, very well."

"His eyes told you that?" Kelly sounded skeptical.

Abbie dipped a fry into a puddle of catsup, "A man's eyes reveal all."

Kelly looked down at his burger.

"So anyway," Abbie continued, "then I asked about Hyacinth's child. Well that sent Vincent Gianninni right over the edge. He started to babble."

"About?"

Abbie sipped her soda. "About Chelsea Castle and Marco and Harley and the Benton Springs Hospital Ball."

"You're kidding."

"Nope." She shook her head.

"The old man babbled about The Darkest Hour?"

"I guess he's more addicted to my crap than you are."

"So what did you do?"

"I left. And I went straight to the studio and rewrote today's taping. I added a scene in which the famed neurosurgeon Dr Jasper Black cures a little, old, bald man in a wheelchair named Mr. G of amnesia and convinces the grateful old geezer that he must reveal information that he has been suppressing for years regarding the identity of a child of a missing woman named Hyacinth."

"You didn't."

"I did."

"You're good."

"I know."

They spent the next half hour discussing the Gianninnis. Abbie filled Kelly in on Father George, and Vincent, and Isabella the cook, and the two guys stationed in the hallway. She kept thinking about the flight plan hidden in her backpack, but couldn't bring herself to mention it to Kelly. He had too much on his mind as it was, this bombshell could wait until after his meeting with Antonio Gianninni.

"You know Bob," Abbie nervously drummed the table with an ice cold french fry as she broached a subject of lingering concern, "tonight...at the meeting...ummm... you have to be nice."

"Pardon me?"

"When you meet with Gianninni, you have to try to be nice."

"I'm blackmailing the man Abbie, I'm not asking him to the prom."

"You see right there, that's going to be your downfall."

"What is?"

"Your lack of diplomacy. Whether you know it or not, you have an abrasive personality."

"I don't think I'm abrasive."

"Have you forgotten our first encounter?"

"I may have been brusque, but we're friends now."

"Yes, now. But at the time I wanted to kill you. And I'm not a mobster with the ability to carry out such a desire. Gianninni is. You get what I'm saying?"

"So you want me to suck up to the guy?"

"Why not? There's no rule that says blackmailers have to be rude. And if Gianninni is anything like his father and his brother, he might not be all bad. Just go in with an open mind, be pleasant and try not to antagonize him."

"If I can't antagonize him, how exactly do I blackmail him?"

"You're clever, you'll think of something." The cell phone rang. "This thing is forever ringing at the most inopportune time," Abbie growled as she dug into her backpack and pulled out the phone, "and its never good news. What?" she answered.

"Well someone is in a pissy mood."

"Hey Meg."

"What crawled up your ass?"

"What didn't?" Abbie replied.

"Sorry to be a bearer of more bad news but it looks like the documents are clean, the signature is legit, and the disk you gave me is damaged."

"Shit."

"What's wrong?" Kelly asked.

"Who was that?" Megan asked

"Nothing," Abbie said to Kelly and "no one," Abbie said to Meg.

"Is that Bob Kelly?"

"Yes."

"What's he wearing?"

"Thanks for your help Megan. If there's anything I can do for you."

"Well, as a matter of fact."

"No."

"You don't even know what I was going to ask."

"I have an idea."

"I don't want the author; he's all yours, although I'm sure you'll manage to let him slip away. What I do want is your little black cocktail dress."

"The strapless."

"That's the one."

"What for?"

"I've got a Giants Tight End that needs some loosening up."

"That dress will do it. Help yourself, it's in my closet."

"By the way have you told Jacky boy that he's history yet?"

"No. And while I'm sure you would love to do the honors, please keep your mouth shut."

"Fine."

"And listen, he's been doing a lot of rehearsing lately so try not to bother him."

"I've got the key. He'll never know I was there."

Abbie hung up the phone and filled Kelly in on the outcome of the handwriting analysis; it wasn't a forgery, Hyacinth Poole had definitely signed those papers. They lingered for a few more minutes until both faced the fact that they had schedules to keep. Kelly walked Abbie to the Jeep where they experienced another awkward moment, kiss on the cheek or smile and nod?

"Call me as soon as you get out of the meeting," Abbie demanded, prolonging their good-bye, "and remember, be nice."

"I'll try my best," he smiled and nodded.

"Try harder," she smiled and nodded back.

Then he leaned over and kissed her on the cheek.

## Chapter 26

Three stops at McDonalds to feed his pain in the ass kids plus two additional pee breaks, a flat tire and several wrong turns caused Dino DeLuca to miss the four o'clock ferry and to nearly miss the seven o'clock as well. At 6:45 the Towncar pulled up to the ticket booth of Tyle Island Navigation, Angie hopped out, teetered to the window and asked to purchase one-way tickets for her family and a pass for the car. The ticket agent, a blonde, dreadlocked, overly tan teen-ager hid the joint that he had been smoking behind a can of Mountain Dew and sold the woman the tickets. He then watched her teeter back to the car. When she opened the door he heard a loud voice yelling at a couple of kids to 'sit fucking still'. The woman got in, and the Towncar proceeded to back onto the ferry guided by a member of ship's crew. It pulled in beside a green Jeep Wrangler, which, Angie declared, "needed a fucking washing."

Once the car was secured in its spot, a crewmember pulled a set of chains across the stern of the ferry then radioed back to the ticket booth, instructing the agent to call John Beale and let him know that a suspicious car was heading over.

"You got it dude," the teenager replied. He finished his joint, downed his Mountain Dew, ate a couple of Twinkies then picked up the telephone but couldn't for the life of him remember who he was supposed to call.

Bob Kelly was led to Antonio Gianninni's office by the receptionist who had made it clear that he was three minutes late. He was tempted to tell off the mouthy broad, but decided that such behavior wouldn't be, in Abbie's words, diplomatic. Outside the office he was frisked by a bodyguard who removed a small tape recorder from the right pocket of Kelly's sport coat and a folded manila envelope from the left.

Kelly volunteered his wallet stating, "Careful, it's loaded."

The bodyguard returned Kelly's possessions without comment then knocked twice on the office door.

"Enter," a voice answered from within.

The bodyguard opened the door and motioned for Kelly to proceed.

Upon stepping into the dimly lit room Kelly was immediately struck by the smell of cigar smoke mixed with, he sniffed to make sure, incense?

"That will be all Dominic," Gianninni dismissed the goon. A twinge hit Kelly's stomach as he heard the door click closed behind him, it was show time and he had but a moment to size up his foe.

Unlike the Hollywood version of the Mafia Don, Antonio Gianninni was not overweight from too much pasta and too many cannolis; with his pale complexion and soft features one wouldn't even guess that he was of Italian descent. He wore a beautifully tailored, jet-black suit with a black silk shirt and black shoes, but for some reason, Kelly noted, had opted for a bright white necktie to complete the ensemble.

"Mr. Kelly," Gianninni, who stood in front of a gold gilded cabinet that was draped with a white cloth, motioned toward a wooden bench situated opposite his sleek, black marble desk, "please, have a seat."

Kelly noticed that there had been no hint of a Brooklyn upbringing in the man's voice. "Thank you for meeting with me Mr. Gianninni," Kelly made a point of being pleasant as he walked across the office. He took a seat on a long, carved pew that came complete with red velvet kneeler, and stared up at the mammoth stained glass window that dominated the room. His mouth hung open slightly, as if confused.

Gianninni followed Kelly's puzzled gaze. "I see you've noticed my artwork," his tone was that of a proud father; as if the mere thought of the window brought him great joy. "What do you think of her?"
What do I think of her? I think that I've been in a lot of offices in my time and I've seen a lot of things hanging behind desks - diplomas, awards, photographs of insignificant people posing with significant people in an attempt to make themselves seem more significant - but this is without a doubt the first stained glass window that I have ever encountered. Kelly thought, but wisely didn't say all that; instead, "it's rather," he searched for a description..."ominous."
Gianninni opened the doors to the cabinet revealing an array of liquor bottles held within. "I'm sure my grasp of the language is not equal to that of a writer such as you," he paused and bowed his head before removing a bottle of wine, "but doesn't the word ominous carry a negative connotation?"
Kelly smiled on the outside while cringing internally. In less than a minute Abbie's concerns regarding his social skills had come to fruition. "It certainly wasn't meant as a criticism," Kelly made a feeble attempt at explaining away his feaux pas, "it's just that I find the scale somewhat daunting."
Gianninni cocked his head as he reassessed the window, "you think its' too large?"
No a fifteen square foot stained glass window is understated, of course its too fucking large Kelly thought, but that too would have been undiplomatic to say aloud, so he shifted the focus away from his bumbling critique of the mobster's décor by asking, "what exactly does the scene depict?"
"The Annunciation," the smiled returned to the mobster's face, "I rescued her from a Cathedral in Sicily that was slated for demolition." Gianninni fell silent, as if mesmerized by the figures portrayed in dark lead and

colored glass. In a hushed, almost reverent voice he revealed to Kelly, "I'm sickened by the beauty that is destroyed in the name of progress." Kelly was about to acknowledge that such a viewpoint was ironic considering Gianninni's pending rape of Tyle Island's most treasured piece of land, but he thought of Abbie and kept his mouth shut. "May I offer you a cocktail?" Gianninni asked.

Kelly held up the tape recorder. "Under the circumstances I don't think I should," he answered as he eyed the bottle of premium Single Malt Scotch that stood at the front of the liquor cabinet where all premium bottles of scotch should stand.

"We are civilized men are we not Mr. Kelly?" Gianninni replied, "Surely we can enjoy a drink while we talk."

Kelly didn't want to further offend his mobster host, and considering the volume of scotch he had ingested over the past six months he honestly didn't think that one drink could diminish his blackmailing abilities, so, he acquiesced. Antonio Gianninni poured four fingers of single malt and added a touch of water as instructed by his guest. He then filled a tall gold goblet with red wine for himself. Gianninni handed Kelly his glass then stood behind his desk, closed his eyes and with both hands raised his goblet in toast, "to your health."

"Amen" Kelly whispered as he took a long, slow drink. God that tasted good.

"Something to eat?" Gianninni held out a simple gold plate that was stacked with small round water crackers.

"No thank you," Kelly took a pass as he shifted on the wooden bench in a futile attempt to get comfortable.

"Now where were we?" Gianninni asked as he took a seat.

"We were discussing your window," Kelly figured that showing an interest in the mobster's hobbies would help to establish a pleasant blackmailing mood. "You said it depicted The Annunciation."

"Yes, are you familiar with the story?"

"I may be a little fuzzy on the specifics, but I believe it has to do with Mary being told that she is to be the Mother of Jesus."

"Very good Mr. Kelly," Gianninni gave him an approving nod. "As you can see," he pointed up to the window as if instructing a course on Art History, "the Archangel Gabriel appears before Mary to announce that God has chosen her to be the Mother of his only Son. Isn't the solemn expression on her face remarkable?"

"She looks," Kelly honestly thought that Mary looked bored, but knowing how well "ominous" went over he substituted, "serene."

"Precisely." Gianninni liked that answer so Kelly congratulated himself with a sip of scotch. The mobster continued to sing the praises of his window. "The artisan was truly a master at capturing the mood of his subject."

"His use of color is very effective," Kelly added. "I don't think I've ever seen a blue quite as spectacular." Kelly found himself rising to the ass-kissing occasion in a manner that would make Abbie proud, so, feeling cocky, he went on. "Rather than the typically demure representation of Mary in softer hues, the stronger cobalt tones make her appear almost majestic."

"And majestic She is," Gianninni picked up his goblet and again raised it in toast. "To the Virgin Mother."

While he was unaccustomed to toasting virgins, Kelly joined his host in another sip. "May I ask," Kelly leaned forward on the rock-hard wooden bench in an act that, while only meant to alleviate the pins and needles now tingling his half-numb butt, made him appear thoroughly immersed in the topic, "which aspect of the window are you more drawn to, the artistry or the subject matter?"

"An excellent question Mr. Kelly," Gianninni clasped his hands together as if in prayer, "I would have to say the latter. While I own many works by the Masters, and I appreciate their material as well as aesthetic value, my true passion lies in salvaging religious artifacts. I get great satisfaction from protecting that which cannot protect itself." Gianninni took a cracker off the gold plate and placed it on his tongue. He then drank some wine and continued. "I have a mosaic of Jesus feeding the masses that I am especially fond of, and I recently acquired a statue of The Blessed Mother which is said to have shed tears of blood."

I bet he didn't get that on e-bay Kelly thought as he took a drink and responded, "You believe in such miracles?"

"Why wouldn't I?"

Kelly shrugged. "The world is full of skeptics."

Gianninni's face grew grim as he assured his guest, "I am not a skeptic when it comes to matters of my faith."

Clearly not, Kelly glanced around the room. In addition to the Bible scene window and rock hard pew, there were a number of crucifixes and religious artifacts adorning the walls, and votive candles were placed about the office like miniature shrines. Antonio Gianninni's office looked more like a church than did Saint Joseph's by The Sea. The intercom button on Gianninni's phone buzzed, he excused himself and picked up the phone.

By now Kelly's rear end had gone totally numb so, feigning interest in an ivory carving of The Last Supper, he stood and walked over to admire the relief. Very detailed, nice work, Kelly wondered what the price tag had been. While Gianninni continued his conversation Kelly continued to browse the mobster's collection. To the right of the carving was a gold crucifix encrusted with rubies and emeralds, to the left was a 5" x 7" black and white photograph in a simple silver frame. Kelly took a closer look at the photo, three people stood in front of The Great Sphinx. He immediately recognized Antonio Gianninni, although the man's now silver-gray hair had then been a light brown; he guessed that the photo was taken circa 1980. Posing with Gianninni was a priest of roughly the same age, presumably his brother Giuseppe although there was little physical resemblance between the two men, and a woman who appeared to be much younger, late-teens or early twenties at most. He felt a twinge in his stomach. There was something oddly familiar about her.

"Has something caught your eye Mr. Kelly?" Gianninni asked as he put down the phone and picked up his glass of wine.

"I see you've been to the Middle East," Kelly commented while trying to jump-start his memory regarding the girl.

"For my fortieth birthday I went on a pilgrimage to the Holy Land. Egypt was a side trip."

"The priest, is he your brother?"

"Yes," Gianninni fondled the knot of his white silk necktie, "Giuseppe."

"Your other companion is very attractive."

"She is."

"She looks familiar."

"I'm sure she's not."

Kelly took a large gulp of scotch. Idle chatter was right up there with diplomacy as one of his strong points and the sucking up routine was wearing thin; however, the proper segue into blackmail had yet to surface so he took one more stab at schmoozing the Don, "did you enjoy your pilgrimage?"

"It was disappointing."

"Really? Why?"

"Too crowded."

Well that's a new one, Kelly thought, you travel half way across the world to retrace the steps of Jesus Christ and are deterred because the line for the restroom is too long. Kelly returned to his bench and, though still sore in the hindquarters, reluctantly sat.

"Please don't get me wrong," Gianninni went on to explain his statement, "I don't mean to belittle the experience, it's just that," a look of sadness came over the mobster's face, "you wouldn't understand."

Kelly took a large swig of scotch, conjured his most sympathetic voice, looked Antonio Gianninni dead in the eye and stated, "But I do understand Mr. Gianninni. You sought a spiritual journey but instead got a guided tour of Bible studies 101 - to your left you'll find the manger and up on your right, the Wailing Wall. While that may be a satisfying experience for some, I'm sure it falls short of inspirational for a man of your obvious faith."

There was an extended silence during which Gianninni stared at Kelly.

Kelly stared back.

"Mr. Kelly."

"Yes Mr. Gianninni."

"I like you."

"I'm flattered."

"Rarely do I meet someone with whom I can discuss my passions for art and religion."

"I too have enjoyed our conversation."

"So I'm going to do something that is extremely out of character for me."

"And that would be?"

"I'm going to give you the opportunity to leave, now, no questions asked."

Kelly laughed light heartedly, "but Mr. Gianninni, the point of my visit is to ask questions."

Gianninni's tone grew somber, "I assure you Mr. Kelly, it would be in your best interest if we were to discontinue this meeting and part amicably."

"While I appreciate your advice Mr. Gianninni, I'm here to do a job." Kelly turned on the tape recorder and asked, "Shall we get down to business?"

Gianninni sighed, "I wish you would reconsider."

Kelly stood firm, "May we proceed?" Kelly raised his glass for a sip of liquid confidence but found that the scotch was gone. His hand shook ever so slightly as he placed the empty glass on the desk. "I assume that you're aware of the reason I requested this meeting."

"Theresa told me that you are writing a book."

"That's correct."

"A biography I believe."

"An autobiography actually, I'm ghostwriting for Nick Scarpelli."

"An interesting term ghostwriter," Gianninni leaned back in his leather chair and gazed into his glass of wine, "if it were to be taken literally it would presume that either the writer's topic is that of ghosts or," Gianninni looked up and met Kelly's eyes, "that the writer himself is a ghost."

Kelly forced a laugh as he reached out for his glass only to remember that it was empty.

"Theresa also informed me that in this book you accuse me of being connected with the so-called mafia."

"If I may clarify," Kelly leaned forward in his pew.

Gianninni held up a hand to quiet Kelly. "I will make the offer one more time, leave now and we part friends. If this conversation persists, I make no guarantees."

An internal tug of war took place between the two Bob Kellys. Old Kelly, the self-centered lush, yelled at him to stand up and run out the door. New Kelly, the love struck savior of Tyle Island who was toting some major scotch muscles, still thought that his brilliant plan of blackmail and manipulation would succeed against the crazy zealot seated across from him. Old Bob pulled one way, new Bob the other until, "I'm sorry Mr. Gianninni, but I have an obligation to see this interview through." New Bob won.

Gianninni sighed, "Have it your way. But if we speak, we speak frankly so as not to waste each other's time." He reached across the desk and turned off the tape recorder. "You will never be able to prove that I am in any way affiliated with the Mob. The Feds have tried, the Gaming Commission has tried, even Geraldo has tried."

"Yes, but Geraldo didn't have Nicky Scarpelli," Kelly rebutted.

"And neither do you."

"I beg to differ."

"Do not beg Mr. Kelly, it is degrading." Gianninni stood and carried both his and Kelly's glasses to the liquor cabinet where he began to freshen their drinks.

"If I may get to the point of my visit," Kelly was struggling to gain control of the conversation. Six months without intelligent banter had left him weak in the realm of repartee.

"An excellent idea," Gianninni filled Kelly's glass with scotch but this time omitted the water. "You claim to be here on behalf of Heart Publishing."

"If you doubt my credentials, please feel free to call Sam Heart," Kelly pointed to the phone, "I'll wait."

"As an avid reader I am fully aware of your credentials Mr. Kelly. You wrote twenty bestsellers during the course of your career. I read some of them. They were quite good." Gianninni handed Kelly his drink then took a seat at his desk.

Kelly leaned an arm along the back of the pew and crossed his legs, trying to assume a pose of casual confidence. "I'm flattered," he instinctively took a swig of scotch.

"Your forte' was fiction." Gianninni took a sip. "Crime stories."

"That's correct."

"I like crime stories. I pride myself on being able to figure out the end well before all of the clues have been presented to me."

"You are an astute reader."

"And as an astute reader I wish you would explain something that has me quite puzzled."

"I'll do my best."

"You had a stellar career."

"It was successful, yes."

"You retired."

"True."

"Then, not six months later, you emerged from this self-imposed retirement to ghostwrite an autobiography."

"Also correct."

"Why?"

Kelly didn't miss a beat. "The genre presented me with new challenges. Crime fiction had grown stale, crime fact held exciting prospects."

Gianninni nodded as Kelly sipped. "That makes sense."

"I'm glad."

"But what doesn't make sense is why Heart Publishing? You had no contractual obligations to Sam Heart and surely your relationship must have been strained."

Kelly leaned forward in his pew and grinned. "Both Sam and I are capable of separating business matters from personal matters where a good story is concerned. Sam had Nicky the Ax and Nicky the Ax had something Geraldo didn't have." Kelly struggled to remove the manila envelope from his coat pocket. When he finally freed it, he tossed the envelope on Gianninni's desk and announced, "Proof."

Gianninni stared at the envelope but did not touch it. "Sam Heart has three biographers under contract. Wouldn't it make more sense to put an experienced biographer on a story of such supposed magnitude?"

"My name sells books Mr. Gianninni," Kelly countered. "Sam could put my name on the phone book and it would sell fifty thousand copies."

Gianninni smiled. "You're not listed in the phonebook Mr. Kelly. I looked. Which leads me to my next question. Where, may I ask, do you currently reside?"

Kelly did not respond. Gianninni couldn't possibly know of his link to Tyle Island? It had never been mentioned in any of his bios. When he moved back home he left no forwarding address. Even Sam, who might have squealed if pressured, didn't know where Kelly was hanging his hat these days. He took a sip as he retraced his steps. The car he was driving was rented by Heart Publishing, as was the hotel room so there was no link to the Island there. He had used cash to pay for meals to avoid a possible trace of his credit card, again no link to the Island. "I don't see how that is relevant," he managed to finally respond.

"But it is relevant." Gianninni slid the envelope off his desk and into the trashcan. He looked up at Kelly and smiled. "The phone call I took earlier was from an old friend and current business partner." Gianninni pointed to the photograph of him and his companions posed by the sphinx. "She's the attractive one."

Kelly looked back at the photograph of the Gianninni brothers and their young companion. A sharp pain struck him square in the gut. How had he not recognized her? Pete had her eyes. Kelly gulped down his scotch as he realized that not only would he not be halting construction of the casino any time soon, he'd most surely end up a part of it; in the foundation under three feet of concrete.

"Mr. Kelly I'm aware that you live on Tyle Island. You are aware that I am developing a piece of land on Tyle Island. You came here thinking that you could somehow persuade me to abandon my plans for building a casino in your backyard, if not through your obvious charm," Gianninni glanced down at the envelope in the trashcan, "then through blackmail. I offered you the door, you chose not to take it."

Kelly had often written scenes describing the final thoughts of a dying man. While he wasn't exactly on his deathbed, he was getting the distinct impression that the cement mixer was being backed up to the building. The thoughts that passed through his mind surprised him. He thought of Pete. He thought of Clara's corned beef hash and wondered what secret ingredient made it taste so damn good. He thought of the ruts in his front lawn that he had never gotten around to repairing and he thought of Abbie, standing on the deck of the Old Coast Guard Boast house with water dripping off the tip of her nose and a fluffy white towel wrapped tightly around her. He closed his eyes, hoping that when he reopened them he would be sitting on that piece of driftwood watching Abbie O'Neal skipping seashells into the ocean off of Madonna's Cove.

"You may be a talented writer Mr. Kelly, but you're no miracle worker," Gianninni stated as he straightened his white necktie and brushed a piece of lint from the lapel of his black suit coat. "I doubt if William Shakespeare himself could come up with a plot twist that would save you or your island now."

Kelly opened his eyes, no Abbie, just the stained glass window. He looked up at Mary towering over him and noticed that there was something oddly different about her; it appeared as if her look of boredom had been replaced by a devilish smirk. And while Kelly would later attribute what took place next to the rapid ingestion of scotch, at that moment, he swore he saw the Virgin Mary look down upon his condemned soul, and wink. It was just the plot twist he needed. It was a miracle.


Once aboard the ferry, an exhausted Abbie curled up on a long wooden bench and fell asleep. Her ill-timed snooze caused her to miss the little old lady who shuffled about the lower deck sprinkling passengers with holy water. She missed the chaos that ensued when the spiked heel of a passenger's red pump became stuck in the metal grate staircase leading to the upper deck. And she missed a chubby little boy and his chubby little sister getting seasick and regurgitating a total of three Happy Meals complete with chocolate shakes and super-sized fries onto the clean white boat shoes of the ferry Captain who had the misfortune of being in the wrong place at the wrong time. Abbie only awoke when the announcement came over the loudspeaker instructing passengers with vehicles to return to their cars in preparation for docking on Tyle Island. Even then, only one hour of sleep in the past thirty-six left her too groggy to register concern over the Lincoln Towncar with New Jersey plates that was parked beside her. When the ferry landed, Abbie was waved off ahead of the Towncar. She headed straight for Chief Tatum's office while the Towncar headed straight for The Water Lily.

Dino DeLuca stood before a petite, antique writing desk in the lobby of The Water Lily and repeatedly rang the little gold bell that sat atop a note that read 'ring bell for service'. A tall slender man who was over-dressed in a navy blue sport coat, khaki slacks, pale blue oxford and burgundy ascot emerged from a back office in response to the incessant ding-a-linging.

"I'm sorry to have kept you waiting," Dino noticed that the man had an accent, "my assistant stepped out for dinner and I'm alone. May I help you with something?"
"You Prescott?"
"Yes, I'm Robert Prescott."
"Mr. Gianninni sent me." Dino smiled and let loose with a right to the stomach. Prescott slumped into a groaning mound behind the desk. "You fucked with the wrong man," Dino declared as he repeatedly kicked Prescott in the stomach and groin. When the man appeared sufficiently battered Dino knelt beside him and whispered, "You finger me or Mr. G and next time you're fucking dead." Dino then pocketed the little bell; Angie would like it, and casually walked out to the Towncar waiting on the street with its motor running. When he

opened the door he could hear Angie yelling at the kids to sit fucking still.
"How'd it go baby?" Angie asked.
"Piece of cake. Let's find this fucking cottage, I'm beat."

## Chapter 27

Antonio Gianninni walked Kelly to his room; the bodyguard followed a few steps behind. "I took the liberty of having your room searched," Gianninni informed Kelly as he inserted the key card and opened the door.

"I would expect nothing less." Kelly stood in the doorway and gave the room the once over. His empty duffle bag lay on the floor beside the bed and Abbie's laptop sat on the dresser exactly where he left it. "Your men do good work. I wouldn't have known they were here."

"That is the point." Gianninni gestured toward the nightstand. The bodyguard walked over and detached the telephone from its wire. "Considering your recent behavior, I think it would be best if we kept our travel plans to ourselves." The bodyguard went into the bathroom and removed the second telephone. "No cell phones Dominic?"

"No sir," the bodyguard grunted.

"I'm hurt that you don't trust me Antonio," Kelly pretended to pout as he flopped down on the end of the bed.

Gianninni smirked, "You've given me such cause."

"You can't blame a guy for trying," Kelly shrugged.

"No Bob, I can't. And I do respect your resourcefulness, which is why there will be an armed guard posted outside of your room at all times. Now, is there anything I can get for you before we say good-night?"

"I missed dinner."

"I'll have a meal sent up. Will a steak do?"

"Is it going on your tab or mine?"

"You are my guest."

"Then make it a t-bone, rare, with a baked potato and,

if it's not too much trouble, a large wedge of cheesecake for desert." He grinned, "I have a sweet-tooth."

"Another scotch?" Gianninni seemed amused.

"No thank you, but a pot of coffee would be lovely."

"Dominic will see to it." Gianninni turned to leave then paused and looked back at Kelly, his glare was penetrating. "I sincerely hope this isn't another trick Mr. Kelly."

"You give me too much credit Antonio," Kelly looked around the room, which was on the twentieth floor, with no telephone, and no method of egress that wouldn't involve surviving bullets or one hell of a drop. "I'm a novelist, not Houdini."

The two men shook hands and Gianninni departed. His bodyguard followed carrying a telephone under each over-developed arm. Once Kelly was satisfied that Gianninni was safely out of ear-shot, he tip-toed to the door, held his breath as he quietly engaged the security chain, tip-toed to the dresser, picked up Abbie's laptop and carried it into the bathroom where he closed and locked the door behind him. He placed the computer on the vanity beside the telephone wire that Gianninni's goon had been foolish enough to leave behind and pushed a button on the side of the computer. The Internet hookup slid out. Kelly smiled, Houdini would be proud.


"I killed him."

"Will you hand me that note pad please?" Chief Tatum asked.

"Did you hear what I said?" Abbie passed a yellow legal pad to the Chief then collapsed onto the chair across from his desk, inhaled deeply, exhaled deeply and announced, "Bob Kelly is dead, and I killed him."

The Chief glanced up from his work and realized that Abbie wasn't going away, so he half-heartedly asked, "How do you figure that?"

"I should have told him about his brother," Abbie whined. "If Kelly had known that Dan was mixed up with the Mob he never would have met with Gianninni." She sighed dramatically, "It's as if I led the lamb to slaughter."

Chief Tatum set aside the flight plans, which, prior to Abbie's declaration of murder, he had been trying to analyze, and leaned back in his chair.

"First of all my dear, Bob Kelly is no lamb, a stubborn jackass maybe, but definitely no lamb. This was his plan and he knew the risks going in. Second, we haven't proven that Dan is involved with the Mob. I know Dan, he's a good man, there's a reasonable explanation. Third and most important, just because Kelly isn't answering his phone, it doesn't mean he's dead. He's probably passed out at a Black Jack table. He'll call when he comes to."

Abbie stared up at the ceiling as she considered each of the Chief's three points. "Nope," she finally concluded, "he's dead."

"Abbie," Chief Tatum picked up the flight plans and put on the dime store reading glasses he had stolen off of Mabel's desk, "could you do me a favor?"

"Sure," she mumbled, her eyes still fixed on an imaginary spot on the ceiling.

"Could you stop feeling sorry for yourself long enough to help me figure out this mess?"

"Excuse me," Abbie lowered her gaze and raised a finger in objection, "but I'm not feeling sorry for myself."

"Yes, you are. You're acting like some love-sick puppy."

"Love sick?"

"Yes."

"Over who?"

"Kelly."

Abbie laughed. "I don't love Kelly."

"Yes you do."

"Please Chief, I'm engaged."

An expression of disapproval spread across Chief Tatum's weathered face. "I know."

Abbie tapped her foot. "Look, I respect Kelly. I might even go so far as to say that I like Kelly despite his fingernails on a blackboard personality. Yes, it's true that I feel affection for him, but I feel affection for everyone I've met since I've arrived. And maybe I have decided to call off my engagement, but that decision has nothing to do with Bob Kelly and everything to do with me. So you see Chief, I don't love Bob Kelly."

"Yes you do."

"Do I?" she cringed.

"Yep."

Abbie slumped further down in the chair, "well that's just great. I killed the man I love."

"Abbie?"

"Yes Chief."

"You're starting to piss me off."

She pulled her knees to her chest and whined, "I'm sorry it's just that..."

"Abbie?"

"Yes Chief."

"I don't care." Chief Tatum's fatherly face took on an axe-wielding Jack Nicholson expression, "and do you want to know why I don't care?" Even with no sleep and the burden of a lost love weighing heavily upon her highly sensitive shoulders, Abbie's judgment was keen enough to tell her that to actually ask "why" would be a mistake. The Chief's voice rose with anger, "because there are five hundred people on this Island who are counting on me to stop this casino from being built, and I'll be damned if I can figure out how to go about it. Bottom line, your love life is not my priority. And if I might add on a more personal level, if you are truly convinced that Kelly is dead, I suggest you spend less time feeling sorry for yourself and more time helping me take down the people who killed him."

Abbie stared at Chief Tatum whose face had grown alarmingly red. "For a man of few words, that was quite a speech." She chanced a smile but his grim expression did not change. "You do realize that you just suggested to an emotionally fragile soap opera writer that she unleash some major avenging-woman rage?"

He nodded.

"Do you remember what Clarice did to Blake with the tweezers and the ball of twine when she found out that he'd been having an affair with Donna?"

He winced and nodded.

"And do you recall the confrontation Eunice had with Marla after her drunken driving accident left Raef impotent?"

He nodded again.

"I was in a good mood when I wrote that shit."

"And now you're in a bad mood?"

"Yep."

"Good. That's just the attitude I'm looking for." She paused. "So you really think he's still alive?"

"Yep."

"All right then," Abbie rolled up her sleeves and asked, "What have you got?"

Chief Tatum explained. "The first flight plan was filed on the morning of April 24th. It shows that Dan flew off Island carrying five passengers. His destination was listed as Allaire Airport in New Jersey. The second flight plan shows Dan departing Allaire Airport at 2:30pm on the same day, this time carrying two passengers. The destination for this flight is listed as Wakefield Airport in Wakefield Mass. That means that somewhere between New Jersey and Wakefield he managed to lose three passengers."

"Or," Abbie tossed out a second possibility, "he lost five and picked up two."

"Good point." They stared at the flight plans waiting for a light bulb of insight to click on. Darkness prevailed.

"Lets forget about the number of passengers," Abbie suggested, "and figure out the logic of his route. While I'm no expert at geography, I don't think Wakefield, Massachusetts is anywhere near Alaska."

"Not even close," Chief Tatum concurred.

"Since you seem to have a certain level of faith in the man, I'll give Dan the benefit of the doubt and say that prior to heading off from New Jersey for a two month trip to Alaska he felt the need to pull a u-turn and run an errand back in Massachusetts. So tell me, what's in Wakefield that would attract Dan Kelly?"

"I don't even know where Wakefield is." The Chief drummed his fingers on the desk, "but that name sure does ring a bell."

"Do you have a map?"

They ransacked Mabel's file cabinets and drawers until they came across a map of New England that looked as if it predated Plymouth Rock itself. The State of Massachusetts had been torn into two tattered pieces but while Chief Tatum laid them out across his desk and used his forearm to press out the wrinkles, Abbie managed to find Wakefield listed in the index. The town was located in area C1 of the map. Chief Tatum moved a stubby finger across the map to column C then down just a quarter of an inch until he came to a tiny black dot just below the New Hampshire border, beside the dot was printed Wakefield.

"That's a mighty rural area," the Chief explained. "There's a ski resort about twenty miles west, but that's about it."

"Sounds like a good place to hide out," Abbie suggested.

"Or," Chief Tatum pounded his fist on the map, "to escape the pressures of a grueling work schedule." He excused himself and walked out of his office.

"You sound like an ad for Club Med," she called out after him.

He returned carrying a stack of newspapers. "I asked Mabel to go through the papers every day and save anything that mentioned the casino." He fished through the pile.

"What are you looking for?" Abbie asked.

He ignored her question and dug through the pile, tossing unwanted newspapers onto the floor. Abbie watched him rummage until "bingo" he pointed to a photograph in a back issue of the Boston Globe.

Abbie stepped over the mound of discarded newsprint and looked to where his finger pointed. It was a black and white photograph of Governor Hardy disembarking a plane at Logan Airport following a visit to Las Vegas. The accompanying article mentioned that following several grueling days of meetings the Governor was heading off to his ski house in Wakefield for a weekend of relaxation.

"This would be quite a coincidence," Abbie peeked up to gauge Chief Tatum's current demeanor, "if I believed in coincidences." The Police Chief sat down heavily in his chair. "I understand that he's your friend, but I think its time you filled me in on Dan Kelly."

Chief Tatum clasped his hands together and rested them on his protruding stomach. "What do you want to know?"

Abbie ran her hands through her hair and began pacing. "The way I see it, there aren't many reasons why someone would get mixed up with the Mob. One would be money. What can you tell me about his finances?"

"As far as I know, Dan is doing well. He and Bob own the house free and clear and a condition of Bob's moving back was that he take-over payment of the taxes and house expenses. Dan figured it was only fair since he'd been keeping up the place on his own for the past twenty years."

"So if anything," Abbie took four steps and turned, "Dan would have accumulated more savings in the past six months than ever before?"

"You would think," Chief Tatum replied. "Plus everyone knows that Bob is filthy rich. If Dan needed a loan he would have gone to his brother not the Mob."

"What about Dan's business?"

"Flying is profitable during the busy season. He picks up extra work off season, either fishing or doing some carpentry, but I think that's more out of boredom than need."

"So this supposed trip to Alaska wasn't made to supplement his income?"

"Nah. Dan claimed that it was an opportunity he couldn't pass up."

"Opportunity, alibi," Abbie shrugged, "what's the difference?" She took four steps, pivoted and turned. "Does he gamble?"

"Not that I know of."

"But you're not sure?"

"Abbie, if you haven't already noticed, when you live on an Island this small everybody knows everybody else's business. If Dan was gambling or owed money to the Mob someone would have found out, which means that every Islander would have known not more than ten minutes later."

"Ok. So money wouldn't have been his motivation. Was he seeing anyone?"

"What do you mean?"

"Romantically, was he seeing anyone?"

"Why do you ask that?"

"If a man is in trouble and it doesn't involve money, it usually involves a woman."

"To be honest, I haven't seen Dan out with a woman since..." Chief Tatum's voice trailed off.

Abbie stopped pacing. "Since?"

"Pete's mother."

"Hold on there Chief," Abbie scowled, "Pete told me that he never met his mother."

"That's true." Tatum nodded.

"So you're saying that you haven't seen Dan Kelly with a woman in seventeen years?"

"That's what I'm saying."

"That's impossible."

"Why?"

"Come on Chief, men have needs."

"And men have obligations."

"Meaning?"

"He had a son to raise."

Abbie shook her head in disbelief. "I'm sorry but that's taking the parental devotion bit to the extreme. If a man goes seventeen years without female affection he's either gay or he's been burned bad."

"Dan Kelly sure ain't gay."

"So he was burned?"

"I guess you could say that," the Chief nodded.

Abbie leaned on the desk, "tell me all about it."

Chief Tatum picked up a pen and began clicking. "Pete's mother was a rich girl from New York City, early twenties, real pretty, but as I remember a little full of herself." He thought a moment then added, "then again most of the blue-bloods that come up here are full of themselves. She rented a room at Hyacinth's house for the summer."

"Is that how Hyacinth earned a living back then? Renting rooms?"

"No," the Chief shook his head, "that was the only time I can remember Hyacinth ever taking in a border. Anyway, the story went that when she got here she looked up Dan and told him that she knew Bob from NYU. She said Bob had told her that Dan would show her a good time during her stay."

"Clearly he did. Go on."

"It was nearly Labor Day when she told Dan that she was pregnant. He proposed, she turned him down, but stayed on until Pete was born the next spring."

"Then what happened?"

"She left."

"That's it?"

"Dan woke up one morning and she was gone. He tried tracking her down but it was if Prissy had fallen off the face of the earth."

"Prissy?" Abbie's tired eyes bulged, "her name was Prissy?"

"Yep."

"As in Priscilla?"

"Probably."

"As in Priscilla Des Pierre?"

The Chief squinted as he tried to recollect. "I can't recall her last name."

"Listen to me Chief, this is very important." Abbie crawled onto the desk, across the tattered map and grabbed Chief Tatum by the collar, "think hard. Think very, very hard. Was Pete's mother's last name Des Pierre?"

"Nope."

Abbie, still clutching the Chief's shirt collar, turned to find Pete Kelly standing in the doorway. "Are you sure?" she asked.

"Yeah I'm sure." He pushed his long hair behind his ears. "Her last name was Steele."

Chapter 28

Abbie couldn't hear the telephone ringing over the cacophony of panic drums beating wildly in her head; Chief Tatum had to pry her fingers off of his collar so he could answer. She knelt on the desk watching his lips move as he spoke. He looked upset. She saw him hang up the phone, open his desk drawer, and remove a gun, which he holstered. He then placed both of his hands firmly on Abbie's biceps and tried, unsuccessfully, to shake her back to reality.

"I've got to go," he explained, "that was Caroline from The Water Lily. Robert Prescott has been attacked."

"No shit," Pete commented from the doorway, "is he okay?"

"No. Doc is on his way."

"Can I come with you?" Pete asked.

"I need you to stay here and take care of her."

Abbie had begun to speak quietly to herself.

Pete cautiously approached. The two men stared at the young woman who, still kneeling on the Police Chief's desk, had begun muttering incoherently.

"What's she saying?" Pete asked.

"I'm not sure," Chief Tatum answered.

Pete leaned in closer. He looked up at the Chief with a puzzled expression on his face. "Do you know what putanesca sauce is?"

"Never heard of it. What else is she saying?"

Pete pushed his long hair behind his ears. "I think she just called the Widow Poole a whore."

"I don't have time for this," Chief Tatum reached for his hat.

"Wait a sec Chief, why was she was asking about my mother?"

"I'm not really sure," Chief Tatum answered honestly.

"Cus, it's weird. You see I found some papers today that mention..."

"We'll talk about it later Pete," the Chief interrupted, "I've got to go. Just keep an eye on her. I'll be back as soon as I can." And he was gone.

"Abbie," Pete poked her in the arm. "Abbie," his voice grew louder. "Abbie, can you hear me?"

She slowly raised a finger, placed it against her lips, and whispered "shhhh."

"What are you doing?" he whispered back.

She closed her eyes. "I'm thinking."

"Are you thinking about my mother?"

"In part."

"Because I found something today that makes me think that I kind of screwed up."

Abbie opened one eye. "Screwed up how."

"Can I trust you?"

"Of course," both eyes were wide open now.

"It all started when I burned down the Widow Poole's place."

"You're the arsonist?"

He nodded.

"Does your Uncle know?"

"He helped."

"Jesus Christ Pete," Abbie yelped then quickly lowered her voice and asked, "what if Chief Tatum finds out?"

"He knows."

"He knows?"

"Yeah. He pretty much used the information to blackmail me into helping him find the Widow Poole by hacking into the Phone Company and credit card company data bases."

Abbie climbed off the desk and into Chief Tatum's leather chair. "I can't believe what I'm hearing."

"That's not all."

"What else could there possibly be?"

"Yesterday the Chief mentioned that Lila had to know how to get a hold of Hyacinth since she was the one selling her house, but she wasn't cooperating. So I kind of went to her house today to see what I could dig up."

"You broke in?"

"Yeah. And I found the Listing Agreement and now I have a really big problem."

"Bigger than being a three time felon at the age of seventeen."

"Yeah. According to the Agreement, Hyacinth didn't own her house."

"Who did?"

Pete pulled the document out of the pocket of his denim jacket and unfolded it, "the owners are listed as Edward and Priscilla Steele." Abbie grabbed the papers and read. "So what I need to know is," he pushed his hair behind his ears, "did I like, burn down my own mother's house?"

Abbie began to talk to herself.

"Oh shit not again," Pete harrumphed as he fell into the chair across from Chief Tatum's desk.

Abbie continued her solo conversation for quite some time; Pete caught snippets of information. She mentioned Vincent Gianninni, Eddie Steele, Hyacinth Peters, prostitution, adoption and Priscilla Steele. She spoke of the Governor, Priscilla Des Pierre, Antonio Gianninni, the casino and the Mob. She mumbled something about a Christmas card then repeated Des-Pierre, her volume rose, Des-Pierre, then practically leapt out of the chair and announced, "I've got it."

"Got what?" he asked, his attention focused more on Chief Tatum's desktop than on Abbie.

"The link between Hyacinth and the Governor," she stood.

"Does it involve my mother?"

Abbie looked down at the young man and debated her reply. She decided that if Pete Kelly could set a fire, hack into the phone company, and break into a house, he could probably handle the truth. She nodded, "I think so."

"Who is Priscilla Des Pierre?"

"She's Mrs. Governor Hardy."

He slid the first of the two flight plans off of the desk, held it up and asked, "And where does my father fit in?" Abbie glanced down at the desktop hoping that the second flight plan had not been seen. "Abbie?"

His look was intense. He deserved honesty. "The day your father left for Alaska, he flew five passengers off Island. That was the same day that the Conservancy Council members can last be accounted for, and two days prior to the announcement of the casino."

"So you think my father is a part of all this? Just because he flew them off," Pete argued, "it doesn't mean he knew why they were leaving. If you think my father is mixed up with this casino bullshit you're wrong. You and Tatum, you're both wrong."

Abbie rethought her earlier decision to be honest, and lied. "You misunderstood me Pete. No one is accusing your father of being involved in the casino deal. Chief Tatum just figures that if your father flew the Council members off Island he might have heard something being discussed during the flight. Maybe he could give us a lead as to where to find The Widow Poole. The only reason he took the flight plan was to see if we could use it to track your father down."

Abbie paused to gauge Pete's reaction to her extemporaneous line of bull. He seemed to have mellowed some, so she put on her best innocent-Abbie voice of sincerity, the one she often used to get her way, and asked, "Do you have a way to reach him?"

Pete slowly shook his head. "He said he would contact me when he could."

From the hound-dog expression that swept across the young man's face Abbie surmised that his father hadn't yet been able. Pete Kelly needed an immediate distraction or the clever young man would start asking questions that

Abbie was not prepared to answer. She clapped her hands together and asked, "So, are you ready?"

"Ready for what?"

"Chief Tatum and Doc Gno are tied up, Clara and John Beale have their hands full with running interference and your Uncle is sitting at a black jack table in Atlantic City having the time of his life, so I guess its up to us to save the Island."

"Us?"

"Yes Pete, us."

"Cool." The killer Kelly grin returned. "What do we do?"

"You schedule me a flight off of this Island for first thing tomorrow morning."

"Where you going?"

"Wakefield."

"What's in Wakefield?"

"I'm not sure. That's why I'm going."

## Chapter 29

One positive about being blind is that the search for dead bodies can continue well past dark. While most Tyle Islanders were snuggled in warm beds with their televisions tuned to the eleven o'clock news, Mildred Ahearn was catching her first whiff of a scent that turned her stomach inside out. She was hobbling her way along the beach below the cliffs, taking advantage of low tide to explore the small caves that had been carved into the landscape by breaking waves, when the odor of decomposing flesh passed by on the tail of a cool ocean breeze. She stopped dead in her tracks. Her black high top Cons sunk in the wet sand as she sniffed, then sniffed again. She hobbled forward three more steps and felt the toes of her sneakers grow wetter. Though she couldn't see, fifty years of Island life told her that she was standing in a tidal pool. Three more steps and she was sloshing up to her ankles in the cold still water. She paused to sniff again. The stench had grown stronger. She held her shotgun out in front of her and tapped at the sand to keep from stumbling over whatever was creating the putrid smell. Slosh, slosh, nothing. Four more steps. Slosh, slosh, nothing. Three mores steps. Slosh, slosh, thud. Mildred swung her shotgun and felt it thud again. The odor had grown unbearable so she held her breath, took one step forward, leaned over and reached out her hand. The peeling flesh felt soft and bloated. She ran her hand along the length of the corpse searching for Hyacinth's baby fine hair that she had rolled in curlers every Saturday night for forty years until finally losing her vision. Tears formed in the corners of Mildred's eyes as she thought of touching the now lifeless old bitch that had once been her best friend. Then her hand ran across something odd. Something unfamiliar. It was sinewy, not soft. She propped her shotgun between her knobby knees and used both hands to feel the appendage. It was large, an odd shape, triangular, like a fin.

"Goddamn dolphin," Mildred's nicotine voice grumbled as she wiped away her tears, picked up her shut gun, turned around, and slowly counted off the 312 paces that would take her back to the staircase that would lead her up the cliffs and take her home to her warm bed and The Tonight Show.

Jack was pleased with how the Polaroids had turned out. He stayed up past midnight gluing them into his notebook. Then on the first page, with a thick black magic marker, he neatly printed the introduction.

'Love scenes are hard, especially when they make you talk. Talking and remembering what to do with your body at the same time is hard, so you should rehearse a lot. The key to good love scene rehearsing is a good partner. As Doctor Jasper Black on The Darkest Hour I have had a lot of partners. Each one has taught me a lot. And now I will teach you (see pictures that follow) my tekniques for making the love scene look hot every time.'

He left the notebook on the coffee table and picked up the following days script. He had spent so much time working on the book that he had forgotten about his big scene with the new cast member. What was her name? He flipped through the pages, Bambi. Nice name, sounded smart. She plays a phy-si-cal ther-a-pist, he read the words aloud as he found the pronunciation difficult. He shrugged and read further. Aqua therapy?

The smart brunette with the long red fingernails came out of the bedroom wearing nothing but a stethoscope.

"Are we done with the photo shoot?" she asked as she slithered over and curled up beside Jack on the couch.

"Yeah," Jack sounded confused.

"What's wrong now baby?" she asked as she began to nibble on his ear.

"Do you know what that means?" he pointed to the words that had him so puzzled.

"Aqua therapy? Sure. That's a type of physical therapy that takes place in a pool," she explained. He still looked clueless. "The water acts as a cushion and reduces the stress that is put on the joints during physical exertion." He still looked clueless. She whispered in his ear, "Let's go fill the bathtub and I'll show you what I mean."

Jack followed the brunette to the bathroom and brought the camera, just in case.

Chapter 30

Clara's Diner was filled to capacity by seven o'clock on Wednesday morning, and a line had formed outside to boot. The news of Robert Prescott's attack had left the already edgy Islanders in near hysteria; even the pacifist lesbian couple that ran the Island's honeybee farm was ready to kick some ass. Clara stood at her griddle flipping pancakes and watching the tears that fell from her cheeks drop onto the hot surface and evaporate in a salty sizzle while Taloy Jobbs sat at the counter staring into a cup of Jamesons that he had cut with a bit of coffee and listened as the crowd grew more hostile by the minute. Just as Father Andrew, God bless him, called upon the demons of hell to rise up and take the soul of the evil bastard that had so violently beaten their fellow Islander, the telephone rang and the diner fell silent. Clara dropped her spatula and answered on the second ring.

"Doc? How is he?" She listened for a moment. "Will he make it?" She listened again. Every Islander was at the edge of his or her seat or stool. "All right, I'll tell them. In your office, yeah, I'll take care of it. Call as soon as you know more." She hung up and sniffled, "he's in critical but stable condition." She used a dishrag to wipe away another tear. "Docs gonna stay with him until he's out of the woods."

The mood quieted for a few minutes until the door swung open and John Beale and Chief Tatum marched in. All heads turned as the Harbor Master announced, "Some little shit on the mainland failed to call in a suspicious car that came over last night on the seven o'clock."

Every Islander fell silent but for Taloy who stared into his cup of Jamesons and asked, "did the car go off on the nine o'clock John?"

The Harbor Master answered, "No."

Taloy looked up, "then he's still here."

"Let's get him," a tree-trunk of a fisherman stood and headed for the exit.

Chief Tatum blocked the doorway. "Hold on there, Jimmy. Let's all relax a minute and think this through." The fisherman ignored the police chief's advice and reached for the door handle, "Prescott might be a nasty little prick, but he's our little prick."

"A lynch mob isn't going to do anything for Prescott," John Beale interjected on the Chief's behalf. "And anyway, this guy isn't alone."

Two more fishermen stood; one stated, "Neither are we."

"He's with his wife, a couple of kids and an old lady," Chief Tatum explained. "Unless you feel like lynching a couple of pre-schoolers, I think you should all do as I say and take a deep breath."

"The Chief is right," Taloy hopped off his stool, pulled a ten-dollar bill out of his pocket and placed it on the counter beside his plate of uneaten eggs. "You boys fuck with this guy and ten more like him will show up tomorrow."

"So what do we do?" the tree trunk asked.

"Nothin," Taloy answered. "Be cordial to our visitors and leave the punishing to the people who know how to do it right."

"Meaning you?" the tree trunk laughed at the pint sized Irishman who, on tiptoe, barely reached his chest.

"Aye, me," the little Irishman laughed back as he placed his hand to his heart. "You see my husky boy, the difference between us Mics and them Dagos is us Mics don't leave em in stable condition." Taloy squeezed past the fishermen and walked to the door where Chief Tatum still stood his ground. Taloy looked to John Beale and then to the Chief and whispered, "He's in that hospital because of me. It will be a clean job I assure you." He patted Chief Tatum on the shoulder, "and I'll do my best to keep it out of your jurisdiction."

Chief Tatum stepped aside.

Pete skipped yet another day of school. He walked into the office of The Tyle Island Conservancy Council at nine a.m. and headed straight for his computer. Abbie had instructed him to do nothing until she returned from Wakefield, but not only was nothing boring, it was unproductive as well. He had other ideas as to how he would spend his morning. He was going to contact his mom.

The idea had come to him during the wee hours of the morning as he lay in bed trying to recall everything his father had told him about his mother, which wasn't a lot. Her name was Priscilla Steele, she was from New York City, she was twenty-two when he was born and only one week older when she abandoned them. During the year that followed his father had tried tracking her down, but he came up dry every time. So he gave up, end of story. Or, Pete considered, was it just the beginning? What would be the first thing someone would do if they didn't want to be found? Pete had asked himself. The answer was obvious; they would change their identity.

The possibility that a woman by the name of Priscilla Des Pierre had brought him into this world had caused Abbie to climb up on a desk and begin choking the Chief of Police. Then there was the semi-catatonic bout of droning during which Abbie had mentioned a whole myriad of names, including Priscillas Steele and Des Pierre, followed by the admission that Priscilla Des Pierre was the maiden name of Priscilla Hardy, wife of the Governor. Then there was the revelation that Hyacinth Poole's house was actually owned by Edward Steele. And finally there was the fact that Hyacinth Poole had been the one to betray Tyle Island by turning over Barron's Hollow to the casino developer. Two plus two plus two plus two could only add up to the theory running through Abbie's brain that Priscilla Steele is Priscilla Hardy and that she is the link between Hyacinth, the Governor, and the casino building Mob.

Now, Pete knew that legitimately proving or disproving such a theory could take forever, and forever he did not have, so he decided to take a more straightforward approach to solving the puzzle. He would operate on the basis that Abbie's theory was correct and drop a line to Mrs. Governor Hardy, a.k.a mom. It would just be a brief 'Hi mom. How have you been? By the way I know you're married to the Governor and I was just wondering if you've seen Hyacinth Poole lately. Would you like to do dinner to discuss or should I tell the others about my suspicions? How does Friday sound? Seven o'clock. You know where to find me. Love always. Your Son, Pete." After all, what harm could it do?

Pete logged onto his computer and listened to a voice advise him that 'he had mail'. He thought about checking the message, then decided that it was probably just a lame joke or piece of porn sent by one of his buddies; he would check it later when he had more time, there were more pressing matters at hand, like obtaining the e-mail address of Massachusetts' First Lady.

The DeLuca family schlepped their blankets, chairs, umbrella, radio, cooler and boogie boards to the beach early that Wednesday morning. The temperature was a chilly sixty degrees and the breeze was blowing in strong off the ocean, but a little adverse weather wasn't going to keep Angela DeLuca from getting a tan. She waded through the pure white sand with her family in tow until she found a seashell-free stretch of beach suitable for soaking up the rays. She then kicked off her red stilettos and peeled off her black stretch pants, revealing a hot pink bikini whose strings struggled to remain tied against the pressure of her bulging girth. Chubby Anna Marie and chubbier Pasquale grabbed their brand new plastic sand buckets and shovels and headed for the waters edge; their Nona followed behind them ever ready to fling holy water at any dirty seagull that dared to venture too close to her grandchildren.

And then there was poor Dino. After making two additional trips back over the sand dunes and out to the car for forgotten suntan lotion (trip number one) and the latest issue of People Magazine (trip number two), he finally plopped his large body onto a small plastic beach chair which immediately buckled under his weight and sent him falling ass-first into the sand. Pasquale and Anna Maria started laughing, Nona started sprinkling, and Angela pointed out that the piece of shit chair had cost eight fucking dollars. Day one on Tyle Island and Dino DeLuca already longed for home.


    Bob Kelly awoke early and asked the armed guard for a breakfast of two eggs sunny side up, an English muffin oozing with butter and a side of corned beef hash. The food came with a copy of the New York Times and a Cuban cigar, both gifts from his anxious host. After finishing his meal, which didn't compare to Clara's, he read the paper front to back, completed the crossword puzzle then, upon entering the bathroom with the intention of showering, noticed a bottle of complimentary bubble bath sitting on the vanity. Kelly realized that never in his life had he taken a bubble bath and since it was quite possible that his life would soon be over, it was high time he gave it a try.

So he fired up the Cuban and lowered himself into the hot, bubbly tub, which he immediately realized was not designed for use by a man of his size. He stared at his pale knees that rose like two hairy mountains out of a thick bubble fog and, while savoring the flavors of premium tobacco, wondered what was taking place beyond the confines of his room. Surely Pete had gotten his e-mail by now. Kelly grinned as he pictured his fellow Islanders clamoring to arrange the details of his latest scheme. Abbie would inevitably play the starring role. Come Friday night, as he and Antonio Gianninni sailed along the western coast of Tyle Island with their eyes fixed on Madonna's Cove, Abbie would appear on the beach, a veil of blue flowing in the soft breeze and her angelic face framed in the moonlight. It would be a miracle, Kelly blew a smoke ring and watched it disappear, a miracle that Antonio Gianninni would surely want to protect.

## Chapter 31

Crosswinds made for a bumpy landing at the Wakefield Airport, which made Tyle Island's airfield seem like JFK. Tom Taylor, a pilot from the mainland and long time friend of the Kelly's, taxied to the end of the short runway and dropped Abbie off in front of an old trailer that acted as the airport's offices. A hand painted sign nailed to a door that was hanging onto the trailer by one rusty hinge read, Please Check In. Abbie thanked her pilot for his services; he agreed to return at four to take her home.

As she watched the airplane taxi back down the runway and take off into the crisp New England sky Abbie realized that she was all alone in the middle of nowhere in search of a man she had never met and more importantly, who probably didn't want to be found. "How do I get myself into these situations?" she asked herself as she approached the trailer. "I mean seriously Abbie, you couldn't be more ill prepared." She was so busy reprimanding herself that she failed to hear the sound of dogs barking. Large dogs barking - with menacing voices. And the source of the barking seemed to be drawing closer. She looked to her left just in time to catch a glimpse of two Rottweilers the size of water buffalo racing toward her; they were no more than thirty yards away. She made a mad dash for the trailer… twenty yards…fumbled with the door knob which dangled like the hinge…ten yards…swung open the door…five yards…stepped in, slammed the door behind her, closed her eyes and leaned on the thin piece of plywood praying that all 125 of her pounds would withstand the impact of three hundred plus pounds of growling, frothing, drooling dog.

"Can I help you Sugar?" she heard a woman ask in drawl that sounded as if it had its origins from somewhere deep below the Mason Dixon Line.

Abbie kept her eyes closed and her teeth gritted as she pushed with all her might against the door, "There's a pair of monsters trying to kill me."

"The puppies?" The woman pooh-poohed her concern, "honey they don't want to hurt you. They just want to play."

"I think we're talking about different monsters." Abbie opened her eyes and pushed harder.

"Were they Rottweilers?" the woman asked.

"Oh yeah," Abbie answered as she braced for impact.

"That's just Lucy and Ethel. My babies."

"I don't mean to be rude, but your babies tried to kill me."

"Don't be silly." The tall slender woman with big bouffant hair walked out from around the counter and asked Abbie to step aside. She opened the door and hollered in a sing-song way, "Lucy –Ethel," then made the kissing noise that is usually reserved for getting the attention of a cuddly kitten entangled in a ball of yarn. The Rottweilers bounded out from the side of the trailer in response to her call. "Have you ladies been naughty?" she lectured in the same sing-song voice. "Did you frighten our guest?" The Rottweilers fell onto their sides and rolled over onto their backs in anticipation of a satisfying tummy rub. "You see," she pointed to her beasts, "as sweet as shoe fly pie. Now Sugar what can I do for you?"

Abbie's heart rate gradually slowed to twice the normal rhythm and she managed to verbalize that she was looking for a pilot.

"Big mistake Sugar." The woman waved a dismissive hand as she made her way back to her counter, "pilots are like poison, once they get into your system," she closed her eyes and gave a playful shudder, "you're never quite the same."

The presence of this bizarre woman in this bizarre place amazed Abbie. "I can't help but notice that you don't have a New England accent."

"Heck, I'm no Yankee. I'm from Peachtree Georgia," the woman responded with pride. "I was voted Miss Peachpit when I was just eighteen years old."

"Congratulations."

"Then I married a Navy pilot when I was nineteen, ooh that man got under my skin something fierce. Well anyway, a year later he got a dishonorable discharge from the military so we packed our bags and moved up here where my honey pie was born and bred. That was ten years ago and you would think that living and working in these God forsaken boondocks would make me want to hightail it right back to Peachtree but ooh Lordy, no sooner am I set to run when that man of mine takes me up in his plane and shows me how to fly and all of a sudden Peachtree Georgia seems light years away. The name's Scarlet Newbaker," the woman held out her hand for Abbie to shake.

Abbie just stared. Scarlet Newbaker was a very attractive woman, a cross between That Girl and Jackie O. Some quick math put her at twenty-nine years of age, just a few years younger than herself, but unlike Abbie the native New Yorker, this woman oozed Mint Julep and grits. Her skin was flawless and not one strand of her chestnut hair was out of place. It stood six inches too high for Abbie's taste, but on Scarlet Newbaker it worked.

"What's wrong with you honey?" the Southern Bell asked. "Are my eyelashes on crooked or something?"

"No, not at all. I'm sorry," Abbie apologized for her breech of etiquette. "I just have a lot on my mind."

"Your pilot," Scarlet raised a knowing brow.

"Exactly."

"Let me guess," she reached for a pot of coffee and two Styrofoam cups, "he's got another woman playing in his cockpit."

Abbie hesitated. What would be easier, telling Scarlet the truth, which she herself wasn't one hundred percent sure of, or going along with the scorned woman chasing after her cheating man scenario? Abbie accepted a cup of coffee and opted for what was behind door number two.

"It's hard for a girl to admit," she forced a sniffle, "but I think he's having an affair."

Scarlet placed a sympathetic hand on Abbie's shoulder, "Oh Sugar I'm so sorry. How can I help?"

Those words were music to Abbie's ears. She began to spin a tale of how her fiancé, she flashed her engagement ring for credibility, had left a few weeks back for a job bush piloting in Alaska. He had told her he would be gone for two months and when he returned they would be married. But then she started hearing rumors that Danny had a girlfriend on the side; a rich girlfriend, a rich married girlfriend. And then, sniffle, sniffle, she heard from another pilot that Dan's plane had been spotted at this airport. And to top it all off, she found out that the other woman owned a house not more than five miles from this very spot.

"A tall man?" Scarlet asked.

Bob was tall and Pete was tall so Dan would presumably be tall as well. Abbie nodded.

"Dark hair and dreamboat eyes?"

Abbie imagined a blend between Bob and Pete. Again she nodded.

"You know Sugar, maybe you should sit down." Scarlet took Abbie by the hand and led her around the counter to her desk. Once Abbie was seated she blurted out, "You poor thing, he was here, and you're right, he was with a woman."

Abbie nearly jumped out of the chair with excitement, and then she remembered that devastation was the more appropriate reaction to the news. "What did she look like?" Abbie asked.

"Well it was hard to tell behind them big ole sunglasses she was wearing but let me tell you she was dressed to the nines. The reflection off the diamonds in her ears nearly blinded me."

Abbie sighed. "I have to be sure."

"We'll Sugar his plane is still parked out back. Has been for a while now. Paid a good penny for us to keep an eye on her."

"May I see?"

"Come on, I'll take you myself."

The two women exited the trailer, being careful not to knock the door from its last surviving hinge. Abbie immediately tensed up when Lucy and Ethel bounded up to them but Scarlet took her by the hand and introduced her new friend to her old puppies. Abbie patted each water buffalo on the monstrous head and watched them fall onto their sides and roll over on their backs in response to the affection; she subsequently rubbed their tummies. The foursome then headed out behind the trailer to a clearing that held several small planes. Scarlet pointed to one about twenty yards away, "Is that her?"

Abbie took a quick look at the serial numbers; it was a match. She trotted up to the plane to peek inside but it was clean, no signs of having transported Hyacinth Poole or anyone else.

"I don't mean to me insensitive to your pain Sugar, but can I ask you a personal question?"

"Of course," Abbie answered as they headed back toward the trailer.

Scarlet hemmed and hawed then blurted out, "Is your man a little kinky?"

Abbie wasn't sure where Scarlet was going with this but she was sure as hell interested in finding out. "No. Why do you ask?"

"Well him and his rich chicky, they weren't alone."

"They weren't?"

"No, they were toting around an old lady. Now I try not to judge, you know to each his own and all, but she was eighty if she was a day and that's just plain icky."

"How were they behaving?" Abbie was chomping at the bit.

"What do you mean?"

"Were they all friendly, or did the mood seem...tense."

"Well you know I tried to give the poor old woman a glass of water, she looked so tired and frail, but that no good rich girl would have no part of it. Kept bossing her around saying 'come on Hyacinth we don't have time'."

"Hyacinth?" Abbie felt faint. "Are you sure absolutely sure she called her Hyacinth?"

"Sure I'm sure. A girl from Peachtree knows her flowers. I even complimented her on having such a pretty name."

"Scarlet," Abbie stopped walking; Lucy and Ethel settled in at her feet, "I haven't been totally honest with you."

"You haven't?"

"No. And you've been so kind to me that you deserve the truth as best as I know it."

"Well go on Sugar," Scarlet seemed ready for anything, "fess up."

"The pilot's name is Dan Kelly. I believe that the woman he was with is Priscilla Hardy, the Governor's wife, and the old lady Hyacinth, I think she's been kidnapped by the two of them."

Scarlet raised a hand to shield her eyes from the morning sun and asked, "Well is he at least your fiancé?"

"No," Abbie shook her head, "we've never actually met. But I am in love with his brother. I'm very sorry I lied to you." Her shoulders slumped as the guilt ridden Abbie began to slink back toward the trailer with Lucy and Ethel romping playfully at her side.

"Wait a sec Sugar there's no need to rush off," Scarlet called out after her. She hurried to catch up then took Abbie by the arm and walked along side. "I don't mind a little white lie from time to time. But tell me, is that story of yours for real? 'Cus it sounds like the plot of a mystery book."

Abbie grinned. "Thank you Scarlet."

"For what?"

"For not saying it sounds like a soap opera."

"Oh please, you're just talking about a kidnapping. You would need affairs, bastard children, blackmail and maybe even a murder to sound anything like a soap opera."

Abbie introduced herself. "Scarlet Newbaker, I'm Abbie O'Neal."

"Well Abbie O'Neal, it just so happens that I know where the Governor's house is located, so what do you say you and I go peek in the windows and see what we see?"

Chapter 32

Scarlet parked her Cherry Red '69 convertible Mustang a quarter mile or so down the road from the Governor's house and she, Abbie, Lucy and Ethel hopped out. The dogs were brought along as an excuse for trespassing as much as for protection; two helpless women trying to subdue their run away dogs was a perfect alibi for venturing onto private property. The women crept through the woods heading due north until they spotted the house.

"That's the one," Scarlet whispered.

"Do you think we can get around back?" Abbie, feeling like an urban fish out of water, asked the woman from Peachtree who surely grew up climbing trees and hopping fences.

"We can sure give it a try," Scarlet sounded upbeat despite having spent the last few minutes lamenting a sap stain on her new khaki capris. "But be careful to hug the tree line, they can probably see us from this distance."

Lucy and Ethel watched with canine curiosity as the two humans darted from tree to tree, advancing, pausing, and advancing again. Abbie fell twice along the way while Scarlet managed to survive injury free but for a slight reduction in the height of her doo. The two spies and their drooling companions settled in behind a towering pine to catch their breaths and determine their next move.

"Abbie Sugar?"

"Yes Scarlet?"

"If the people in that house don't know who you are, why are we sneaking around?"

Abbie pulled a wayward piece of pinecone from her hair. "There just may be the wife of a government official in there with a woman whom she kidnapped and a large, presumably strong man who assisted her. They might be edgy. I prefer to sneak."

"That's a fine point." Scarlet patted Abbie on the back as if proud of her insight, "so what should we do?"

Abbie scouted the area. The distance from the edge of the forest to the back deck of the house was about thirty feet. Abbie noticed that the sliding glass door was open. Only a short sprint and a screen door stood between her and Hyacinth Poole.

"I'm going to sneak up to that back window and look inside."

"Oh Sugar, are you sure you should do that?"

"We've come this far, I can't turn back now."

Abbie gave Scarlet a thumbs-up and, staying low to avoid being spotted, scrambled out across the lawn. Lucy and Ethel, considering this a new form of play, scrambled with her. Abbie stopped in mid-scramble and whispered, "stay." Both dogs sat. "Good girls," Abbie praised them before continuing on. She took ten more steps and made it to the deck unnoticed.

Her heart was racing and her senses on high alert as she crouched beside the wooden steps. As she collected her thoughts and prepared to mount the stairs, she sensed movement from behind; every muscle in her body tensed, the presence was just inches away. Though she was known to watch horror movies with one hand covering her eyes, and had more than once been ejected from a theater for yelling at the mindless ingénue not to go down the basement steps, Abbie couldn't help but ever so slowly turn around, and look fate directly in the eye.

Four eyes looked back. Lucy and Ethel just loved playing this odd human game. Scarlet, sensing Abbie's growing frustration over her dogs, scooted out of the woods, across the lawn and joined the three of them at the deck.

"I'm so sorry Sugar," she whispered, "They think you're playing."

"Scarlet?"

"Yes, Sugar."

"You should be back in the woods."

"I know Sugar but I was getting jittery being all by myself out there and then I realized that I've got to tinkle."

Abbie closed her eyes, "why didn't you just go?"

"Out there?"

"Yes."

"Excuse me, but I'm a lady. If it ever got back to the folks in Peachtree that Scarlet Newbaker tinkled behind a tree, let me tell you, I would just die."

"Well you can't ask to use the bathroom."

"Why not? Wouldn't that be as good an excuse as any to get inside? We can say we were out walking our dogs when I was overcome by the need to tinkle and may I please borrow your powder room? I won't be but a minute."

Abbie thought a moment then agreed, "That might actually work."

"Do you need to tinkle too?" Scarlet asked.

"No."

"Alrighty then, I'll go first."

And before Abbie had a chance to stop her, Scarlet was up the deck stairs and knocking on the sliding glass door to the Governor's ski house. To Abbe's great relief no one answered. To Abbie's great dismay Scarlet let out a "yoo-hoo, anyone home" that could have been heard clear as day in the next county. Abbie instantly rethought this entire search and rescue mission, realized it was a tad bit insane and bounded up the steps to drag Scarlet away. But just as she grabbed Scarlet by the sleeve of her powder blue cotton cardigan a slightly younger, slightly taller version of Bob Kelly slid open the screen door.

"Well hello there Sugar," Scarlet turned on her southern charm, "remember me?"

Oh my God, Abbie was floored by the resemblance; she now understood why Pete looked so much like his Uncle, his father did too. Dan Kelly took a moment to assess the two strange women standing uninvited on his back deck then, finally recognizing Scarlet, he replied, "From the airport?"

"That's right Sugar, you've got quite a memory."

He flashed the Kelly killer grin. Oh yeah that's him, Abbie thought as Dan responded, "You're a hard woman to forget."

"I'm sorry to bother you honey, but my friend and I were out trekking through the woods when I was suddenly overcome by the need to tinkle. Being a lady I didn't want to soil my reputation by relieving myself in the wild, so I was just wondering if you would be so kind as to allow me the use of your facilities."

Dan hesitated. "I'm sorry I can't let you in."

"Oh Sugar it'll just take a sec." Scarlet batted her eyelashes and swept her hand playfully across his bare forearm.

"Give me a minute," he instructed, then closed the screen door and disappeared inside.

"Oh Abbie Sugar, if his brother looks anything like him, you are one lucky girl."

"He is gorgeous." Abbie paused. "And Bob does look just like him." She paused again. "Bob's actually better looking." Her focus blurred for a moment, recalling that devilish Cary Grant raise of an eyebrow that had first caught Abbie's wandering eye, but then she remembered that her Kelly could very well be dead, never to raise a devilish eyebrow again and the people responsible were quite possibly inside that house. The blood of the scorned soap opera writer began a slow, steady boil.

"So what's our next step?" Scarlet asked.

Abbie sprung into action. "He won't let us in if Priscilla is here so if he OKs your pee break, they're probably alone. I want you to look for the old lady while I deal with Dan. If you find her, verify that her name is Hyacinth Poole and ask if she's being held against her will. Tell her that Tyle Island is falling to pieces without her and we've come to take her home."

"It's as good as done," Scarlet whispered just as Dan returned.

"You can come in," he slid opened the screen door, "but please make it quick."

Scarlet and Abbie entered the house which did not possess what one would call a woodsy feel. It was as if someone had thrown up post-modern-minimalism all over the place. Typical new money, Abbie shook her head in dismay, all cash, no breeding. Then Abbie wondered about the source of the wealth that had mis-decorated the log cabin in late nineties chic. Was all this kitsch bought with blood money? Abbie felt her blood pressure begin to rise.

"The bathroom is just past the kitchen," Dan pointed the way.

Scarlet headed off, and just as he was about to follow, Abbie declared, "Scarlet is a big girl Dan, I think she pee on her own."

"Do I know you?" Dan Kelly's handsome face grew grim.

"Nope." She picked up a piece of black art glass and checked the bottom for an artists mark. There was none - mass produced, it figured. "But I know you."

"Really." His tone was rightfully suspicious.

He may have his brother's looks, Abbie thought, but he sure doesn't share his gift for intelligent banter. His brother whom she loved. His brother who was probably lying at the bottom of the Manasquan River with cement blocks tied to his feet.

"Well, if we're being literal I don't actually know you per say, but I know your brother and I know your son and I know all the people on Tyle Island who for some misguided reason consider you to be their friend."

"What are you talking about?" Dan's mouth denied knowledge but his eyes said 'oh shit.'

Abbie smirked, a man's eyes reveal all. "What amazes me is how everyone on Tyle Island considers a son of a bitch like you to be the good Kelly, and a man like Bob to be the bad."

"Who are you?" Dan approached her in a manner that, from where Abbie stood, appeared threatening.

"Abbie O'Neal," she placed her hands on her hips, raised her chin and responded defiantly, "I've come to liberate the Widow Poole."

"Well then Abbie O'Neal," Dan Kelly grabbed her by the wrist, "you wasted a trip."

A combination of pain and shock caused Abbie to squeal. This was a high-pitched squeal. The kind of high-pitched squeal that only dogs can hear. And they heard. Before Dan knew what was happening, Lucy and Ethel crashed through the screen door and charged the large human who was hurting the nice woman who had scratched their tummies and let them play her funny human game. Fur flew, drool flew, a piece of Dan Kelly's flannel shirt flew as the puppies made the point that their new friend should not be mishandled. The melee would have gone on indefinitely if Scarlet hadn't rushed in and made the kittenish kissing noise that called off the dogs. Lucy and Ethel returned to Scarlet's side and enjoyed a long bout of tummy rubbing while Dan Kelly lay on his back, slightly bloodied and very much prone.

"So Dan," Abbie looked down upon her prisoner, "where is she?" He did not respond. "Scarlet, would you please do me a favor and search the place?"

"Sure thing Sugar." Scarlet spent the next several minutes running from room to room checking under beds and inside closets for anything that resembled a little old lady. She came up empty; no Hyacinth Poole.

Again Abbie asked the question, "Where is she Dan?" Again he remained silent. The avenging soap opera writer was losing her patience. "Hey Scarlet."

"Yes Sugar?"

"Do you watch soap operas?"

"You betcha."

"Do you watch the Darkest Hour?"

"Who doesn't?"

"Remember the incident that took place about a year ago between Clarice and Blake when she found out that he had an affair."

"Sure do."

"Dig through those drawers and find me some tweezers and a ball of twine."

"You're not gonna?" Scarlet sounded both thrilled and appalled.

"Oh yes I am."

Scarlet got to digging.

"Now Dan, as you've probably already surmised I'm not in the mood to play games. In the past few days I have had little sleep, which has left me irritable, and it is safe to say that your continued belligerence will in no way help to raise my spirits. Lucy and Ethel are lap dogs compared to me when I'm cranky, and I assure you that I am getting very cranky. Any luck there Scarlet?" Abbie called out.

"No tweezers or twine, but I've got pinking shears and a roll of duct tape."

"That'll do, bring them over." Scarlet practically skipped her way into the room. "All right Dan this is your last chance to save yourself from some major discomfort." Abbie opened and closed the scissors for effect. "I already know that Hyacinth Poole fraudulently turned over Barron's Hollow to the casino developers who plan to build on Tyle Island. I also know that you flew the get-away plane that took Hyacinth and the other Council members off Island. If my instincts are correct, which they usually are, I'm pretty sure that Priscilla Hardy is the brains behind the whole operation. So the only point I need you to clarify is where the hell can I find The Widow Poole?"

Dan did not reply. Big mistake.

## Chapter 33

Bob Kelly ordered another t-bone for lunch, deciding that if he was going to die he might as well die well nourished. His food arrived during the second commercial break of The Darkest Hour. He had been watching intently, awaiting the scene that Abbie had added between Doctor Idiot and the old man Mr. G. It came in the closing moments, just as Kelly had started on his cheesecake.

    Mr. G: (With a thick New York accent) Doc, I don't know how to thank you for bringing back my memory. I'm a wealthy man. I have power. Is there any way I can repay you?
    Dr. B: (with an intense look that, to Kelly, seemed more like a battle with constipation than deep thought) As a matter of fact Mr. G, there is something you can do for me.
    Mr. G: Name it.
    Camera pulls a tight close-up on Mr. G's face as Doctor Jasper Black utters.
    Dr. B: You can tell me where to find Hyacinth Poole's child?
    "Holy shit she really did it," Kelly yelped as he raised a cheesecake-covered fork in triumph.
    Mr. G: I, I, I don't know what you're talking about. (Beads of perspiration shimmer off the old Man's bald head.)
    Dr. B: (A tight close-up on Dr. Blacks' face - his electric blue eyes still looked constipated) You can't hide behind your amnesia any longer Mr. G. It's time to come clean. Lives are at stake. (His voice rises with anger) Tell me, where is her child?
    Mr. G: (Closes his eyes) You're right Doc. There have been too many lies for too long, but I can't

tell you. (He opens his eyes and looks directly into the camera) I must tell Abbie.
Show over. Fade to black.

   There was nothing quite as unappetizing as watching the DeLuca family eat lunch. Tartar sauce dripped from their mouths and chunks of fried cod fish were spat across the table as they argued loudly and crudely without first swallowing their food. Chubby Pasquale squeezed whole handfuls of French-fries into tight potato balls before shoveling them into his already overstuffed mouth. Billy Prior, the owner of The Nest, who was both appalled and frightened by the feeding frenzy, telephoned Clara at the Diner and insisted she rush right over to witness the display. She arrived just in time to sees chubby Anna Marie, at barely five years of age, ingesting an entire foot long hot dog in four gargantuan bites.
   "HELL has come early this season," Billy commented as he mixed up a couple of Bloody Mary's, heavy on the Absolut.
   "This is only a glimpse of what's to come if we don't stop that damn casino." Clara accepted her drink, removed the celery stalk, dropped it on the bar and drank.
   "Do you really think we can pull it off?"
   "To be honest Billy, up until this morning I wasn't sure. But after seeing those fellas at the diner getting all worked up over Prescott, I get the feeling that come hell or high water we will win this war."
   "It may be a bloody battle."
   "It already is."
   They sipped their drinks and watched Angela DeLuca dismember a lobster with her bare hands then lean her head back and allow the juices to pour out of a claw and into her cavernous mouth.
Billy winced at the image. "You know who has surprised me the most?"
   "Kelly?"

He nodded. "A week ago he was a grouchy bastard who barely opened his mouth, and when he did it was only to order a scotch or say something sarcastic. Now he's a hero. What do you think caused the change?"

"Loneliness."

"Loneliness?" Billy looked skeptical. "How do you mean?"

Clara took a long, slow sip of her drink before explaining herself. "Somebody famous, I don't know who exactly, once said that writing is the most solitary of professions."

"Yeah. So." Billy wasn't following.

"Think about, for twenty years it was just Kelly and his typewriter."

"He must have had friends."

"He wrote twenty books in twenty years, and they weren't trashy books Billy, they were bestsellers. I'd be surprised if Kelly had time to go to the bathroom let alone go out and form friendships."

"So you're saying that Kelly is risking his ass because he wants to be liked?"

"That, and I think he wants to like himself as well."

"That's very profound Clara." Billy took a sip. "I would have figured that he was just doing it to get into Abbie O'Neal's pants."

"Oh don't get me wrong Billy, I'm not saying that cute little figure of hers didn't play a part in the change, but I doubt any man, let alone Bob Kelly, would go head to head with a mobster just to get a piece of ass. Nope that Abbie has shown our Bob that there's more to life than a warm bed and a bottle of booze. He's in love and I'll tell you something if you can keep a secret." She leaned in close knowing damn well Billy Prior could never keep a secret. "According to Tatum, she loves him right back."

Billy raised his glass, "To love."

"And war," Clara clinked his glass with hers, "an unbeatable combination."

John Beale ferried to the mainland with Doc Gno's package. The address label was made out to The Center for Disease Control in Atlanta Georgia; it was being sent to the attention of Dr. Lorraine Macy. The Doc had telephoned from Prescott's hospital room and given him strict instructions to personally take the package to the Federal Express Office on Route 2 and request priority-overnight-super rush-needed it yesterday service. Next Tuesday was fast approaching and if they were to keep construction workers off of Tyle Island, they would need quarantine posted a.s.a.p.

The telephone at the Old Boat House rang at 2:02pm. It would have rung earlier if Vincent Gianninni had not wasted two minutes locating Abbie's number and wheeling himself to the phone. He got the answering machine, so he hung up, and dialed again, and got the answering machine again. This went on until 2:37 when Vincent's arthritic dialing finger finally gave out. So he wheeled himself out of the bedroom and to the top of the stairs where he hollered down to Fric and Frac seated in their armchairs to get their useless asses upstairs fast. Fric, the leaner of the two goons, beat Frac up the steps. Vincent handed him the piece of paper with Abbie's telephone number on it. "Get me the address that matches that number."

"You got it boss," Fric answered, as Frac, the heavier of the two finally made it huffing and puffing up the steps.

"And don't mention a word of this to my boys. You do, and you're dead."

"Yes boss."

Fric headed off down the steps while Frac remained behind, huffing and puffing, to continue guarding Mr. G.

## Chapter 34

Dan Kelly sat on the bathroom floor with his Levis around his ankles that were, like his hands, bound together with duct tape. His entire chest and half of a leg were now hairless thanks to the application then speedy removal of duct tape from skin. It hadn't been until Scarlet rather giddily stripped him down to his boxers and threatened the crown jewels with a squeeze of the pinking shears that he began to talk.

"Jesus Christ, you women are nuts," he screamed as the cold metal scissors brushed against his nether regions.

"That's true," Abbie agreed from her seat on the toilet, "and you sir, will soon be nutless."

"You know Sugar," Scarlet interjected, "I'm sure the puppies could bury these little fellas somewhere out in the woods." Lucy and Ethel, who were dozing in the bathtub, whimpered as if they knew they were being discussed.

"Good idea Scarlet, eliminate the evidence."

"And we've got turkey vultures around these parts that could pick this beautiful body clean in ten minutes flat if we need to dispose of the rest of him as well."

"Scarlet my friend, you are truly an asset to this investigation."

"Thank you Sugar," she smiled, closed her false eye-lashed eyes and began to squeeze.

"Ok, enough," Dan yelled. "Hyacinth is with Priscilla. They're at the Governor's Mansion."

"That would be Priscilla as in Priscilla Steele-Des Pierre-Hardy?" Abbie asked.

"Yes."

"Pete's mother?"

"Yes."

"You flew the council members off Island?"

He nodded.

"Where are they now?"

"I don't know."

"Are they alive?"

"Of course." He seemed appalled by her implication to the contrary.

"Are you sure?" Abbie asked. Dan thought a moment then looked away. Abbie took his chin in her hand and forced him to look at her. "What does Priscilla have on you Dan?"

He spoke through gritted teeth, "I can't say."

Abbie let go of his handsome face, smacked him squarely on the back of the head and leaned back on the toilet. "You know Scarlet, that is a lovely sweater you're wearing, I would hate to see it get ruined." She stood, stepped over Dan and draped a lavender bath towel around Scarlet's powder blue cardigan. "I imagine that the blood from those little guys will spurt quite a distance."

"Thank you Sugar, that's very considerate. Now stand back, I don't want you getting caught in the crossfire."

Every muscle in Dan's hairless body tensed and just as Scarlet was about to clamp down on the pinking shears he whispered, "I can't lose my son."

"Did you say something?" Abbie asked.

"He said he can't lose his son," Scarlet helped out.

"Oh, did he?" Abbie knelt beside Dan and placed an arm around his shoulder. "Priscilla is married to the Governor. Stepping forward to reclaim a child whom you abandoned seventeen years ago is not a wise political move. She knows that, you know that, and I know that. You've got ten seconds to come up with the truth."

"She won't take him, she'll destroy him."

"How?"

He closed his eyes.

"How?" she repeated as Scarlet applied cold metal scissors to warm inner thigh for effect.

"She'll tell Pete that I'm not his father."

Abbie laughed. "Priscilla told you that you weren't Pete's father and you believed her? What are you a moron? The kid is the spitting image of you. Who else could be his father?"

A pregnant pause followed during which Abbie added up two and two and got…"oh shit".

She stood and leaned on the sink for support. She took a deep breath and looked in the mirror. There were large bags under her once bright eyes and her shiny hair was matted with tree sap and pine needles. What the hell are you doing here Abbie? She asked her weary reflection. What has happened to you? Have you totally lost your mind? Those are real scissors and real balls and this is really the Governor's house. You need to leave. You need to drive back to the airport with Scarlet and her dogs and beg her husband to fly you home, home as in Manhattan, not Tyle Island. You need to stop off at a spa and spend a few hours getting pampered and primped then you need to meet Jack for dinner at Po and eat putanesca sauce until it spills out of your ears. Then you need to return to your luxury apartment and have sex with your highly desirable fiancé, and in the morning, after having sex again, you need to go to work, write yourself a soap opera and live happily ever after.

"Abbie Sugar," Scarlet's voice broke the spell, "are you feeling all right?"

Abbie glanced over at her new friend with her now defunct bouffant spilling down into her eyes who was still holding Dan Kelly's testicles hostage, and a small smile began to form on her beleaguered face. She looked at the three hundred pound lump of dog snoring merrily away in the Governor's bathtub and the naked, half-hairless man sitting on the ceramic tile floor. Then she looked back at her reflection and watched her small smile grow wider. "You haven't lost it Abbie," she whispered, "you're a soap opera writer, and everyone knows that soap opera writers don't know the first thing about happily ever after.

So, to hell with Manhattan, and Jack, and the job and the pampering, the clock is ticking and you've got an Island to save." Her grin stretched from sappy ear to sappy ear.

"As a matter of fact, Scarlet," Abbie slipped her engagement ring off of her finger and tucked it into the pocket of her jeans, "I have never felt better." She then turned to address her potential future brother-in-law by asking, "Does Bob know that Pete is his son?"

Dan shook his head.

"Your Bob?" Scarlet sounded puzzled.

Abbie nodded.

"Your Bob has a seventeen year old son?"

Abbie shrugged.

"Oh Sugar, you are way too young to be playing stepmom to a teen age boy."

"Scarlet?"

"Yes Sugar?"

"Would you excuse us for a moment?"

"Sure thing." She dropped her scissors and left the room.

Abbie took a seat on the edge of the bathtub. "You know Dan, this isn't really a big deal." She drummed her fingers on Lucy's massive head as she contemplated this latest plot twist; the dog let out a tired snort in response to the attention. After a good minute or so Abbie came to the astute conclusion that, "I'm sorry I was wrong, this really is a big deal."

"No shit."

"And I'm not looking at this from your perspective. Although I'm sympathetic toward the possibility of you losing your son, I'm more concerned about Pete's reaction to learning that Bob is his biological father. I've sensed some tension in their relationship and have witnessed what one who has gone through many years of therapy might call an unhealthy family dynamic."

"They hate each other."

"Precisely." Abbie leaned forward placing her elbows

on her knees, "Do you mind if I ask what caused the friction in the first place?"

"You won't believe me."

"Two weeks ago I wouldn't have believed that I'd be sitting in the Governor's bathroom threatening a mans private parts with a pair of pinking shears in order to get him to spill his guts about an eighty-year-old lady on the lam. Try me."

So Dan explained. "Pete and I went to the docks to meet my brother the day he moved back home. You have to understand that the kid spent his whole life idolizing his Uncle the famous writer. Well, Bob must have christened his retirement with a bottle of scotch, because when he stumbled off the ferry he walked right past us. Pete called out to him, Bob asked who he was, and when Pete said that he was his nephew Bob told him that he looked more like his fucking niece. Then he told Pete to cut his hair, leaned over and puked."

"Ouch." Abbie, recalling her original meeting with Bob, had no trouble envisioning the altercation.

"Pete responded with something like 'go to hell you drunk bastard', which I couldn't really blame him for, then Bob countered with his own line of insults. Not exactly the family reunion I had been hoping for."

"I admit it was an awkward moment, but eventually Bob sobered-up. Didn't he apologize?"

"Are you sure you know my brother?"

"Cranky, sarcastic, quick-witted, looks just like you but with chest hair?"

"You know my brother."

"So it's because of a few drunken insults that they don't speak?"

"Neither will give in. They're both stubborn to the core."

"Well, if it makes you feel any better they seem to be bonding."

"Really?" Dan's furrowed brow showed the depth of

his skepticism.

Abbie nodded, "Yeah, they burnt down the Widow Poole's house together."

"Really?" he grinned.

"Really."

"Well good for them," he responded with family pride.

Abbie considered telling Dan about his missing brother, but something told her that he would chew through the duct tape, pull up his Levis and head straight for the airport if he knew the truth, and while that course of action would have been appreciated a half hour earlier, it didn't jive with the plan know brewing within her twisted little mind.

"Dan, if you're willing to sit tight and do exactly as I say, we may be able to get you out of this mess with your family intact."

"I'll do anything."

"Good." Abbie looked up and saw Scarlet standing in the doorway. "What about you?"


Jack West finished taping early. He had lunch with his new costar, the aqua therapist, and the two headed back to his place for some rehearsal. He liked Bambi and was pleased that she would be his new love interest. After all, she was prettier than Nurse Rhonda, and more than willing to go back to his apartment to rehearse their first love scene scheduled to shoot the next day.


Megan got out of court early, and with no other appointments scheduled for the afternoon decided to swing by Abbie's place to pick up the little black strapless for her date with the Giant. She checked her purse to make sure she had the key; sure enough it was still on her key ring. She hailed a cab and headed downtown.

John Beale stopped in at the office of Tyle Navigation before boarding the ferry back home to inform the administrative staff that the union dockworkers would be going on strike the next day.

Clara drove past Mildred Ahearn who was standing in the tall grass along West Side Road. She pulled over her pick-up truck and jogged back thirty yards to where Mildred stood. "Are you all right Mildred?" she hollered as she approached.
"Who the hell is that?"
"It's Clara. What's wrong?"
"Somethin' ate my god damn shoe."
Clara bent down to examine what had Mildred in such a pickle. The laces of her black high top Con were wound around a road spike. "Oh Mildred, you could have gotten hurt."
"What the hell is down there?"
"You're stuck on some spikes Joe Morgan put together to stretch across the road when the construction trucks come over."
"Well unstick me goddammit."
Clara worked the shoelace off of the spike. "All done," she yelled. "Why don't you let me take you home?"
"I can't go home," Mildred argued, "I got work to do?"
"Still looking for Hyacinth?"
"Yup. She's dead. I'm sure of it."
"I hope you're wrong."
"I ain't wrong. Now move along, that perfume of yours is confusing my nose."
"You want to have dinner with me tonight?" Clara asked.
"What you cooking?"
"Whatever you like."

"Bluefish. I can smell them running."

"Then blues it is. I'll see you tonight."

"I sure as hell won't see you," Mildred mumbled as she made her way along the side of the road, sniffing for decaying carcasses and prodding the brush with her shotgun.

## Chapter 35

Having thoroughly enjoyed his soak in the bubble bath, Kelly decided to give the complimentary lemon verbena facial treatment a try. With the television tuned to Oprah and a mound of pillows propped behind him for support, he lounged in the king sized bed while allowing the healing properties of the herbal mask to rejuvenate his sun-damaged skin. There was a soft knock on the door then, "Mr. Kelly," the now familiar voice spoke, "may I have a word with you?"

"Come on in," Kelly called out. Gianninni opened the door and peeked in; a wide grin spread across the mobster's face when he saw Kelly relaxing in his white hotel bathrobe, navy blue dress socks and bright yellow mask. "What can I do for you Tony?" Kelly asked. Another Cuban cigar that had been sent up with lunch remained clenched between his teeth as he spoke.

Gianninni stepped in and closed the door behind him. Then, as an afterthought, he engaged the privacy lock. "I'm glad to see that you are taking full advantage of the amenities."

"Have you tried this stuff?" Kelly held up the half empty tube, "it's fabulous."

"I've been told." Antonio approached the bed.

"Now I know why women pay so much to get slathered with mud and wrapped in seaweed."

"Relaxing?"

Kelly took a deep drag on his cigar then blew out a smoke ring. "I feel as if I don't have a care in the world."

"I'd give anything to have that feeling." Gianninni let out a dramatic sigh.

"Rough day?"

The mobster nodded.

"Come," Kelly patted the mattress, "sit down and tell me all about it."

Gianninni removed his black leather wing tips and joined Kelly on the bed. "What are you watching?" he gestured toward the television.

"Oprah."

"I know its Oprah. Who is her guest?"

"It's make-over day." Kelly explained, "All of these women are either terminally ill, survivors of spousal abuse or struggling to support twelve kids on $8.50 an hour, so Oprah is treating them to a make-over. New hair, wardrobe, the works."

"Why?"

"Apparently it's good for the self-esteem. The better you look, the better you feel."

"I always look flawless, but I rarely feel well."

Kelly took another long drag on his cigar, exhaled and asked, "Why do you think that is?"

Antonio reached for a stray pillow and gave it a fluff. "Can I trust you to keep a secret?"

Kelly looked around the empty room. "Who would I tell?"

Antonio paused then casually confessed, "I've been doing a great deal of soul searching lately and it seems that I am no longer satisfied with my position."

"Owning a casino doesn't make you happy?"

"Not that position; the other position."

"Oh."

"To be honest Bob, I can't recall ever being truly happy. I've always felt like a fish out of water. In countless ways my life and I just don't fit."

"For example?"

"I don't like tomato sauce."

"No shit?"

"I abhor the stuff. I ask you, what Italian hates their Momma's gravy?"

Kelly studied Antonio's soft features and noticed for the first time that he had hazel eyes. "Has anyone ever told you that you don't look Italian?"

"Yet another way that I just don't fit."

"Hey Tony," Kelly's mind began to race, "how old are you?"

"Sixty." Gianninni hugged the pillow to his chest. "I'm sixty years old and all the money, the power, my life, means nothing to me. Do you have any idea what that feels like?"

"As a matter of fact," Kelly smiled supportively, "I do."

Both men grew silent. Gianninni fondled his white silk necktie. "May I confess another secret Bob?"

"You may."

"I've always had a fantasy."

"About being a priest?"

"Is it that obvious?"

Kelly nodded. "Let me ask you something," he pointed at Antonio with his cigar, "if you were the Gianninni with the penchant for religion, how is it that your brother became the priest while you became the...well... how should I put it..."

"The mobster?" Gianninni supplied the noun. "Poor timing. My brother Giuseppe is a year older than I. The eldest son in a devout Italian Catholic family such as mine is destined to become a priest."

"Which left you, the second son, to succeed your father in the family business."

"Correct."

"So your father needed to have two boys."

"And he got us, but I think Momma would have preferred that I were a girl."

"Why do you say that?"

"She fawned over Giuseppe, but to me she was cold and distant."

"Interesting." Kelly leaned over and flicked his ash into a water glass. "I suppose there's no way you could apply for early retirement and join the priesthood."

Gianninni shook his head. "Our severance packages are non-negotiable."

A loud round of applause coming from the television interrupted their conversation. A woman wearing a chic navy pantsuit and sporting a trendy hairdo clutched Oprah in a death grip. The woman wept openly and thanked the talk show host for changing her life. The terminal illness would soon take her, but Oprah's miracle would allow her to go happily and in peace. The audience sobbed. Oprah sobbed. The picture shook as if even the cameraman was sobbing. Kelly was about to comment on the ludicrousness of such melodrama when he heard Antonio whisper, "my miracle is only a day away, then I too can go happily."

This was getting way too deep for Kelly. "Here," he handed Antonio the tube of lemon verbena facial treatment, "it's not exactly a sauna and a massage, but maybe it will help."

"You know Bob," Gianninni unscrewed the cap and took a whiff, "I own a spa."

"Really. Where?"

"The fourth floor."


Megan slipped past the doorman who was helping an elderly tenant into a taxi; being announced was an unnecessary formality since she had the key and strict instructions not to interrupt Jack if he was in the middle of rehearsal. She hurried to the elevator, jumped in, and hit the button for the eleventh floor. Once off the elevator she fished her keys out of her bag as she walked the long corridor to Abbie's apartment. She quietly inserted the key into the lock and slowly turned until she heard a gentle click. She opened the door, entered the apartment and upon seeing that no lights were lit, assumed that she had the place to herself.

Thank God she said, there was no way in hell that I would be able to converse with that moron without letting slip that Abbie plans to dump his sorry ass. Megan left her briefcase and purse in the foyer and headed toward the bedroom. She paused for a moment in the hallway when she thought she heard something, water running perhaps, but when the noise did not persist, she continued onward. She entered the bedroom and nearly fell over a pile of clothing that was lying in a heap on the floor. "Stupid and a slob to boot," Megan muttered as she turned on a light, kicked the pile of clothes aside and made her way to the closet where she rifled through Abbie's wardrobe until voila', she located the dress. She held the dress up to herself and admired her reflection in the full-length mirror. Satisfied that she would tame herself a Giant, she flicked off the light and headed out the door. She stopped. Shoes. She remembered Abbie's strappy sandals with the rhinestones that worked so well with the dress. Megan returned to the closet, snatched up the sandals and made her way into the living room where she stopped again. Abbie's an eight, I'm a nine, she thought, I sure don't want to lug these things uptown if I'm not going to wear them. So she slung the dress across the coffee table and plopped down on the couch. She slipped off her lawyerly pumps, slipped on the sexy sandals, and rested her feet on the coffee table to admire the shoes. They are hot even if they are a bit on the snug side. She smirked, realizing that she was planning on spending more time on her back than on her feet so the fit wasn't really of consequence. She slipped the sandals off, put her pumps on, and once again, was on her way. She was just about to grab her purse and briefcase when she realized she forgot the dress. So she went back to the living room, retrieved the dress, took a few steps toward the foyer and heard something fall to the floor. She looked down at the item that had made the soft thud. It was a notebook, a black and white marbled composition book to be exact. What was written on the cover? An Actors Guide to Rehearsal? By Jack West? You've got to be kidding. Megan tossed the dress on the sofa and picked up the book, noting that Jack could barely read let alone write. She flipped open to page one and read Jack's introduction. Oh dear Lord this man is dumber than dirt, she said aloud. Then she turned the page and…what the hell…she closed the book tight. Did she just see what she thought she just saw? She opened the book and took another peek. Oh yeah, she saw what she saw. She flipped through the pages of photographs. Those cannot be real she commented, if those were real they would be hanging down to her waist. And my God Jack, I can assure you that there is no medical reason to put a stethoscope there. Just as she was about to flip the page, she heard the noise again. It sounded like splashing. Megan put down the notebook and went to investigate.

    She tiptoed down the hallway and was steps away from the guest bathroom when she thought she heard a voice. She stopped and listened. It was Jack's voice. What was he saying? She strained to hear. "But Bambi my darling, we must follow all water safety rules." What the hell was that all about? Then she heard him say, "Let me try that again, I didn't like my inflection." He cleared his throat, "But Bambi my darling, we must follow all water safety rules." The jackass was just rehearsing, Megan began her silent retreat when she distinctly heard a female voice respond, "No problem Doctor Black, I'm a certified life guard as well as a physical therapist. Just let me wrap my legs around you and I promise we'll float." There came more splashing followed by moans and groans not related to any water sport with which Megan was familiar.

    For the first time since infancy Megan Cole was speechless. Should she burst through the bathroom door and catch Jack in the act? That was more of Jack than

Megan cared to see. But she couldn't let him get away with this. She thought of the notebook. That piece of self-made porn was all the evidence she would need to take down the scum-sucking-low-life-two-bit cheating piece of trash. So Megan spared herself an eyeful and crept her way back down the hall. She gathered her things, including the dress, sandals and notebook and left the apartment, making sure to lock the door behind her. She hurried to the elevator, rode down to the lobby, marched out onto the street and hailed a cab. She needed to figure out how to best use the evidence to destroy Jack while, at the same time, not destroying Abbie.

"She went where?"
"Wakefield."
"Aw crap," Tatum tossed his pen on the desk, "when did she leave?"
"This morning. Tom Taylor flew her off."
"You know that little girl is turning out to be a thorn in my side."
"I like her." Pete pushed his hair behind his ears.
"Well I like her too, but she doesn't listen very well."
"That's probably because she's usually talking."
"Hey Chief," Mabel hollered from the outer office, "you've got a call on line one."
"How many times do I have to tell you Mabel, we only have one line, so you don't have to say line one."
There was a pause then she hollered, "Hey Chief, you have a call."
"Who is it?"
"Abbie O'Neal."
He grabbed for the phone. "Abbie?"
"Hi Chief."
"Where are you?"
"The Governor's house in Wakefield."

"Are you all right? You sound strange."

"I'm fine. We're in a bathroom so the acoustics are a little funky."

"Who is we?"

"Me and Dan and Scarlet, and Lucy and Ethel. You aren't acquainted with the last three."

"I see," the Chief hesitated, "so you found what we were looking for?"

"If you asking if I found Dan, the answer is yes. Why are you being so cryptic?"

"Pete says hi."

"Oh. Sorry. Should I call back?"

"No, no, go ahead."

"Ok this is the scoop. I found Dan and you were right; he's a good guy who got mixed up with the wrong woman. He confirmed my suspicions; Mrs. Governor Hardy is the former Priscilla Steele, Pete's mother. She used Pete as leverage to blackmail Dan into flying the Council members off the Island. He strayed. He's sorry. I've forgiven him. Hyacinth is currently with Priscilla in Boston. The other council members are unaccounted for."

"I thought you said that Priscilla Hardy's maiden name was Des Pierre?"

"I did. Des Pierre was a very clever alias."

"Good work Abbie. When are you coming home?"

Abbie smiled, she liked the way that Chief referred to Tyle Island as home. "I'm getting picked up at four. Dan is going to stay put for a while. In the meantime I need you to do me a favor."

"Anything."

"I need you to run a background check."

"On?"

"Eddie Steele. He was from Brooklyn."

"Was? Where is he now?"

"Dead."

"You want me to do a background check on a dead man?"

"Yes."

"Why?"

"Has Pete mentioned that he broke into Lila's house?"

"No." He glanced up at the young man who was awaiting news of Abbie. "He hasn't mentioned anything about Lila's house." Pete began to back out of the office but Chief Tatum's glare stopped him in his tracks.

"Pete found a Listing Agreement that shows that Eddie and Priscilla Steele own Hyacinth's house. Eddie Steele was Vincent Gianninni's best friend. Vincent Gianninni is the father of our casino developer Antonio Gianninni."

"So Eddie Steele is our link between Hyacinth, the Governor and the Mob?"

"Bingo."

"Too bad he's dead."

"We've got a bigger problem."

"Which is?"

"This is all just a theory."

"Meaning."

"It needs to be proven."

"You just said we have the papers on the house to substantiate the relationship between Hyacinth and Steele."

"True, but I still have to prove that Priscilla Hardy and Priscilla Steele are one in the same. I need you to confirm that Eddie had a relative, most likely a granddaughter, named Priscilla. Get her vitals - date of birth, blood type, fingerprints if possible. And I know this is asking a lot Chief but I need you to also see what you can do as far as making a solid connection between Eddie Steele and the Gianninni."

"I'll do what I can."

"And Chief, this has to be done on the qt. If Dan's involvement gets out it will kill Pete."

Chief Tatum looked up at the boy who had again been attempting to skulk out of the room. "I hear you."

"I'll be at the Nest by seven tonight."

"See you then." Chief Tatum hung up the phone.

"Is she okay?" Pete asked.

"She's fine."

"Good. I gotta go."

Chief Tatum ordered Pete to stop.

"Sorry Chief but I have to get to school. Don't want you to arrest me for truancy. See you later," and off he went.

The Chief began to smile but forced himself to stop. He called out to Mabel, "do you have the file on the Poole fire?"

"You closed that one Chief," Mabel called back.

"I know I closed it, may I have it anyway?"

She walked into the office, threw the file on his desk, turned and left. Chief Tatum leaned forward in his chair and opened the folder. He removed the pen from his shirt pocket and clicked it repeatedly as he scanned the report. When he got down to the line that listed "Cause" he scratched out "accidental" and wrote in "arson." The first step in any arson investigation is to question the owners for possible motive.

Oh, and for the record, Pete didn't go to school.

## Chapter 36

Abbie made it back to Tyle Island by 5:00, went straight home, opened a bottle of burgundy and slipped into the hot tub for a therapeutic soak. As the churning water soothed her weary muscles she thought of Kelly. What unspeakable atrocities was he suffering at the hands of the Mob while she was indulging in a frivolous dip in a spa? Racked with guilt she corked the bottle and climbed out of the tub. After taking a quick shower, ice cold as penance for her selfishness, she reached for the telephone and noticed that the machine had logged over thirty messages. There were over thirty annoying hang-ups and without caller ID she had no idea as to the source of the harassment. She cleared the memory and got down to business. Her first call was to her lawyer. She needed to know the legal ramifications of what she was about to do. Again she thought of Kelly. He hadn't been concerned with legalities when facing the mafia; he had been willing to pay the ultimate price. What a selfless man, it was no wonder she loved him so.

"You're killing me," Kelly moaned as the hands of the therapist expertly maneuvered their way through a deep tissue massage. "Tony, you really have to try this."

The mobster was being attended to by five different therapists, all blonde, all beautiful, all dressed in white. One massaged his scalp while the others focused on his feet and hands. "I'm doing just fine here Bob," he managed to reply.

"Do you have plans for this evening?" Kelly asked.

"I'm having dinner with my father," Antonio replied.

"Oh," Kelly sounded disappointed.

"What's wrong?"

"Well you know all I do all day is sit around and wait for the weekend. It gets a little frustrating."

"You're right. I'm being unfair. How about tomorrow night we do something special?"

"Really?"

"Of course. What are friends for?"

The DeLuca family returned to the Nest for dinner. They slurped down countless clams on the half shell before moving on to bowls of chowder followed by cheeseburgers all around. Dino had three. The Islanders watched in awe as the visitors from New Jersey consumed every morsel on their plates, including the parsley garnishes and the lemon wedges. Then they wanted dessert.

"I'm sorry," the waitress, the younger sister of the purple barretted girl from the grocery store apologized, "we don't have any dessert tonight."

"Why the hell not?" Angela barked as she stared into the mirror of her compact and used a tine of her clam fork to pick a stray piece of parsley from between her front teeth.

"Miss Ellie, who bakes our deserts," the young girl explained, "has the flu."

"Don't you have any fucking ice cream?" Dino barked.

"No sir," the young girl innocently replied. "The ice cream parlor sells ice cream."

"Where the fuck is that?"

"It's on Water Street. But it doesn't open until Memorial Day weekend. The grocery store sells ice cream too, but they're all out."

"What sort of place is it," Dino roared, "where I can't get a fucking bowl of ice cream?"

"It's an island sir," the young girl eyed the bartender who was fondling the baseball bat that he kept on hand just in case, "would you like some coffee?"

"You got espresso?"
"What's espresso?"
Tyle Island was gonna kill Dino DeLuca.

"Define extortion."
The last voice Megan had been expecting to hear was Abbie's; she placed her martini glass atop Jack's notebook, "What's going on?"
"I need you to define extortion."
"Why?"
"Because I'm going to do it."
"Please explain."
"Do you remember when you told me that I have to be prepared to find a creative way out of Tyle Island's troubles?"
"I recall. "
"Well, I'm getting creative."
"How creative?"
"Darkest Hour creative."
"Will you be in danger?"
"I plan on using protection."
The comment made Megan think of Jack. She shook off a mental image of Doctor Black splashing in the bathtub, picked up her martini glass and gulped. "What's you're game plan?" she wheezed as the vodka burned its way down her throat.
"I'm going to link the First lady of Massachusetts to both the Mob and Hyacinth Poole."
"The dirty Council member?"
"Exactly."
"That's an interesting love triangle you've got going there." Again Megan pictured Jack hence more martini. "How exactly do you intend to use this information?"
"By threatening to reveal the First Lady's questionable affiliations if they don't cease and desist with the casino project ASAP."

"You now Abbie this is good dirt. Why don't you take it all the way; bust up the administration and slam the Mob?"

"Because. Well. To be honest, I don't have proof."

"You don't have proof?"

"No."

"Then what do you have?"

"A gut feeling combined with too many coincidences, and you know I don't believe in coincidences. But don't worry, I haven't totally abandoned my attempts at obtaining proof, its just that I'm running out of time so I'm going with the creative angle and trusting that the proof I require will surface when I need it."

"Abbie dear, I don't think you fully appreciate what you're proposing."

"It's true that I have no experience with a mob-politics-extortion story line so I'm actually venturing into uncharted waters, but it can't be all that different from when Tiffany used the formula for Ecstasy perfume as leverage to extort child support from Malcolm. So my question is, will I go to jail?"

"Only if you get caught. And if you get caught, I'll get you off."

"On what grounds?"

"Insanity."

"Thanks."

"You're welcome. So how's the writer?"

"He's missing."

"Pardon me."

"That's the other reason I called. He had a meeting with Antonio Gianninni and we haven't heard from him since."

"That's a problem."

"I know. So can you do me a favor?"

"Sure."

"Could you hook me up with one of your PI's? I need someone to go to Atlantic City and hunt him down and I'm too swamped with the extortion thing to break away."

"Where was he staying?"

"The Rio. I don't know his room number but he was driving a rental car. It was a dark blue Taurus, I don't know the plates."

"When was the meeting supposed to have taken place?"

"Seven o'clock last night."

"And the reason for the meeting?"

"Blackmail."

"Your boyfriend called a meeting with a mobster in order to blackmail him and you're surprised that he is now missing?"

"He went in undercover."

"As?"

"A writer."

"That's a stretch."

"He used his own identity and requested a meeting under the pretense that he was working on a book for Heart Publishing?"

"What sort of book?"

"A tell-all autobiography of a former mafia hit man."

"And you considered this to be a good idea?"

"It sounded good at the time."

"And in retrospect?"

"I was wrong."

"I'll see what I can do. Meanwhile do me a favor and watch your ass. This isn't the Darkest Hour. If things get rough you can't just cry 'cut' and try take number two. I'll call you on your cell as soon as I get a line on your missing author."

"Thanks Meg, I owe you big."

"How about you let me tell the putz that he's history and we consider ourselves even?"

"You would enjoy it too much."

Megan glanced down at Jack's notebook and conceded, "You're right, I would."

"Oh," Abbie added as an afterthought, "did I forget to mention that you were right and I am in love with Kelly and if I get him back alive I plan on telling him so?"

"Does that mean your move to Tyle Island would become permanent?"

"I haven't thought that far ahead. Why?"

"I want your apartment."

"You always were the sentimental type Meg."

"Can't help it, I'm just a hard ass at heart. Now get going and have fun catching the bad guys." Megan hung up the phone, downed the rest of her martini then called downstairs to the lobby and asked for her car to be brought around. She then went into the bedroom and changed into Abbie's little black cocktail dress and strappy sandals. She would put her best man on the Kelly case all right, Megan grabbed Jack's notebook and shoved it under her arm as she headed out the door, and the best man for the job was this fine looking woman.

Pete sat at the bar of the Nest with Chief Tatum and John Beale. "When did she say she would get here?" he asked for the third time in ten minutes.

"Seven o'clock," Chief Tatum answered again. "She said she needed some time to get cleaned up. She mentioned something about getting pine tar out of her hair."

"Pine tar? Is that some sort of code word?" John Beale asked.

"Code word?" Tatum scowled. "Have you been reading more of Kelly's books?"

The Harbor Master shrugged.

"I can't believe she would stop off to do her hair at a time like this." Pete spun a quarter and watched it dance across the bar.

The bartender chimed in, "You know I saw on Oprah today that women feel better and think better when they look good. It's a self-esteem thing."

A brief conversation followed regarding man's inability to understand women that was interrupted when Clara and Abbie sailed through the door.

"How's the Crap Shoot progressing?" Abbie asked as she hopped up onto a stool beside Pete and ordered a pint of Harp.

"The dock workers are going on strike tomorrow," John Beale informed her, "and we lucked out, the non-union employees are pulling a sick out in sympathy. No ferries will run until I say it's a go."

"Damn John," Clara smiled, "you are powerful." The Harbor Master blushed.

"We've got the hit man under around the clock surveillance," Chief Tatum explained.

"A disgusting job," Clara cringed, "especially at meal time."

"How's Prescott?"

"Stable. Doc is flying back tomorrow."

"It sounds like you've got everything under control," Abbie took a sip of beer.

Pete leaned over and whispered, "I need to talk to you."

"We'll talk over dinner," she assured the anxious young man. "But first I need to speak with the Chief." Abbie gave Chief Tatum the eye and added, "In private."

"Let's move to a table," Tatum picked up his drink and led Abbie to the back of the bar.

Once they were seated Abbie leaned in close and asked, "Have you told anyone about Dan?"

"I've got enough trouble keeping these people from lynching the hit man, I don't need them turning on Pete in retaliation for his father."

"Any progress on Eddie Steele?"

"Have you ever heard the term consigliore?"

"Yeah, Robert Duvall was Brando's consigliore in the Godfather."

"Well Eddie Steele was Vincent Gianninni's consigliore in real life."

"You're kidding."

"Nope."

"How did you find that out?"

"I called the New York City DA's office."

"And they just offered up that information over the phone."

"Yes." There was a pause then Chief Tatum looked away.

"It was that simple?" Abbie was skeptical.

"I'm law enforcement young lady," he looked down at the table and spoke into his chest, "I'm investigating a crime that might have Mob ties, of course they cooperated."

"You want to look me in the eye and repeat that?"

"No."

"What aren't you telling me?"

The Chief reluctantly admitted, "I have a connection high up in New York City politics." He mumbled, "He made a few phone calls on my behalf."

"Who is he?"

"You'll get angry if I tell you."

"Why would I get angry?"

Chief Tatum judged the length of Abbie's arms then pushed his chair far enough back from the table so as to be out of striking distance. "Because his name is Stewart West."

"My future father-in-law!?"

"I thought you weren't marrying Jack."

"I'm not."

"Then he's not your future father in law now is he?"

"But still…"

"Look young lady, do I have to remind you yet again that this investigation is not about you? Stewart West is a landowner on Tyle Island. He has more invested in the place than you do. Now trust me, I wasn't specific. I merely said that I was investigating a possible arson case and could use the help of the DA to track down a couple of leads. Stewart just opened the door for me, that's all."

Abbie stared into her beer, refusing to speak.

"Stop pouting," Tatum growled.

"I'm not pouting," Abbie growled back.

"Then what's your problem?"

She looked up and met Chief Tatum's eyes. "Tell me Chief, is land ownership the only barometer you people use to determine a person's worth? To Stewart West that house on Madonna's Cove is a tax shelter, not a home. I love it. He merely visits from time to time. And if I may remind you, besides Bob Kelly, no Islander, yourself included, has risked more than I have to stop this casino from being built, so don't you dare tell me that just because Stewart West is a taxpayer that he has more invested in this Island than I do."

Chief Tatum smirked.

"Are you mocking me?" Abbie asked through gritted teeth.

"No."

"Then what's with the stupid grin?"

"Owen Brady would have loved you."

Abbie took a sip of beer to help force back her smile. "So is that your idea of an apology?"

"I apologize for insinuating that your concern is not sincere, but not for involving Stewart."

"Fine. Apology accepted. And maybe I did over-react. Stewart isn't really a bad guy. I never got along with him because he didn't try to hide his obvious contempt for Jack; brilliant attorneys with political aspirations don't like to breed soap opera actors with questionable IQs."

"I'm glad you understand, because he also got me the name of the lawyers handling Eddie Steele's estate. I telephoned but it was after business hours. I'll try again in the morning."

"It's progress." Abbie conceded.

"So have you got anything more on your end?" the Chief asked.

"As a matter of fact, I have another plan."

"Oh no," Chief Tatum pushed his chair back even further, "not another plan."

"I'm going to set up a meeting with Priscilla Hardy to discuss her family background and her ties to the Mob."

"You think your inside info will make her back down?"

"I'm cautiously optimistic."

"What if she doesn't bite?"

"Then I will take the proof that you are sure to uncover and go to the media."

The chief crossed his arms and rested them on his chest as he silently appraised the situation. After a moment of consideration he declared, "That might work."

"I know. Now I just have to figure out how to get her here."

"Well my plate is full, so you're on your own for that one. Any word on Kelly?"

"No," she shook her head, "but I have a PI going to look for him."

"He'll be fine Abbie."

"You think so?"

"I know so. Now let me buy you another beer."

They joined the others back at the bar where Pete immediately accosted Abbie, demanding, "I need to talk to you, now."

## Chapter 37

Talk about mixed emotions. On one hand Abbie was ecstatic that Pete had solved the problem of how to lure Priscilla Hardy to Tyle Island. On the other hand, a potential encounter between pissed off mother and long lost son would no doubt reveal the deep, dark secret that Abbie had just sworn to protect. Abbie's solution to the dilemma at hand was to run interference and pray. So, assuming that the First Lady would have no cause to stop by Madonna's Cove when tracking down her clever son, Abbie moved Pete into her place. Abbie then took up residence at the Kelly house so that when Priscilla came a knocking, she would be the one answering the door. Pete, who liked the idea of spending several days at a beach house equipped with a hot tub and fully stocked bar, did not object to the move. He did suggest that they run by the Conservancy Council office to check his e-mail for a response from long-lost mom, but Abbie assured him that Mrs. Hardy was too smart, and in too deep to correspond in a manner that could be electronically traced. "Trust me Pete, if she is your mother and she received that e-mail, she'll be here, but she'll show up unannounced."

Next came the matter of a protective stakeout. Clara called in her tree-hugging squad and established a schedule of five-hour shifts during which the Kelly house would be closely monitored by teams of two. Each team was given emergency air horns, provided by Joe Morgan's hardware, and strict instructions to blow away if anyone other than a known Islander or the First Lady came to visit.


Megan insisted on parking her own car thereby bypassing the valets and gaining access to the garage and, potentially, Bob Kelly's Ford Taurus. Unfortunately blue Ford Taurus' are popular vehicles; she counted twelve with New York plates on the first two parking levels alone, so she abandoned her investigation of the casino's perimeter and headed inside.

 Years of experience in the realm of cross-examination told Megan that questioning management regarding a disappearance involving their employer would be ineffective, so she avoided the neatly dressed corporate types stationed at the front desk and, recalling Abbie's comment that Bob Kelly was a drinker, headed for the one place an alcoholic visiting Atlantic City would frequent, the bar. She showed a picture of Kelly torn from the jacket of his last novel to the bartenders and wait staff, but none remembered seeing him. However, a bartender who clearly appreciated the fit of Abbie's dress on Megan's body was kind enough to point out that the hotel had seven other bars as well as three restaurants. Her next stop was the Lido Lounge.

 Father and son Gianninni dined at Vincent's brownstone. Isabella had prepared a meal fit for a king, starting with a cold antipasto, finishing with babba au rhum, and, ever aware of Antonio's aversion to red sauce, serving stuffed veal chops as the entrée.

 The two men ate in silence. Antonio's guilt regarding his desire to leave the family business weighed heavily upon him as he sat across from his elderly father who stared down at his own crumb filled plate, distracted by the guilt of a long held secret and a girl named Abbie O'Neal.

 "When does Giuseppe come home?" Antonio finally broke the silence.

 "Monday," the old man replied.

 "Oh," Antonio sipped his coffee.

 "Oh what?" Vincent asked.

 "It's nothing papa."

 "If you got somethin' to say, say it."

Antonio removed the napkin from his lap, carefully folded it and placed it on the table. "I've had some business matters arise that must take me away this weekend."

Vincent pulled the napkin out of his shirt collar and tossed it in a lump beside his plate. "So you ain't coming for Friday night dinner?"

"I don't think so." Antonio, still unable to look his father in the eye, shook his head.

The old man sipped his coffee. "Business is business. I understand."

"Are you sure you'll be all right?" Antonio asked as he silently prayed that the old man would say yes.

"I'm not a baby," Vincent reprimanded his son.

"All right then," Antonio perked up, having cleared the only hurdle that stood between him and the miracle waiting on Tyle Island.

"All right then," Vincent Gianninni perked up as well. With his sons out of the picture, there was nothing to keep him from going to find the girl Abbie on that place called Tyle Island and telling her what he had always suspected about his boy Antonio and his old friend Hyacinth.

Six bars and three restaurants later Megan had made no progress in tracking down Bob Kelly. She sat on a barstool sipping a dirty martini and rubbing her feet that were throbbing thanks to the sexy sandals that were a full size too small.

"The spa is open all night."

"Excuse me?" Megan stopped rubbing and looked up at the source of the voice.

"You look like you're hurting. There's a spa upstairs that gives a great foot massage." The advice came from a sparsely dressed cocktail waitress standing at the service bar waiting for an order to be filled. "Wearing these all night is a killer," she lifted a foot and flashed a four inch stiletto, "so when I have a good night, I treat myself to a massage."

"Do I need an appointment?" Megan asked.

"Not at this time of night." The waitress removed the paper wrappers from three drinking straws and stuck the straws into the pina coladas that the bartender had placed on her cocktail tray. "It's on the fourth floor. Ask for Yvonne and tell her that Sammy sent you."

Jack looked everywhere for his notebook. It wasn't on the coffee table where he swore he had left it, and it hadn't fallen on the floor. He checked under the sofa - no notebook. He looked in the kitchen - no notebook. He checked his bedroom, the guestroom, the foyer, the bathrooms and even the closets and still, no notebook. Then he sat down on the sofa and racked his small brain. Had he taken it with him to the set? No. Had the cleaning woman come? No. Physical Therapist Bambi was sound asleep so clearly she hadn't taken it. He began to panic. Had he lost his book? He thought of Abbie who was probably still collaborating with that old guy. His muscles began to flex. He had to put an end to their collaborations. Book or no book, he would go to Tyle Island this weekend and reclaim his woman once and for all.

Megan was fully reclined in an energy zapping massage chair when the therapist, a tall Nordic woman entered the small private room, introduced herself as Yvonne and got to work. Not two minutes into the foot massage Megan was feeling as if she could dance the night away - in larger shoes of course.

"So you're a friend of Sammy's?" Yvonne commented, her voice a hushed whisper despite the fact that they were alone.

Megan's eyes remained closed as she answered, "Actually we just met downstairs."

"So you're new?"

"This is my first time."

"And you're already working the floor?"

"Pardon me," Megan opened one eye.

"Damn girl," Yvonne raised a blonde eyebrow as if impressed, "you must be good."

Megan opened the other eye, "at what?"

Yvonne laughed, "At what? You even have the cover down. Don't worry," Yvonne winked, "you can trust me. I worked the floor for three years before they moved me up here to service the regulars."

It was at that somewhat awkward moment that Megan realized she was being massaged by, as well as mistaken for, a prostitute. Ordinarily such a mix up would have caused her to leap from the chair and tear the bottle blonde hair from the head of her accuser; however, she sensed that the sisterly bond between ladies of the evening might help with her investigation so she remained calm and played along.

"So you're not really a massage therapist?"

"Oh, I'm certified," Yvonne nodded. "Fifty percent of my clients come in for legitimate massage, but let me tell you, this work," she lifted one of Megan's feet, "is harder than hooking."

"And how's business?"

"Usually steady. It was slow today because the boss was in."

"Antonio Gianninni?"

"The one and only. He brought a friend in for the full treatment so we closed down for a couple of hours."

"The full treatment?" Megan wasn't sure she wanted to

know what the full treatment entailed, but she had a job to do, so she asked for clarification.

"Massage, mud baths, herbal wraps, manicures, pedicures, you name it those two got it."

"What about sex?"

"The boss isn't into sex. It's too bad, he's in good shape for an old guy and his friend Bob was hot."

"Bob?" Megan struggled to free herself from the all-consuming grip of the comfy massage chair. "His friend's name was Bob?" Yvonne nodded. Megan finally broke loose, grabbed her purse and fished out the picture of Kelly. She showed it to Yvonne, "Is this Bob?"

She nodded. "Great eyes."

"Do you know how I could get a hold of him?"

"I didn't get a room number," Yvonne shrugged, "but he's coming back in the morning."

"What time?"

"Eleven. But it's another private session. You won't be able to get in."

"Shit." Megan fell back into the chair.

"I can give him a message, but it'll cost you."

Megan thought of Jack's notebook. "How much?"

"Two hundred. Cash."

"The boss can't find out," Megan warned.

Yvonne eyed her well-dressed client and made another demand.

Chapter 38

It was a picture perfect Thursday morning on Tyle Island. The air was crisp, the sun was shining, the birds were singing and Dino DeLuca was yelling "fuck, fuck, fuck," at the top of his lungs. He had awoken early and gone outside to smoke a big, fat cigar when he got his big, fat butt got stuck in a skinny beach chair. Despite her best efforts, Angie was not able to extract her husband's bottom from the jaws of the aluminum monster. After half an hour of struggling, Nona finally emerged from the cottage to save the day; she doused her son-in-law's buttocks with olive oil, lubricating him such that he could finally squeeze free. As the monstrous and now slippery hit man stood in the yard with his blood a boil and a slick of Bertolli extra-virgin pooling at his feet, Angie announced, "Move your ass Dino, we're going for breakfast then to the beach."

"I'm not going back to that fucking beach Angie," Dino roared.

"Oh yeah you are," Angie roared back as she teetered toward him. "And you're going to build a fucking sand castle," she poked his hairy chest with her long, red fingernail, "and you're going to ride the fucking boogie board in the waves with Pasquale," she poked him again as if putting an exclamation point on the end of her sentence.

"I ain't going in that water Angie," he argued. "Its forty fucking degrees."

"Oh yes you are," she reached up and grabbed her husband by the gold rope chain that hung around his thick neck, "or you're answering to me."

Dino slinked inside, showered off the olive oil, donned his pink and black Hawaiian print swim trunks and black guinea tee, loaded the Towncar with towels and chairs and blankets and buckets and headed to Clara's Diner for breakfast followed by another fun-filled day on the beach.

With no vacancies at the inn, Megan had been forced to spend the night on a pew in a chapel; she awoke to the sound of slot machine bells proclaiming that a jackpot had been won in the casino just outside. After confirming that she was alone, Megan hurried to the altar and used the Baptismal font as a washbasin, ridding her body of the shroud of casino odors that clung to her skin. She then returned to her pew, pulled out her cell and phoned Abbie. The call was immediately forwarded to Abbie's voice mail; Megan left a message informing her that Kelly had been spotted, alive, approximately fifteen hours earlier. She spared her friend the details surrounding the context in which Kelly had been seen, half-naked, and avoided the subject of her black strapless cocktail dress which was now hanging in the closet of an Atlantic City hooker while she was being forced to wear a "Just Say No" tee shirt, sweat pants with the likeness of Joe Camel printed across the rear end and a pair of hot pink plastic flip flops purchased from a seedy boardwalk vendor the night before. When Megan heard the chapel doors open, she cut the line and stashed her cell in her black beaded handbag, the only vestige of style remaining following tough negotiations with Yvonne, and, hunkered down in the pew so as not to be seen dressed in her current fashion "don'ts".

Several minutes passed, Megan grew bored, and curiosity got the best of her, so she chanced a quick peek to see who else might be seeking sanctuary in a casino chapel at such an early hour. She expected a vagrant but instead found that a handsome and well-dressed older man had taken a seat in the rear. Megan then took a closer look and recognized the bastard.

Antonio Gianninni entered the Chapel of the Little Flower located between the craps tables and slot machines on the main floor of the Rio and, thinking he was alone as he usually was at such an early hour, he slipped into a back pew, closed his eyes and began to pray. This wasn't his typical morning Novena. Today Antonio was seeking guidance. There, on his knees, ruining the crease in his three thousand dollar suit, he posed the burning question to his Almighty Father, "Should I build on Tyle Island?" He asked God for a sign that might lead him down the proper path, and he vowed that whatever God's decision, he would obey.

When Antonio opened his eyes a homeless and clearly destitute woman stood before him. Startled by her presence he gasped aloud; he hadn't heard anyone come or go, from where had this lowly creature of the streets emerged? The woman did not speak. She did not have to. Her message, God's message, was clear.

Gianninni removed his money clip from his pants pocket and offered the thick wad of cash to the lost soul. She stared down at him with contempt, refusing his blood money. As she walked away, the sound of her movement, like the beat of Poe's Tell-Tale Heart, echoed through the quiet chapel, flip-flop-flip-flop-flip flop.

Abbie sat on the Kelly sofa with an afghan wrapped around her shoulders and a Bob Kelly novel resting on her lap. She had slept little, having spent most of the night nervously awaiting the blast of an air horn. Hungry, she wandered into the kitchen, checked the time, 8:53, fished through the refrigerator and found little in the way of nourishment besides the once delicious, now rancid roast beef she had sliced for Kelly less than two weeks prior. She did manage to locate coffee, cereal and a quart of milk that hadn't quite gone sour; not exactly four-star fare, but it would suffice. As Abbie ate her Capt'n Crunch, berries first, she flipped open her small notebook and reviewed her game plan. Priscilla had been contacted, check. The Chief was working on proof, check. Megan was tracking down Kelly, check. Pete was well hidden, as was Dan, check, check. The ferries were no longer running, check. The hit man was being tailed and Tyle Island's emergency alert system had been lowered to Defcon 1. All that was left was to wait. The hand of the clock moved from 9:01 to 9:02.

After finishing her cereal, Abbie wandered about the kitchen, opening cabinets and drawers, looking for nothing in particular, just looking. The hand of the clock moved from 9:06 to 9:07. She made her way into the living room, nothing exciting going on there, and then down the hall, where she decided to check the weather. A burst of crisp spring air rushed into the house as she opened the front door.

"Morning Abbie," a head popped out of the brush on the other side of the narrow road. "Did you sleep well?"

Abbie stepped out onto the porch and held back her hair to keep it from blowing across her face. "Just fine thank you." She had seen the woman at the diner but did not know her name. "Would you like some coffee?"

The woman waved a silver thermos over her head. "No thanks, I brought my own."

"Is that Abbie?" a voice called out from the backyard.

"Sure is," the woman hiding in the bushes called back.

Abbie peeked around the side of the porch and saw a head pop out from behind a tree in the backyard. "Morning Abbie."

"Morning Billy." Abbie was well acquainted with Billy Prior, the owner of The Nest. She repeated her offer of coffee, which was answered with another wave of another silver thermos. "It sure is windy today," Abbie commented loud enough so that both could hear.

"There's a small craft warning posted," Billy explained.

"And planes can't land in gusts like these," the woman added. "I doubt we'll be getting any visitors today."

"Probably not," Billy agreed.

Abbie sighed, just what she needed, more waiting. The woman returned to her bush, Billy returned to his tree, and Abbie returned to the kitchen, 9:09. It was going to be a long day.

Thanks to the on-going assistance of Stewart West, the Brooklyn DA faxed over twenty year old surveillance photographs of Eddie Steele with Vincent Gianninni. While outdated, they served their purpose; Chief Tatum now had an indisputable link between the Steele and the Gianninni families.

The second leg of Chief Tatum's task was not going as smoothly. Baldwin, Capra and Baldwin, Attorneys at Law, were not exactly free flowing with information regarding their client. The Chief explained that he was investigating an arson case that involved the Tyle Island property belonging to the late Eddie Steele. One of the Baldwin's, or was it the Capra, denied any knowledge of Tyle Island or the property thereon. Chief Tatum offered to fax the listing agreement between the party of the first part and Lila the belligerent Realtor but the Baldwin's/Capra were uninterested. He was then expeditiously disconnected.

A six-foot tall by six foot wide Italian man led Kelly to the spa then blocked the doors with his enormous body, assuring that no one without the benefit of a Sherman tank, could pass by. Yvonne rushed to greet her client.

"How are you feeling today Bobby?"

"I'm well," Kelly stood with a cigar clenched between his teeth and his hands shoved into the pockets of his white terrycloth Rio Hotel & Casino robe, "and you?"

"Hanging in. What did you have in mind for this morning?"

"I'm open to suggestions."

Yvonne looked down at Kelly's navy blue socks, sans shoes, and suggested, "Why don't we start at the bottom and work our way up?" She led him into a private room, the type usually reserved for 'regulars', and patted a plush leather chair. "Make yourself comfortable, I'll get you something to read."

While Kelly settled in and took off his socks, Yvonne carefully removed a copy of Sports Illustrated from her oversized shoulder bag. The notebook was stashed between the pages.

"You look like the sporting type," she commented as she handed Kelly the magazine. Kelly smiled politely thinking that Yvonne looked like she had gone a few rounds in her day as well. "There's a good article on page ten, you should read it."

Kelly opened to page ten and discovered the notebook, which, naturally, he removed from the magazine and held up for closer inspection.

"Keep it down," Yvonne warned.

Kelly glanced around, they were alone in a locked room so he didn't quite understand the urgency in her voice, but since she had a tight grip on his big toe he did as she asked and shoved the notebook back between the pages before taking a better look. "What the...?" he said aloud as he read what was written on the cover.

"Your friend gave it to me last night," Yvonne whispered. "I took a peek, pretty kinky shit."

Kelly opened to page one. Written in red lipstick over Jack's grammatically incorrect introduction was a note which read "B. - WILL TELL A. THAT YOU'RE OK. THOUGHT THIS WOULD INTEREST YOU". It was signed M. Cole, Esq. He flipped through the pages muttering a series of slanderous profanities which culminated with 'oh Jack, you are one dumb schmuck'.

"He may be dumb, but he's hung like a horse," Yvonne grinned up at Kelly as she rubbed the balls of his feet. "He looks familiar, is he a friend of yours?"

"No." Kelly closed the notebook and drummed his fingers on the cover. "The person who gave this to you, will you see her again?"

Yvonne shook her head. "But I'm supposed to call to let her know if you got the goods."

"Will you give her a message for me?" Bob asked.

"It'll cost you."

"How much?"

She thought a moment then answered, "Two hundred, cash."

Kelly reached into the pocket of his robe, pulled out the money he had brought along for the purpose of tipping and asked for a pen. Yvonne pulled a blue Bic from the bun in her bleach blonde hair and handed it to him. He wrote on the back of a fifty, "TELL A. WILL SEE HER FRI ON THE BEACH. WILL HANDLE J.W." He gave Yvonne the money and made her read the note aloud. He added another fifty to insure that his message would be passed along.

"May I keep the magazine?" he asked. She nodded. "Thank you," he slipped the notebook back into the magazine, tucked it firmly under his arm, slung his navy blue socks over his shoulder, left the room, walked up to the behemoth guarding the door and explained that he was not feeling well and asked to be brought back to his room.

Vincent Gianninni summoned his henchmen to his bedroom to advise them of his travel plans. He instructed them to get a car and a map and figure out how to get to a place called Tyle Island Massachusetts. He then dismissed the goons and wheeled himself closer to the television. Tomorrow was the Benton Springs Hospital Ball and he was dying to find out who Ashley was taking as a date.

Abbie looked at the clock that read 12:56. God she was bored. A knock on the door nearly caused her to jump out of her skin. She hadn't heard the air horn, which meant that her visitor was either known or alone. She approached with caution, her heart raced and her hand trembled as she reached for the knob. She took a deep breath to calm herself then opened the door. Clara held up a brown paper bag, "Thought you could use some lunch."

The spiritual smell of a greasy cheeseburger with a side of fries blew in with the wind. Abbie inhaled deeply and replied, "You are an angel." She unlatched the screen door allowing Clara to enter.

"The Chief asked me to tell you that the airport isn't letting any planes land and the seas are too rough for small boats, so you're on hold 'til tomorrow. He also wanted me to give you this." She pulled an envelope out of her L.L. Bean tote bag and handed it to Abbie.

Abbie led Clara into the living room where they both collapsed on the couch. As Clara began unpacking lunch, Abbie opened the envelope and pulled out the FBI surveillance photos; attached to each was a Post-It note identifying the subjects of the photographs; Eddie Steele "Consigliore" and Vincent Gianninni "Don". Abbie smiled, she was half way home.

Megan sat in a dingy diner, drinking cup after cup of watered down coffee and impatiently awaiting Yvonne's call. She had had enough of Atlantic City; in less than twenty-four hours she had been mistaken for being both homeless and a whore. Even the street people who wandered into the diner to beg for spare change looked at her sympathetically. At just after eleven, her black beaded handbag began to ring. It was Yvonne and the news was good; the hand-off had gone down without a hitch. Megan disconnected with the hooker, called Abbie and again reached her voice mail instead of her friend. She tapped her pink flip flopped foot on the dirty black and white tile floor as she awaited the tone that would allow her to leave a message. "It's me. I made contact. Your author says he'll see you Friday on the beach. Now I'm going home to slay me a Giant so we can both live happily ever after. Try not to screw this one up kiddo. Ciao." She hung up and strutted out of the diner, flip-flop-flip-flopping all the way home.

Chief Tatum was failing miserably at his task of proving kinship between the former Eddie Steele and the present First Lady of Massachusetts. He clicked the end of his pen as he stared at his doodle-covered legal pad; besides curly cues and little hearts, he had scribbled only one name repeatedly, Pete Kelly. The Chief was sure that Pete could break into the Baldwin, Capra and Baldwin mainframe to see if their ignorance of Tyle Island property sincere, but asking the kid to help hang his mother seemed like bad form. The Chief tossed his pen on the desk and once again picked up the file on the Poole arson case. As he re-read the contents for the hundredth time it became very clear that the only person who could supply the needed answers was Hyacinth herself. Abbie had said she was hiding out at the Governor's mansion. As he glanced at the telephone a silly thought crossed his mind. Nah, he said to himself, he couldn't just...could he?

Dino DeLuca had had enough of Tyle Island. Boring did not begin to describe his feelings regarding the act of sitting on a big ass empty beach and looking out at a bunch of blue fucking water for five goddamn hours a day. His already fragile mood shattered completely when, after having spent forty five minutes riding that piece of shit boogie board in the frigid frigging water, he emerged from the ocean, shriveled and shivering, only to have a cold wind kick up, leaving his hairy wet body caked with painfully abrasive grains of sand. The hit man roared for Angie to pack up her fucking things while he gave his children thirty seconds to get their fat asses back to the car. Nona sprinkled holy water as she hurried with her daughter and grandchildren over the dunes.

The strong winds hindered Mildred's sniffing ability so she called off her afternoon hunt for dead bodies and settled into her ramshackle cottage for a much-needed rest.

As Chief Tatum dragged Pete out of the hot tub he assured the cute blonde in the orange bikini that he would be returning the young man shortly.

"Where are we going?" Pete complained as the Chief led him, barefoot and soaking wet, to the Police truck.

"I need a phone number," the Chief explained as he opened the passenger door.

"Dial information."

"This one isn't listed."

Pete sighed, "Can I at least have some shoes?"

The chief looked the boy up and down and answered, "No. We're running out of time."

As they drove Chief Tatum apologized for interrupting Pete's tryst and filled the young man in on what he needed from this last hack. When they arrived in town they let themselves into the Conservancy Council offices where Pete, in his dripping wet swim trucks, sat down at his computer and logged on. Again a voice informed him that 'he had mail', again he ignored the prompt, focusing on the more urgent matter at hand. Twenty minutes later

Pete handed over a list of private numbers wired into the Governor's Mansion.

"I've got to check my e-mail," Pete announced before disconnecting.

"No, you have to clean up that puddle." Chief Tatum pointed to the pool of water that had formed beneath Pete's chair, "and I need to use the phone."

So Pete logged off. While he mopped up the hardwoods with a wad of toilet paper, Chief Tatum dialed the first of the unlisted numbers. A recording of a woman's voice apologized for not being available and requested that the caller leave a message - not what he was looking for - he hung up and tried the next number. After two rings a youthful sounding voice answered, "Hello."

"Hello is this Amy Hardy?" the Chief asked.

"Yes, who's this?"

"My name is Police Chief Tatum," he declared in his most official of voices.

"Is something wrong?" the girl asked.

"I certainly hope not. I'm looking for someone. I was told that she's staying with your family."

"Auntie Hyacinth?"

"Yes, Auntie Hyacinth," Chief Tatum repeated the girl's words for Pete's benefit. Pete stopped mopping and listened as the Chief asked, "May I speak with her?"

"She's gone."

"Gone where?"

"Mom said she was taking her home."

Taloy Jobbs sat on the deck of his hotel and gazed down on the docks where lobstermen and fishermen had gathered to discuss the day's catch. When he saw the Towncar pull into the ferry parking lot, Taloy picked up his Bloody Mary and hurried across the Street. He watched the hit man march his way down the length of the narrow dock, stopping at every boat where a fisherman was unloading his haul or hosing down his equipment. A young deck hand rushed ahead of the goon, passing along word that the he was trying to arrange a charter.

Taloy casually wandered over toward the "The Mary Rose" where her skipper, Milo Donaghue, was seated on an overturned chum bucket cleaning a pile of bluefish while drinking a warm can of Bud. As the hit man approached, Taloy leaned over and whispered to Milo to take the charter. Milo looked at Taloy as if he was crazy; Taloy repeated 'take it', and winked. So when Dino DeLuca, yet unsuccessful, barreled up to the two men and demanded to go fishing the next morning, Milo suggested a six a.m. departure. Dino marched back down the wooden boards of the dock which vibrated under his girth, got into his town car and screeched away, pleased that he wouldn't be spending another goddamn day on the beach.

"What the hell you make me do that fer?" Milo asked Taloy who was grinning from ear to Irish ear.

"The less you know the better my friend," Taloy responded. "Where would you be taking him tomorrow?"

"The blues are running," Milo rubbed his brow with an oily rag. "I'll take him out about a mile on the South side. Even a fecking moron can catch a fish out there."

Taloy reached into his pocket and pulled out a thick roll of bills. He peeled thee hundreds off the top, showed them to Milo then stuffed them into the old man's shirt pocket. "You be there at nine and if anyone asks, I didn't give you this money."

Milo looked into his pocket. "What money?"


Kelly sat in a red velvet wingchair studying a chessboard and sipping a scotch. "I have a favor to ask," he said as he moved his rook to within striking distance of

Antonio's king. Gianninni looked up from the board awaiting Kelly's request. "I have no Will."

"Bob," Gianninni anticipated Kelly's chessboard strategy and moved his knight to block, "let's enjoy the evening and not speak of such things."

"I have a brother and a nephew who don't need to fight with the State of Massachusetts over my assets. I have friends who I would like to take care of, and," Kelly swirled the scotch and water in his glass, "there's a woman."

Gianninni looked up. "I wasn't aware." He paused then asked, "Do you love her." Kelly nodded. "Does she love you?"

"God I hope not," Kelly replied.

Gianninni appeared puzzled. "Why wouldn't you want this woman to love you?"

"No good can come from loving a dead man." Kelly moved his Queen and declared, "Check."


Dan Kelly had just finished repairing the screen on the sliding door when he heard a car pull up the long dirt driveway. He stowed the toolbox under the sink, buttoned his shirt to hide his new hairlessness, then grabbed a soda out of the fridge and dove onto the sofa, using his body to cover a tear in the leather suffered during his scuffle with Lucy and Ethel. The door swung open and in stormed a seething Priscilla Hardy; shuffling along in her wake was none other than Hyacinth Poole. Dan Kelly grinned, an unscheduled visit, Abbie was right.

## Chapter 39

Scarlet Newbaker awoke at dawn. She lay in bed fantasizing, as she did most every morning, about flying. She pictured herself in the cockpit of Cessna, gazing out upon a bright blue sky speckled with pure white clouds that looked like giant cotton balls suspended from heaven. Off to her right appeared a magnificent rainbow that reached out to the horizon and beyond. She slowly leaned over to kiss her husband who is manning the controls. Wait a minute. Rewind. That wasn't her husband; that was Dan Kelly flying the plane.

A naughty grin stretched across Scarlet's face. Ever since she and Abbie had left the Governor's house, she hadn't been able to get that pilot out of her mind. The sad story about his son who wasn't really his son had pulled at her heartstrings, while his wavy hair and dreamboat eyes had pulled at other parts of her anatomy. She opened her eyes and glanced over at her snoring husband. His Elvis Presley pompadour had deflated after a restless night sleep and his thick sideburns, which two days ago seemed sexy, now looked ragged and ridiculous. He smelled of whisky and cigarettes and Scarlet knew that when he finally awoke he would stumble into the bathroom and make that guttural hacking noise until he coughed up whatever mucous and nicotine was still lodged in his lungs from the night before. Maybe he would shower, maybe not. Then he would wolf down a plate of eggs and grits and head off on another run to Canada, leaving her alone in her rusty trailer in the middle of nowhere New England.

Scarlet sighed as she closed her eyes and resumed her fantasy.

Dino arrived at The Mary Rose at 6:00 on the dot. Upon boarding, Milo handed him a Styrofoam cup filled with strong black coffee and a bottle of Jim Beam to add if desired. Dino desired. After a few cursory checks to make sure they had adequate supplies of bait, food, beer and booze, Milo released the ropes and hit the engines. The Mary Rose chugged out of Old Harbor heading due south, just as he had promised Taloy she would.

    Kelly spent most of the night composing his Last Will and Testament. He had divided the bulk of his financial holdings equally between Dan and Pete. He also made provisions for Clara, who had been dreaming of a new griddle and Doc Gno, who longed to continue his Lyme Disease research but never quite had the time nor the funds required to undergo such a pricey endeavor. Kelly earmarked resources for a scholarship fund to be established in the name of Owen Brady that would provide Tyle Island High School graduates with the means to further their educations if they so desired. He also made substantial donations to the Fisherman's Widow and Children's Fund as well as Volunteer Fire Department and Emergency Squads. The balance of his estate would be placed in a trust to be used for the purpose of buying and preserving undeveloped parcels of land on Tyle Island, a practice that had once been under the auspices of the now defunct Conservancy Council. He signed and dated the Will, hoping that in the event of his demise, it would be honored despite the fact that it was un-witnessed and un-notarized.
    When Antonio Gianninni, full of enthusiasm and eager for a miracle, came to Kelly's room to roust him for breakfast, Kelly asked him to review the document. Gianninni silently scanned the Will. When finished reading he asked, "What about the girl?"
    Kelly who was seated on the end of the bed struggling with the difficult decision of whether to wear the worn

out loafers or the newer, less comfortable boat shoes asked, "Can I trust you Tony?"

To which Gianninni solemnly replied, "Of course."

"I mean really trust you." Kelly emphasized the importance of what he was about to reveal.

Antonio nodded.

Kelly reached for the loafers, preferring to go out comfortably rather than in style. He put on his shoes then stood and began folding his clothes and packing them into his duffle bag.

"There's a house on Tyle Island that I want her to have."

"That's a very generous gift."

Kelly tossed the boat shoes into the bag. "The problem is the house isn't for sale."

"That is a problem," Gianninni concurred.

"I also know that once you begin construction real estate prices will soar." Kelly struggled to properly fold his navy blue blazer. "If the house were to go on the market she could never afford to buy the place, even with help from me."

"So what do you intend to do?"

"I'm going to convince the current owner that he should sell it for a loss."

Gianninni laughed. "Even I would have trouble negotiating that deal."

Kelly realized the futility in trying to fold the sport coat. Who cares if it wrinkled, he'd never be wearing it again, so he rolled it into a ball and stuffed the jacket in the bag.

"I am in possession of certain material that the owner, who has political aspirations, would not want made public."

Gianninni rose, removed Kelly's balled up sport coat, folded it neatly and returned it to the bag. "So you plan on using this material to blackmail the owner into giving your friend the house?"

"Yes."

"You really do have a romantic notion of blackmail as a bargaining tool don't you Bob?"

It was Kelly's turn to laugh. "I admit that I screwed up on my previous attempt, but this time I'm sure it will work. However, I don't want to part with the original bargaining chip so if you would be so kind as to permit me use of a photocopier before we leave I'll shoot off a duplicate and forward it to the homeowner along with a note outlining my wishes. I'd appreciate it if you would arrange for the documents to be delivered to the interested party this morning along with my Will."

"Your Will?" Gianninni looked puzzled. "Is the man you plan to blackmail your attorney?"

"No," Kelly answered, "but he is an attorney."

John Beale, Clara and Chief Tatum waved to the landscape photographer who was staking out the rear of the Kelly house as they entered through the back door for one final meeting before zero hour arrived. The winds had subsided making it safe for planes to land and ships to sail; Priscilla Hardy would soon be paying a visit to Tyle Island.

They found Abbie asleep on the sofa, snoring, drooling and still dressed in the clothes she had worn the day before. There was a half empty scotch bottle on the coffee table and a stack of Bob Kelly novels piled high on the floor. Clara nudged Abbie ever-so-gently on the shoulder, but the sleeping beauty did not respond. The next nudge was less gentle; the third bordered on assault. Abbie awoke, jumped to her feet then lost her balance and fell back onto the couch.

"Have you been drinking?" Clara could hardly contain her outrage at finding their savior in such sad shape.

"Yes," Abbie replied.

"Do you think that was wise?"

"No," she rubbed her tired eyes. "But I also know that facing Priscilla Hardy after going seventy-two hours without sleep would not have been considered a wise battle tactic either. I decided to have one drink to relax me, but," she shrugged, "one didn't work."

"So you had more?"

Abbie checked the level of the scotch bottle that had been newly opened the night before and answered, "Yes."

"What time did you finally crash?" John Beale asked.

"What time is it?"

He checked his watch. "Just after eight."

She thought a moment before responding, "seven forty five."

"Dear Jesus," Clara cried as she grabbed Abbie by the arm and dragged her across the living room, "we have to get this girl sobered-up or this Island is in deep shit. Chief, put on some coffee. John, you, you, help him with the coffee. We'll re-group in ten." Clutching Abbie by the back of her shirt collar, Clara whisked her up the staircase, down the hall, and into the second floor bathroom.

Abbie objected to Clara stripping her naked, fruitlessly complaining that she had no clean clothes to wear, but Clara wasn't listening and Abbie was too exhausted to fight the buxomly redhead who was freakishly strong.

"Now get in that shower and scrub," Clara demanded.

Abbie, resigned to the fact that she was not getting out of the bathroom alive if she did not quickly recuperate, did as ordered while Clara stormed down the hall to Kelly's bedroom and fished through his dresser drawers until she located a navy blue Henley and a pair of gray sweatpants. She marched back, flung open the shower curtain, poured shampoo on Abbie's head and demanded that she lather. When Abbie was squeaky clean and smelling of Irish Spring, she was permitted to exit the shower and towel off.

"Put these on," Clara ordered as she held out the clothes.

"What are they?"

"I found them in the room down the hall."

"Kelly's room?"

"There are three Kelly's living in this house young lady. The room belongs to one of them, which one is of no concern to me."

Abbie held the clothing up to her face. They smelled like a musty dresser drawer. She grimaced at the odor then caught a glimpse of Clara's snarl, so she dropped the towel and quickly dressed. As Abbie rolled up the extra long shirtsleeves so that her hands could protrude, Clara ran a brush through her hair, taking pleasure whenever a knot was found. Abbie cinched the drawstring on the sweatpants as tight as it would go then borrowed a toothbrush and scraped her mouth clean of its cottony scotch residue. She spat, rinsed then checked herself in the mirror. She looked quirky, mismatched, rumpled ...literary.

The two ladies proceeded downstairs. Abbie detoured to her backpack for a few dozen squirts of Chanel to mask the musky odor clinging to the clothes, then collapsed at the kitchen table with the Chief and John Beale who had helped themselves to heaping bowls of Capt'n Crunch. While Clara filled two coffee mugs Abbie reached into the box, pulled out a handful of cereal and shoveled it into her mouth in the manner that would make a DeLuca proud.

"So what's up?" she asked.

"Priscilla took the bait," Chief Tatum smiled, "she's on her way."

"How do you know?" Abbie accepted the coffee and poured in a spot of slightly sour milk.

"I called the Governor's mansion. Amy Hardy told me that her mother had taken her Auntie Hyacinth home."

Abbie smirked. "You little devil. What inspired you to call the mansion?"

The Chief shrugged. "I figured that Hyacinth was the only one that could fill in the rest of the blanks. You knew where she was staying. I knew how to get a hold of her."

"But you weren't able to actually speak to Hyacinth, so we still don't have proof substantiating the relationship between Priscilla Hardy and Eddie Steele?"

"Not officially, no."

"That's alright," Abbie smiled, "I think I've managed to unravel this twisted storyline of ours."

"Tell us..." all three prompted.

"Ok, but it's a long, complicated story," Abbie popped a crunch-berry, "so I'll summarize. Try to keep up." She took a deep breath. "My interview with Mildred Ahearn revealed a few sordid details about the beloved Widow Poole's past. One, she was a hooker." Both men cringed upon hearing the news, so Abbie clarified, "when she was a teen-ager." Both men looked relieved. "Second, during her prostitution days, Hyacinth associated with a couple of young mobsters named Eddie Steele and Vincent Gianninni. I have proof from Hyacinth's own photo album to back me up on that one. Third, when Hyacinth was nineteen she got pregnant and had a child whom she gave up for adoption. Again I have proof in the form of letters written by Hyacinth to Mildred. Fourth, after giving birth, Hyacinth took on a new identity and moved from New York City to Tyle Island. The Widow Poole was never actually married. Her real name is Hyacinth Peters, she and Mildred made the name Poole up while swimming one summer afternoon. Remember the name Peters, it will come up again."

All three sat with mouths agape as Abbie continued her tale.

"It is my assertion that Eddie Steele was the father of Hyacinth's child. He purchased the Tyle Island property in exchange for legal custody of his baby who he and his wife adopted and raised. We have proof that Eddie Steele held the title to Hyacinth's house." The Chief nodded confirmation while Clara and John Beale exchanged looks of shock and disbelief. "I'm guessing that this child in turn had a child of his own. A little girl named Priscilla; a little girl who grew up and spent a summer on Tyle Island with her "Auntie Hyacinth", the summer during which Pete Kelly was conceived. Peter, an interesting choice of names wouldn't you say? Now its common knowledge that after Pete was born Priscilla disappeared. Well, I say to you that Priscilla Steele saw the opportunity to escape the confines of the life of a mafiosa, so she and Hyacinth created a new identity for her, just as Hyacinth had done for herself some sixty years prior. Priscilla Steele became Priscilla Des Pierre. Des Pierre - "of Peter", of Hyacinth Peters, the woman I believe to be not her dearest Auntie, but in fact, her biological grandmother." All three gasped. "But wait, there's more. Priscilla, upon her grandfather's death, resurfaced for the purpose of cashing in on her inheritance. A kindly priest informed me that Eddie Steele's estate was being contested. I suspect that Priscilla was the one contesting the Will. Priscilla who had denounced her mob tied family years prior, was in turn denounced by her grandfather and left out in the financial cold. Now I ask you, how does a woman who was expecting a handsome inheritance react to getting the royal shaft? She seeks retribution from someone who did get a piece of the pie, a piece of the Tyle Island pie, Hyacinth Poole. The wheels were set in motion this past Christmas when, after a seventeen year hiatus in their relationship, Priscilla sent Hyacinth a greeting card. Well people, I say that card was no harmless 'hello and happy holidays', it was a wake-up call meant to tell the Widow

Poole that Priscilla Steele was back in town. With a politician in her pocket and a casino-developing mobster as an old family friend, the road to wealth was paved with her bad intentions. All she needed was the land, and that she secured by threatening to reveal Hyacinth, the pillar of Tyle Island society, for the fraud she truly was."

Clara looked astonished. John Beale looked ill. Chief Tatum looked doubtful. He asked, "Are you sure about all this Abbie?"

Abbie responded with a definitive "No. But we've got nothing else to go on."

"You're amazing," Clara muttered.

"No," Abbie replied triumphantly, "I'm a soap opera writer."

Vincent Gianninni sat in the back seat of a black Mercedes watching I-95 pass him by; Fric was driving while Frac navigated.

"How long it's gonna take?" Vincent asked his goons.

"Without traffic, about four hours."

"That ain't too bad," Vincent answered.

"Then we have to fly."

"We havta what?"

"We have to fly," the goon repeated.

"Why do we havta fly? We got this nice car."

"It's an Island boss," Frac put down his map and turned around to address the old man. "We can't drive to an island."

"I ain't flying nowhere," Vincent's jaw was set firm. "I ain't never flown before and I ain't gonna start now."

"But boss."

"I'm not a bird. I don't fly. Find another way."

"There's a ferry boat," Frac suggested, then added, "but it'll take longer."

"A boat ride sounds nice." Vincent had fond memories of the Staten Island Ferry. "We go by boat. But first you gotta find a place with a TV."
"Why a TV boss?"
"I gotta see my show. Today is the hospital ball."

"We will be sailing out of Newport," Antonio explained as he and Kelly settled into the private jet that he kept housed at Allaire Airport.
"This is quite a toy," Kelly ran his hand along the soft leather seats. "I know someone that would kill to fly this baby."
"You're referring to your brother?"
Kelly forgot about the plush leather and stared at Gianninni. "How did you come to know about Dan?"
"The same way I learned about you."
"Priscilla?"
Gianninni nodded.
Kelly started to play with the controls of the small television screen in front of him. "The moment I recognized her standing with you in front of that Sphinx, I knew I was screwed." Kelly tuned into The Darkest Hour. "So tell me, how does Prissy Steele fit into all of this?"
"Priscilla is an old family friend who also happens to be married to the Governor of Massachusetts."
"Ah," Kelly buckled his seat belt as he felt the plane begin to taxi down the runway. "Having friends in high places helps to get casinos built."
"Actually, the idea to build on Tyle Island was entirely hers."
"Oh, I'm sure it was."
"She told me that the two of you used to be friends."
"She lied."
"You sound bitter."

"I have cause." Kelly watched the ground fall away. "Priscilla Steele destroyed my brother's life."

"How is that?"

"She got pregnant." Kelly could tell that his news had caught Gianninni off guard. "After the kid was born she took off and left my brother holding the bag." Gianninni appeared skeptical. Kelly held up three fingers as if reciting the Boy Scout oath. "Good old Prissy left her newborn son in the hands of a twenty year old kid. Then, on the kid's first birthday she telephoned me to let me know that the boy was really mine."

"What did you do?"

"Nothing."

After a prolonged silence Antonio asked, "Why are you confessing this?"

"Because Tony, despite everything that has happened or will happen between us, I like you. We have a lot in common. You might think Priscilla is your ally, but take it from one who knows, she's a snake. Watch your back, she can strike at any minute."

Gianninni leaned back in his seat as the plane leveled off. "I appreciate your concern for my well-being, but I assure you that Priscilla is under control. Now let's try to think pleasant thoughts. Is there anywhere in Newport that you'd like to have lunch?"

Scarlet was feeling so melancholy that she couldn't even find it within herself to apply her lashes or bouffant her doo. Seated at her makeshift vanity, four orange milk crates topped by a piece of plywood draped with a remnant of Laura Ashley fabric, she lacked the energy to press the spritzer on her jar of Aqua Net. When the phone rang she leaned over to the nightstand and answered, her signature "hey there Sugar" replaced with a deadpan "hello." When she discovered that it was Abbie on the other end of the line, her spirits lifted.

"Oh Sugar," Scarlet oozed, "it is sooo good to hear from you."

"We're all set," Abbie informed her.

"Today?"

"Yes, today. Is that a problem?"

Scarlet reached for her teasing brush, "No problem at all."

"Good. You know what to do?"

"I know exactly what to do."

"Excellent, take down this phone number, I recently moved."

Scarlet used Avon midnight blue eyeliner to write the telephone number on a Kleenex, hung up the phone and started spraying. Danny boy was coming and she wanted to make a lasting impression.

The First Lady of Massachusetts emerged from her lair looking as if she had just survived a Gap store explosion. The uptight businesswoman who had stormed in the night before had been miraculously transformed into a Martha Stewart wannabe, complete with denim shirt, khakis and clogs.

Dan, noting that a wolf in sheep's clothing is still a wolf, couldn't resist asking, "What's with the wardrobe?" He poured tea for Hyacinth who sat at the kitchen table silently nibbling a Milano cookie. "Planning on doing a little antiquing before lunch?"

"No Dan," Priscilla inserted her large diamond stud earrings into her lobes, taking the 'casual' out of 'casual chic'. "I'm going to Tyle Island; I felt I should dress the part."

"I hate to disappoint you, but no one on Tyle Island dresses like that."

"Not yet," she sneered, "but they will."

"So what takes you to the Island?" he asked. "Casino problems?"

"Its nothing I can't handle."

"If you're going to the Island, why did you come here?"

"I need a flight."

"You could have flown direct from Boston."

"The Q&A is over Mr. Kelly," Priscilla glared. "Our ETD is four o'clock sharp."

Dan shook his head, "Hyacinth doesn't look up for traveling."

Priscilla tied a pale blue scarf around her neck. "Hyacinth isn't going."

Doc Gno finally made it back to Tyle Island. His nurse picked him up at the airport, chattering incessantly as she drove, filling him in on the latest happenings, finally remembering to inform him that he had received a call earlier that morning from a Dr. Lorraine Macy of the Center for Disease Control. Doc instructed the nurse to head straight for the office. That was one call he needed to return. She picked up the pace and as they took the bend on Airport road they nearly sideswiped a station wagon going the other way.

"Was that Lila?" Doc Gno asked as he looked back and watched the car drive off down the road.

"Looked like her," the nurse replied.

"Wonder why she's going to the airport," he commented.

"Maybe she finally took the hint and is leaving."

"Maybe," Doc continued to stare back in the direction Lila had driven, "maybe."

Lila parked her station wagon in the airport's empty dirt lot. She left the doors unlocked and the keys in the ignition as Priscilla had instructed. She then hurried into the office and asked Marjorie, full time ticket agent, part time pilot, for a flight to the mainland. Marjorie informed her that there were no pilots available. Lila suggested that Marjorie fly her. Marjorie explained that she couldn't leave the airport unattended. Lila removed her wallet from her purse and asked how much it would take for Marjorie to leave the airport unattended. Marjorie changed her mind.

Dino DeLuca was the best charter Milo ever had. The guy drank a lot, ate more, and swore like a Merchant Marine. They were having a successful morning of fishing when off in the distance Milo spotted a pleasure boat headed their way. He told an off-color joke involving a priest, a rabbi and a prostitute while keeping one eye on Dino and the other on their visitors. When the boat was no more than thirty yards off of their bow, Milo nudged Dino who had been concentrating on his line and gasped, "Good Lord will you look at that."

Dino spotted the boat and more to the point, the boaters. Five big-haired women with large breasts and teeny bikinis were sunning themselves on the deck.

"Now this is what I call a fucking vacation." Dino gave Milo a pat on the back that nearly sent him overboard.

The boatful of scantily clad women circled The Mary Rose; large breasts flailed about as the woman enthusiastically jumped up and down and waved greetings to their fellow seamen. Dino enthusiastically jumped and waved back. Milo did not, for he had noticed the name 'Irish Ayes' painted in emerald green along the bow of the vessel.

"Do you want me to be re-bait yer line for ya there Dino my boy?" Milo asked as he inched away from the target.

"I think I've had enough for today Pops," Dino put down his pole and fished through the cooler for a fresh beer. He found an ice cold Bud, popped the top and turned back to admire the view, but found to his great dismay, that the ladies were gone. The deck was empty, no more big hair, no more bouncing breasts.

"Where the fuck did they go?" Dino scratched his mammoth head. As he removed his sunglasses to get a better look, two men stepped out onto the deck with guns drawn. Milo, not wanting to be caught in the crossfire, climbed onto the side rail. He heard a loud "oh fuck" followed by two gunshots, then he dove, and when he hit the water, he swam like hell.

Chapter 40

Chief Tatum was immersed in a challenging game of FreeCell when he heard a commotion in the outer office.
"Good Lord what the hell happened to him?" Mabel screamed. The Chief stared at the computerized playing cards displayed across his screen and tried to ignore what he had just heard.
"You'd better get out here Chief," Mabel hollered. "This ones a doozy."
Chief Tatum sighed, then reluctantly abandoned his game and went to investigate this so called doozy.
What he found was Milo Donaghue standing in the middle of his Police Station with a wool stadium blanket wrapped around his shivering shoulders. Milo's hair and clothing were soaking wet and when he took a step toward the Chief water squished out of the tattered seams of his canvas sneakers. The Chief repeated Mabel's original query. "What the hell happened to him?"
Sammy Long, a local lobsterman, stepped forward to inform the Chief that he had pulled Milo out of the icy water less than a half hour earlier.
"What was he doing in the water?" the Chief asked.
"The back stroke," Sammy replied.
Chief Tatum closed his eyes. He slowly reopened them then addressed the quaking old man, "What happened to you Milo?"
Milo tried to respond but his teeth were chattering so furiously that he couldn't manage a single word. The Chief instructed Mabel to retrieve the bottle of Wild Turkey he stored in his bottom desk drawer. Milo shook his head in the negative as his trembling hands pulled a fifth of Jim Beam out of a watery pocket of his olive drab army jacket. The Chief uncapped the bottle for his shivering friend. Milo placed the bottle to his pale blue

lips and drank. After several substantial gulps Milo was able to relay the story of his misadventure at sea.

A few of the details had grown fuzzy, perhaps from the time spent in the cold Atlantic waters, perhaps from the booze, but more likely from the three hundred in cash provided by Taloy. The name of the boat carrying the gunmen had somehow slipped Milo's mind, and he was unable to give an accurate physical description of either assailant. He did, however, tell them all about the bluefish that were practically jumping into the boat, and the titties that were spilling out everywhere, and Dino DeLuca's final words, "oh fuck," and the two gun shots, pop-pop, and diving into the ocean and swimming like hell.

When both he and the fifth of Jim Beam were finished, Milo asked Chief Tatum if he would contact the Coast Guard and arrange for the retrieval of the Mary Rose. The Chief assured Milo he would see to it straight away. With the excitement subsiding, the handful of locals who had wandered in during the questioning dispersed to perform their civic duty and spread word of the hit man's demise. Chief Tatum returned to his office and telephoned The Harbor Master who had already heard a slightly embellished version of Milo's tall tale. The Chief suggested that the men take out a rescue boat and have a look for themselves before calling in the Coast Guard. John Beale agreed.

"By the way John," the Chief added, "have you seen Taloy today?"

"He's sitting right beside me Chief. Has been all morning."

"Tell him well done."


Scarlet's make-up was flawless, her hair raised to new heights and the pink sweater she wore accented both her coloring and her cleavage. She sat behind the counter in her rusty old trailer, sipping an iced tea and waiting for her flyboy to arrive.

No flights came or went all day, causing the hours to pass as slowly as a sultry summer night in Georgia. It was just after four when Scarlet finally heard a car drive up. She snuck a peek outside; sure enough handsome Dan was sitting in the passenger seat of one of those gas-guzzling Sports Utility Vehicles that was all the rage with Yuppie housewives. Priscilla Hardy was behind the wheel. The old lady didn't appear to be with them. Scarlet hurried back behind the counter and awaited her guests. Dan entered first; he flashed Scarlet a knowing wink, causing those parts of the anatomy that a lady did not discuss, to quiver.

"May I help you Sugar?" Southern charm dripped from Scarlet's voice.

Dan tried to hide the little grin that began to form at the corners of his mouth, but failed. Priscilla, who caught a glimpse of the exchange, dismissed it as a mere flirtation and muttered, "Please Dan, surely you can do better than her."

Not since the Battle of Gettysburg had the relationship between the North and the South been so strained. Dan, getting the distinct impression that the south was indeed about to rise again, stepped in to calm the waters.

"I'm Dan Kelly. You've been keeping an eye on my plane."

"Among other things," Scarlet batted her thick black lashes before setting her sights on Priscilla. "So honey, where's your sister?"

"My sister?"

"The lovely woman who was with you last time you stopped in."

"That wasn't my sister," Priscilla scoffed at the notion as she adjusted the knot in her powder blue scarf.

"Well you all could have been twins." Scarlet grinned then returned her attention to Dan. "Your airplane is waiting for you right out back," she touched his hand playfully and felt sparks run down her spine. "Shall I show you the way?"

"I'm sure we can find it," Priscilla took Dan by the arm and dragged him outside.

Scarlet followed them out of the trailer. She stood at the top of the steps holding the squeaky screen door open and warned, "Keep an eye out for my puppies. They get nervous around strangers."

"I think we can handle a couple of dogs," Priscilla snarled as she stormed away.

Dan paused and reached up to Scarlet who stood on the top step of her dilapidated trailer looking like a low country Juliet awaiting her very own Bubba Ray Romeo. Dan took Scarlet's hand in his and gently kissed it. "Thank you for everything," he whispered, and then silently mouthed the words, "she's at the house."

"It's been my pleasure," Scarlet brushed her hand along Dan's tanned cheek then slowly turned around to give him an eyeful of her other assets. She reentered her trailer and, feeling slightly overheated from the encounter with her dream pilot, sauntered back behind the counter to sip from her glass of iced tea. She listened to a series of playful barks. Then she heard Priscilla Hardy scream.

"Oh, those silly girls," Scarlet giggled as she pulled a Kleenex from her purse and dabbed at the beads of perspiration which had formed on her neck and chest. "Always wanting to play with strangers."

She tossed the damp Kleenex back in her bag and waited until she heard the plane's engine come to life, then she stepped outside and watched Dan Kelly's Cessna taxi across the grassy field. As it sped down the runway Scarlet hurried over to the Mustang and called in her sing-song voice for Lucy and Ethel to join her.

They were the oddest threesome in the marina. Gianninni was, as usual, dressed from head to toe in black but for the white silk necktie, while Kelly wore wrinkled khakis, an NYU sweatshirt, Yankee baseball cap and his favorite pair of worn-out loafers with the one sole coming loose. Dominic opted for a purple and black poly-blend running outfit that he accessorized with a bright orange life jacket that barely buckled around the bodyguard's enormous circumference. Not exactly the breed of boaters Newport was accustomed to.

First Gianninni, then Kelly boarded a luxury fishing boat that made the private jet look like a wind-up toy. Dominic handed a wicker picnic basket to Kelly then joined them on deck. While Dominic untied the docking ropes, Gianninni climbed up to the glass-enclosed tower that housed the controls. Kelly followed, whistling as he got his first glimpse of the elaborate bank of gadgets that drove the magnificent vessel.

"Would you like to do the honors?" Gianninni asked.

"I'd need a degree in rocket science to decipher this panel," Kelly answered with a laugh.

"It's not difficult. I'll take her out to open waters then you can try your hand."

As they cruised out of the marina Kelly felt like the envy of every pretentious boater in Newport for whom sailing was just another opportunity to flaunt one's wealth.

"Hey Tony?" he asked as he waved to a couple of kids in a rowboat. "You don't seem like much of a seaman. Where did you get the boat?"

"It belongs to a business associate. I borrow it from time to time. There's something about the sea that makes me feel at peace."

"Yet another link to the priesthood," Kelly patted Gianninni on the back. "The apostles were fisherman. Perhaps it's a sign."

Gianninni stared out at the endless horizon and quietly replied, "I've already received my sign, and I've told you of my family obligations." Kelly considered voicing his growing doubts regarding Antonio's family obligations, but before he got the chance to comment Gianninni added, "And speaking of families, I have a question for you."

"Fire away," Kelly stated, then cringed at his choice of words.

"Why didn't you ever claim your son?"

It was a question Kelly had asked countless times over the past sixteen years. "I suppose a kid just wasn't part of the plan."

The boat entered open waters. Gianninni stepped back from the controls so Kelly could have a try and stated, "What is it they say about the best laid plans?"

A gnaw hit Kelly's stomach and it wasn't seasickness.

A shift change took place at the Kelly house at five o'clock sharp; for the next five hours the two pregnant Islanders would perform surveillance. Single-birth mom was stationed behind a tree in the back yard, while multiple-birth mom was resting comfortably on a lawn chair behind the tall brush across the road.

Vincent Gianninni arrived at the Tyle Island Ferry to a chorus of "no money, no freight" being chanted by a group of burly longshoremen.

"What the hell is this?" Gianninni pressed the button that made his car window go down as they drove past the line of strikers. "Pull over and find out what this shit is all about."

Frac exited the car, approached one of the picketers and had a brief conversation. He then returned to the car and informed Fric and his boss that the union was on strike and the ferries weren't running in sympathy of the walkout.

Vincent stared out the car window, he had to get to Tyle Island, Abbie was waiting.

"I guess we gotta double back to the airport and fly," Frac commented.

Vincent continued staring out the widow; his gaze fixed on a tall, handsome man standing at the ticket booth. He looked familiar. When the young man turned, allowing Vincent a full frontal view, the old man gasped. Did his aging eyes deceive him or was that the one and only Dr. Jasper Black standing only fifty feet away? He pushed the button making the window lower all the way and called out, "Dr. Black. Dr. Black." The young man heard. He shielded his eyes from the glare of the slowly setting sun and ambled over to the car. "Doctor Black, is it really you?" Vincent reached out of the window and took Jack West's hand in his own. "It's so good to meet you. What are you doing here?"

Jack tousled his hair and flashed his pearly whites; he loved the recognition that accompanied his craft. "I was going to Tyle Island, but the ferries aren't running."

"I know, I know," Vincent's voice carried the enthusiasm of someone seventy years his junior. "That's where we were going too."

"You know any other ways of getting there besides flying?" Frac asked.

"You could sail," Jack suggested.

"In what?"

"A boat."

"No shit."

Vincent smacked Frac on the back of the head, "Don't you disrespect Dr. Black. He's a goddamn brain surgeon."

"Sorry," Frac reluctantly apologized as Vincent explained, "You see Doc the thing is we don't have a boat."

"There's a rental place about a half mile down the road. I was thinking about it," Jack shrugged, "but I'm short on cash."

"I got cash," Vincent struggled to open his door, then again smacked Frac on the back of the head. "Stop being so goddamn rude and let the Doc in."

Frac got out of the car, opened the door for Jack then returned to his place behind the wheel.

"So where is this joint?" Fric asked.

"Just go straight, it'll be on your right."

"So Doc," Vincent Gianninni patted Jack on the knee, "how was the ball?"

Pete Kelly sat on the end of Abbie's king sized bed and stared out at the ocean. God, he was bored. While he was under house arrest his friends were partying at the bluffs. He was dying to join them, if only for a couple of hours, but he knew that Chief Tatum would kick his ass if he went against orders and skipped out. Then again, Pete thought, the Chief was so busy that the odds of him ever finding out were slim. He could go for one beer and be back before anyone knew he was gone. Abbie's Jeep was parked in the driveway and he had the keys. "Oh what the hell," he said as he stood, his head brushing against the linen canopy that draped across the four poster bed, "one lousy beer can't hurt."

This time there would be no sneaking around the woods for Scarlet Newbaker. She pulled her car right up to the front door of the Governor's house and honked the horn twice. Then she and the girls got out, marched up to the front door and knocked. No one answered.

"Hyacinth," she called out, "it's Scarlet Newbaker, from the airport. There's been an accident, I was sent to get you."

Scarlet heard the sound of a deadbolt being disengaged and watched the door slowly open. A china doll of an old woman, with soft gray hair and mother of pearl eyeglasses peeked out; she appeared frailer than Scarlet had remembered. When Hyacinth finally recognized Scarlet as the woman who tried to give her a drink of water, she opened the door wider and asked, "Is she dead?"

"Who?"

"Priscilla."

"No."

"Shit," Hyacinth turned around and disappeared into the house. Scarlet, Lucy and Ethel waited a moment then went in after her. After some searching they found the Widow Poole in a bedroom packing a bag.

Scarlet stood in the doorway and explained. "I'm sorry that I lied to you about there being an accident and all, but I needed you to invite me in so we could talk."

"You've come to get me haven't you?"

"Well... yes... I suppose," Scarlet nodded.

"It's about damn time."

"Pardon me?"

"I've been waiting weeks for someone to rescue me. I was starting to think that every last one of those freaks on Tyle Island had forgotten about me."

"Forgotten about you?" Scarlet stepped into the room, "Mrs. Poole they've been trying to find you."

"Well what do they need, a trail of breadcrumbs?" The old woman shook her head in disgust, "I always knew Tatum was a lousy Chief of Police, and this proves it. The man couldn't find a grain of sand on the beach." She closed and locked her suitcase then looked to Scarlet, "Well what are you waiting for? Take my bag."

"Take your bag where?" Scarlet asked.

"You came to get me, let's go."

"Oh, no, no, Mrs. Poole, we aren't going anywhere, yet. Abbie asked me to come speak with you."

"Who is Abbie and why should I care about what you have to say?"

"Abbie is from Tyle Island."

The old woman adjusted her eyeglasses and pursed her coral colored lips. "You are mistaken young lady. I know every single person on Tyle Island and there is no one named Abbie."

"She's Bob Kelly's girlfriend."

Before Scarlet had a chance to react, Hyacinth Poole's suitcase hit her squarely in the shins. If Scarlet had been shorter, and Hyacinth taller, the blow would have done some series damage to those parts of her anatomy of which Scarlet was too much of a lady to speak.

"Who are you?" Hyacinth hollered. "Did Priscilla send you to kill me?"

With Lucy and Ethel nowhere in sight, they had returned to the cool porcelain of the bathtub to doze, Scarlet was left to defend herself. "Calm down Mrs. Poole," Scarlet held up her hands to protect her face as she cautiously limped toward the luggage wielding old woman. "I've already explained."

Hyacinth was a fluster. Her words came rapidly and were difficult to understand. "You said Bob Kelly has a girlfriend, and I know Bob Kelly doesn't have a girlfriend. He couldn't have a girlfriend; he's a miserable drunk and a verbally abusive S.O.B."

Fearing that Hyacinth would have a coronary and drop on the spot, Scarlet backed up a distance and tried to calmly explain. "Abbie has been trying to stop a casino from being built on Tyle Island. She is luring Priscilla Hardy to the island in order to confront her with some sort of gossip about Priscilla's past. Something about being related to a mobster."

Hyacinth lowered her suitcase, "I'm listening."

"Abbie is planning to blackmail her. She figures that rather than exposing herself and her husband to a scandal that would ruin his political career, Priscilla might be willing to use her influence with the builder, Antonio Gia-something, and convince him to stop construction. Are you following me so far?"

"I'm following. Go on."

"Assuming that Priscilla would most likely want to keep you away from Tyle Island, you being the Benedict Arnold that gave up the land in the first place," Hyacinth scowled at the analogy but Scarlet ignored her and went on, "Abbie sent me here to beg you to come forward and admit that you falsified town records. You see Sugar, if you're sweet enough to do that, then the casino can be stopped whether that horrible Mrs. Governor Hardy cooperates or not, and everyone will live happily ever after."

Hyacinth put down her suitcase. "Everyone but your friend Abbie."

"Whys that?"

"Something has happened in the past day or so to put Priscilla in an awfully sour mood," Hyacinth sighed, "and she's got a gun."

Scarlet's eyes grew as wide as saucers. "I have to warn Abbie." She rummaged through her purse, pulled out the Kleenex, unfolded it and discovered that the telephone number had become an illegible blur of Avon Midnight Blue eyeliner. She stared at the still damp tissue recalling how, following her adulterous flirtation with Dan Kelly, she had used the Kleenex to blot beads of perspiration from her still heaving bosom. Scarlet collapsed onto the bed, placed her head in her hands and began to weep.

"Don't you worry dear," Hyacinth took Scarlet by the wrist, "I know who to call. Just get me to a working telephone. Priscilla had this one shut off when Danny moved in."

Scarlet grabbed her purse and whistled for the dogs. They all rushed out of the house, climbed into the Mustang and sped down the bumpy, country roads toward the airport. Ten minutes later they pulled up in front of the trailer. Scarlet helped Hyacinth out of the car and led her inside where Hyacinth immediately went to the phone and dialed the Tyle Island Police Department. Ten rings, no answer. Unaware that he was dead, she next dialed Owen Brady's house and again got no answer. She tried the Harbor Master's office. Ten rings, no answer. She dialed Clara's Diner. No answer. Doc Gno, no answer. And last but not least she dialed Mildred Ahearn. Mildred was sure to be home, Mildred never went out. Ten rings, no answer. She placed the phone on its cradle and informed Scarlet that, "It appears that no one on Tyle Island is home."

"How can we get there?" Scarlet pleaded for an answer.

"There's a ferry," Hyacinth scowled, "but it's too long a drive, we'll never make it in time."

Scarlet threw her body across the counter and wailed.

"We could always..." Hyacinth paused.

Scarlet looked up. "We could always what?"

"Fly."


Abbie spent the day rearranging the kitchen cabinets, putting the books in alphabetical order by author and title (not a complicated task since most were Kelly novels), cleaning Kelly's bedroom and doing two loads of laundry. As she hurried out to the back yard to take the second load of wash off the clothesline she heard the sound of an airplane engine in the distance. She looked up into the darkening sky and saw a small plane begin its approach. It was too far off to check the numbers, but something told her it was Dan Kelly's plane. She dropped the laundry basket and hurried inside.


"Are you sure you know what you're doing?" Hyacinth asked as she fastened her seat belt.

"Don't you worry Sugar, I've seen it done a thousand times." Scarlet finished buckling Lucy and Ethel into the rear of a four-seat plane. She then went through the checklist that her husband religiously followed every time he prepared for takeoff. Once assured that every switch was appropriately flicked and every knob turned to the right position, Scarlet took a deep breath and started the engine. She then slowly taxied toward the runway allowing herself time to get a feel for the controls. Lucy and Ethel were whimpering in the rear and Hyacinth's pale skin had grown paler, but Scarlet wasn't worried, she felt alive. When the tires hit tarmac she opened her up, sped down the runway and pulled back on the controls until she felt the ground fall off from underneath her. Scarlet Newbaker was airborne.

## Chapter 41

It started like a gas bubble, slight discomfort, a twinge here and there. Then came the cramping, nothing too severe, just enough to let one know that something out of the ordinary was taking place. Then her water broke. Right there in the tall bushes across the street from the Kelly house, multiple-birth mom went into labor. She took several deep breaths to calm herself then slowly raised herself out of her lawn chair. With one hand supporting her lower back and the other her protruding front, she waddled across the road and into the backyard.

"Where are you?" she called out in a semi-whisper.

"Over hear," she heard a strained voice answer from behind a wide tree.

She waddled over toward the source of the voice and announced, "My water broke." Then she looked down and found single-birth mom lying on her back panting the short quick breaths taught in Lamaze. Through gritted teeth that warned of an oncoming contraction single birth mom responded, "So did mine."

The airport was empty. Dan parked his plane in its customary spot and shut off the engines.

"So what's next Priss?" he asked, taking pleasure in knowing that her troubles were just beginning while his would soon be coming to an end.

"We're going to your house."

"I'm not going anywhere," Dan laughed.

Priscilla pulled the gun from her purse and pointed it at him. "Yes, you are."

He stopped laughing.

"There's the coastline," Hyacinth pointed toward the ocean then looked down at the aerial map of the Massachusetts Coast that Scarlet had pulled off the wall of the trailer before setting off on their journey. "Make a right."

The sun was starting to set and Scarlet was starting to panic. As she had never before landed a plane, the possibility of making her first attempt at dusk, on a tiny island, was causing her some distress. Hyacinth sensed Scarlet's concern and reassured her in a grandmotherly voice, "We're almost home dear, and you're doing remarkably well for a beginner."

"Thank you Sugar," Scarlet whispered as she gripped the controls and banked right.

While John Beale navigated, Chief Tatum and two of his newly deputized fisherman searched the waters for signs of The Mary Rose. They had already spent hours circling the island and had turned up naught; the Chief was starting to fear that she had been sunk or had drifted into the shipping lanes and taken a long ride on the current. Just as he was about to throw in the towel, one of his deputies called out that he had spotted something due east. Chief Tatum raised his binoculars to his eyes and scanned the area where the fisherman had pointed. It was a small motorboat carrying...he adjusted the focus, four people. Sensing that the boaters were in distress he instructed John Beale to move in.

Doc Gno marched through Barron's Hollow with a king sized white cotton bed sheet dragging behind him; Clara did the same twenty yards to his right. Every so often they would stop to inspect their catch. Doctor Macy of the CDC would be flying in the following morning, which meant Doc Gno had less than twelve hours to collect enough deer tick specimens to support his claim of a Lyme Disease outbreak of pandemic proportion. Not only was the Hollow's future at stake, his future in medicine hung in the balance. The last he had heard, the CDC didn't take kindly to false claims of health threatening insect outbreaks or unwarranted requests for quarantines.

   Abbie had not been expecting a knock at the backdoor, but no blow of an air horn meant that all was still well. When she opened the door to discover two women in the throws of childbirth, all thoughts of Priscilla's pending visit disappeared.
   "Our waters broke," multiple-birth mom announced.
   A series of "oh shit, oh shits" followed as Abbie assisted first one, then the second mother-to-be into the house. They waddled their way across the kitchen and carefully lowered their oversized bodies onto undersized wooden chairs.
   "What do we do? What do we do?" Abbie asked one child-bearer, then the next.
   Single birth mom, struck by a contraction of seismic proportions told her, in a demonic voice, to call the f-ing doctor. Abbie ran to the telephone, then stopped dead in her tracks and asked, "What's his number?" Multiple-birth mom recited the number while Abbie dialed. She waited through eight rings then slammed the telephone down. "He's not answering," Abbie whined as she rushed to one of the newly arranged cabinets pulled out a pot, took a look at the two women and exchanged the four-quart capacity for a lobster pot, filled it with water and set it to boil. When questioned as to what the hell the water was for she admitted she had no frigging clue, but thought it might come in handy. Single-birth mom, who was now between contractions, calmly suggested that Abbie call the Police Station and have Chief Tatum track down Doc Gno. More dialing, more ringing, but still no one home. Multiple-birth mom, hit with her first toe curling contraction, demanded that Abbie do something,

NOW. What to do, what to do, the panic drums beat wildly. Then, struck by a moment of clarity, "The air horns" she said aloud, "If I blow an air horn this whole Island will come running." She started for the front door then realized the backyard was closer. She pivoted, ran past the women assuring them that help would soon be on the way, checked the water, not even a simmer, then swung open the screen door and came face to face with Dan Kelly. Behind him stood Priscilla Hardy, and in her hand was a gun.

 

While Dominic manned the controls, Kelly and Gianninni reclined in deck chairs and nibbled on a sampling of crusty breads, cured sausages and zesty cheeses that Antonio had packed for the journey. As the sun began to set Gianninni popped the cork on a bottle of champagne and filled two tall flutes; even a scotch drinker couldn't pass up Crystal. They watched as the sky was slowly transformed from a pallet of soft blue to vibrant orange then to fiery red; it was as if the sun was performing for them, aware that this would be Kelly's final Tyle Island sunset and giving him a spectacular show.

"We should make our way to the west side," Kelly suggested between bites of parmegiano-reggiano. "But stay far enough off the coast so that our presence doesn't sound an alarm."

Gianninni studied the tiny bubbles bursting in his glass, "Why would a pair of pleasure boaters be a cause for alarm?"

"We don't belong."

"But..."

"Trust me Tony, if the people of Tyle Island knew that you were sitting a half mile off their coast they would catch, kill, stuff, and mount you over the bar at the Nest. You, my friend, would make the ultimate trophy fish."

Gianninni paused to consider Kelly's imagery then responded, "It's remarkable."

"The sunset or the wine?" Kelly drained the last of the champagne from his glass and reached for the bottle.

"Neither," Antonio held out his glass so Bob could refill it. "It's the fact that you are actually concerned for my well being that astounds me."

"All I ever wanted was for you to find another site for your casino," Kelly topped off the Antonio's glass. "I never wanted you dead."

A combination of joy and dread struck Scarlet when she saw Tyle Island come into view. She was grateful that having miraculously stumbled upon the Island they would not be lost at sea, but now she was faced with the challenge of landing. Hyacinth sensed Scarlet's increasing apprehension and assured her, "The airport is smack dab in the center of the Island. Just aim for the middle and we'll be fine."

"I'm glad you have so much confidence in me Sugar, 'cus I'm damn near ready to piddle my pants."

Scarlet spent the next several minutes replaying in her mind the steps that her husband had always followed when preparing for landing. When the process was complete she took a deep breath and began her descent. Lucy and Ethel whimpered while Hyacinth held on for dear life and prayed. As Scarlet cut back on the power, the engine began to sputter out. She made a quick adjustment that caused the engines to quickly spring back to life.

"Sorry," she whispered.

"You're forgiven," Hyacinth whispered back.

"I'm gonna take her down now Sugar, so hold on tight."

The plane skimmed the treetops and tilted a little too far to the left. Scarlet compensated, then over-compensated and tilted too far to the right, then she evened her out, decreased altitude, lower, and lower until the tires ever-so gently kissed the tarmac. They bounced, touched back down again, bounced twice more, then skidded to the end of the runway, off the tarmac, and finally stopped.

Scarlet cried and Lucy and Ethel barked with joy as Hyacinth unfastened her seatbelt and embraced her new southern friend.

"Mrs. Newbaker," Hyacinth wiped a mascara-trailed tear off of Scarlet's flushed cheek, "you are one hell of a pilot."

"I did it," Scarlet yahooed, "I flew."

"We have to get to town," Hyacinth glanced back at the shed that handled arrivals, departures, concessions, and every other airport service, and noted that it appeared deserted and locked up tight.

"How far is it?" Scarlet asked as she reattached a stray eyelash that had come loose with the tears.

"Too far to walk." Hyacinth sounded defeated.

"Why walk?" Scarlet managed to get the lash realigned, "when we can drive."

"But Scarlet dear, we don't have a car."

"No Sugar, but we do have a plane." Scarlet restarted the engine and taxied the small airplane across the airfield and through the adjacent dirt lot. "Which way?" she asked when they reached the paved Airport Road.

"Right," Hyacinth directed.

Scarlet turned right and headed to town.


"The young guy looks familiar," John Beale commented as they approached the motorboat that was dead in the water. Two overdressed men were paddling the crippled vessel while the familiar looking young man waved down the rescuers. As they drew closer Chief Tatum realized, "It's Doctor Jasper Black."

"Abbie's fiancé?"

"Former fiancé," the Chief corrected.
"She dumped him?"
"She did."
"For Kelly?"
"I do believe."
"Then what is he doing here? And who are his friends?"
"I'm not sure. Let's find out."

When they had gotten within shouting distance of the crippled craft, the Chief called out, "What seems to be the problem?"

"Motor died. You got here in the nick of time." Jack was clearly flustered by the harrowing ordeal, "We might have died."

"No need to be so dramatic," John Beale threw a line to one of the goons. "You're not even a mile from shore. You would have made it sooner or later."

Jack, finally recognizing his rescuers, flashed his pearly whites and asked, "Haven't we met?"

"We have," the Chief looked suspiciously at the two goons. "Have you seen any other boats in the area? We're looking for an old Boston Whaler named The Mary Rose."

"Haven't seen her," Jack replied.

"Who are your friends?" the Chief asked.

"This is Vincent," he pointed to the old man, "and these are his drivers."

"What sort of man needs two drivers?" Chief Tatum asked.

Fric and Frac weren't talking and Vincent sat silently trembling from the cold. The Chief instructed the two fishermen to secure the towropes and invited the four stranded men aboard.

"I've got to get to Abbie in a hurry," Jack explained as he grabbed John Beale's hand for balance while transferring between the two boats that rocked with the tide.

The Chief assured Jack that he would be getting to Abbie soon enough. After the rest of the men had been helped aboard, John Beale whispered to Tatum, "If he goes looking for Abbie, he might spoil the plan."

"Give the old man coffee and a blanket then take the long way home. I'll keep an eye on those two," he gestured toward Fric and Frac. "They're trouble if ever I saw it."

"You armed?" John Beale asked.

Chief Tatum shook his head no.

Anticipating a possible infiltration by the enemy Joe Morgan and his son went out to West Side Road and moved the spikes into place.

As Mildred hunted through the tall grass along West Side Road, a familiar scent caught the attention of her high-powered sniffer. It was a pleasant smell, not the rotting flesh that she was hunting. It was the subtle scent of class and breeding. She raised her nose up into the gentle breeze and inhaled - ahh, Chanel.

Scarlet was cruising down the narrow, winding roads of Tyle Island oblivious to the carnage she was leaving in her wake. Rose bushes and honeysuckle that grew wild along the route fell victim to a wing expanse that exceeded that of the street. Even the typically fearless deer scurried into the brush when the giant machine threatened to decapitate them as they nibbled the roadside greenery. When she arrived at a fork in the road she looked to Hyacinth for directions.

Hyacinth pointed to the left, "Take West Side Road, its quicker."

So Scarlet went left, and, despite the s-curves and increasing darkness, was making pretty good time until, ka-boom, a tire blew. The plane skidded out of control, struck a rock wall head-on, sputtered twice and died.

"What on earth was that?" Hyacinth asked as Scarlet unbuckled her seatbelt and stepped out to inspect the plane. After a quick assessment, she poked her head back in and announced, "It looks like we're walking."

Undaunted, Hyacinth unfastened her own seatbelt then released the dogs. "The Kelly house isn't far. I'll call Chief Tatum from there."

Scarlet's heart fluttered at the sound of the Kelly name. She assisted Hyacinth out of the plane then the two women set off on foot with Lucy and Ethel romping playfully behind them.

One beer turned into six, and before Pete knew it the party was breaking up. He didn't feel like going back to Abbie's, there was nothing to do there, and Friday night television sucked. If he stopped by The Nest the Chief would surely find out, so that was out of the question. Then he came up with the brilliant idea of stopping by the Conservancy Council office and liberating his computer.

Abbie had spent the past twenty-four hours imagining the moment when she would come face to face with Priscilla Hardy. None of the scenarios had included women in labor, a man held at gunpoint, or a pistol toting Martha Stewart groupie. She had envisioned the First Lady as a viper, tall and sleek with a killer wardrobe and an attitude to match. Instead she had come face to face with soccer mom. Granted soccer mom was armed, but still, Abbie was at a complete loss for how to handle the situation. That is, until Priscilla Hardy finally spoke.

"Where's that son of a bitch Bob Kelly?" she growled, her dark brown eyes narrowing and her rhinosplasty enhanced nostrils aflair. Only a soccer mom behind the wheel of a Suburban, fighting over the last available parking spot at the mall could have mustered such venom. Abbie breathed a sigh of relief. Now this was a character that she was accustomed to dealing with. Soap operas were short on cupcake baking housewives, but evil bitches were a dime a dozen. The Emmy award winning soap opera writer would simply pretend that she was in Benton Springs and write herself out of this latest dilemma. The scene would be a breeze. Dialogue worthy of The Darkest Hour began to flow.

"Bob has been off Island," Abbie snarled back, "since Monday."

"He's back. I know he's back."

"I'm sorry, but you're mistaken."

"Where's my son?"

"If you mean Pete," Abbie's voice rose to a dramatic crescendo, "you won't find him here."

"Who are you?" Priscilla seemed puzzled by the odd woman in the baggy sweatpants who seemed to be emoting.

"My name is Abigail O'Neal," Abbie raised an eyebrow, "Mrs. Governor Hardy I presume?"

Priscilla did not respond. Instead she stared blankly at Abbie as if she was some sideshow freak.

"Please Priscilla Steele-Des Pierre-Hardy, don't be shy, I know all about you. That private e-mail that Pete sent you," Abbie grinned, "was not so private after all."

Priscilla now appeared as if the bearded lady had just been joined by sword swallowing Siamese twins.

"The truth is," Abbie crossed her arms and slowly circled the woman who held her gun dangerously close to Dan Kelly's head, "everyone on Tyle Island is privy to the fact that you were the brains behind the Barron's Hollow land scam. We know that your supposed country club blue blood is tainted with mafia platelets. What did you think would happen when you got here Mrs. Hardy? Did you honestly think that Pete would feel some long lost loyalty to the mother who abandoned him? Or does that gun in your hand tell us that you were coming to quiet your long lost son forever?" Abbie longed for a pen and paper; this was Emmy winning dialogue being wasted on an audience of three.

"Who is this woman?" Priscilla asked Dan. "Some kind of nutcase?"

"Oh, I am no nutcase Priscilla. I am your judge and jury. It's High Noon and I'm Gary Cooper. It's all over lady," Abbie held out her hand as if awaiting the relinquishment of the weapon.

"Excuse me," Priscilla interjected, "but correct me if I'm wrong. Isn't the person with the gun usually the one with the upper hand?"

"You wouldn't be foolish enough to pull the trigger."

"And why not?" Priscilla appeared outwardly amused as she waited for what was sure to be a lengthy and over-acted reply.

"You're on an island. What do you plan on doing, shooting your pilot then swimming for freedom?" Abbie grinned with satisfaction, she had been triumphant, the tables had turned. God she was good.

"You know you actually have a point," Priscilla stepped away from Dan and placed the gun against the temple of multiple-birth mom whose deep rhythmic panting quickened when she felt the cold steel barrel press against her skin. Single birth mom cried out in a combination of frustration and pain. "This way my pilot stays healthy and I still have the upper hand. Thank you for the suggestion. Now shut up and sit down."

Abbie grimaced. Kelly was right, real life was way more complicated than soap operas. Cut. Take two.

## Chapter 42

There are people who handle pressure well. People for whom adrenaline is a drug that peaks their creativity and hones their cognitive powers to a deadly point. People who view a pit of quick sand as a day on the beach, and an insurmountable obstacle as just one more bump in the road. People like trauma surgeons, firefighters, Wall Street brokers and big city cops. The greatest of athletes, the most decorated of soldiers, and even on occasion, a writer facing a deadline.

Abbie cleared her throat and announced, "I have to pee."

It was Dan's turn to gawk. "That's all you have to say? You have to pee?"

"Well I do," Abbie shrugged then looked up to Priscilla, "may I?"

"No."

"The bathroom is right there," Abbie pointed to the door. "I assure you that there are no windows by which I can escape and you have my word that I can not, nor would I care to, flush myself down the toilet."

"Will it shut you up?"

Abbie nodded.

Priscilla pointed the gun barrel in the direction of the bathroom. "Then go."

"Thank you." Abbie reached for her backpack.

"Hold it right there."

Abbie stopped reaching.

"What's the bag for?" Priscilla asked.

"I need a..." Abbie looked to Dan then back to Priscilla and mouthed the word 'tampon'.

"Just go." Priscilla's tone expressed her astute conclusion that her hostage was insane.

Abbie grabbed the backpack, hurried to the bathroom, closed the door, took a seat on the bowl, unzipped the bag and rummaged through the contents until she found - voila - her cell phone. She flipped it open and discovered that she had messages.

She first listened to Megan's voice explaining that Kelly had been spotted alive. Abbie was pleased, but too preoccupied with pregnant ladies and big black guns to fully appreciate the fact that the love of her life was still breathing. A second message followed, also from Megan, passing on word that actual contact with Kelly had been made. Abbie's brow furrowed as Megan went on to inform her that Kelly would see her Friday on the beach. What Friday? Abbie asked herself, and what beach?

"Hurry up in there," the First Lady bellowed from the other side of the door.

Abbie quickly dialed the only Tyle Island phone number she had committed to memory but reached the answering machine instead of Pete.

"I said hurry it up," Priscilla repeated. The edge in her voice growing sharper by the second, so Abbie, picturing Pete lounging in the hot tub instead of dutifully answering the phone, waited for the beep then whispered that it was her and that she was in trouble and that he should send Chief Tatum and a large posse of his deputies right away. Then she stood, flushed, hid the cell phone in the medicine cabinet and hurried out to find Priscilla still holding the gun to the sweaty head of multiple-birth mom.

"Now where was I?" Abbie asked the group. "I needed to pee, did that, oh, that's right, I was about to inform Priscilla that earlier today an associate of mine liberated Hyacinth Poole from The Hardy family vacation house. The Widow is currently in protective custody and singing like a canary." Abbie took a seat next to Dan, placed her backpack at her feet and asked, "Was that better than I gotta pee?" She then re-addressed Priscilla. "At this very moment your Mob affiliations and your involvement with the fraudulent land scam are being made a matter of public record. Might I suggest that, under the circumstances, you allow me to get these women some medical attention before you add murder to your list of felonies?"

Priscilla appeared un-phased by Abbie's rambling monologue.

"I can see from your rumpled brow that you doubt both my sanity and my sincerity so I will offer you some legitimate proof to substantiate my claims. Show her your chest Dan." Dan unbuttoned his shirt and revealed his new hairlessness. "This past Wednesday my associate and I paid a visit to Wakefield where we found Dan hiding out in your post-modernist pseudo-Swiss chalet. After charming our way through the back door, we confronted Daniel regarding Hyacinth Poole's mysterious disappearance. He remained steadfast and refused to talk so," she shrugged, "we did what any pair of young, intelligent and might I say very resourceful young woman would do in our situation, we tortured him into submission. It's amazing how utilitarian a tool duct tape can be. Under great duress," she glanced down at Dan Kelly's crotch, "he confessed that you blackmailed him into flying the get-away plane that carried Hyacinth and the other traitorous Conservancy Council members off Island."

Priscilla remained stoic so Abbie added, "and if you still don't believe me, a black leather sofa dominates your living space, you've got lavender towels in the guest bath, and the black piece of art glass that you're trying to pass off as Murano is a fake."

That got her attention.

Priscilla slowly lowered the gun. Multiple-birth mom let out a faint moan as she felt the cold steel move away from her temple. Abbie knew that the fate of the women, their unborn children and she and Dan for that matter hung in the balance. "Dan will fly you anywhere you want to go Priscilla. This is your chance to get away."

The room was silent except for the slow, rhythmic breathing of the mothers-to-be, the quiet hiss of the water simmering in the lobster pot, and the thump, thump, thump of footsteps climbing the back stairs.

Thump, thump, thump? What thump, thump, thump?

Priscilla returned the gun to multiple-birth mom's temple and watched the doorknob slowly turn. Abbie held her breath. The door swung open and in walked Scarlet Newbaker followed by none other than Hyacinth Poole.

"Hyacinth!" Dan gasped.

"Hyacinth!" Priscilla grinned.

"Hyacinth?" Abbie whined as she dropped her head to the table and banged it, hard.

Pete stumbled up the staircase, entered the Conservancy Council office and smiled at his computer. He lovingly stroked her monitor and informed the machine that it was time to go home. He considered checking his e-mail before dismantling the system; however, the sun was down, the sky dark and the stars a twinkle. He realized that he was seriously AWOL and needed to get back home before being discovered. So he disconnected every cable and plug and carefully loaded his computer into Abbie's Jeep. Then he hurried back to Madonna's Cove before his presence could be missed.

Doc Gno and Clara gave up foraging after it had grown too dark to see. As they drove back to his office with the few deer tick specimens they had been fortunate enough to gather, Clara assured the doctor that she would return to the Hollow at dawn to continue the hunt. Doc Gno, his spirits atypically low due to the pending loss of his medical license, told her there was no need. The diner required her attention; after all he might need a job as a short order cook once the AMA got wind of his shenanigans. When they pulled up in front of his office they were met by a group of Islanders assembled outside. Doc Gno stepped out of his truck and inquired as to the problem.

"Lyme," one woman answered as she placed her foot on the truck's bumper and lifted her pant leg revealing the bulls-eye like rash that was a sure sign of a bite.

"We all got it," another Islander concurred.

"I don't understand," Doc Gno checked one rash after another using his high beams to light the way. "So many cases at one time?"

Clara scanned the faces in the group, placed a hand to her mouth and declared, "Sweet Jesus, they're all my tree-huggers."

"Your what?"

"My volunteers. They've spent the past week and a half chained to trees in the Hollow or crouching in Kelly's yard. They must have all gotten bit."

"Somebody oughta do something about these damn ticks," someone growled.

"I intend to," Doc Gno breathed a sigh of relief, "tomorrow."

After making a grilled cheese sandwich and grabbing a can of Pepsi from the fridge, Pete set about hooking up his computer in Abbie's library/den. With six beers under his belt it took several attempts before he was able to successfully set-up his baby, but when he finally turned her on and she sprang to life, Pete Kelly was once again content.

Priority one was to check his much neglected e-mail. There were a bunch of dirty jokes, several notices by fellow computer junkies sharing newly discovered software secrets which Pete saved to read when sober, and a heads up from the Puddle Of Mud fan club telling him that the band would be playing in Boston this coming July. Pete chugged some soda and burped as he scanned down the list of e-mails and came upon an unfamiliar address. Who the hell was ABBIEO11? When he clicked the READ prompt his jaw dropped to his chest:

    Pete -

    Urgent. Madonna sighting needed. Cove - 5-18 - 9:00 pm.

    Only chance to save my ass.

    Abbie will know what to do. Wish me luck kid.

It was signed Uncle Bob.

"Oh shit," Pete muttered, today was the eighteenth; he checked the clock, and it was 8:56. He had exactly four minutes to find a Virgin and get to the beach and since there were no women handy; he was on his own. His Doc Martins pounded up the wooden steps to the second floor where he entered Abbie's bedroom and began rifling through her drawers; tossing clothes everywhere as he searched for something Virgin-like to wear. Torn jeans and oxfords didn't quite fit the bill. He spun around and was headed for the bathroom when he stopped dead in front of the bed. He grinned, if it was the Madonna his Uncle needed, it was the Madonna he would get.

The Kelly kitchen was getting crowded. Scarlet and Hyacinth joined the others at the table, unfortunately Lucy and Ethel had been left to wait outside. Priscilla, still holding the gun to multiple-birth mom's head spoke on her cell phone. She was discussing delayed flights and apologizing for having missed dinner. She told whoever was on the other end, presumably the Gov, that she would return first thing in the morning. Then she asked to speak to the kids.

"Abbie Sugar, are you all right?" Scarlet whispered to her friend who was slumped forward on the table like a life-sized rag doll.

Abbie raised her head, answered dryly, "I'm just swell," then dropped her head back down on the table with a loud and painful sounding thud.

"So what happened?"

"What happened to whom?" Abbie asked, her head still lying on the table and a bit of drool spilling from her half open mouth.

"What happened to make her," Scarlet's eyes darted in the direction of the First Lady who was insisting that whomever was on the other end of the line finish his or her homework, "go wacko."

"This isn't wacko Scarlet," Abbie explained. "On Tyle Island this is par for the course."

"Well Sugar, I don't know what sort of course you're used to playing on, but I assure you that having the Governor's wife standing in your kitchen holding a gun to the head of a pregnant woman just ain't normal."

"Is threatening a man's testicles with mutilation by pinking shears normal?"

"Well no, I suppose it's not," Scarlet glanced across the table at Dan and pictured him naked.

"You see," Abbie insisted, "par for the course."

Scarlet shook the image of Dan's muscular thighs from her mind and demanded, "You can't compare the two Sugar. We did what we did because we were desperate. What's her excuse?"

Abbie considered Scarlet's curiously keen observation. Oddly enough she made an excellent point. Their actions had been motivated by desperation. Priscilla's behavior didn't make sense, unless... Abbie sat up straight and listened to Mrs. Governor Hardy promise a very special gift for whichever child to whom she was now speaking.

"Oh Sugar," Scarlet smiled hopefully, "you feeling better?"

Abbie used her sleeve to wipe the away the trail of drool that ran down her cheek. "Scarlet, you're right."

"About what, exactly?"

"This situation," Abbie drummed her fingers on the table top, "it's fucked up."

"Now, now," Scarlet objected, "I did not use those foul words."

"I apologize, I paraphrased, but you are right all the same." Abbie leaned over so she and Scarlet were shoulder-to-shoulder and whispered, "She's the first lady for Christ sakes. She's a responsible human being with a successful husband, a couple of kids, and hell, she's probably even got a Golden Retriever named Max to complete the portrait of Baby Boomer over-achiever utopia."

"She drives one of those SUV's," Scarlet added, "I saw it for myself."

"You see, twenty first century Norman Rockwell." Abbie's foot began to tap in time with the finger drumming. "She's semi-attractive, although her roots are beginning to show, and clearly she's an intelligent and motivated person, having conjured up this whole land scam scheme, yet something caused this otherwise stable and well-adjusted woman to jeopardize everything she has attained during her lifetime by coming here waving a weapon. I only know one person who is capable of inciting such rash behavior and poor judgment in a fellow human being."

"Who?"

"Bob Kelly."

"Your Bob?"

"Yes," Abbie, now downright excited, nodded furiously, "my Bob. I'm telling you Scarlet, he got to Gianninni, halted the casino deal and Priscilla came looking for revenge."

"Are you sure?"

"Positive. The clues were there I just didn't piece them together."

"What clues?"

"When Priscilla came busting through that door she wasn't looking for Pete; it was Bob she was after. I told her he had been off Island since Monday but she insisted he had returned; not that he was here all along, but that he returned which meant that Priscilla knew where he had been and most likely why."

"Oh Abbie Sugar," Scarlet let out a hushed squeal, "you're good at this who-dunnit stuff."

"Then I got a message on my cell phone telling me that Bob would see me tonight on the beach. I dismissed it earlier but tell me, how could a man who was blackmailing a mobster be coming home alive unless he had been successful?"

Scarlet thought for a second then responded, "It would have to be a miracle."

"This is real life Scarlet, not a soap opera, there are no miracles."

Scarlet summed up the situation. "So the casino is called off which is good news, and your boyfriend is coming home which is good news too, but we still have a problem in that she still has a gun."

"That is a problem," Abbie concurred.

"So what do we do?"

Abbie shrugged, "I left a message for Pete that we were in trouble. I suppose all we can do is stall for time until help arrives?"

Single birth mom let out a deep, guttural moan.

"Oh Sugar," Scarlet winced, "I know we're good, but I don't think we're good enough to stall what's happening there."

Priscilla snapped her cell phone closed and placed it on the counter. "That's enough out of you two."

"Here we go," Abbie gave Scarlet a conspiratorial nudge, then, "excuse me, Mrs. Hardy," she raised her hand as if in the classroom, "may I ask you a question?"

"No."

"Please."

"No."

"It's important."

"I don't care."

"I just want to know where the other council members are."

"That's none of your business."

"Prissy paid them off and sent them away," Hyacinth answered.

"Sent them where?" Abbie asked.

"Shut up," Priscilla demanded.

Hyacinth ignored her. "Some fancy around the world cruise. They left out of New York City and won't be back for months."

"So they're alive?" Abbie asked.

"Of course," Hyacinth sounded confident. "Priscilla has always had a nasty temperament but this violent streak is new."

"Well Mrs. Poole I must ask, if they are alive and cruising the world, why aren't you with them?"

"Good question Sugar."

"Thank you Scarlet.

"You're welcome."

"I'm glad you asked," Hyacinth adjusted her mother-of-pearl eyeglasses, "maybe now I can clear up a misconception that seems to be going around this Island regarding my part in this plan to build a casino."

"Oh please," Abbie leaned her elbows on the table, rested her chin in her hands, and urged, "do tell."

"Priscilla did not let me go with the others because she knew very well that at the very first opportunity I would have jumped ship, come home and spoiled her plan."

"Be quiet Hyacinth."

Abbie, like Hyacinth, ignored her captor and argued, "Come on, you can do better than that. You signed the minutes, making you an integral part of Priscilla's plan, and for the record, I had your signature authenticated so don't try denying that it was yours."

"It's true I signed those papers, but I didn't want to, I had to. If I didn't she would have..."

"I said shut up you old bat," Priscilla roared.

"How dare you use that tone of voice with your grandmother," Abbie scolded.

"My what?" the sideshow freak expression returned to the First Lady's face.

"Your grandmother," Abbie repeated.

"She's not my grandmother."

Abbie looked to Hyacinth, "You're not her grandmother?"

"Good Lord no."

Abbie rubbed her tired eyes, "I am so confused."

"Why dear?" Hyacinth asked.

"Priscilla Hardy was originally Priscilla Steele. Then she changed her name to Des Pierre. Des Pierre means 'of Peters'."

"Yes," Hyacinth nodded, "I suppose it does."

"And before you changed your name to Poole, it was Peters, correct?"

"Yes," Hyacinth nodded. "That's correct."

"So I just figured that you chose "of Peters" because Priscilla was your granddaughter and you wanted her to hold onto a piece of you as she traveled alone through this cold cruel world?"

"You have quite a flair for the dramatic, don't you young lady?" Hyacinth replied.

"Well if that wasn't the reason," Abbie whined, "then why?"

"You do know that Peter is also her child's name."

"So she chose Des Pierre as a way of holding onto Pete as she traveled through this cold cruel world alone?"

"No, not really."

"Oh Hyacinth, please just tell me why?"

"It sounded French."

"Huh?"

"If I remember correctly we were down to Smith, Jones or Des Pierre. Des Pierre had more mystique."

"You know Sugar," Scarlet voiced her opinion, "Des Pierre does sound nicer than Smith or Jones."

"All right, fine," Abbie was losing patience, half because she was so very tried and half because the basis upon which her whole Hyacinth-Priscilla link theory was dead wrong. "Like a typical writer I sought some symbolism behind the choice of names, but I will concede that I looked for depth within people who have none. I believed that you aided and abetted this bitch because you and she were blood. I now know you're not, so tell me Hyacinth, in ten words or less, if she's not your granddaughter then why the hell did you give her Barron's Hollow?"

"She had no choice," Priscilla, who clearly did not like being referred to as a bitch, and was sick and tired of being ignored, answered for the Widow Poole. "That land is rightfully mine."

Single birth mom screamed, threw back her head, spread open her legs, and started to push. Scarlet took a peek under the young woman's housedress and announced, "Abbie Sugar, I can't stall this."

"Do something," Priscilla ordered, quickly pointing the gun toward Scarlet before turning it back on multiple-birth mom.

"I don't know nothing about birthing babies," Scarlet did declare.

Dan stood and headed for the phone. "You're all insane. I'm calling for help." He picked up the receiver and began to dial.

"Put the phone down Dan," Priscilla ordered. He did not obey. Priscilla fired. Dan went down. The receiver dangled over his motionless body and slammed against the wall. Scarlet screamed and ran to his aid. Abbie rushed to single birth mom, squatted, placed her hands under the mother-to-very-soon-be's dress and prepared to catch the baby. Multiple-birth mom began pushing too. Lucy and Ethel began barking wildly and scratching on the back door. Hyacinth Poole calmly and quietly confessed.

"Sixty years ago I had a baby of my own," she smiled, "the sweetest little boy with hazel eyes and light brown hair, just like me." The smile faded, "I was only allowed to see him for a moment before they took him away." She looked to Abbie as if pleading for understanding. "I had to give him up, I was young and irresponsible and in no position to raise a baby."

Abbie was the wrong person from whom to seek compassion. Short on patience and therefore shorter on tact she clarified, "you were a knocked up hooker, a kid didn't fit into your plan, and would you mind speeding this story along," she grimaced as she peered between the legs of single birth mom, "it's getting messy under here."

Hyacinth dutifully quickened her speech. "I had already decided to give my baby up for adoption when one morning I was walking down Broadway and who did I run into but Eddie Steele." Since Abbie clearly knew the truth about her jaded past, Hyacinth decided not to waste any more time by trying to sugar coat the sordid details. "I spent a lot of time with Eddie and his friends before I got pregnant." She paused, "his friend Vincent was one of my regulars."

"Vincent Gianninni?" Abbie asked.

Hyacinth nodded.

"Is he the father?"

Hyacinth looked down, "I honestly don't know."

"That's enough reminiscing," Priscilla ordered.

"I've been silent for far too long Priscilla. It's time the truth came out." Hyacinth continued her tale. "I knew they were mobsters, but the mobsters were the ones with the money, and they were nice enough fellows, sharply dressed and well groomed." For a moment it looked as if Hyacinth was drifting back to the good old days, but an evil eye from Abbie made her u-turn from her jaunt down memory lane. "Eddie saw that I was pregnant and told me that he knew someone who would take the baby if it turned out to be a boy. The man was desperate for a son. He and his wife had one child but could not have another; money was no object, I could name my price. I agreed and gave Eddie my terms. He drew up the papers. Three weeks later I gave up my baby boy in exchange for my house on the hill and the property you now know as Barron's Hollow. I didn't need all that land, I just wanted a nice home and a quiet place to live, so after moving here I formed the Conservancy Council, donated the land and had the property designated as a Nature Refuge."

"But the land wasn't yours to give." Priscilla interjected. "The agreement that you signed permitted you to live in that house until the time of your death, but my father held the legal title to the house and all of the land."

"A fact which you uncovered after your father, Eddie Steele, died six months ago." Abbie was finally beginning to see the light even though she had both eyes fixed between single-birth mom's legs. Still no baby.

"I hadn't spoken to the old bastard since the day I left this God forsaken Island, and even then it was just to tell him that I wouldn't be coming home, ever."

"But ever only lasted until it was time to claim a piece of the old bastard's estate."

"I deserved an inheritance."

"Your father didn't think so."

"We never saw eye to eye."

"So rather than abide by your father's wishes, you opted to contest the will."

"At first."

"The attorneys handling your father's estate denied any knowledge of the Tyle Island property. Why?"

Priscilla's grin snaked across her face. "They were unaware of said asset."

"And how was it that you became aware of said asset?"

"Quite by accident. I returned to the Brownstone following Daddy's death in order to retrieve the personal possessions that I abandoned when I escaped my old life."

"Escaped your old life? You sound as if your father tortured you."

"You have no idea what it was like to be a child of the Mob."

"Wealthy, spoiled, boo-frigging-hoo. Get on with the story."

Priscilla grimaced but went on. "Daddy, like so many empty nesters, had turned my childhood bedroom into a home office."

"So he traded your Barbie Dream House for a fax machine."

"And file cabinets," she smiled, "lots of file cabinets. I suppose when you're consigliore to Vincent Gianninni it's wise to keep your records close to home. I found some very interesting reading material, but none intrigued me more than a file marked Tyle Island. Imagine my surprise when I read the contents of that dusty old folder and learned that the sweet old lady whom I had called Auntie was not only a former call girl, but also the biological mother of Antonio Gianninni. And imagine my glee when I realized that Daddy had taken this dirty little secret to the grave."

"Vincent doesn't know Hyacinth is Antonio's mother?"

"Please," Priscilla scoffed at the notion, "my father couldn't tell Vincent that the mother of the next Gianninni Don was a two-bit hooker, and he certainly couldn't tell Hyacinth who was adopting her baby; she might try to lay claim to him later on down the road. So Daddy wisely kept those details to himself. The deal he cut was ingenious.

The soap opera writer was immersed in the twisted tale. Abbie was prepared to prod for details, but Priscilla, seemingly proud of her father's shrewdness needed no motivation. "He made arrangements for Vincent to pay an initial lump sum which he used to purchase the house and land on Hyacinth's behalf, but in his own name. Then every year Daddy would take a stipend from one of Vincent's illegitimate and therefore un-audited business holdings to pay for the property taxes as well as Hyacinth's modest living expenses."

"The yearly stipend explains the on-going relationship between your father and Hyacinth."

"He did have a warm spot for her. Perhaps she was better at her job than I give her credit for."

"And since the Tyle Island properties were mob business there was no reason for it to show up as part of your father's personal estate."

"Exactly."

"So you had hit the jackpot," Abbie filled in the rest of the blanks. "But you had a problem in that the wife of the esteemed Governor couldn't just step up to the plate and demand the return of a nature refuge for her own monetary gain." Abbie chanced a quick glance away from single-birth mom's private parts and made eye contact with Priscilla. "But I'm sure that providing Antonio Giannini with the site for a casino would provide a finders-fee that would more than make up for the loss of any inheritance."

Priscilla met Abbie's glare. "Antonio was an old friend and a wise businessman. He was very receptive to my suggestion for the site."

"And your husband was equally receptive to the revenue that gambling would bring to his state."

"Those so-called Indian tribes down in Connecticut were stealing our tourism."

"I believe Native American is the politically correct term," Abbie looked at the gun, "not that political correctness is a priority of yours. But anyway, that's beside the point. You had to get your hands on the land without getting them dirty, so you set your little scheme in motion. It all began with a Christmas card sent to dearest Auntie Hyacinth, the current tenant on your father's land."

"You found the Christmas Card?" Priscilla nodded as if impressed.

"Now let me see if I have this right. After slithering your way back into Hyacinth's life, a large payoff guaranteed that the rest of the Council Members would climb on board. Then you blackmailed Dan into secretly flying them off Island, thereby making the trail difficult to follow. He dropped them off at an airport in Jersey where you were waiting, then you and Hyacinth and Dan flew back to Wakefield where he stashed his plane at Scarlet's airport then hid out in your vacation house. You, of course, returned to the Capital and not fully trusting Hyacinth, dragged her along for the ride. Then you put her house on the market, listing your father and yourself as owners."

"You did what!" Hyacinth cried.

"Don't worry," Abbie shrugged, "the house wasn't sold."

"Oh thank God."

"We burned it down instead."

It appeared as if the old lady was about to keel over so Abbie explained. "I'm truly sorry about the loss of your home, but you must admit that you came across as quite the disloyal Islander. From where we all stood, you had signed away this Island and such behavior could not go unpunished."

"But...," Hyacinth complained.

"Shhh," Abbie quieted her, "I'm on a roll." She took a peek under single birth mom's skirt - still no baby. "So your plan was going along smoothly until an unexpected turn of events landed Bob Kelly in Atlantic City with your business partner. Face it Priscilla, you underestimated the resourcefulness of the common Tyle Islander. You assumed that these backward hicks would just roll over and play dead, but they didn't. Under Kelly's leadership they rallied and beat you at your own game. Not only is the casino deal off, but Bob isn't here, so your hopes for revenge are out the window as well. Face it lady, it's just not your day, so why don't you just cut your losses and go home. We'll keep this little love-in of ours a secret, right guys?" Everyone lying and sitting and bleeding around the room nodded in unison, "right."

"I've lost nothing," Priscilla smirked. "Antonio Gianninni isn't the only developer in the world."

"No, he's not," Hyacinth agreed.

"Hyacinth," Abbie interrupted, "I really think you should let me handle this."

"This is my Island, I'll handle it."

"But Hyacinth," Abbie argued, "I don't think you know what you're saying." Single birth mom moaned, pushed and "oh shit," Abbie muttered, "I see the head."

"I know exactly what I'm saying." Hyacinth stood. "Barron's Hollow was granted to Mr. Gianninni, not to you Priscilla. If he doesn't build the land will never be developed."

Priscilla moved the gun away from multiple birth mom's head and aimed it at Hyacinth. "Do I have to remind you that you had no legal right to grant the land in the first place. I can sue you or..." she grinned.

"Or what?" Hyacinth asked.

"Use of the land is yours only until the time of your death. Then it becomes mine. Sorry Auntie," Priscilla stepped closer and aimed the gun at Hyacinth's head, "but I want my land."

Abbie peeked out from under the skirt, looked up at Hyacinth and said, "You really should have let me handle it."

## Chapter 43

Kelly's heart was racing as they eased the boat into the cove. A cool breeze carried a mist across the water while a thin veil of fog began to shroud the starlit sky. Conditions were ideal for a Mary sighting. Once anchored, Gianninni ordered Dominic into the cabin while he and Kelly remained on deck to await the Virgin.

"Where should I be looking," Gianninni whispered, his voice reverent in tone.

Kelly, with a gnawing in his stomach so severe he could barely stand erect, pointed toward the beach. As he pulled his arm back he casually checked his Timex, 9:03. The best laid plans...

Kelly closed his eyes and prepared for death. He thanked his maker, whoever he or she was, for having given him a second chance at life. The past few weeks had changed him. He had, for the very first time, experienced the feeling of omnipotence that comes with falling in love. Even love at forty, and unrequited, had left an unsatisfied man with his sights set on self-destruction feeling like a child on the first day of summer vacation; filled with the hopeful promise that anything was possible, even tangling with the Mob. After twenty years of playing the noble role of creative recluse dedicated to ones craft, he learned that there was nothing noble about being alone. People were to be treasured, whether it was the crazy redhead who cooked his breakfast or a quirky mobster who longed to be a priest.

And speaking of quirky mobsters, Kelly's philosophizing was interrupted when Antonio Gianninni let out an audible gasp. Kelly opened his eyes to find that a heavenly figure, a majestic figure, a really tall figure, had materialized on the beach, and was slowly walking, no gliding, along the waters edge. The figure was draped in a billowy fabric that danced softly across the sand. Dark hair cascaded past the shoulders of the mysterious figure, shielding its face from their view, which was a good thing, since the Virgin needed a shave.

Gianninni dropped to his knees and began praying, when, as quickly as she had surfaced, The Madonna disappeared into the night. The mobster wept.

"Thank you Bob," he uttered, his voice choked by emotion. Kelly was speechless. He had expected Antonio to be pleased but this reaction seemed extreme. "She was beautiful."

"Yeah," Kelly thought of Abbie as he placed a hand on Antonio's shoulder, "more beautiful than I remembered."

Gianninni cleared his throat and wiped away his tears. He stood, brushed off his Armani slacks and straightened his white silk necktie.

"Dominic," he called out. The bodyguard appeared. "Give me your weapon and leave us alone."

The bodyguard, sensing Gianninni's delicate condition, pleaded, "Let me do this for you boss."

"I said give me your weapon and leave us alone." Gianninni's icy tone relayed the message that now was not the time for Dominic to assert himself. The bodyguard turned over his gun and retreated to the safety of the stateroom. Gianninni waited until the goon was out of sight before addressing Kelly.

"I don't know if what I just witnessed was real, or merely a bit of your magic," Antonio smiled warmly, "but it doesn't really matter. Go."

"Go where?" Kelly looked around the boat.

"Home."

"You mean?" Kelly pointed overboard.

"You can swim can't you?"

"Well yes," Kelly's eyes were fixed on the shoreline. Fifty yards to freedom. Just a jump, a splash and a little kicking stood between him and home. But home would never be the same. Kelly still had to convince Gianninni not to build. He turned to face the mobster, "What about the casino?"

"I called off the deal."

Kelly couldn't believe what he was hearing. "Why?"

Gianninni grinned. "On the evening of our first meeting you impressed me with your willingness to play the role of martyr. Based upon your reputation, it wasn't the behavior that I expected. Granted, I'm fairly sure that the scotch you were drinking may have added to your zeal, but I respected your conviction just the same."

"So you intended to call off the deal all along?"

"No," Antonio shook his head, "I liked you Bob, but not that much. However you did raise some doubts in my mind, so I went to Chapel yesterday morning and prayed for guidance. I asked The Lord if I should build a casino on Tyle Island."

"And The Lord told you not to."

Gianninni nodded.

"You spoke to God?"

"Not directly. He sent a sign."

"What sign?"

"As I sat in the chapel a homeless woman appeared before me. She wore a shirt that read "Just Say No."

Kelly removed his Yankee cap and scratched his head. "So you're telling me that an anti-drug message plastered across the chest of a homeless woman was a sign from God that told you not to build a casino on Tyle Island?"

"That," Gianninni nodded, "and her flip flops."

"Pardon me?"

"I offered the sad soul money, but despite her obvious need, she refused. It became clear to me that she had been sent by God to teach me a lesson."

"And what lesson was that?" Kelly had to ask.

"That I must open my heart to the needs of others. Your needs and the needs of your friends for whom you were willing to sacrifice your life."

"Oh."

"The woman wore a pair of pink plastic flip flops and as she walked away from me, with my outstretched hand still offering a money clip thick with bills, the sound of her shoes echoed through the chapel." Gianninni paused and made the sound, "flip flop-flip flop." He shuddered, "It haunts me still."

"You're seriously telling me that a tee shirt and a pair of flip flops made you call of the project?"

"No Bob, God made me call off the project. The flip flops and the tee-shirt were just the instruments He used to show me the way."

"Well hell, Tony," Kelly complained, "Why didn't you tell me this yesterday?"

"I wanted my miracle," Antonio shrugged. "You gave it to me. Now you can go."

"Seriously?"

"Seriously."

"You're not going to kill me?"

"I wouldn't dream of it."

"And you're not going to build a casino."

"No."

"Well that's great." Kelly held out his hand. "It's been nice knowing you Tony."

Gianninni reached out, took Kelly's hand in his own and gripped it firmly, "You too Bob."

Kelly walked to the side of the boat and looked down into the cold dark water. He took a deep breath, placed one foot up on the rail and then the other. As he balanced precariously he looked back and saw Antonio Gianninni slowly raise the gun and place the barrel in his mouth.

Kelly cried out, "no," then leapt. His worn out loafers with the one sole coming loose hit boat deck, not water, as he rushed Antonio and grabbed for the gun.

"Don't do it," Kelly struggled for control of the weapon.

Gianninni, twenty years his senior but twice as physically fit, held firm. "I can't go back to my old life."

Kelly pulled the gun toward him, "You don't have to."

Gianninni pulled the gun back, "I have an obligation to my family."

"You have no obligation," Kelly grunted as he pulled with all his might, "if you aren't a Gianninni."

Kelly fell ass over elbow as Antonio let go of the gun. "What did you say?"

"I said you're not a Gianninni," Kelly lay on the deck panting from the struggle, "or at least," he paused to catch his breath, "there's a good chance your not," another breath, "and I think a good chance is worth looking into don't you?"

"Why don't you think I'm a Gianninni?"

Kelly sat up. "You mean besides the hazel eyes and dislike of tomato sauce?"

"Yes," Gianninni nodded, "besides that."

"I think I know your birth-mother."

"My birth-mother?"

"Her name is Hyacinth Poole. Sixty years ago she had a child whom she gave up for adoption. She knew your father. It's only a hunch, but I'm telling you Tony, the resemblance is uncanny."

Antonio placed a hand to his chin as he processed the information. "That would certainly explain the lack of nurturing on my mother's part."

"And when it comes to the identity of your real father, I have to be honest, Hyacinth was a hooker when you were conceived so pretty much anybody with twenty bucks could have been your dad." Gianninni's mouth dropped open at the revelation that his biological mother was a woman of questionable reputation. "What's the big deal?" Kelly commented, "Mary Magdalene wasn't exactly squeaky clean and Jesus didn't hold it against her."

Gianninni couldn't argue that. He reached out a hand and assisted Kelly to his feet.

"Even if what you say is true, and I'm not a Gianninni, I can't just retire. I know too much. I'd be eliminated if I ever tried to leave the family."

"They can't eliminate you," Kelly smirked, "if you're already dead."

Gianninni frowned. "What do you mean?"

"Dominic saw how shaken you were after seeing the Madonna. He's worried about you, correct?"

"Correct."

"Well, I'll go in there and tell him that you're acting all moody and depressed. Meanwhile," Kelly looked around until he spotted the gun lying under a lounge chair just a few feet away, "you pull the trigger and dive in. Can you hold your breath for a while?"

"Forever if need be," he replied.

"Stay under water and swim like hell," Kelly pointed to the far side of the cove. "With the fog that's rolling in, if you make it that far, he'll never see you."

"What will you do?"

"I'll be right behind you. Just remember when you jump, take the gun with you, I don't want Dominic taking his frustrations out on me."

"Do you honestly think it will work?" Gianninni asked.

"Miracles happen," Kelly grinned. "You can hide out with me and Pete for a couple of days while the Coast Guard searches the water. They'll come up empty, assume you've become shark bait and Antonio Gianninni the mobster will be pronounced dead, may he rest in peace."

"Why are you helping me?" Gianninni asked.

"I'm a sucker for second chances," Kelly patted Gianninni on the back. "Wait for me on the beach."

Kelly went below deck and found Dominic sitting in front of a big screen TV. A DVD was playing, The Godfather, what else.

"What the fuck do you want?" Dominic growled.

Kelly shrugged, "Mr. Gianninni sent me down here to wait with you."

"Wait for what?"

Then came the gunshot. Dominic ran for the deck. Kelly, impressed with the big man's response time stepped in his way, slowing him down just long enough for Antonio to get safely into the water and a good distance from the boat. Kelly followed Dominic, and as the bodyguard searched the water for signs of his boss, Kelly slipped over the side, took a deep breath, and disappeared.

"That was definitely a gunshot," Chief Tatum declared as he pointed toward the west. "Get moving."

John Beale gave the boat full throttle, causing his passengers to fall backwards into a writhing mound. This angered Fric and Frac who jumped to their feet and went blow for blow with the two deputized fishermen. Still not having a firm grasp of who were the good guys and who were the bad, Doctor Jasper Black, in a moment of typical stupidity rose to his feet and threw a punch. One punch. The fishermen, whose ability to maintain their footing on a speeding boat far outweighed that of the city slickers, quickly won the battle. The mound of goombas and soap star no longer writhed, but lay in a state of semi-consciousness at the feet of their employer/fan.

Chief Tatum spotted the vessel anchored off Madonna's Cove. Armed with only a flare gun, the rescue boat proceeded with caution. As they approached the ship one of the deputies, keeping low to avoid losing his head, pointed a flood light at the ship. On the deck stood an enormous man wearing a purple and black running suit; a tiny orange life jacket was strapped to his hulking chest. The man raised his hands above his head and called out that he wasn't armed. Chief Tatum kept his flare gun aimed directly at the orange target in the middle of the big man's chest.

"He shot himself," the man cried out.

"Who shot himself?" Chief Tatum yelled.

"My boss."

"Who's your boss?"

"Antonio Gianninni."

"Antonio Gianninni the mobster?" Chief Tatum asked.

"Antonio Gianninni my son," Vincent whispered. "Hyacinth's son."

Mildred swore she heard a gunshot, followed immediately by the sound of dogs barking. As she drew nearer to the source of the noise she noticed that the scent of the Chanel grew stronger. Mildred paused to get her bearings. She had counted her paces, and by consulting the map of Tyle Island that was permanently engraved in her mind, she deduced that she was headed for the Kelly house. There was trouble brewing and from the smell of it, her friend Abbie was involved. Mildred hoisted her shotgun, stuck her nose in the air and quickened her pace. As she stepped from pavement to grass she noticed that the barking seemed to be coming from the rear of the house; hence Mildred, being no old fool, would go in the front.

She searched her memory bank for a picture of the Kelly house, recalling that there was a wide lawn, then three porch steps, then, if she remembered correctly, which she did, four steps across the lemonade style porch dodging a few old white wicker chairs if the boys hadn't junked them, then a screen door with handle on the right. Mildred was so absorbed in the mental lay of the land that she didn't pay attention to her footing, and whoops, thud, she stumbled over the ruts in the lawn created by Abbie O'Neal's dirty green Jeep.

"Goddamn Kellys," she muttered, "too lazy to care for their damn grass. Damn near got me killed." She felt around for her shotgun, located it and used it like a crutch to help hoist herself to her feet. While her body was not wounded, her temperament was experiencing an extra dose of ornery. She carried on more cautiously until one Converse hit something solid. Mildred bent down and felt a step. One, two, three she slowly climbed, then came the four long strides across the porch. She held out her hand and felt the door handle on the right, just as she remembered. She turned the knob and went in.

Abbie was not happy. Kneeling in bodily fluids with her hands up a stranger's groin was not how she pictured this meeting coming to an end. And while there had been moments during the past few weeks when she had wished Hyacinth Poole dead, her actual death was not something to which she wanted to bare witness. She glanced over at Scarlet who was applying pressure to Dan Kelly's wounded shoulder, and at multiple birth mom who had begun the same teeth gnashing and face contorting that had been the precursor to the appearance of the small head which was now crowning before her. It was time to try rationalizing with the irrational.
"Please Priscilla," Abbie begged, "if you truly wanted Hyacinth dead you would have killed her weeks ago. I know that deep down you are a good person who is in a bad situation. I know you don't want anyone to die, so please just put down the gun."
"You talk too much." Priscilla untied her scarf and, threatening Dan with another bullet, forced Scarlet to gag Abbie.
"Oh Sugar, I'm so sorry," Scarlet wept as she tied a loose knot.
"Ids ok Scaled," Abbie grunted, then she glared defiantly at Priscilla and mumbled, "Uuu arn gunna ged

awaaa wid dis."

"That's where you're wrong. I am going to get away with this, and do you know why? Because the only people who could implicate me are in this room and I have enough bullets to silence you all. I will have my land, and I will build my casino and there is nothing that Antonio Gianninni, Bob Kelly or any other Tyle Islander can do to stop me."

"Abbie!!!! Where the hell are you, Abbie?" a nicotine voice called out from the living room.

Startled, Priscilla moved the gun off of Hyacinth and aimed it at the doorway. She watched, with gun barrel trembling, as an ancient looking woman who wore thick dark sunglasses despite it being past nine o'clock at night, stepped into view. The old hag was bent like a question mark, curlers dangled from her unkempt pale blue hair, and two bright splotches of red rouge gave her the appearance of a circus clown. Oh, and she balanced a shotgun on her hip.

"I said where the hell is Abbie?" Mildred hollered, struggling to hear herself over her own deafness and the barking of the dogs. She took another step and walked straight into the doorjamb then she bounced off the wall, took two quick steps to maintain her balance and stumbled over Dan Kelly's legs that were stretched across her path. Priscilla saw the mishap and realized that the uninvited guest was blind.

"Abbie's not here," Priscilla pointed the gun directly at Mildred's chest, letting all in the room know that one false move would cost the old woman her life.

"Who the hell are you?" Mildred barked as she took another awkward step and sniffed about like a bunny rabbit foraging for food.

"I'm a friend of the Kellys."

"Why them damn dogs barking?" Mildred asked as she tried to zero in on the source of the Chanel. Her already bent body leaned further downward; it seemed as if the perfume trail was emanating from the floor. Why the hell would Abbie be sitting on the floor and not answering?

"They're hungry," Priscilla answered.

"Then why the hell don't you let 'em in and give 'em some food." Mildred took another deep whiff. Sure as shit the smell was coming from the floor. If Abbie was on the floor and not talking it could only mean one thing.

"I would, but they don't like strangers. I wouldn't want them to harm you. May I help you with something?" Priscilla aimed the gun

"What kind of perfume are ya wearing?" Mildred hollered.

"None," Priscilla answered as she closed one eye and prepared to pull the trigger.

"That's what I thought." Mildred cocked her shotgun and just as the First Lady was about to fire, the bathroom medicine cabinet began to ring. Priscilla hesitated. Mildred, who couldn't hear the cell phone, did not. She fired

As shards of cherry wood cabinetry and green Fiestaware sprayed across the kitchen, single birth mom gave one final push and a slippery but beautiful baby girl slid into Abbie's arms. Hyacinth ducked under the table, joined by multiple-birth mom who, despite ongoing contractions and near delivery, wanted no part of the gunfight at the Kelly Corral. Scarlet, who had thrown her own body over Dan's when the shooting began, looked up to find that Priscilla was bleeding but still on her feet. Mildred had missed. The First Lady was frantically searching for something. Scarlet spotted the gun on the floor. So did Priscilla. They both dove... but it was the south that rose again.

With slivers of wood hanging from her bouffant hair and her left eyelash loose and a flutter, Scarlet turned the weapon on Priscilla. Gambling that Scarlet wouldn't have the guts to shoot, Priscilla stood and ran for the door

- the back door - where Lucy and Ethel were impatiently waiting.

Pete Kelly stood in front of the mirror in the master bathroom of the old Coast Guard Boat House. The wet, sandy bed canopy lay in the bathtub, and clumps of his once long, dark hair were strewn across the floor. He dropped the scissors in the sink and admired his new clean-cut look; Destiny the psychic had been right, a woman had made him cut his hair.

Kelly and Gianninni, wet, tired and sandy, slowly made their way up the beach toward the Boat House. Kelly could see that a light was lit on the second floor. Abbie was probably unwinding after an award winning performance. He would surprise her. Sneak up the steps and unburden himself with a heart-felt declaration of love. He placed an arm around his soggy friend and asked, "Do you mind spending your first night on Tyle Island alone?"
"Looking for your girlfriend?"
Kelly pointed up at the light, "I don't have to look far."

When they arrived at the Boat House they let themselves in. Gianninni headed for the first floor bathroom to dry off while Kelly went upstairs. He snuck down the hallway and stood outside the bathroom door. He heard the water running in the sink and imagined the love of his life with her hair pulled back, cleansing her perfect skin with some sort of lemon verbena facial treatment before slipping into a pair of silk pajamas and cuddling up in bed. His stomach was twisted into the most glorious of knots and a lump was rising in his throat that threatened to keep his words choked down forever if he didn't spit them out soon. So Kelly held his breath, opened the door, stepped into the bathroom and announced, "I love you."

A young man with short, dark hair, shaving cream smeared across his face, and a towel wrapped around his waist stood before the sink with a pink Lady Bic razor in his hand. "Gee Bob, I love you too."

It was Pete's voice, and Pete's body, but the hair? Kelly looked down and saw piles of once long hair strewn across the bathroom floor. Then he looked into the tub and saw the mound of wet, sandy fabric.

"It was you?"

Pete nodded.

"But you looked so...pretty."

"I know," Pete rolled his eyes, "more like your niece than your nephew."

"Where's Abbie?"

"I haven't seen her in a couple of days."

"Why not?"

"She's been hiding out at our place waiting to meet my mother."

"What?"

"She figured out that my mother was at the bottom of all this casino bullshit so she called her in to have a face to face."

"Priscilla is here?"

"I'm not sure," Pete shrugged, "you know I thought I wanted to meet her but then I realized, between you and Dad, I have all the family I can handle."

Kelly took a second to savor the sentiment then turned and bolted down the steps. He pounded on the door to the first floor bathroom. When Gianninni emerged Kelly asked, "You said the casino was Priscilla's idea?"

"That's right."

"How did she react when you called off the deal?"

Gianninni squinted, "Not well."

Pete, now wearing Abbie's robe, joined the two men on the first floor. Kelly ran for the kitchen, grabbed the phone off its mount, and as he dialed his telephone number made the introductions.

"Antonio Gianninni this is my nephew, Pete Kelly."

"Pleased to meet you Pete. I've heard a lot about you."

Pete looked dumbfounded.

"Don't be rude," Kelly ordered as he listened to an endless busy signal.

Pete held out his hand, "Antonio Gianninni the mafia dude?"

"Antonio Gianninni our house guest." Kelly corrected as he disconnected the line and started to punch in the number to Abbie's cell.

Pete still looked dumbfounded.

Kelly explained. "Look, he didn't want to be a mobster any more so we're pretending he's dead and he's going to hide out with us until the heat dies down."

"You're shitting me right?"

"No." Kelly finished dialing and put the phone to his ear.

"But what about the casino?"

"There will be no casino. The deal was called off."

"So it's all over?" Pete sounded hopeful.

Then came the shotgun blast.

## Chapter 44

The sound of an air horn began to blare as Kelly raced towards home in Abbie's dirty green Jeep. A rescue boat had shown up off the cove so Pete stayed behind to run interference in case Chief Tatum stopped in and stumbled across Tyle Island's "Most Wanted".

Kelly pulled the Jeep into his driveway, he was followed by a pick-up; Doc Gno and Clara jumped out. All three ran around to the back of the house where they were greeted by a pair of Rottweilers who had large swatches of khaki and denim hanging from their drooling mouths. Mildred Ahearn stood between them holding the air horn in one hand and her shotgun in the other. When she sensed that people were approaching she dropped the horn, raised her shotgun and called out, "Who's there?"

"It's me," Clara shouted, "I'm with Doc Gno and Bob Kelly."

"Well Doc," Mildred gestured toward the house, "they'll be needing you inside."

"What happened?" Kelly asked as Doc Gno cautiously passed by the Rottweilers then rushed for the stairs.

"Who the hell knows?" Mildred shrugged, "I can't see a damn thing. All I know is there are people moaning and crying and it smells God awful in there."

"We heard a gun shot."

"That was me," Mildred chuckled, "not quite sure what I hit."

It was Kelly's turn to rush for the steps, dreading the carnage he would find in his home. He swung open the wooden door that was covered with claw marks, stepped into his kitchen and gasped at the sight. His brother, who was supposed to be bush piloting in Alaska, leaned against the far wall; his hairless chest was stained with damp blood and he had what appeared to be a tampon, with strings dangling, protruding from a wound to his shoulder. The Widow Poole knelt on the floor littered with cherry wood splinters and shards of Fiestaware, and used a kitchen towel to wipe the brow of one of the formerly pregnant Islanders; the new mother dozed as she clutched her sleeping infant to her chest. A very attractive but disheveled woman with big hair and one crooked eyelash sat cross legged on the floor cradling a second infant whose perfect little hands flailed about as his strong lungs let out a healthy cry. Doc Gno knelt between the legs of an exhausted but relieved young woman, and cooed to the newest Tyle Islander, a baby girl, born just seconds earlier. And in the corner, bloodied and bitten, sat Priscilla Steele-Des Pierre-Hardy. A pale blue scarf was shoved in her mouth and her wrists and ankles were bound by duct tape.

Where was Abbie? Kelly's heart sank and his stomach churned until the newborn took a break from his wailing and Kelly heard a voice coming from the next room. He stepped over the bodies splayed across his floor, paused to check on his brother who smiled reassuringly despite the feminine hygiene product plugging up his wound, then followed the sound of that angelic voice into the living room where he found her, drenched with blood and sweat, a cell phone wedged between her shoulder and ear, pouring a touch of water into a tumbler size glass of single malt scotch. Kelly cleared his throat to get her attention. Abbie turned, saw him, blew the bangs away from her eyes, raised her glass and smiled, "Happily ever-after, who would have thought?"


There were loose ends that needed tying up, in Tyle Island knots.

Bob Kelly placed a late night call to Governor Patrick Hardy, identified himself, explained the events of the past few hours and gave the man two suggestions as to how he might handle this delicate political and personal scandal.

Suggestion number one was to retrieve his psychopath of a wife, return her to the mainland and have her immediately committed to a very reputable mental institution where she would receive the much needed treatment that might some day, far, far in the future, allow her to return to society. Any claims to ownership of land on Tyle Island held by the First Lady would be rescinded and the possibility of gambling ever again coming to Tyle Island would be squelched by executive order. If the Governor were to opt for this first course of action, the details of his wife's kidnapping, blackmailing, gun wielding rampage would remain a Tyle Island secret, thereby not adversely affecting any future political aspirations that the Governor might entertain.

Then there was a second possible course of action. The Governor could choose to defend his wife's actions and support her claim of ownership of land on Tyle Island, and, as the Chief Officer of the fine state of Massachusetts support the rights of the many to gamble as opposed to the rights of the few, to not. If the Governor were to follow this line of thinking, 60 Minutes would be immediately notified regarding Priscilla Steele-Des Pierre Hardy's bloodline and blood thirst.

Ever the politician, Governor Patrick Hardy chose what was behind door number one.

After contacting the Coast Guard regarding the disappearance and presumed death of Antonio Gianninni, Chief Tatum, along with a group of the Island's biggest and burliest escorted the grieving Vincent Gianninni, his two goons, the big guy from the luxury yacht and the remaining DeLucas to the mainland, where he advised them to drive away quickly and not look back. This time he was armed. They took his advice.

Doc Gno placed a phone call to the Center for Disease Control and left an urgent message for Doctor Lorraine Macy. She returned his call minutes later. He apologized for the late hour and any inconvenience he may have caused her, but explained that he had just that minute discovered that his initial assertion of a Lyme Tick epidemic on Tyle Island was inaccurate. Further interviews of infected patients showed that each had spent a substantial period of time in a nature refuge on the island. This was a common link he had earlier missed; therefore, he could no longer support his claim that there was a widespread outbreak, rather just too many careless Islanders not taking the proper precautions when trekking through the high weeds on one particular parcel of land.

Doctor Macy's professional recommendation was that the foliage in the area of concentration be mowed down, thereby eliminating the host environment.

Doc Gno preferred to keep Barron's' Hollow intact and accept Bob Kelly's generous offer of research funds. With the best fishing on the east coast, a small family practice and now medical research right in his own backyard, Doctor Gnocuchuk was one happy Islander.


Hyacinth Poole was one unhappy Islander. She stood at the base of her driveway staring at the pile of charred rubble that had once been her home. Clara passed her a bottle of cream sherry. Hyacinth took a hit and handed it back.

"I can't believe it's gone," Hyacinth sobbed.

"I'm so sorry Sweetie," Clara apologized before taking another sip of sherry and placing the bottle in Mildred Ahearn's awaiting hand.

"Sixty years worth of memories gone up in flames," The Widow Poole signaled for Clara to pass the bottle back.

Clara pried the sherry from Mildred's reluctant fingers and handed it over.

"I know you see sixty years worth of lost memories when you look at what's left of your house, but do you know what I see? I see the chance to start all over. This Island is strong and our lives will go on and you can start brand new memories."

"I suppose you're right," Hyacinth handed the bottle back to Clara.

"You know what I see?" Mildred asked while reaching out for the bottle.

"What?" both women asked

"Nothing, I'm blind. Now stop your whining, you're not goddamn dead, and we've got more important things to discuss."

"Like what?" Clara asked.

"You think Abbie and Kelly are doing it?"


Scarlet Newbaker telephoned her dilapidated trailer, dreading the encounter that would take place when Hank picked up the line. Instead of her husband, a gentleman by the name of Federal Agent Stephen J. Dugan answered the phone. He informed Scarlet that her husband had been arrested for drug trafficking. Hank Newbaker had been making drug runs between the US and Canada three times a week for the past four years. The airport in Wakefield was a front for his smuggling operation.

"Well I'll be damned," Scarlet whispered then apologized to the nice agent for her use of profanity. She explained that a respectable girl from Peachtree Georgia never swore and it would tarnish her reputation for all eternity if anyone ever learned that she had let a vulgarity pass over her lips while conversing with a man of his prominent position.

Federal Agent Dugan blushed through the phone line. He expressed his sympathy for poor Scarlet who had

been taken in by a cretin such as Hank Newbaker.
Scarlet thanked the nice agent for his concern and asked if it would be at all possible for her to return to her trailer to retrieve some of her personal items. She explained that, under the circumstances, she had no desire to remain Mrs. Hank Newbaker.

The Federal Agent offered to help Scarlet pack.

Scarlet hung up the telephone, walked down the long white hospital corridor and took a seat beside the handsome young man with short dark hair that sat in a chair outside room 1101.

"You're daddy is going to be just fine Sugar," she patted Pete Kelly on the knee and gave him a friendly wink. "He's a real toughy."

"I know."

"Then what's got you so down in the mouth?" Scarlet asked

"I just don't understand why he got involved with Priscilla. Why didn't he just say no?"

Scarlet, recalling the truth about who truly sired young Pete, took a deep breath, "I'm sorry to be the one to tell you this Sugar, but your Mamma, she's a crazy lady, and your Daddy, he just loves you to death. He didn't want that woman hurting you in any way, that's why he got mixed-up with her." Pete did not respond. "You wouldn't believe the torture he suffered on your behalf." Scarlet glanced over and noticed that the mention of torture had piqued the young man's interest, so she went on. "Pete Sugar, do you know what pinking shears are?"


Abbie asked Chief Tatum if she could have a moment alone with the prisoner. Tatum gave her the key to the cell then excused himself; he went into his office and closed the door. Abbie unlocked the cell, went in and sat next to Jack.

"What happened Jack?"

"I hit a deputy."

"Why?"

"I was defending a fan."

"You were defending a mobster."

Jack mussed his hair and flexed his muscles. "A fan is a fan. They love me, I love them."

Even the baby hairs on the back of Abbie's neck were too exhausted to react. She calmly asked, "What are you going to do?"

"I called my father."

"What did he say?"

"He wouldn't take the call. Mother says he received a package containing some disturbing information and she didn't think it would be wise to put me through."

Abbie patted him on the knee. "I'll talk to the Chief and see if I can get the charges dropped."

"Thanks."

There was a long awkward silence. "You know Jack, we need to talk about us."

"I know Babe. I've been doing a lot of thinking and...I can't marry you."

"You can't?"

"No."

"Why not?"

"I don't think I can forgive you."

"Forgive me for what?"

"For collaborating with that old guy." Jack's face contorted into a pained expression, "no matter how hard I try, I can't erase the image of you two together, naked, sweaty, collaborating."

Had the shotgun blast damaged her ears or did he just say naked? And sweaty? And then it dawned on her, "Jack, do you know what collaborating means?"

He sighed dramatically, "Of course I do. What do you think I am, stupid?"

She felt no need to answer.

349

# Chapter 45

Kelly held his stomach as he laughed uncontrollably. Abbie, seated beside him on the large piece of driftwood, shoved him playfully, "It's not that funny."

He wiped a tear from his eye. "He honestly thought that collaborating meant..."

She nodded and, despite herself, began to giggle too.

"You know Abbie, it's not such a bad idea."

"What? Our collaborating?"

"No," he glanced at her, "our...well...you know."

Again she shoved him, this time harder. "Jesus Bob, I just ended my engagement."

"Well, I hate to be the one to point this out to you, but technically Jack just ended your engagement, and while I agree that had you been the dumper it would indeed be bad form to hop into bed with another man so quickly, but since you are the dumpee, I don't see a problem."

"Has anyone ever told you that you're very wordy?" Abbie asked.

Kelly chuckled, touché.

"And while I find your logic extremely insulting, I have to admit that you make a valid point." She placed a hand on his knee and smiled seductively letting his hopes rise before crushing them with a blunt, "But still, I'd feel funny about sleeping with you so soon after my break-up."

Kelly picked up a seashell and tossed in into the water. "But, just to clarify, you're not entirely ruling out the possibility of sex?"

"Between us?"

"Yes."

"No."

"So you're merely postponing the inevitable."

"Precisely."

"For how long?"

She took a sip of wine while debating her response. "You know Bob, I'm not really sure what the appropriate period of mourning should be under the circumstances." She took another sip.

"A week?" Kelly raised the Cary Grant brow.

"Oh good God," she nearly choked, "not that long."

Kelly held up a can of Pepsi and clinked it against her glass of wine. "I like the way you think."

She glanced at the soda and asked, "No scotch?"

"Not thirsty," he replied.

They sat together silently listening to the ripple of the ocean as it gently rolled across the rocky shoreline, and watching a pair of Coast Guard Cutters search the water off Madonna's Cove for the body of Antonio Gianninni. Little did the men aboard those ships know that the former mobster was alive and well and sitting only fifty yards away enjoying a long overdue reunion with his Mother.

Abbie sighed as she buried her bare feet in the cool sand.

"What's wrong?" Kelly asked.

"I'm going to miss this place."

"Where are you going?"

"Home."

"But this is your home," Kelly argued.

"Oh really. Where am I supposed to live?"

"With me."

"Between you, Dan, Pete and now Antonio Gianninni, the Kelly house, which is minus a kitchen, is a little crowded. And anyway, I have a sneaky suspicion that Scarlet has dibs on being the next to move in."

"We'll buy the Boat House."

"It's not for sale."

"It will be."

"How do you know?"

"I know all."

Abbie studied him. There was something that he didn't know, something big. He deserved to know that he had a son. "I don't think you know as much as you think you do."

"You're wrong Abbie."

"I'm being serious."

"So am I."

"It's about Pete."

"There is nothing you can tell me about Pete that I don't already know."

"But."

"Abbie look at me."

She looked into Bob Kelly's deep blue eyes as he repeated, "Abbie, I know."

A man's eyes reveal all.

"So you see," he smiled, "you have nothing to worry about. You love me, there's no use in trying to deny it, Chief Tatum told me so, and to be honest," his stomach twisted into a wonderful knot as he said the words, "I love you too. So you'll move up here and we will continue to live happily ever after."

"You've got this all figured out haven't you?"

"I've had a lot of free time in the past few days."

"All right then, what about my job?"

"I'm rich, you don't need a job."

"Could you imagine all this pent up energy without an outlet? Trust me Kelly, I need a job, and if I've learned one thing over the past few weeks, it's that I'm never going to be a great American novelist. I am a soap opera writer and I sure as hell can't write soap operas while living in Tyle Island, Massachusetts."

Kelly was not about to give up. "What is the plot of your great American novel?" he asked.

Abbie shoved her feet deeper in the sand and refused to answer.

"Let me guess, family angst set during the Civil War. Lost love set during World War II. Or better yet, Jane

Austin mixed with Hemingway in a heart-wrenching tale of The Old Man and the Thames."

"Remember what I said about a week being too long of a mourning period?" she scowled, "I just made it a month."

"Abbie," Kelly sat forward and looked her straight in the eye, "rule number one of writing well is writing what you know."

She dropped her head to her knees and whined, "But all I know is soap operas."

"What about the past few weeks?"

She peeked up at him.

"It would make one hell of a book."

"You think?"

"I think. And I also think you're just the one to write it." He placed his arm around her waist and whispered in her ear, "Tell me, how would you begin?"

"I can't."

"You can," he gave her a reassuring squeeze. "Don't try to be Jane Austin or Ernest Hemingway, just be yourself and give me an opening sentence."

"Ok," she propped her wineglass in the sand and took a deep breath, "here goes nothing. Are you ready?"

"I'm ready."

Abbie rested her head on Kelly's shoulder, stared out at the horizon and said, 'Dino DeLuca never should have gone deep sea fishing.'

THE END

Printed in the United States
64099LVS00005B/12